A. D. 'Tony' Parsons has worked as a p
sheep and wool classer, an agricultural journalist,
a news editor and rural commentator on radio, a
consultant to major agricultural companies, and an
award-winning stud breeder of many animals. He
owned his first kelpie dog in 1944, and in 1950 he
established 'Karrawarra', one of the top kelpie studs
in Australia, and bred the first of his many trial
winners in 1954. In 1992 he was awarded the Order
of Australia Medal for his contribution to the propa-
gation of the Australian kelpie sheepdog.

Since 1947 he has published hundreds of articles,
many in international publications, as well as several
technical books, including three on the working
kelpie. He is also a short story writer and columnist.
The Call of the High Country is his first novel.

Tony lives with his wife in Queensland, where he
still breeds and shows merino stud sheep and main-
tains a stud of kelpies.

The Call of the High Country

Tony Parsons

Penguin Books

The publishers would like to thank Ian and Jill Watson of Watson's Mountain Country Trail Rides in Mansfield, Victoria, for their assistance with the cover photography.

Penguin Books

Published by the Penguin Group
Penguin Books Australia Ltd
250 Camberwell Road, Camberwell, Victoria 3124, Australia
Penguin Books Ltd
80 Strand, London WC2R 0RL
Harmondsworth, Middlesex, England
Penguin Putnam Inc.
375 Hudson Street, New York, New York 10014, USA
Penguin Books Canada Limited
10 Alcorn Avenue, Toronto, Ontario, Canada M4V 3B2
Penguin Books (NZ) Ltd
Cnr Rosedale and Airborne Roads, Albany, Auckland, New Zealand
Penguin Books (South Africa) (Pty) Ltd
24 Sturdee Avenue, Rosebank, Johannesburg 2196, South Africa
Penguin Books India (P) Ltd
11, Community Centre, Panchsheel Park, New Delhi 110 017, India

First published by Penguin Books Australia Ltd 1999

16 15 14 13 12 11

Copyright © Anthony Parsons 1999

Typeset by Midland Typesetters, Maryborough, Victoria
Printed and bound in Australia by McPherson's Printing Group, Maryborough, Victoria

National Library of Australia
Cataloguing-in-Publication data:

Parsons, A. D. (Anthony David), 1931– .
  The Call of the High Country.

  ISBN 0 14 026461 2.

  I. Title.

A823.3

www.penguin.com.au

To my mother, Evelyn Margaret Parsons, who was thrilled that this book was on the way, but who did not live to see its publication.

Author's Note

It was once suggested to me by a visiting American friend that I should write a work of fiction in which the working kelpie played a prominent role. The suggestion stayed in my mind for several years; in fact, through all the years in which I was heavily engaged in writing three technical books on the working kelpie. I kept thinking back to my early years in the sheep and wool business when I had spent a lot of time in the Liverpool Range region of New South Wales. It was there that I met the sheepdog breeders and handlers and saw the dogs that would shape my future thinking on sheepdogs.

Nearly all of the great dog men who lived in the country at the head of Half Moon Creek and Jimmy's Creek have gone. The incomparable Quirindi master, Frank Scanlon, has gone, and I doubt that we shall see his like again, or the likes of the dogs he and his contemporaries worked with in the high country of this story.

The she-oaks still sigh along Half Moon Creek but the great stations like Collaroy and Brindley Creek are minuscule in area compared with what they were in the early days.

There are no such places as Yellow Rock or Wallaby Rocks but there are places just like them. I know because I have ridden over them and I have watched the eagles soaring above the peaks.

David and Andrew MacLeod are composites of several men I came to know and call my friends, and Anne MacLeod is an amalgam of several dozen women who put up with me and fed me while their menfolk passed on the knowledge and information that I sought with such zeal. Even Sister Kate Gilmour had her counterpart in my travels.

In truth, this book is a blend of fact and fiction. There are names in it, surnames specifically, which are well-known in some country districts, but in no instance do such names represent any person, living or dead. Other things have been altered to suit the purposes of fiction, such as the size and procedures of the Merriwa Hospital.

A lot of Merriwa people were very kind to me in many ways. It is a long while since I rode a borrowed black mare up onto the tops, and saw for the first time the kind of country that Tom Bower and the Cronins worked their dogs over. I regret that it has taken me close to fifty years to do something worthwhile to acknowledge the kindnesses of these people.

And of course we should not forget the late Athol Butler, who worked the legendary Johnny and scored the possible 100 points at the National in 1952. I was there when they did it. A colour picture of Johnny hangs beside my work table as a reminder of that dog and the genius who handled him. Perhaps we shall one day again see someone achieve what he did. It is something to think about and to dream about.

The details I have given for the National Trials are not precisely accurate, but have been changed to suit the story. I am sure that I will be forgiven for the licence I have taken. It is a long time now since those first trials were held at the lovely Manuka Oval, and many great handlers and their dogs are now only memories. I look back on those early days of the National with real affection.

And who could forget the day Queen Elizabeth II and the Duke of Edinburgh honoured the National and the Australian sheepdog fraternity by attending the National Trials? It was 1970, held up as the centenary of sheepdog trials, and one of my kelpies, Karrawarra Sergeant, obtained the highest score for a kelpie. A grand day and a grand trial. I hope that all of those people associated with the National draw some pleasure from what I have written about it.

What I have sought to do is present a background that represents the kind of environment that is reasonably typical of the high country. Horses play a major part in the handling of stock in hill country and some of the top sheepdog men, notably Frank Scanlon (to mention only one), were also outstanding horsemen. The same applies today.

I hope that this book fulfils the hopes of that first American who suggested it and also of the many other people who encouraged me to give its writing first priority. I loved writing it because so much of it is close to my heart and took me back to my early years when everything associated with the working kelpie was full of wonder.

Tony Parsons, OAM
East Greenmount, Queensland

Prologue

High, high above the top country of the Liverpool Range a wedge-tailed eagle hung in suspended animation. It was so high in the sky that it was nothing more than a speck, lost from time to time in the white fleecy clouds that drifted across the range. The eagle's nest was on Oxley's Peak, but its wonderful soaring flight carried it way beyond the Peak and it was now directly above High Peaks, where, among the broken, lightning-riven rocks and the caves, rock wallabies and rabbits found sanctuary.

Sitting on his pony on Yellow Rock, the highest point of Andy and Anne MacLeod's High Peaks property, David MacLeod watched the eagle and envied it. From up there in the sky, the eagle would be able to see all of High Peaks and much, much more. Some bushmen said that eagles were bad news because they killed lambs, though David had never seen this. To him the eagles were wild and free and

1

they belonged to the high country, just as he felt he did. As always when he watched the flight of an eagle, his spirits lifted. He never tired of watching the great birds. He knew where all their nests were on High Peaks and the eagles' secret places were safe with him.

David had never wanted to live anywhere other than High Peaks, except, perhaps, for the Whites' place next door. It ran right to the top of the range, like their own property, but it also had a wonderful, grassy valley where Wilf White ran his brood mares and yearlings. In this valley lucerne grew so well that you could get several cuts a year without irrigation.

As David watched, the eagle dropped like a stone towards Wallaby Rocks on the Whites' place. He lost sight of it momentarily and then it rose, clumsily, appearing with a rabbit hooked in its claws. Its huge wings propelled it upwards and then it banked, just like an aeroplane, and flew towards Oxley's Peak. It crossed the creek, genesis of the Hunter River, and was lost to sight.

David knew he was going to be late home for lunch, but that was nothing new. He was always late when he rode off into the hills with a kelpie running beside his pony. The range country of High Peaks seemed to cast a spell over him; a spell so powerful he could not resist it. He was content to simply sit and gaze at the landscape around him, to watch the creatures and birds that inhabited it. At other times he put his pony to feats which, if his mother had known about them, would have brought grey hairs to

2

her head and probably resulted in his confinement to the homestead area. There was no fun in riding down an established track; the real fun was making your own.

David MacLeod was not very old when he realised that he had a special feeling for High Peaks. He had heard his mother telling people that her son 'loved' High Peaks. He wasn't sure he knew the meaning of the word love, but he did know that there could be no place else like High Peaks – and he was part of it. He didn't like leaving the property for even half a day, so the times he spent away from it at school were almost intolerable. But at least he could see the range through the windows of his classroom. And at lunch-time he could sit and look at the peaks and remind himself that come the weekend he would be riding them.

What David really lived for was the day when he would be finished with school and could spend all his time at home. He didn't need to know all the things they were trying to stuff into him. It wouldn't make him a better stockman or judge of stock.

'No, David, it won't make you a better stockman, but it will make you a better man,' his mother chided. 'There are more things in life than properties and dogs and horses. The sooner you realise that fact, the better it will be for you. Besides, there is more to being a successful property owner than you imagine. Keeping a good set of books and records is also important. Even your father went to school,' Anne reminded him.

'Not for long,' David replied.

'That was a great pity. Your father is a very intelligent man and it was a real shame that circumstances forced him to leave school prematurely.'

'Well, I want to be just like Dad. That's good enough for me,' David said with as much conviction as a ten-year-old boy could put into words.

There was another good reason why David MacLeod virtually haunted the high country – it gave him the chance to work one of his father's kelpies. It was very difficult country to muster; so difficult that odd sheep missed out on getting mustered when they needed crutching, drenching and shearing. Crutching kept the britch end of the sheep free of stains and dags, but flies also struck sheep on the body, especially after rain in spring and autumn. Old hands told of fly seasons so bad that flies would strike sweaty saddlecloths and even crushed thistle leaves. A sheep struck by flies and left untreated will eventually lie down and die. So if you saw a struck sheep you first of all had to catch it, which was not always easy in the high country, and you then had to cut the wool away with dagging shears to expose the maggots. Fly dressing was applied to the affected area and the sheep was released. Catching and holding a big range wether was no easy task for David, although he was much stronger than most boys his age. He had done his share of axe work, helping out when his father was 'ringing' trees.

The trick in catching a wether was to try and work

it into a blind gully. This was difficult to do if a sheep was on its own, but quite often the 'rogue' sheep ran in twos and threes. The first thing they would do when they sighted boy and horse was to bolt for the most inaccessible spot they could find. The job of winkling them out then had to be left to a hill-wise dog.

As David sat watching the eagle, he saw movement in the scrub below him. It was a very rough hill, covered with low scrub and odd kurrajong trees. He thought it was probably either a wallaby or a roo, but patient watching revealed it to be not one but three wethers. Two were crutched so would have been drenched at the home yards, but the third sheep had been neither crutched nor shorn. It had missed last shearing, which suggested that it could be a pea-eater. These were sheep that ate a weed called the Darling Pea and became quite mad, virtually impossible for a dog to handle. They didn't survive very long. The problem was that in dry times the Pea was often the only green plant on the hills and some sheep wouldn't leave it alone. On the other hand, the unshorn sheep might be a pure and simple rogue which had hidden in the scrub when mustering was in progress and could not be flushed out with whip cracks.

David considered the situation and resolved to try and take the sheep back to the shed. It was a long way to pull three sheep, but if he let the woolly one go, it would probably get struck and they would lose it. His father hated losing sheep.

It was lucky that he had old King with him. King was an old blue and tan kelpie his father had won a lot of trials with over the years, and he was considered to be one of the best and brainiest dogs Andy MacLeod had ever handled. David looked down at the dog and hissed, but he need not have worried – King had seen the wethers and was watching them intently.

'Keep out, King,' he said softly, so as not to disturb the sheep. He wanted King behind them before they realised there was a dog around.

King slipped away up the hill, knowing, from all his years of experience in the hills, that as soon as the sheep saw him they would bolt for the tops. That usually meant a lot more hard work to get them back.

David took up the reins of his pony and waited for King to make his lift. The two crutched wethers saw him first because they had been 'wigged' and had better vision than the woolly. They milled and were undecided what to do. David soon realised that the woolly wether was a rogue. Its first instinct was to bolt. King blocked it several times and turned it back to the other two wethers. It was then that David witnessed a wonderful piece of dog work. As King drove the sheep down the hill and away from the scrub, the rogue turned and jumped for the gully which ran right up to the tops. King leapt and snapped his teeth not six inches from the wether's head. It crashed to the ground, got up, and meekly joined the other two.

David rode down the hill after King and the sheep

and then took up point position ahead of them. In this fashion he eventually brought the three sheep back to the home yards. There, the tall figure of his father was waiting for him.

'Mum's worried as hell about you, Davie. Can't you ever get home on time for meals?'

'Sorry, Dad. I found this unshorn wether and I reckoned the best thing I could do was bring him back. He's a bit of a rogue and took some handling.'

'Where did you find him?' Andy asked.

'The Whites' side of Yellow Rock,' David said.

'That's some trip. How did you keep them clear of the other sheep?'

'It wasn't easy. I had to make a few detours. That's why it took so long. Did I do the right thing in bringing this woolly in?'

'I reckon you did, but I don't know how you managed it.'

David grinned. It really hadn't been all that difficult. Not with King to do most of the work.

'King did an amazing thing up at Yellow Rock. He's still a beaut dog, Dad.'

Andy nodded. 'He knows it all, Davie. Dogs get better with age. They know all the short-cuts and learn to outguess sheep. They get to know what sheep will do in certain paddocks. Now, you'd better scoot for the house. Tell your mother you're sorry you're late and explain what you did.'

Andy shook his head as his son ran off. He found it hard to believe that even David could have brought three wethers a distance of three miles, most of it rough country and grazed by a couple of thousand sheep. He had thought the boy was too young to work at the local sheepdog trial, but it was clear that he was wrong. He would have to let him have a go. The boy was a freak. He could be a pain in the arse the way he worried his mother, but he was a hell of a kid for all that. He reckoned he'd been damned lucky to have one like him. And damned lucky to get a wife like Anne, for that matter. She could have done a lot better for herself than marry him. Anne and David. Andy could do anything, face anything, with them to come home to.

He thought about shearing the woolly straight-away, but knew that David would be back to see him take its wool off as soon as he had bolted down his lunch. He pushed the three sheep up the race and then went inside the shed and loaded up his hand-piece. Yes, he would definitely enter David in the local trial. The locals would reckon he had gone off his rocker, but his boy would make them eat their words. What a joke it would be if a kid beat Angus Campbell. Wouldn't he blow a gasket! Angus thought he was God Almighty where stock and dogs were concerned. In fact, he thought he was God Almighty where everything was concerned. But that was the Campbells. They thought they were better than anyone.

For all his snobbish ways, Angus Campbell had his good points, as had his father before him. Old Angus senior had helped Andy in various ways, but he had never been his mate. And Angus junior would never be a mate either. Not in the way Wilf White was. You lived your life and you let Campbells live theirs. You helped out when you were needed, and sometimes the favours were returned. That was the way life was in the bush, and that was what made it so worthwhile. It could be a hard life, but the good things certainly made up for the hardships. Especially when you had a son like David. Yes, he reckoned he had been damned lucky the day he met David's mother.

Chapter One

Merriwa was, by nature of its location, a place where people took a good deal of interest in other people's affairs. Somebody had once described Merriwa as 'landlocked'. Muswellbrook, three-quarters of an hour away by road, was the town's closest large neighbour and it was the favoured place for a day's shopping. Over the range there was the village of Willow Tree on the New England Highway, just a few miles on the Sydney side of Quirindi. Forty miles north of Quirindi was the city of Tamworth. To the north-west there was the village of Cassilis and from there the road led on to Coolah and the Warrumbungles. To the south-west lay the town of Mudgee, the second-oldest settled town west of the Blue Mountains, and north of it was Gulgong, with its narrow, crooked streets which were a reminder of the roaring days when the town was a magnet for people everywhere and 'gold' was the word on everyone's lips.

Back in the early days when Merriwa was a small hamlet off the beaten track, most of the surrounding countryside had been divided between two very large properties, Collaroy and Brindley Park. Little by little these properties were whittled away by settlement so that the area that was once occupied by two owners was now owned by scores of farmers and graziers.

Like a lot of towns, Merriwa thrived on gossip. It was difficult to hide anything. So when Anne Gilmour had first arrived there it did not take long for the news of her to spread. Anne was, if not exactly beautiful, very nice looking and, according to those who made early contact with her, a bonzer girl into the bargain. Her posting at the local school was regarded as one of the major events of the postwar years.

Everyone in the district knew that Andy MacLeod was working his guts out on High Peaks. So when news came that he was to marry the good-looking teacher, Anne Gilmour, it made quite an impact. A couple of the more prosperous young graziers reckoned they had the inside running with Anne. That might have been partly true for a while, but only until the night Anne met Andy at the local dance.

The first time she had seen him, something turned over inside her. Andy was a big man, ruggedly good-looking, and there was an aura of strength about him. But for all his strong, silent image, Andy liked to dance – and he danced very well. He was light on his feet in the manner of all top horsemen, but Anne could feel the hardness of his shoulder muscles as he guided her about the dance floor. They danced together for most of the night, with nobody daring to cut in on Andy MacLeod.

The following weekend there had been another dance, and when Andy didn't turn up, Anne nearly made up her mind to leave the hall. She didn't realise that Andy was a long way from Merriwa on a shearing job. She hadn't yet learned the full story of Andrew MacLeod's struggle to hold High Peaks. She had made some discreet enquiries – as discreetly as was possible in Merriwa – about the big quiet young man who was responsible for the strange emotions inside her, and had learned, in bush jargon, that Andy was a 'battler', a 'gun' shearer, a hell of a man in a fight, and a top bloke with a horse or a sheepdog. She also learned that Andy's father had been a little too fond of whisky and had allowed the family property to sink into debt, and later had been killed while coming down off Yellow Rock on his horse.

Anne came to learn of Andy MacLeod's background by degrees. MacLeod himself was not a man to talk much, and most of her information came from Jane Campbell, who was wife to Young Angus.

Nobody in the district – other than Angus Campbell, of course – was in a better position to discuss Andrew than Jane. Not only did the Campbell property adjoin High Peaks, but Andrew often shore the Inverlochy rams and handled the odd horse for them. He was also viewed by some as one of the most eligible bachelors in the district, simply because he was, to use Fiona Cartwright's words, 'such a hunk of man'.

For upper-crust graziers like the Campbells, tennis was one of the main social pastimes. Most of the Merriwa set had splendid tennis courts. A few outsiders were admitted to join their social events, the most notable being local bank managers and their wives – even some of the top graziers had big overdrafts. The fact that Anne Gilmour was both attractive and single made her a prime subject for conversation at such gatherings.

Not long after she had met Andrew at the local hop dance, Anne was invited to a tennis party at Inverlochy. This was considered something of an honour, and it signified that she had been given initial approval. The invitation might have been inspired by the fact that some of Anne's pupils had carried home rave reports about their new teacher.

During Anne's first visit to Inverlochy, her mind was consumed with the image of Andy MacLeod. She had not seen him since the night of the dance and that fact had been gnawing away inside her when she accepted the invitation to Inverlochy. She knew that his property adjoined the Campbells'.

After her first game of tennis, Anne sat down on a white cane chair in the shade of a massive jacaranda tree, looking up towards the range. The tops towered

13

away into the distance, not as grandly or as high as the mountains of Europe and western Scotland she had seen on her memorable overseas trip, yet there was something wild and wonderful about the Australian mountain country.

'A penny, Anne,' Jane Campbell said, presenting her with a cold glass of lemonade.

'I was thinking how grand the mountains are. There seems to be a kind of magic about high places.'

'The mountains can be very dangerous too, Anne,' Jane said as she sat down beside her.

'Is yours the last property on the road, Jane?' Anne asked, knowing full well it wasn't. They had very quickly assumed first-name status and Jane was discovering that she liked Anne very much.

'No, there are four properties up the road to our right, but the MacLeod place is the only one at the end of this road. Andrew MacLeod joins us a mile or so up, and then along our eastern boundary until you get to the White place. Wilfred White is a rather eccentric fellow who breeds thoroughbreds. Races them, too. His twin brother was killed in the war, and Wilfred was never the same again.'

'Do you see much of Mr MacLeod?' Anne asked.

'Oh, now and again. Andy has been shearing our rams for some time and he handles all our horses.'

'Does he? Someone was telling me he is a wizard with sheepdogs. I used to love watching the sheepdog trials at the Sydney Sheep Show.' This was a slight exaggeration because she had been only once.

Jane looked at her and put her fingers to her lips. 'Shhh, I'll let you in on a secret. Angus and Andrew are deadly rivals at the local sheepdog trials. Well, I'm not sure whether Andy looks at it in that light, but Angus sure enough does.'

'How far is the house from here?'

'About three miles. When you turn the bend you can see High Peaks homestead standing on a slight rise.'

'Do you go up there very often?'

'To tell you the truth, I haven't been there at all. I've never had any reason to go. Andy doesn't entertain, you see. He's not like that. He is not a social person. A real bushman, Angus says. Angus goes up there now and again. It's a wild place and when it rains – rains a lot, I mean – the low-level bridge gets covered and High Peaks is cut off by road. Sometimes artists go there to paint. Apparently there are some wonderful views from up on top – that's the highest part of the range up there. I said that mountains could be dangerous places and that's true of High Peaks.' Jane pointed to where one peak overshadowed all the rest. 'That's Yellow Rock. Andy's father came off his horse there. I believe Andy climbed down the side to recover his father's body. Angus and Grandfather Campbell were with him. It was the talk of the district. But that is Andrew. Pity he's such a bushie.'

'What do you mean, "bushie"?' Anne asked.

'Andy is hard. I think he would be hard on

women, too. It's the way he's lived. He doesn't realise there is more to life than work. Work is all he knows.'

Jane Campbell was blonde and very pretty. She was also just starting to show her pregnancy. She was a tall young woman with lovely manners, which was to be expected of a person with her schooling.

'When is the baby due?' Anne asked.

'In August. I am going back to Mother's in Sydney before then. Angus is hoping the first one will be a boy. Carry on the line and all that. The Campbells go back a long way. It's funny, you know, but back in Scotland the Campbells and the MacLeods were on opposite sides of the fence. The Campbells sided with the English and were hated by the Highland clans.'

Jane went on to explain that Old Angus was the son of a Lowland Scot and, although not as tall and powerfully built as Andrew MacLeod, he was a man of formidable presence. Both he and his son, Young Angus, were of similar complexion, being a shade on the florid side. They had the same piercing light-blue eyes, and where the younger man had sandy, reddish hair, his father's was now a silvery grey. Old Angus had a real parrot's beak nose, which was less pronounced on his son. It was said of Old Angus that he still had the first penny he earned and that his bark was worse than his bite. It took some people a few years to discover that Old Angus had a softer side to his nature, but nobody took him lightly. Old Angus was chairman of the Pastures Protection Board and president of the local branch of the Country Party.

Young Angus was a marginally softer man, and although a few years older than Andrew MacLeod, the two got along well enough. It was a rather peculiar relationship because although Young Angus considered himself top of the grazier pile, he had the greatest possible respect for Andy's ability with sheepdogs and stock horses. He had never managed to beat MacLeod at a single trial, which was a source of mortification to him, as Angus believed he owned the best of everything. He couldn't understand how his border collies got walloped by MacLeod's kelpies every time he came up against Andy at a sheepdog trial.

There had been many arguments over dogs between Andy and Angus in the past. Andy was a kelpie man through and through while Angus favoured the border collie, as his father had before him. Angus could never understand how a man with Andy's Scottish lineage could prefer kelpies to collies, but could not very well criticise – at least not openly – a man who had beaten him so often and so convincingly. It would look like sour grapes.

Angus was one of the most successful graziers in the whole Liverpool Plains region. He owned one of the best horned Hereford studs to be found anywhere, as good a flock of merino sheep as money and good sheep classers could make it, and three times the area of land owned by Andy MacLeod. Angus also owned a lot more good bottom land on which he could fatten cattle and run breeding ewes.

As Jane told her all this, Anne began to warm to her. Fantastic a thought as it probably was, she hoped the two of them could share a neighbourly friendship.

Her reverie was broken when Jane asked, 'Have you met him?'

'Who?'

'Andrew MacLeod.'

'Oh, only once. I had a few dances with him. He told me he had a property in the hills.'

'I see,' Jane said and gave Anne a quick smile. 'I believe there are several young women, and one or two older ones, who wouldn't mind dancing with Andy MacLeod.'

'Is that so? And what does Mr MacLeod think of that?'

'Andy is far from being a ladies' man. My impression is that he doesn't know they exist at all. I predict that he'd want someone very special. His mother was a rare gem, I believe. They lived up on High Peaks all through the war while Andrew's father was overseas. She could do almost anything. She milked the cows and had a lovely vegetable garden. She was killed when her husband crashed his car into the creek. It was up there at the bridge. I am told Andy hardly spoke to his father again.'

'It must be hard on him, having to cross that bridge all the time,' Anne suggested.

'I agree, but fortunately Andy is a very practical person. By the way, is he a good dancer?'

'Very good indeed, but after all you've told me I

find it a little strange that a man like that would go anywhere near a dance hall.'

'A lot of hardworking men like to dance. Where else can they go to meet women? Andrew isn't any different in that regard. He is one of those rare people who is good at almost everything he takes on. His mother taught him to dance when he was quite young,' Jane said. Then, coming closer and whisper-ing in Anne's ear, she added, 'Just between you and me, I think Angus is rather jealous of Andy's sheer ability, especially when it comes to sheepdogs.'

'But I thought that Angus was the livestock king of the district.'

Jane laughed in her musical, tinkly way. 'Yes, but when you've spent a lot of money importing a dog from Scotland only to see it beaten by your neighbour's homebred kelpies, it can affect you quite deeply,' Jane said.

'Well, well. That's something I've learned today,' Anne said and laughed.

'What have you learned?' Angus said, surprising her from behind.

'That that peak up there is the highest point of the Great Dividing Range for a fair way north and south,' Anne replied, thinking very quickly.

'Yes, it is, and a dangerous place it is, too.'

Anne made a mental vow that she would make it to the top of Yellow Rock even if she had to do it on foot – the most likely possibility anyway, as she had never ridden a horse. *That* was something she was going to have to correct.

It had been a most enjoyable afternoon at Inverlochy, but it could have been so much better if only she had found some excuse to visit High Peaks. Anne sighed as she opened the door of her little car. She took a last lingering look at the tops, purple now, before she headed the Morris back towards town. He is up there in those wonderful hills; a little empire all to himself, she thought. The more she heard about Andrew MacLeod, the more he fascinated her. It seemed that he was perhaps the only real man she had ever met. Damn him, she thought. The yearning for him was still there. There had to be some way she could meet him again without compromising her reputation. There just had to be.

Chapter Two

It was a warm, steamy night and some of the men had drunk too much before coming to the dance. Johnny Miller was one of a few men who had beer in his car and would slip outside periodically. Normally he didn't drink so much, but it was a hot night and he had a thirst up.

Johnny was employed at the local post office when he wasn't chasing young women in Muswellbrook and Mudgee. He was a good-looking young man with dark, wavy hair and blue eyes. Anne's mother would have called them come-to-bed eyes. They had lit up the first time Anne Gilmour came into the post office. She was easily the best-looking woman he had ever seen in Merriwa. Only Angus Campbell's missus came anywhere near her. Johnny had an enormous ego to go with his looks, and his many victories with women had imbued him with the belief that he was irresistible.

Anne thought that Johnny looked quite presentable, but it only took her half a dance to discover what he was really after. They were near the back verandah of the hall when the music stopped and Johnny quickly had her through the door and outside. One hand came round and cupped a breast while he kissed her neck. She could smell the beer on his breath.

'Johnny, stop it! Let me go.'

Johnny's ego ignored Anne's words as he reached down and put one hand on her thigh. She was just about to kick him when she heard a deep voice coming from the direction of the doorway.

'Let her go,' it said.

'Piss off and mind your own business,' Johnny said, without even glancing to see who was speaking. He continued to bury his face in Anne's hair and kiss her.

The next moment, he felt a pair of hands like steel bands on his arms lift him bodily into the air. Despite his struggles he was powerless to do anything. He was carried down the back stairs and then sat down hard on the ground. Then a stream of water was being sprayed all over him.

Johnny got to his feet with fists flailing, but there was nobody there to hit. He made out a large figure heading up the back stairs two or three at a time but he couldn't see who it was. He raced after his assailant and was almost at the top of the stairs when the big man turned and looked at him. 'Go home, Johnny. Go home before you get hurt,' the deep voice advised.

Johnny quailed. There were only a couple of men in the district who really frightened him and one of them was staring him straight in the face. Andrew MacLeod. Nobody in their right mind antagonised Andy MacLeod. There were less painful ways of committing suicide than at the hands of Big Andy.

'Sorry, Andy. I didn't know she was your girl,' Johnny said meekly.

'She isn't. But that doesn't mean she wants to be mauled by you. Now go on home and everything will be all right.'

Johnny backed down the stairs and disappeared into the darkness. Anne was standing by the back door of the hall when Andy turned from watching Johnny's sudden departure.

'You didn't, did you?' he asked.

'Didn't what?' she asked.

'Didn't want to be mauled by him?'

'Of course not. And thank you for your timely appearance.'

'Johnny Miller thinks he's God's gift to women. I doubt that he will worry you again. Would you like to dance?'

'I would now,' she said with a slight emphasis on the last word.

'Good,' he said, taking one of her hands and leading her out onto the floor.

Anne closed her eyes and let him guide her about the room, feeling that while she was with Andrew

MacLeod she did not have a worry in the world.

'I was up near your place recently,' she said after they had danced together for some time. She had lost count of exactly how many dances there had been, but it did not matter in the slightest while Andrew held her in his strong arms.

'Were you?' he asked with his dark-grey eyes looking down into hers.

Anne shivered. 'Yes. The Campbells told me you're great with animals.'

'Did they indeed? Do you know much about live-stock?' he asked.

'Not a thing. But one of my current objectives is to learn to ride a horse.'

'I see. Would you like me to teach you?'

'Could I have a better teacher?' she asked, with her nerves tingling.

'That's a matter of opinion. If you would like to learn to ride, I'll teach you. However, I'm a bachelor and I live alone. If you don't want to risk your rep-utation, you might choose to bring an escort.'

'You mean to your property?'

'That's where the horses are, Miss Gilmour,' he said with a smile.

'Anne,' she said, trying hard to control her breath-ing. 'I will come on my own and I will bring a picnic basket,' she said with a rush of words. 'When?'

'It will have to wait until I finish my shearing run. That's a few weeks away.'

'Oh.'

'I'll contact you when I am finished. Sundays are best for me.'

'You won't put me on anything too fierce, will you?'

'Of course not. My mother's old mare will be ideal for you. She is a real lady.'

'What should I wear?'

'Trousers of some kind. Jodhpurs might be best. Have you got any boots?'

She shook her head. 'No boots.'

'You'll need something stronger than shoes. If you can afford a pair of elastic-sided boots, I suggest that you buy Baxter's or R. M. Williams, depending on your pocket. And you should wear a wide-brimmed hat.'

'You mean a sombrero?'

'A sombrero is a Yank or a Mexican hat. Any old wide-brimmed felt hat will do. Don't want you getting sunburned straight off.'

'Will we be going up Yellow Rock?' she asked with much trepidation.

He grinned. 'That's not likely. We'll just have a gentle hour or so about the lower country. If you aren't used to riding, your bottom gets a bit sore, and more so if you're climbing. You'll want to get hardened up well and truly before you venture into the high country.'

'Thank you,' she said, smiling up into his warm, open face.

The weeks dragged by as Anne waited for Andy to contact her. To fill in the time, she visited the local emporium. She had no trouble purchasing the items Andy had suggested. Later, when she tried them on, she was quite satisfied, even pleased, with their practicality and appearance. Please, please, God, make me a natural rider, she thought. She also blew some of her savings on a picnic basket, which she planned to fill with tasty treats for the big day – if it ever eventuated.

When Andy finally rang and made arrangements for her to visit him the following Sunday, Anne almost wept with relief.

The real excitement came on the actual day when she passed Inverlochy and drove on towards High Peaks. The bend in the road appeared and then she was heading for the big homestead which stood on a rise on the other side of the creek. The road dipped rather sharply to the wooden bridge that spanned it. Anne wondered if this was where Andrew's father had run his car off the road. The creek was lined with she-oaks and looked tranquil enough right then.

The Morris rattled across the boards of the bridge and pulled up in front of a high mesh fence which surrounded the homestead. Andrew came down the front steps off the wide verandah and walked out to greet her. Anne's heart skipped a beat when she saw him. He was dressed in grey gaberdine trousers, a plain blue shirt and his wide-brimmed hat, which had seen decidedly better days. Yet he looked – well, just right.

'Welcome to High Peaks, Anne,' he said with a broad smile. 'And I must say you certainly look like a rider.'

'Thank you, Andrew. Boy, what a wonderful spot. Can I have a look around or do we head straight off?'

'Whatever you like,' he said.

He took her around the house and showed her the area his mother had devoted to the vegetable garden. Anne also noted the trees and shrubs she had planted. In the vegie garden there was silver beet mainly, some lettuces and a row of healthy-looking tomatoes.

'I don't get much time to look after the garden,' he said.

'What do you mean? It all looks to be doing well,' she observed.

'Sheep manure. I bring it across from the grating floor where the sheep stand behind the shearing board in the shed.'

They toured the house next, and Anne wandered from room to room in a state of subdued excitement because deep down she wondered if this would be *her* house one day. She tried not to look too interested and certainly not too nosy as her eyes took in the kitchen. In the middle of the room there was a huge and well-scrubbed pine-board table which she guessed was about eight feet long. From a large dresser cups hung on hooks and shelves were stacked with plates. Two drawers probably held cutlery and, in the deeper drawer, tablecloths. At the far end of the room there was an enormous recessed range, beside which was a box containing split firewood. No doubt Andrew had plenty of dead wood to keep this monster going in winter. But she was pleased to see a kettle and a toaster next to a power point. Jane Campbell had explained to her that because bulk electricity hadn't yet reached this end of the road, power and light were supplied by generators.

A wide verandah led off the kitchen and beside the door to this verandah there was a rather elderly refrigerator. Whether it was run by the generator or kerosene she didn't like to ask. Outside, at the far end of the back verandah, there was an old meatsafe and another great stack of split firewood. When they left the kitchen and walked up a wide hall she counted three bedrooms. A quick peep was all she allowed herself. The furniture was older in style and solid and she thought it would come up beautifully with some loving polish. Anne was sure it had seen none since Andy's mother had died. One bedroom was papered in cream and gold and the other two were simply tongue-and-groove pine like the big lounge room.

'It's a lovely house, Andrew,' she said, 'and you have kept it very tidy.'

'For a man, you mean?' he said, grinning.

They came at last to the lounge room with its massive fireplace, over which hung a large oval mirror. Its base rested on a mantel shelf. Years of fires had darkened the mirror's surface but a touch of gold frost and a good clean would do wonders,

Anne thought. To one side there was a sideboard of dark wood. In the centre a woman's picture held pride of place. She was handsome with a wonderful head of dark hair, but it was her eyes and smile that held Anne. She could see Andrew in that face. There was a smaller picture, of a quite good-looking man in military uniform. He had to be Andrew's father. There were two other framed pictures of a small boy, taken some years apart, which she was sure were of Andrew. In between these photos and on the mantelpiece were cups and other silverware. They were all prizes won by Andrew with his dogs and horses. Scattered about the room were big easy chairs.

Anne turned from reading the inscriptions on the trophies and said, 'I must go and see your dogs. I really must, before we do anything else.'

'Do you like dogs?' he asked.

'I think I do. We had a dog in Sydney. It was Father's dog really; a wire-haired foxie. Dad used to get it clipped. I went to the Sydney Sheep Show and the best part was the sheepdog trials. Some didn't seem to be very well looked after and were awfully scrawny, but when they worked they were so clever you forgot about their appearance.'

'You can't keep working-dogs in fat condition,' he said. 'They wouldn't be able to do the job. Sheepdogs need to be in hardworking condition; if you've got them in good shape, they will run all day. It's hard work mustering sheep in these hills on a hot day, but at least here they have plenty of water close by. Out on the plains, you can be a long way from water for a long time. There's times you need to carry water with you or else the dogs will overheat.'

They walked down the front path, out through the gate in the high fence that surrounded the house, and then down a slight slope towards a thick belt of trees. 'The high fence is to keep the chooks and guineafowl out of the garden,' Andrew explained. 'Mum was great for chooks and I still have a few ... they keep me in eggs 'cause I sure hate shop eggs. Wilf White gave Mum the guineafowl.'

There were large, hollow log kennels beneath the pepperinas and kurrajong trees. Tied by a long chain to each log was a prick-eared, short-coated kelpie. Some were black and tan, others a kind of slate-blue, and one was a red or brown with tan markings. A little distance away from the adult dogs was a low mesh pen in which several pups were playing with a much chewed bone.

'Oh, the darlings. Andrew, can I pick them up?' Anne pleaded.

'If you want to. They'll probably get you dirty.'

'What's a bit of dirt?' she said.

He registered the remark in his mind. It gained Anne her first tick of approval.

The pups wriggled and tried to lick her face as she held each in turn. 'I like the black ones with the tan markings the best,' she said after she had held each pup.

'That was the original kelpie colour,' he explained. 'The bitch that made the breed famous was called Kelpie and she was a black and tan. Colour doesn't mean anything so far as working ability goes, but the black and tans are the easiest colour to keep looking right. Them and solid blacks.'

'Can I see one work?' she asked.

'I thought you came to learn to ride,' he said.

'I've heard so much about your dogs I feel I must see one in action. Then can we ride?'

'You're not getting chicken, are you?' he said, by way of testing her mettle.

'Andrew MacLeod, when you know me better you will learn that I don't scare easily.'

'All right, I'll show you a dog in action and then it will be time for smoko. I've got the horses saddled and all we'll have to do is pack the saddlebags.'

'Why are we doing that?'

'I thought we'd boil the billy and have lunch down the creek a bit. What do you reckon?'

'That sounds very nice. I brought a fair bit of stuff and it might not all fit in your saddlebags.'

'Not to worry. We'll fit enough.'

He went across to where a blue dog with tan spots over its eyes was standing on top of its log. 'This is King. I won the local trial with him last year. He's a pretty fair dog in the hills. We'll walk up the hill a bit to where I keep a few sheep for the purpose.'

Beyond the dog area with its shady trees there was a small paddock which adjoined the homestead and

31

its outbuildings. 'This is what I call the cow paddock. Mum used to keep her house cows here and we also run the killer sheep for the table in it. There's a few here now.'

Anne couldn't see any sheep because of the dips in the ground.

'How big is it?' she asked. She was trying to come to grips with acres in relation to properties.

'About twenty-five acres. I've been trying some fertiliser on it. Looks like it's working, too. Here, King. Way out!'

The blue and tan dog left Andrew's side and ran out in a wide arc to the right. He reached the far fence and raced up beside it, disappearing every now and again in the dips and gullies.

'Will he find the sheep?' Anne asked.

'No trouble in this little paddock, not for King.'

Presently a dozen or so sheep appeared from nowhere, and after them Anne could just see the dog. He was directly behind the sheep and seemed to be pointing them back towards where she and Andrew were standing. The dog kept them coming in what was virtually a straight line, standing far enough off them so that they did not gallop but came at a steady walk. It was as if the dog had the sheep on a string. King brought the little mob right up to within a few feet of where they were standing, and held them together so well that Andrew was able to catch one. He held it and invited Anne to open its wool.

'Is that a male sheep?' she asked, noting its small horns.

Andrew laughed. 'Half and half, Anne. It's a male sheep that was castrated as a lamb. It's called a wether. I run mostly wethers because a lot of this country is not suitable for ewes and lambs. These hills are regarded as purely wether country. I do run some ewes on the lower country that adjoins Inverlochy. Most of my cattle are there, too.'

'No bulls, I hope.'

'Only one at the moment, and he's a quiet old fellow. I call him Bob after Bob Menzies.'

Anne patted King on his broad head. The dog had never for a moment taken his eyes off the sheep and still held them in a tight bunch. 'He's a lovely dog. Will they all do what he just did?'

'They will when I've finished training them. That wasn't a very difficult job for King. He can do a lot better than that. What I like about King is that he is such a sensible dog; he reads my mind. Really good dogs are like that. He's never been a fussy dog. What I mean is that he isn't all over you like a rash, as my mother used to say. He's there beside you like a shadow and, fair dinkum, you'd think he was a dopey old dog, but the moment there's something to be done, he's into it. Smart as paint, too. Look here.' He dropped King's leather lead on the ground and walked away a few yards. 'Crikey, where's that lead? Must have lost the damned thing. King, you seen that lead?'

The dog was standing above the lead with his head half turned towards Andrew. 'Well, pick it up, King,' he said.

King picked up one end of the lead and walked towards them. Then he stood on his hind legs and presented the redhide lead to Andrew.

'Why, Andrew, that's wonderful,' Anne said. 'He seems almost human.'

'He's probably more human than some people, Anne. Comes a lot from having so much to do with me. I talk to my dogs all the time, treat 'em like mates. Some people never do. The more you talk to them, the more they come to know. Lazy people never make dog trainers. You tie a dog up all the time and forget about him and you'll never have a smart dog. I can put a saddle, a hat and a whip on the ground and King will sit beside each when I tell him. What it gets down to is that you've got to work with a dog. Course, some dogs are smarter than others. You look for the smart ones right from the time they're pups. You pick those fellas out and start developing them. Come on back to the house and we'll have a drink of tea.'

Anne produced some fruitcake and cream cakes, at which Andrew whistled. 'You'll spoil me with this tucker. I only get this sort of thing occasionally when I go to Campbell's. And sometimes Gertie – she's Wilf's sister – brings me a slab of cake. She and her husband come up from Sydney once or twice a year to see Wilf. I wouldn't have time to do any fancy cooking even if I knew how. I buy a bit of cake when

I see it, but otherwise I stick to biscuits and bread. Mum used to be great on cake. She won a lot of prizes with her cooking.'

'Do you find it at all lonely here on your own?' Anne asked when they were sitting at the big kitchen table with their tea. 'After you lost your mother, it must have been quite hard for you,' she said rather boldly.

'It was lonely at first, but I always keep busy. I don't have time to think about it.'

This wasn't the answer Anne had sought, but she pressed on. 'Who feeds your animals when you're away shearing?' she asked.

'There's a young chap by the name of Shaun Covers on the back road who comes up here and does that. I pay him to keep an eye on things. He likes the dogs and is good with them. In fact, I gave him a dog to get him started in trials. It works out pretty well. Now, want to ride?' he asked, after draining his cup.

'Sure, Tex, bring on them cayuses.'

He grinned and nodded. It seemed she had a good sense of humour. That earned her a second tick of approval.

He led the way out to the horse yard where two horses were already saddled and bridled. One was a big old chestnut mare with a kind eye, something like that of a Jersey cow. The other was a younger-looking bay mare. Andrew buckled two saddlebags onto the bay's saddle and then led the chestnut up to Anne.

'This is Lady. She *is* a lady so don't be scared of her.'

'She's so tall,' Anne protested. 'I couldn't get up there.'

'Nonsense. Just put your left foot in the stirrup and pull up with your arm. Like this.'

Andy was up in the saddle and looking down at her in a flash. Then, in a second fluid motion, he was on the ground again beside her.

Anne made two ineffectual attempts to climb into the saddle but failed miserably each time.

'Once more,' Andrew urged.

She felt the firm pressure of one large hand on her leg just above the ankle as she was lifted up and over into the saddle. 'See, nothing to it,' he said, grinning.

'Huh, not with a man mountain helping you. What do I do now?'

'Gather the reins like so and hold them down low. Now, place your feet so that the balls are taking your weight. Keep your heels down and your feet parallel to the mare's sides. That's the shot.'

He moved over to his own mare and vaulted into the saddle so quickly and smoothly that it seemed to be done in the blink of an eye. 'Okay, now just put a little pressure on your rein to turn her. Use your leg against her side when you do it. All good horses are broken in to respond to leg as well as rein pressure. All right, let's go.'

'Not too fast, Andrew, please,' she protested.

He took a length of redhide from his back pocket and, leaning across, clipped the end of it to the old mare's bridle. 'That should ease your mind. She can't get away. Keep your back straight and your elbows close to your sides. They shouldn't flap about.'

They walked the horses past the dog yards and down to the first gate, which led towards the high country beyond the homestead. Andrew bent across his mare to open the gate, led Lady through and then turned and shut the gate. 'Now, where would you like to go?' he asked.

'Nowhere too difficult. Can we just go to the creek? It doesn't look too rough.'

'Sure we can. If we follow the creek down far enough we come up against Angus Campbell's boundary fence.'

'How far is that?' Anne asked fearfully.

'Not real far. Maybe two miles.'

'Two miles. I don't think I could last two miles. Then there's two miles back.'

'We don't have to go so far. And I'm sure you can make it.'

When indeed they did reach the boundary, Andrew unclipped the lead. 'You don't need that any more.'

Apart from the strain on her legs and a slight soreness in her rear end, Anne found that she was coping quite well. After a while she began to loosen up and could even take an interest in the surrounding countryside.

They turned back from the boundary fence and retraced the route they had taken. It was roughly parallel with the creek, which was lined for most of its distance with she-oaks. In several places the creek deepened and widened and Andrew said that he had often swum in those holes.

When Anne looked at her watch she found that they had been riding for about three hours. Time had simply flown. Whether Andrew had sensed that she was tiring or whether he had always meant to stop under the big apple gum Anne did not know, but the next moment she felt herself being lifted from the saddle and placed gently on the ground. It felt a little strange for a few moments, although after she had walked up and down a few times, the stiffness almost left her.

'You'll feel it later on,' Andrew said as he watched her. He had gathered sticks and started a small fire while she was trying to ease the stiffness from her legs. He took a billy from the chaff bag on his saddle, filled it from the creek and set it against the fire. He then unsaddled the horses and spread Lady's saddle blanket beside the trunk of the gum. 'Sit yourself down on that,' he said.

Anne gratefully sank to the ground.

'Once you get used to riding, you won't have a problem. It's just that your muscles are being used in different ways. If you rode a bit each day for a week or so, you'd be right as rain. Have a bath as soon as you get back to the house. That will ease a lot of the stiffness.'

Anne considered this suggestion. Taking a bath in the home of a man you were going out with for the first time seemed a rather intimate course of action.

She enjoyed the lunch and was pleased she had gone to the trouble of selecting some nice ham to go with the lettuce and tomatoes. She had also included some cold baked potatoes, which she noted Andrew seemed to fancy. The tea, laced with condensed milk, was something else. There was more fruitcake to go with the tea. Andrew ate every crumb, and so did she. She hadn't felt so hungry in years.

'Do you do this often?' she asked.

'My mother and I used to have a lot of picnics. I can remember coming here from when I was a very small boy. I had a pony that my grandfather bought for me as a birthday present. She was my first pony and a real beauty.'

'What happened to her?' she asked.

'A rotten snake killed her. A big brown. She was too quiet and got too close to the mongrel. Why anyone ever put snakes on earth God only knows.'

'God must have had a reason,' she said. 'Perhaps it was to eat mice.'

'They wouldn't eat enough mice to make a difference. One minute you've got a horse or dog worth a lot of money and the next they're dead. I'm real crooked on snakes. Snakes, foxes and rabbits. They're all rubbish, in Australia at least. On one property between here and Cassilis I heard they killed two hundred and fifty thousand rabbits in six months. The trappers were running traps three times a day.'

'I suppose nobody knew how much they would multiply,' Anne said as she accepted a second cup of steaming tea. 'They probably thought rabbits would be useful as food,' she suggested.

'More likely they brought them for sport, like they brought the mongrel foxes.'

'I've read that some people think sheep have caused problems, too. They say they've contributed to erosion,' Anne said.

'Maybe there has been some erosion through overstocking, especially when the rabbits were bad, but sheep are very useful animals,' he said as he settled himself against a log. 'Sheep would be one of the most useful animals you could have. They'll clothe you, feed you and you can even make cheese from their milk. No kidding. Cattle are good too but they are damned expensive things to feed.'

Anne sat back, enjoying hearing Andrew talk about his thoughts and feelings. She sensed that there was so much under his big, rough exterior.

'Sheep put this country on its feet,' he continued. 'Some people would say it's queer me being so keen on sheep after what happened in Scotland.'

'What happened in Scotland?' Anne asked. She knew from her history lectures that a great many Scots had been executed, imprisoned and deported after Culloden. Surely that was too long ago to affect the feelings of a bushman like Andrew MacLeod?

'Between the English and the great and noble clan chieftains, the Scottish countryside – or at least large areas of it – was cleared of people to make way for sheep, mostly Cheviot sheep. Crofts and houses were destroyed and people were either left to starve or forced to accept deportation. People who had depended on their lairds for a thousand years or more were simply told to leave. And when sheep didn't return enough money, many ancestral areas were sold to wealthy Englishmen. What do you think they did with those ancient holdings? Used them as game parks for their English friends. Game parks! They even kept tallies of their kills. These ran into thousands. And the new owners donned the kilt and strutted like the lairds they replaced.

'People trumpet about British justice but there was very little evidence of it where the Scots and the Irish were concerned. There was very little justice and very little prosperity for the average person in Britain, and conditions didn't improve until the royalty lost most of its powers. Not that many politicians are much better – they're only interested in short-term solutions which make them look good. At least we can throw them out every few years.'

'You do have some strong views, Andrew,' Anne said.

'Sorry. I don't usually sound off. People say I don't talk much. Grandfather Tormid used to say that what a man did counted for more than what he said. That's my thinking, too.'

'Having sheep also gives you plenty of opportunities for working your sheepdogs,' Anne suggested, keen to keep Andy talking.

'That too. But there's more to it than that.

Owning a piece of land gives a fellow a kind of independence. Maybe it is there in the MacLeod blood because the family were great landowners in Scotland. Some people would say that High Peaks is just a rough hill-country property, but it's *my* rough hill-country property, and while I keep paying back the bank nobody can take it away from me. I can do as I like on it, within reason anyway.'

'It really is lovely up here, Andrew,' Anne said with a smile. 'What are we going to do now?'

He grinned in the way she was coming to like very much. 'If it was dark we could go eel-bashing. You ever been eel-bashing?'

'Eel-bashing! What in heaven's name is eel-bashing?' she asked, raising her long eyebrows.

'There's eels in this creek. Lots of eels. They're like short snakes. You walk into the creek with a torch or a lantern and belt them with a piece of steel. You can use a twenty-two calibre rifle with the barrel under the surface, but it doesn't do much for the rifle. When you catch your eel, you pull the skin off like a glove and cut it into short pieces for cooking. You can fry them, with or without batter, or steam them. They make a change from mutton and beef.'

'I don't think I'd like to "bash" anything, Andy, but it sounds like the sort of thing my young sister would like. She's coming to stay with me for a few days, in only a couple of weeks now. Can we leave the eel-bashing until then?'

'Sure we can. Is your sister like you?' he asked with

his eyes fixed on hers. Anne thought she had never met anyone with such honest, direct eyes.

She shook her head vigorously. 'Oh no. Kate is much more outgoing than I am. She is a double-certificate nursing sister and is doing her third certificate right now. I can just see her eel-bashing. If she fell in a deep hole she would only laugh. I'm an old sobersides in comparison with her.'

'I think you're just right the way you are,' he said with such candour that she was momentarily overwhelmed.

'Why, thank you, sir,' she said, flashing him a dazzling smile.

'You're a lot like my mother,' he added. 'She was a doer, not a talker. It might sound silly to an outsider, but I think her spirit is still here. Sometimes I can hear her voice.'

'It is good to remember if the memories are precious,' Anne replied, and in the next breath, 'I'm sure I am taking up a lot of your time. Is there anything you have to do?'

'Well,' he said, and hesitated. 'If you feel up to it, perhaps we could ride into the next paddock and have a look at the sheep in there. You need to keep a close watch on them at this time of the year. Flies are the problem.'

Despite her stiffness, Anne consented with a show of enthusiasm. 'Of course I'm all right. Let's pack up and go.'

But by midafternoon, Anne was feeling very stiff

indeed. Andrew must have noticed her wince because he suddenly turned his horse and headed back towards the creek.

'Where are we going?' she asked.

'Home,' he answered. 'I've seen enough.'

Anne did not want the day to end. For the first time in her life, she was in the company of a man she really liked. And she had a very good idea that he liked her in just the same way.

A fortnight later, Anne found herself back at High Peaks for another day's riding, this time in the company of her visiting sister, Kate. The pair had been invited to spend a few nights on Andrew's property. Kate, who had ridden horses in several countries and considered herself to be an adequate rider, had jumped at the chance to spend a day in the saddle in hill country – and she was equally thrilled by the prospect of eel-bashing.

The trio rode and rested in turns, and Anne was pleased to discover she was not quite so stiff on this occasion. They ate lunch in a clearing up by Yellow Rock, which Kate was eager to tackle on horseback. Andrew had had to put his foot down because, although he could see that Kate was a fair rider, only the most experienced riders were up to handling Yellow Rock.

'You're a spoilsport, Andrew MacLeod.' Kate taunted him in a way Anne would not have dared. 'I've been in much higher and rougher country than this.'

'I don't want to spoil the day by having to go down Yellow Rock to pick up your pieces,' Andrew replied. And despite the jocular tone in his voice, Anne – and indeed Kate – knew that his words were not to be taken lightly.

They rode back to the homestead in the soft enchantment of a perfect early summer evening. Andrew left the women to enjoy the setting while he fed the dogs and horses.

After dinner, when the sun had set, he hooked up a trailer to the grey Fergie tractor he had swapped for a shearing job, threw in a bale of straw for Anne and Kate to sit on, and headed for the creek. It was a bumpy ride and there were a lot of squeals before they reached the creek.

'Andrew MacLeod, I'm sure you put us over those bumps on purpose,' Anne said.

Andrew grinned. 'Just trying you out, Anne.'

'Where are these eels, Andrew?' Kate asked.

'All in good time,' he said and began to strip off his clothes down to a pair of green swimming trunks. Anne and Kate had changed into shorts and brief blouses. Andrew took up his torch and handed them each a length of flat steel with a makeshift handle.

'You'll want to take it in turns so you don't hit each other,' he said as he waded out into the creek. Anne and Kate followed in his wake. The water was clear in the light of the torch and Kate screamed with excitement when she saw the first dark shape undulate

45

through the water. Andrew chopped at it with a powerful downward slash, tucked the basher under his left arm and thrust his right arm down into the water. It came up holding a wriggling eel. He stuffed it into a sugar bag he had tied round his waist and then waded out into slightly deeper water. Kate made an enormous swipe at the next eel, missed entirely, lost her footing and fell into the creek. She came up spluttering and laughing. She recovered sufficiently to eventually claim one eel. Anne made several ineffectual swipes and finally opted for holding the torch while Andrew did the bashing. When he had put half a dozen in the sugar bag, he suggested they'd had enough. They retired to the bank where he lit a fire and boiled the billy. The warm night and the warmth of the fire soon partially dried their clothes and induced the young women to feel relaxed and sleepy. It had, after all, been a long day. 'It would be good to sleep here by the fire,' Kate suggested.

'Maybe next time,' Andrew replied.

'We could have a barbecue here by the creek,' Anne said.

'But I won't be here then,' Kate protested.

'You'll return eventually,' Anne said, wondering how anyone could resist the allure of the high country.

The next morning Anne and Kate were still asleep when Andrew came back to the house after doing the outside jobs. He was having his breakfast when Anne and Kate appeared in the kitchen.

'*We* were going to get breakfast for *you*,' they said, almost in unison.

'Then you'll need to get up a lot earlier than this,' he joked.

'What is that in front of you?' Anne asked, pointing to the brown jug on the table.

'Milk, fresh from the cow this morning.'

'You didn't tell me you milked.'

'You didn't ask. As it happens, I don't, generally. Maybe once or twice a week, if I have time, but I thought you would appreciate some fresh milk. I can show you how it's done tomorrow morning, if you like – if you can get out of bed early enough, that is,' he said.

'It would have to be very early indeed,' Anne replied. 'I have to be at school by eight-thirty.'

So the following morning, Andrew roused them out just before five and, after an early morning cup of tea, they made their way out to the cowshed where a Hereford and Jersey-cross cow was chewing on some hay. 'She's bred from my mother's old pure Jersey by my Hereford bull. The old cow was a better milker and gave more cream, but this one is good enough for me and the pups.'

'Wow, look at those horns, Kate,' Anne said as she eyed the cow with concern.

'She's as quiet as a lamb and, anyway, her head goes in that stall so she can't move it very much,' Andrew explained.

He put some feed in a tub and the cow put its

47

head through and began eating the meal. Andrew secured her by pushing a piece of timber against her neck and holding it in place with a steel pin. That done, he pulled the near side rear leg back with a length of cord and tied it to a post. He sat down on a round stump about a foot off the ground and washed the cow's teats with warm water. The steel bucket was placed under the udder and he began to milk.

'See, nothing to it,' he said as the milk frothed up in the bucket. 'Who wants a go?'

Anne and Kate took a teat each and began to pull. Between them they managed no more than about a thimbleful of milk.

'No, like this,' Andrew said, pulling up and down on the near teats. Fortunately, it was a very quiet and tolerant cow, and while Andrew kept adding small quantities of meal to her trough, she endured the milking quite happily. It took over half an hour for Anne and Kate to get half a bucket. They felt a little deflated when Andrew told them that his mother had been able to fill a two-gallon bucket in under ten minutes.

'Practice, that's all it is,' he said. 'Practice gives you the right technique. If you had to milk every morning, you'd soon get it right.'

He put aside some of the milk for the pups and took the remainder back to the house. 'My mother used to separate every couple of days so we had our own butter during the war when most people were on rations. That's one advantage of being on a property. You need never go hungry, if you're willing to put in a bit of effort. A lot of people couldn't be bothered as it's so much easier to buy everything at a shop. No shops close by here, so I milk.'

'I wouldn't mind making my —' Anne began and stopped suddenly. She blushed and looked away. She hadn't meant to push herself but the words had just slipped out.

'No, I shouldn't think you'd be lazy,' Andrew said. 'Either of you,' he added.

'I get the impression that hard work ranks very highly on your list of priorities, Andrew,' Kate suggested rather audaciously.

'Got no time for slackers and bludgers, Kate. I had enough of that with my father and everything went down the drain. If you don't want to work, you shouldn't be on the land. Some, like Angus Campbell, can afford to employ people so they can act the part of squire, but most of us have to work damn hard to keep things going. And you've got to want to do it.'

'Will you whip your wife if she won't work?' Kate asked even more audaciously.

The big man grinned. Anne relaxed. Andrew could take a joke.

'I don't even whip my animals, Kate. And I wouldn't expect my wife to be a slave. I'd just expect her to pull her weight.'

'And what would you be offering her?' Kate quickly replied.

'Me, and this place, a place to call your own . . . and a good, clean life. The chance to build a decent future. Something to pass on to your children. Is that enough?'

'I reckon it is,' Kate said, and looked sideways at Anne. There was a prior claim on Andrew MacLeod and she realised she should say no more.

As a thankyou for letting them stay, Anne and Kate made Andy a massive breakfast, which he ate with little effort before helping them carry their bags out to Anne's car.

'Thank you for everything,' Anne said.

'And especially for the eel-bashing,' Kate added as the car drove away.

Andrew lifted his hand to his hat and walked back to the house.

Kate sighed. 'Now that is a real piece of man,' she said as the Morris crossed the bridge over the creek. 'And he certainly likes you.'

'You think so?'

'Of course. I can tell just by the way he looks at you. Bet you ten bob he asks you to marry him.'

'It would be worth losing ten bob for that,' Anne said very softly.

'You mean you like him enough to marry him?' Kate asked.

'I love the big devil,' she confessed. 'And it's making me miserable. I have wanted him from the first night we met. I just wish to God he would make up his mind what he wants.'

Chapter Three

The following year was one of the happiest Anne Gilmour experienced in her life. Years later, as she looked back on this period, she realised that Andrew MacLeod had been a much wiser person than had been apparent at the time. She was so concerned that Andrew wasn't really serious about her that she failed to realise he was actually preparing her for a life on High Peaks.

While they continued to go to dances, more and more time was spent on High Peaks, out on the hills on horses. Anne found herself enjoying her greater mastery of the old mare. There were also many trips together to sheepdog trials and camp-drafts, which are similar to sheepdog trials except a horse is used instead of a dog. In the dog trials, Andrew won the Maiden and Open Trial with a black and tan kelpie called Ned, and in the final of the Open, Ned was the only dog who penned his sheep. Angus Campbell ran fifth, and his dog didn't even seem in the same class.

The weekend after the trial, Andrew picked Anne up in his old truck and they headed out to Murrurundi for the Hunter River championship campdrafts. Anne was full of interest in the drafts, but at the end of the day she decided that the dog trials appealed to her more. She did like horses, but it seemed to her that there was more science in working a dog in trials.

She said as much to Andrew on the way home.

'You're right, Anne,' he said. 'There's more to dog trialling than campdrafting, and anyone who has ever tried the two would agree with you. An old hand once said to me that having two reins in your hand to control your horse is an easier option than trying to control a dog a hundred yards away. You can exert a positive influence on your horse by your own actions, but if you haven't trained your dog well enough to be able to stop him at a distance, you won't win a sheepdog trial.'

The next time Anne went out to High Peaks she found a new grey gelding in the horse yard. 'Where did you get this fellow, Andy?' she asked immediately.

'He was going to waste so I cut him out by shearing; got the horse in return for his value in labour,' he said. 'I reckon you're ready for a bit more horse than the old mare. He's yours.'

'What? You mean he's really mine? A present?'

'I reckon,' Andy said.

Anne turned around and couldn't resist kissing him. 'You're so sweet,' she said.

'You just going to look at him all day or are you going to try him out?'

'I reckon I'll try him out,' Anne said, imitating Andy's deep voice and bush drawl.

'Right. Get a saddle on him and let's be off. The day is nearly done.' It was only nine a.m. but by then Andy had usually put in a couple of hours' work.

'Yes, sir. Right away, sir,' she said, bowing her head in the fashion of an obedient servant. She was going to try taking the mickey out of him just to see how he would take it.

'I didn't mean it like that,' he said gruffly.

'That's all right, Andy,' she said softly. 'I know you didn't. If I thought you did I would tell you what you could do with your horse and with High Peaks. As it is, thank you very much. A few months ago I couldn't even get on a horse and now I own one. I can't thank you enough.'

She named the gelding Turk, and in time she came to truly love him. He was a very calm horse with lovely manners and he could handle the hills just about as well as the homebred horses. On Turk, Anne could ride almost anywhere – except up Yellow Rock.

The day she mastered Yellow Rock was memorable in many ways. It came about three months after Andy had presented her with Turk and marked the day she passed Andy's test of horsemanship. At the time, there was no indication that this day would be different from any other. It was a delightful autumn morning with a crispness in the air that presaged the coming winter. The hills were green from the autumn rains and there was not a cloud in the sky.

'Better pack for the day,' Andrew said when they had finished breakfast. 'It might be a long one.'

Anne nodded. They were often out all day, especially when mustering for crutching and drenching. She could now handle these long days without a twinge in her body. Moreover, she could take one of Andy's older dogs and muster sheep on her own. The sheep she collected would then be taken to Andy and together they would inspect them for flies or, alternatively, drive them down to the shearing shed.

This time the day began very much as usual, except that when they reached the foot of Yellow Rock they did not ride to right or left of the big mountain. Andy looked across at her and smiled. Anne thought that when he smiled he was as handsome as any film star. 'I reckon it's time you tackled Yellow Rock,' he said casually.

Anne caught her breath and looked up at the side of the mountain. 'If you say so, Andy,' she said, with absolute faith in his judgement.

'It's not all that bad going until you hit the last third or so. Of course it's not that easy either. But the real test is near the top. The track becomes very narrow and if you take a wrong step you can go over the side. What makes it worse is that the last part of the mountain is pretty thick with big carpet snakes. A lot of horses can't handle snakes. It's the only thing I am not sure of with your grey horse. When we get up a bit I'm going to put a rope round your waist. If the worst comes to the worst and the horse goes over the side, I'll have hold of you. You'll see why when we get up there. Still want to give it a try?'

Anne nodded. She couldn't possibly let on how scared she was really feeling. She sensed that this was Andy's ultimate test of her.

'Andy, I'd follow you to hell and back,' she confessed. 'Let's do it.'

He nodded and smiled again. 'Good girl. Just do as I tell you and pay attention to your horse.'

The first part of the climb was steep enough, although the track was reasonably wide. But the higher they climbed the narrower it became. It was much rougher, too, because they were climbing through a maze of broken rocks, some massive and some partly worn away by erosion. They also passed caves and dense pockets of scrub.

After climbing for around half an hour they came to a small grassy clearing edged by scrub and stunted gums. Andrew dismounted and uncoiled the rope that was tied to his saddle. He looped the end and handed it up to her. 'Put this over your head and round your waist,' he said.

Anne did as he asked and he tied the rope so that it would not slip.

'I want you to go first,' he said. 'That way I can

watch you and I'll have time to react. If you're behind me, you could be over the edge before I have the chance to do anything.'

'That's comforting,' she said nervously.

'Keep a firm pressure on the reins, but if anything happens and you feel the horse going over, kick your feet out of the stirrups and leave the rest to me.'

'It just gets better and better,' she said grimly.

'Want to turn back?'

'Not on your sweet life . . . not if it kills me.' God, the things a girl does for the love of a man, she thought.

'Okay, away you go,' he said.

The grassy plateau gave way almost immediately to a grotesquely angled track that reared skywards and was perhaps three feet wide. The confusion of rocks became greater as they climbed.

'Landslides,' Andy called from behind, by way of explanation.

Two dark-furred wallabies spun away from a tiny patch of grass beside the track and with wonderful agility jumped from boulder to boulder and disappeared into the labyrinth of rocks and caverns.

Anne noticed there were lots of smashed trees and big splintered branches littered around them, and Andy, as if reading her thoughts, said, 'Those trees were smashed by lightning. The ironstone rocks up here act like a magnet.'

'Remind me never to be here during a storm,' she said.

The track dipped a little and then narrowed. The mountain plunged away to the left and just ahead Anne could see where there had obviously been a considerable landslide. Tons and tons of earth, shale and rocks had poured down off the uppermost section of the mountain and across the track. Over the years this had built up into a huge deposit across a steeply plunging gully.

'We found my father just beyond that slide,' Andy said.

'You mean you went down there?' she said, looking over her shoulder at him.

'Don't look back. Keep your eyes on the track. Are you okay?'

'I'm petrified, but I guess I'm okay.'

'Once we get past this bit of track the going gets slightly better. The track turns back to the right.'

'Andy, don't tell me you can bring sheep down from here?'

'I've taken a few down this way, but mostly we cut the fence into Wilf's and take them down the hill to the bottom country and in through the lower gate.'

'But there's no grass up here.'

'There is on the other face, and that's where most of them feed. They come up here in the evening to camp.'

'Whew,' Anne breathed to herself. The words of the poem *The Man from Snowy River* kept coming back to her. She began to have some idea of what it would be like to ride the Monaro Range.

Turk twitched his ears and looked to the right.

'He's smelling the snakes, Anne. Pull his head back and keep him pointed up the track.'

Anne's heart skipped a beat and then, almost miraculously, she found that they were over the very steep section of track and were turning away from the actual face of the mountain. She was now riding through a narrow gully that seemed to bisect the very peak itself. Water was trickling down the ravine and Turk lowered his head to drink.

'Keep him going, Anne,' Andy called.

She nudged the grey and he responded immediately. They rode on through the gully until it widened into a very small clearing seemingly gouged out of the mountainside. There was no track there, only a steep slope of shale and rocks.

'We'll have to leave the horses here, Anne. We'll go the rest of the way on foot.'

Andy was beside her knee and untying the rope from around her waist. He helped her out of the saddle. She had thought her legs were well conditioned for riding but they still shook as she felt the ground beneath her. They were unsteady from the continual pressure of having kept her legs tight against the horse as they had climbed.

Andy collected the saddlebags and handed the empty billy to her. 'There's a spring behind that rock, Anne. Why don't you fill the billy and then we'll attack this slope?'

Anne found a tiny spring bubbling clear water, which she used to fill the billy.

As they set off, Andy cautioned her, 'Don't try to climb straight up the slope. Climb across. If you get into trouble, I'll be right behind you.'

It was with this security in mind that Anne managed to climb to the top. She could hardly believe she had made it there, right to the top of Yellow Rock. She pulled herself to her feet and looked around.

'Wow,' she said, with wonder in her voice.

'It's quite a view, isn't it?' Andy said as he came up to her.

The immensity of the view stunned her. It was as if they were in another world, the only two people for miles around.

To their right was another peak, equal in height to the one on which they stood, and farther away still was another big peak, showing darkly against the horizon. Andy caught Anne's gaze and pointed. 'That's Mount Oxley. It's four and a half thousand feet high,' he said. 'And right across there is Murrurundi and Wingen, where we went to the campdrafts. Now, if you look away to the left, you can see the homestead. It's just a speck from here. And back behind us in that haze is Merriwa.'

'Is that Wallaby Rocks across there?' she asked.

'It sure is. The boundary fence is between here and that peak. Wilf White owns all that country down through there. That's his house there by the dark-green patch. It's his lucerne paddock, see?'

She nodded. 'And one day you would like to add all that land to High Peaks?'

'I sure would. It would make a very decent property then. Wilf's lower country is pretty good and I could run more cattle and also make a fair bit of hay. I'm not geared to making hay on High Peaks because I haven't the equipment to do it. Wilf has some farming plant and he's got that fairly level bit of country, which I don't have. Now, are you ready to eat?'

'I've never been more ready in my life,' she said.

There were pieces of storm-hit trees even on the peak, and in his wonderfully dexterous bushman's way Andy soon had a fire going and the billy boiling.

'This is heaven,' Anne said as she sat eating her sandwiches and sipping tea. 'The view is absolutely unreal.'

'Worth the effort?'

'Oh, yes, worth the effort. Mind you, I wouldn't want to do it every day of the week.'

'I can understand that.'

'Today was just the right day for the climb, and Turk was a perfect gentleman. Lady wouldn't have made it, would she?' Anne asked.

'Not now. She used to do it years ago when Mother would come up here on her own.'

'I dips me lid to your mother,' Anne said gravely.

'You two would have got on very well,' Andy said. He looked down into the valley of the White

60

property for a few moments before turning back to her.

'Have you ever thought about becoming Mrs Andrew MacLeod?' he asked.

'Oh, once or twice,' Anne said with a smile. If he had meant to surprise her, he had succeeded, but up there in that world beyond the world, could anything be surprising?

'You have, eh? What do you think of the idea?'

'Well, I've never heard you say that you love me. Do you?'

'I don't know,' he said with surprising candour. 'If what I feel about you is love, then I love you,' he said. 'You're the only woman I've met who I want to have with me on High Peaks. I feel differently about everything when you're with me. The place seems empty when you're gone. If that's not love then I don't know what it is. I sure like you an awful lot.'

'But you've never even kissed me, not even when I've kissed you.'

'I didn't want to risk losing you ... didn't want you to think I was someone like Johnny Miller.'

'There was never any danger of me thinking that, big fella. You could have tried to kiss me any time you liked. You know a hell of a lot about the bush, but you know very little about women.'

'Maybe you could teach me,' he suggested.

'Perhaps I will,' she said.

'Does that mean you'll marry me?'

'Does that mean you're asking?'

'What?'

'Ask me properly.'

'Ask you what?'

'Ask me to marry you.'

'Anne Gilmour, will you marry me?'

'There, that wasn't so hard, was it?'

'No, it wasn't too hard. So what do you say?'

'Of course I'll marry you. I'd nearly given up waiting for you to ask. Are you ready to kiss me now?'

Andrew's response was immediate and overwhelming. Anne felt herself being lifted off the ground so that her eyes were several inches higher than his and he gazed up at her. Then she was lowered until their lips met and she surrendered to his passionate kiss.

'Wow, that was worth waiting for,' she said afterwards, regaining her breath.

Andrew held her crushed to him for an eternity until she took his hand and held it tightly. 'Try it again,' she said. So he did and it was even better the second time.

'We are going to be very happy here on High Peaks, aren't we, darling?' she said.

The look of joy on Andy's face gave her the answer.

A little later he sat with his arms around her while they surveyed their kingdom. Andrew had his back wedged against a large piece of rock. He was feeling very pleased with himself, having won the woman he had wanted since the first time he saw her, the woman he had thought might be out of his reach.

'I wonder what it would be like to stay up here all night,' Anne said with her lips close to his left ear.

'Perhaps it would be a bit like looking down from heaven and watching one side of the world fade into darkness,' he said.

'That's a thought,' she said. 'I'd like to try it sometime.'

'Try what?' he asked.

'Staying the night up here.'

'I think we ought to leave that until after we are married,' he said. 'It might be more than a man could stand.'

She blushed and he pressed her closely to him.

'Speaking of which, when is the marriage to be?' he asked. 'I can't guarantee my impeccable conduct for too much longer.'

'I was beginning to think you only wanted me for my domestic value,' she said and chuckled.

'You're having me on. I don't give a damn for all that. I've always managed on my own. I just want you.'

She reached up and ran her fingers through his thick brown hair. 'We've never talked about children. I suppose you do want children?' she asked.

'Of course. No good a man busting himself to make a good life and then have nobody to leave it to. I reckon three or four kids would be great. This is a good, clean, healthy place to rear children, and I think you'd make a great mother. But enough of that. We'd better get going if we want to make it down the mountain before nightfall.'

So they came down off the peak of Yellow Rock, both in a kind of daze.

'How on earth am I going to concentrate on getting down this slope now that I'm engaged?' she said.

'You'd better,' he replied. 'I don't want to lose you now.'

Chapter Four

Anne and Andrew had a very brief engagement. They were married three months after Andy's proposal in the small church near where Anne had been brought up. It was the second trip to Sydney for Andrew. After Anne had agreed to marry him, he had driven down to meet her parents, Jack and Mavis Gilmour. Jack was a no-nonsense fellow who ran a small printing business. His hobbies were fishing and following the St George rugby league team. The two men hit it off immediately. Jack was impressed by Andrew's honesty, and admired the fact that he didn't make out he was better than anyone else simply because he owned a sheep property.

Looking back later, Anne thought it was a lovely wedding. It was not large in terms of numbers, but those who were there were all dear friends and close relatives. Andrew looked terrific, big and strong and even more ruggedly good-looking in his smart attire.

Paddy Covers was Andrew's best man. Paddy, old now, was Andrew's automatic choice, having been more a father to him than his own father had been. Paddy was the greatest man he knew – apart from Tim Sparkes, who was away to blazes on the rodeo circuit.

Andrew couldn't believe how beautiful Anne looked as she came down the aisle on the arm of her father. He reckoned the night he met her at that dance was the luckiest night of his life. Later, with Anne dressed in her going-away outfit, he thought it seemed incredible that she had become his wife.

Andrew and Anne had had a couple of minor differences of opinion about the wedding arrangements. Andrew agreed to have the wedding in Sydney as he felt it was the bride's prerogative to choose. He demurred about going away for a honeymoon because of the cost, not only of the honeymoon itself but also because he would have to pay someone to look after High Peaks while they were away for the three weeks Anne proposed. When it got down to the money, Anne shamed him by offering to pay for half. This he could not countenance.

For her part, Anne, while very much looking forward to becoming mistress of High Peaks, realised full well that this was probably the only time she would be able to have a decent holiday with Andrew. His idea of a break was a day at a sheepdog trial or campdraft, but she finally got him to agree to a honeymoon in Queensland with the lure of a visit to the Sparkes property north of Rockhampton.

So as she left the wedding reception on Andrew's arm her heart was singing. There were to be three lovely weeks in Queensland and then it would be back to High Peaks. What more could a girl ask of life?

Tim Sparkes was a horsebreaker who followed the rodeo circuit and was regarded as one of the best all-round cowboys in the country. When he wasn't attending rodeos and breaking in horses, Tim was helping out on his Uncle Bob's cattle property near Rockhampton. Bob Sparkes maintained a top stud of stock horses, and Andy reckoned that as they were within a bull's roar of Rockhampton it would be downright bad manners not to drop in on Tim – and have a look at the horses Tim was always raving on about.

Bob Sparkes was a bachelor who ran a heap of cattle and had time for only three things in life – stock horses, whisky and his nephew, Tim. He was a lean, sandy-haired bushman with grey eyes that seemed to bore right through you. Tim had told his uncle a lot about Andrew MacLeod, and Bob reckoned his nephew wouldn't have been laying it on. For all Andy's size, Bob thought MacLeod sat a horse as well as anyone he had ever seen. He was even more surprised to find that Anne, originally a city girl, could sit a horse pretty well, too.

Bob insisted on taking the newlyweds to see the whole property. Bearing in mind the size of the place, this was something of an undertaking, especially for

Anne. Andrew had shorn and broken in horses on some very big properties, but Anne had never been on a property so large, nor had she seen so many cattle. By the end of the day she was feeling very rocky. And that was not the end of it. After dinner – which Bob and Tim threw together and was mostly comprised of pieces of steak as large as a plate – there was the yarning. Over several glasses of whisky, Anne heard so many wild and often improbable stories that her head was spinning. She whispered in Andrew's ear that if she didn't get to bed soon, she would fall asleep right there in her chair.

The next day Bob ran in about thirty steers so they could have an on-the-spot campdraft between Andrew and Tim with himself as judge. Andy cleaned up Tim and won the unofficial 'championship'. Bob told Anne, who had sat on a horse beside him for the whole time, that it was one of the best days he had ever put in.

'You've got a great lot of horses here, Bob,' Andy said when they had been at it for most of the following day. 'A real even lot of horses. Some of those mares are the best I've ever seen, and there's a couple of colts that could be real bottlers. That bay colt could make anything. They're such a good-tempered lot, too. There's good horses in our Hunter River Radiums but some are a bit hyper and cattle-mad. Whatever else you put in them has done the job.'

Bob grinned. The big man knew his horses all

right. 'Next time Tim is heading down your way I'll send you something along with him,' he said.

'Better let me know what you want for it, Bob. Money isn't real plentiful back home. I'm still paying off the bank and blasted death duties.'

'You send him a good horse and I'll pay for it,' Anne said. 'It will be my wedding present to Andy.'

'Forget the money, young woman,' Bob said gruffly. 'I can tell a man who appreciates good horses, and let me tell you that I've never seen a better horseman than your new husband. Besides, Tim tells me he can stay at your place any time. The horse will be a wedding present from Tim and me.'

So that was how Andy came to get his first Sparkes colt. Maybe now he would be on the road to breeding the kind of horses he had always set his heart on.

'Good old bloke, that Bob,' Andy said as he and Anne drove away from the Sparkes property that afternoon. 'Got a big lump of country with a heap of second-rate cattle yet he's got as good a lot of horses as there is in the country. I'm afraid that the property is going downhill, though. Did you see the fences? Needs a young, active bloke to pull it into shape. You'd think Bob would get Tim to stay and run the place. Either that or employ a good man. The old fella must be worth a heap. The blasted whisky has got the best of him and he doesn't care any more ... except about his horses. If only Tim could stop chasing rodeos around the country.'

'They sure are a pair,' Anne said. 'I heard Bob

telling Tim that you were strong enough to hold a bull out to piss and yet you had hands like a feather on a horse.'

'I'm shocked, Anne. I never thought I would hear you say something like that.'

'Only repeating what I heard,' she laughed.

'Well, I hope you never hear some of Tim's yarns. You wouldn't believe the stories he tells from life on the circuit.'

Andy and Anne talked and laughed all the way back to High Peaks.

'I must say it's been a lovely three weeks,' Anne said when they finally arrived home. 'Now it's time to do some work before school starts again.'

And work she did. Most of her goods had been moved up to High Peaks from the house she had been renting in town. It had been decided, mainly for financial reasons, that Anne would carry on teaching for the time being. She had only another three weeks before that came around. She loved teaching and, as much as she wanted to spend time at High Peaks, she didn't want to give it up. She worked ferociously those first three weeks, because after school began she would have only weekends and holidays to get High Peaks homestead and its surrounds the way she envisaged it all could be. There was so much she wanted to do that she almost didn't know where to begin. The vegetable garden had languished for years, and she set aside two hours every morning to extend Andy's limited efforts. There was plenty of water because Andy had installed a petrol engine down by the creek which pumped water into an overhead tank and provided good pressure for quite an area of garden. Andy carted in sheep manure and dug it into the soil, and Anne planted more silver beet, tomatoes and lettuce, and added a variety of herbs, such as thyme, sage, parsley and mint. The rest of the garden was in something of a mess, too, but the vegetables were given priority. 'They will save us some money and there's nothing like eating your own home-grown produce,' she said as she surveyed the fruits of her first week's toil. Andy looked at her admiringly. She was dressed in a pair of brief shorts, a blouse and a wide-brimmed straw hat. She certainly looked a picture.

Anne also mastered milking the cow, and in a matter of weeks she had reduced her milking time to just over ten minutes. She was determined to get it under ten minutes, and before the next school holidays came around she had achieved that goal.

After she finished in the garden she would cook and sew in the big, cool house. All the curtains needed replacing and some of the rooms needed repainting. Andy repaired the poultry pens and yards to keep the foxes out and Anne purchased a new lot of chickens. There were not many of the old brood left and Anne wanted to have her own fresh eggs and cockerels for the table. She would never kill a fowl but didn't mind the plucking and cleaning. She also took over the care of the kelpie litters. If there were horses in work or being prepared for campdrafting, she fed and watered them, too.

When Andy came home from a day in the hills or from shearing or horsebreaking somewhere in the district, Anne had usually taken care of most of the outside chores. This gave Andy more time to handle his young dogs or to work a horse. Anne loved to watch him at work with his dogs. There were two paddocks set aside for this, and fresh sheep were kept on hand in both for when overworked sheep needed resting.

What with all this work on top of her teaching, Anne had no trouble sleeping. Sleep had often eluded her before she and Andy were married because she had been so excited with the anticipation of marrying the man of her dreams. It had been even worse before they were engaged because she would lie awake for hours wondering whether Andy really wanted her. Now she slept right through the night and often didn't even wake when Andy got up. She requested that he wake her when he rose, even though that was always before sunrise. Andy could never be found guilty of being in bed when the sun came up.

Andy soon realised that he needed Anne to be able to look after High Peaks when he went away shearing. She would not entertain the idea of getting anyone in to look after the place. She knew it would be lonely without Andy, especially at night when the wind made the she-oaks moan right along the creek and the mopokes called from high up in the hills, but it would have to be endured.

One of the really scary things about living on High Peaks, and, Anne realised, the land generally, was that you had to keep your eyes open all the time for snakes. The brutes were plentiful throughout the district, especially along the creeks. There were browns and blacks and even, way up on the peaks, carpet snakes. Blacks were bad enough but seemed to get out of your way quicker than the browns. These, Andy drummed into her, were deadly mongrels. He had lost several good dogs to snakes, mostly browns, and, despite what the National Park rangers and others said, he reckoned the only good snake was a dead one. So Andy bought Anne a .410 shotgun and taught her how to use it. He cut up pieces of an old hose and got her to shoot at those. But shooting a snake in a real-life situation was quite another matter.

Anne's first confrontation came one Saturday when she was on her own and Andy was away up in the hills. She walked out the back door to bring in some washing and there, stretched out on the lawn, was a very large brown snake. Her heart missed a beat. She had been just about to step off the verandah. She stopped and slowly backed into the house. Oh, God, don't let it move, she thought. If it moves and goes under the house, I will die.

She took down the gun and rammed in a shell. On tiptoe she walked back out to the verandah. The snake was still there, stretched out in the sun. Its tongue was flicking in and out and its head was moving slowly from side to side. Anne lined the gun's sight up just behind the head and pulled the trigger. The explosion was followed by a violent thrashing from the snake. It coiled itself into knots and still seemed very much alive. Anne pushed in another shell and, walking a little closer, fired again. She leant against the wall of the house for support. Her heart was racing. She was between crying and laughing. The shock of seeing a big snake so close still affected her, and now she had killed it! This, she reflected later that day, was just another test she had to pass on her way to becoming a real country woman.

When the snake had stopped thrashing about, she picked it up on the rake and hung it over the back fence. Andy saw it there that evening. 'Well done,' he said as he came into the house. 'Did he give you any trouble?'

'No trouble, Andy,' Anne answered easily. She wasn't going to tell him about the glass of brandy she'd had to drink to calm her nerves. 'Just lined up on the brute and fired.'

Andy nodded. It was what he had expected of her.

Before the summer was over Anne had killed two more browns and a massive goanna which had been taking eggs from some of the hidden nests the hens had made outside their yards. The second big brown had been coiled up in the sun near the water trough in the horse yard and was still there when Anne crept back with the shotgun. When Andy returned from the hills that evening, the snake was hanging over the fence of the horse yard. After that episode he was sure that his new wife was going to be okay. But it took much longer than that for Anne to overcome her fear of snakes.

When Anne went back to teaching there was no time to do more than a couple of early jobs – like milking and feeding the pups and chickens – before breakfast, and then it was time to drive into Merriwa. The evenings were better, especially in summer when it was light until after seven. Later, as the days closed in and it was dark not much after five-thirty, there was little time to do much else outside feeding-up after driving home from Merriwa. In winter, it was sometimes pitch-dark when she finished her jobs with the aid of a lantern. When Andy was home, things were much more manageable.

Although summer could be trying with its heat and flies and snakes, it was winter that really tested her. This was when Andy went away shearing at his Queensland sheds and did not come home for months at a time.

She hated him being away. She missed him so much, and she knew how hard he worked to earn money. He had to 'ring' all the sheds he worked in, and he worked like the devil to do it. It was hard coming home to a house with no Andy in it. When he was away, the kelpies had to be let off for exercise. They loved the weekends, when Anne would take them along with her for big gallops. Sometimes they would go as far as the creek where Andy had first introduced her and Kate to eel-bashing. The young dogs would charge into the water then swim around in tight little circles before emerging, water dripping everywhere, to roll around in the grass. The older dogs would stand halfway into the water, lapping sedately. Ben drank like a dingo, submerging his snout in the water and dashing up water in quick grabs. But Ben was a law unto himself. Sometimes, Anne thought, he was more human than dog.

She would sit on a log and after the dogs had finished their splashings in the creek they would all sit nearby and watch her with their agate-coloured eyes. At her first movement they were up and ready for anything. She also tried to watch the sheep for flies, and she often rode out to inspect their small Hereford herd. One thing Anne never did was ride up Yellow Rock alone: Andy had expressly forbidden it.

'I would sooner lose every wether on High Peaks than have you ride up there without me,' he had told her.

There were several people prepared to help Anne out while she was on her own and who called in regularly to see her. Paddy Covers was now a very old man, but he was still quite sprightly and was sometimes accompanied by his son, Shaun. Paddy had been the manager of High Peaks when Andy was a small boy. He came from a pioneer family and lived on a small area of country just the other side of the turn-off to Poitrel, the Whites' property. Paddy had reared a large family, mostly daughters. Shaun was his youngest son. Andy owed most of what he knew about sheepdogs, horses and stock generally to Paddy. Paddy's youngest daughter, Eileen, had had her eye on Andy for years and nothing would have pleased old Paddy more than to have her marry his protégé before he passed on. But it hadn't happened, and Eileen was looking elsewhere. Shaun was the only one of the boys who had any real aptitude with sheepdogs and he worked dogs at the local trial. Shaun was always looking to earn extra money, so Andy employed him when he needed another hand. He reckoned he owed it to old Paddy to help any of the Covers.

The Campbells, Young Angus and Jane also came to see Anne, together at first, but as time progressed Jane began to come on her own. The two women had become very friendly since Anne had first invited Jane up to see her. She had waited until the interior of the house was repainted and the new curtains were in place along with some new furniture and rugs she had purchased from her savings. The once neglected gardens had been tidied up, and in some cases new shrubs had replaced ailing specimens. The vegetable garden drew special praise from Jane.

Old Angus and Sarah had retired to the coast and Young Angus now 'reigned' in his place. That was what Anne wrote to Andy: *He always carries on as though he is a lord of the realm.*

That is Angus, Andy wrote in his reply. *He's a mite big for his boots and regards himself as the king-pin grazier of the district. Perhaps he is. He's certainly got the best cattle, probably the best flock of sheep and one of the best properties for miles around. He's regarded by some as a silvertail who's had it all handed to him on a plate. I will say this for Young Angus: snob he may be, but he's always there when the whips are cracking.*

Wilf White was another caller who often turned up when Anne needed a hand with the animals. Wilf had a special kind of relationship with Andy, which stemmed back to the time when Wilf had been very kind to Andy's mother during the war years. But after his twin brother was killed in New Guinea, Wilf became a real recluse. Andy never charged him a cent for breaking in his young thoroughbreds, and when Andy did his crutching, Wilf paid him in sheep.

Wilf would never visit High Peaks without a box of chocolates or some beef for Anne. In return, she would always send him away with a chocolate cake or a cream sponge because she knew he had such a sweet tooth.

The best times of all were the weekends when Andy was home. Sometimes he didn't come home for long periods at a time, because as soon as one shed was cut out he would have to go on to the next. These were a long way from High Peaks and he couldn't get there and back in a weekend. But when he was home, if he was not working in the hills, he and Anne would get up very early and drive off together to a sheepdog trial or campdraft. More often than not they would come home with a nice bonus cheque.

Anne did not have much spare time to consider the changes that had taken place in her life, and when she did it amazed her how smoothly they seemed to have happened. She had been reared in a Sydney suburb and her only contact with animals had been the family dog and a few laying hens. Yet now, at times, she found she was running an entire sheep property.

Andy had often told her that 'farming is the beginning of everything', and Anne found herself agreeing with this view more and more. He said that life on the land could be damned hard but also damned satisfying. For him, one of the most satisfying aspects of it was looking at good livestock in prime condition. But Anne knew that what really drove Andy was, primarily, his determination to free High Peaks of its debt and then, ultimately, to acquire Wilf's property next door. If added together, High Peaks and Poitrel would give Andy the area of country he was seeking, not just for him and Anne, but for the children they hoped to have. Moreover, he was principally a real MacLeod: a descendant of the MacLeods of western Scotland; and he felt he had a duty, like the other MacLeods scattered around the world, to show that he could prosper in a new land. Andy's father had been one of the few MacLeods who had not bettered himself, and Andy still retained a lot of bitterness about it.

Nearly all the proceeds Andy earned from wool and, to a lesser extent, cattle, went to pay off the bank loan. What Andy earned was paid into a special account that helped to run High Peaks. Anne's teaching money went towards buying their clothes, food and things for the house.

Their first year together was like one long honeymoon and it seemed to fly as quickly as most honeymoons do. Anne did not take any precautions against pregnancy because she did not see any reason for postponing a family. They would lose her salary if she fell pregnant, but things would be manageable. Andy earned quite a lot of money, but he needed to with the size of his debt. What's more, there were the iniquitous death duties. A farmer paid taxes all his life and then, when he died, his family had to pay additional taxes. It seemed so unfair.

'Andy, what would you say if I told you I was going to have a baby?' Anne asked him one night as they sat in the lounge after dinner. He was reading *Country Life* newspaper and she was attempting to check school papers.

He put down the paper and looked at her. 'Well, Anne, I would say that you probably are, you being a straight-up-and-down young woman.'

'Well, I am. Are you pleased?'

He got up and came across to her. 'Stand up,' he said.

She stood up and locked her gaze with his. Slowly, he bent down and kissed her, with all the passion of his first kiss on top of Yellow Rock.

'I'm awful pleased, Anne. Have you been to see the doctor yet?'

'No, but I don't think there's any doubt.'

Andy sat down on a chair and put Anne on his knees.

'What did I ever do to deserve you?' she asked and kissed him on the cheek.

'Other way round, Anne. Couldn't believe my eyes the first time I saw you. There, I thought, is the girl for me. I was right, too. I'm the lucky fellow.'

'I disagree, but we won't argue about it. And now I'm going to have a baby. Can we manage? I mean, you might not be able to go away as much, at least until I've had the baby.'

'And not for a while after, either. I'll try and do a bit more locally and maybe up the horse and dog sales. We'll manage, and you're not to worry your head about money. We aren't broke.'

The fact that Anne was going to have a baby was the best bit of news Andy had heard for a long time. Now there was going to be a child on High Peaks. Having children on the place would make everything worthwhile. He wished his mother were alive to see it. She and Anne would have got on so well. Boy or girl, it didn't matter, although if he were given the choice, he would like a son first. A son and then a daughter.

Chapter Five

According to Jane Campbell, Anne had had a good pregnancy. Jane had been very sick when she was carrying Stuart. If it hadn't been for her strong desire to have a daughter, she might never have tried to become pregnant again. As fate had it, Jane fell pregnant just a couple of months after Anne.

Andy had not gone away shearing that year, not to the big Queensland sheds. He had stayed close to home and was there with Anne every night. Towards the end of the pregnancy, Anne had trouble convincing him to go away for even a day at a time. She assured him that if the pains started she would ring Angus or Jane who would come for her at any notice.

At this time, Andy had an outstanding blue and tan male dog called Ring which he reckoned might be the best trial dog he had owned. There was a big trial at Forbes, and Andy thought Ring was plenty good enough to at least take out the Maiden award if not win the double of the Maiden and the Open. If he left very early in the morning, he could work the Maiden and be home the same night. Anne pressed him to go. The baby was not due for another fortnight and Shaun Covers had assured them that he would feed up that day.

Andy was in two minds because although he wanted to win the trial for the kudos it would bring him and his dogs – and the money would come in handy – he was very reluctant to leave home with the baby so close. He was also concerned about the location of a low-pressure system off the New South Wales coast. He listened to the weather forecasts and reckoned there might be a fair bit of rain due.

It had actually started to rain when he left – not heavily, but the sky was leaden and he thought it would probably set in. The rain followed him to Forbes, and when he arrived he found that there were so many dogs entered in the big Maiden event he would not be working until the next morning. He almost decided to scratch Ring then and there and drive back home. Instead he went down the town and rang Anne with the news that if he wanted to work Ring he would have to stay the night, as they would be starting at seven-thirty the next morning in order to get all the dogs through. Anne assured Andrew that she would be fine and that she would get Shaun to stay the night.

He rang again that evening and Anne told him

that she was quite well, but a bit worried about the rain. It had been raining quite heavily all day and it was forecast to continue doing so. Shaun would stay and milk the cow and do the other morning jobs before going home.

Andy was camping at the showground and the rain was coming down fairly heavily. He again almost decided to give the trials away and drive home through the night. The creek at High Peaks was a horror in big rain. Several times it had covered the bridge and on two occasions they had been cut off for a couple of days. If that should happen this time and the baby decided it was time to be born, there could be real trouble. He finally decided that seeing he had stayed the day he might as well see the trial through.

It was a wet, gloomy showground when the handlers who had camped there got up next morning. Andy had not come prepared to camp, except that he always carried his swag with him. He reckoned he'd work Ring and then have breakfast down the town before heading off. The other handlers wouldn't hear of that, and he was soon set up with steak and eggs and a big pint of tea. He loved the friendliness of sheepdog workers. It made trialling a very satisfying sport. They really are a great bunch of fellows, he thought.

Ring was the second dog to work that morning and fourth last of the Maiden dogs. He took the dog for a run in the rain, thankful that he had brought his wet-weather gear. Ring was a real show-off dog.

It was as if he knew he was a king-pin trial dog. It was a sin, having made the trip to Forbes, not to allow such a dog to display his talents. Ring didn't give a fig for the rain. Once he sighted sheep he was majestic. A man would be a heel not to let him work. Yet deep down he realised he should get the hell out of Forbes. There would always be another trial but there was only one Anne.

The sheep were a bit doughy and disinclined to run in the rain. This didn't give Ring the best chance to show off his footwork and holding ability. It was really a very easy trial for him after the touchy hill-country wethers he had worked on High Peaks. He still managed to come out with a score of 96, which was seven points higher than the other leading dog.

'A great run, Andy. You've got a dog there you could take to Canberra,' Hugh Shorter said as Andy and Ring came off the ground. Hugh worked kelpie and border collie-cross dogs and owned a property east of Goulburn.

'Don't know that I will ever get to Canberra, Hugh. I've got a lot of commitments at home.'

'That's a real shame. You're the best kelpie handler around. You should give it a go.'

'Right now I've got to head for home. Our first baby is getting close and we've got a bugger of a bridge to cross. I sure don't like the look of this rain.'

'Congratulations, mate. I hope it all works out. Pity you have to leave, though. Ring would have been a good chance to take the double.'

'I'll be happy to win the Maiden this time,' Andy said.

Of the last three dogs, one was disqualified for crossing and the other two didn't score very well, so Ring came out the winner.

Delighted as he was with his success, Andy couldn't get away quickly enough. The rain was belting down and he was as worried as he could be about it. He had been a fool to leave Anne even for a minute.

He called her before he left Forbes and heard that it was absolutely pouring at High Peaks. The creek seemed to be up and it was roaring worse than she had ever heard it.

Andy didn't like the sound of that. 'Listen to me, Anne. You get out of there! Get Shaun to drive you into town and take a room at the Federal. Stay there and I'll see you tonight.'

'Jane rang and suggested I go over to Inverlochy,' Anne replied.

Andy did a quick mental check of the creeks between Inverlochy and Merriwa. 'No, it's too risky. The only place for you is in town. If that creek comes up and you need to get to the hospital in town, you won't get in from Inverlochy. Is Shaun still there?'

'He's down looking at the creek now,' she said.

'Tell him I said he's to take you to town. Pack up now. Tell him to come back when he can and feed up. If not tonight, tomorrow. I might get stuck in town for a day or so. This could be flood rain.'

'All right, Andy. Now tell me, how did you go at the trials?'

'Ring won the Maiden, but I'll tell you all about that later. I have to leave now.'

Anne hung up the phone and went out on to the front verandah. It didn't take long for the first big gust to hit her. She shivered and looked first at the road that led out the front gate and down to the creek, and then she turned her eyes towards Yellow Rock. She could see the road as far as the dip to the creek but beyond that everything was hidden by mist and rain. Yellow Rock was completely obscured, hidden by an impenetrable curtain of mist. There was so little visibility it looked as if there were no mountains at all.

Presently Shaun appeared through the rain. Although he had driven down to the creek, he now returned on foot.

'Where's your ute, Shaun?' Anne asked as he came up the front path.

'Down near the creek. I'm afraid it's stuck down there. I just couldn't get it to start.'

'Oh, dear. I really needed you to get me to town. I was going to stay at the Federal.'

'We could always take the truck, except it might be a bit rough for you,' he said.

'How is the creek?' she asked.

'The water is just running over the bridge, but I reckon it's rising. This is the heaviest rain I've seen here.'

'Let's go and get the truck then, quickly.'

But the battery of the truck was dead flat. 'Bugger it,' Shaun said vehemently. 'Missus, we've got a problem. I reckon you had better ring Angus and see if he can come and get you.'

'Wait a tick and I'll see what he says,' she said, heading towards the house. She reappeared a few minutes later and Shaun could tell from the frown on her face that it was bad news. 'I can't make it out. The phone is dead. It was quite all right when Andy rang a while ago.'

'The wind has got a lot stronger since then. It's either twisted the wires or else they've come down completely,' Shaun suggested.

He looked up at the heavily pregnant woman, the wife of the man he most admired and respected in all the district. 'Not to worry, Mrs Mac. I'll saddle a horse and scoot down to Inverlochy,' he said with a quick smile to try and ease her obvious concern.

'Would you, Shaun? It will be a nasty ride in this rain,' she pointed out.

'I've got good rainskins.'

'What will you do after that?' she asked.

'It might be best if I come back here while you're gone,' he said. 'If this rain keeps up, Andy might not get back here for a couple of days. There's dogs and horses to feed and Moss has a big litter of valuable pups on her.'

'Thank you, Shaun. We really do appreciate this. There's plenty of food for you and the dogs. You know where it all is, just help yourself.'

'Righto, Mrs Mac. Well, I'll saddle up and be on my way. We'll be back inside an hour, so you just sit tight.'

He put a saddle on one of Andy's mares and cantered her down to the creek. There was now more than a foot of water over the bridge. The creek was definitely rising – and fast. Shaun rode the mare into the water and was immediately thankful for the quality of Andy's horse. The water was rushing across the bridge at frightening speed, and nobody could have crossed away from the bridge. The mare's legs did not create too much resistance in the water so he simply had to keep her in the middle of the bridge to make his way across. When he reached the far side he turned and looked back at the crossing. Soon no car would be able to make it over. Angus would need to bring his truck quickly. Shaun turned and put the mare to a fast canter, with the rain beating endlessly into his face.

Angus Campbell had been trying to raise Anne MacLeod by telephone but her phone line was dead. He walked out on to the front verandah and looked up the road towards High Peaks. All he could see now was a grey wall of rain. As he watched and worried about what he should do, a single horseman appeared out of the mist and deluge.

Seeing Angus on his front verandah, Shaun rode up the drive and dismounted at the front steps.

'G'day, Mr Campbell. Jeez, what a bugger of a day. Talk about rain. Never seen anything like it.'

'G'day, Shaun. What are you doing here? Is there trouble up at High Peaks?'

'I reckon. My ute's on the blink and the truck has a flat battery. The creek is running like hell, must be getting close to two feet over the bridge by now. I need to get Mrs Mac to town. Andy reckons it isn't even safe to bring her here, in her condition.'

Angus Campbell knew what was required of him. As he turned away, Shaun added a final caution.

'You'll never cross the bridge in a car.'

Angus turned back to him. 'It's that bad?'

Shaun nodded. 'I reckon you could do it okay in your truck, but come maybe a couple more hours and even that wouldn't make it.'

Angus nodded his acknowledgement. 'I'll get the truck. We can look after your horse here and you come back with me. That all right?'

'Sounds like we've got ourselves a plan.'

Anne had all her things packed and ready to go. She had actually been packed for days and had only to add a toothbrush and extra clothes for her stay at the Federal. She filled the combustion stove and then went back to the front verandah to wait for Angus.

It was then that she heard the pup crying. Perhaps Mossy had heard the horse leaving and had climbed out of her kennel to investigate. Sometimes a pup attached to a teat could get dropped outside the

kennel and left there. A small pup would die of expo-
sure in this weather. She could not possibly leave it.

She donned her coat, stowing a towel beneath it,
and put on her galoshes and wide-brimmed hat. This
was not easy in her condition. The rain hit her in
great welts as she plodded towards the dog yard. The
dogs were all in their logs and kennels except for
Moss, who was standing over one of her pups. The
rain was streaming off her sides down onto the shiv-
ering, crying pup.

Anne pulled the towel from beneath her coat and
rubbed the pup as dry as she was able. It was a little
black and tan bitch, between two and three weeks of
age. She put it back with the other pups and then
tried to rub Moss dry. It was too hard for her to bend
over and she dropped down on her knees. 'You'll
make your pups as wet as you are,' she said as she
rubbed her. Moss didn't wait long and jumped back
into her kennel. There was a board across the front
and it was high enough to keep the small pups
inside.

Anne made it to her feet and turned to go back
to the house. The ground was very slippery and she
felt momentarily light-headed. Her feet slid away and
then she was falling, falling. She put out her right
arm to try and cushion the fall and felt pain shoot
up into her shoulder. Her whole body shook as she
fell. Her stomach heaved, and as she lay with the rain
beating down at her, a sudden pain gripped her. 'Oh,
God. Not now. Not here,' she groaned. She realised

she had to get up and somehow make it to the house. She pushed herself to her feet and found that she had a job to stand upright. Something was wrong inside her. 'Can't stay here,' she muttered to herself through clenched teeth.

Slowly and painfully Anne pushed herself back to the front verandah. It was all she could do to get up the stairs and collapse into a big cane chair.

It was there that Angus and Shaun found her. Between them they managed to get her into the truck. The creek was now a frightening prospect and even the big truck felt the force of the water as it inched across the bridge. Anne was too far gone in her pain to fully comprehend the scene around her and Angus did not mention just how concerned he really was. Instead he concentrated on getting her across safely. Anne's head was on his shoulder and she was trying hard not to cry out. The pains were coming and going with a severity she had not expected.

The truck inched up the far bank and Angus lowered the window and waved goodbye to Shaun on the opposite bank. Rain and wind beat at the windscreen and he could feel the truck tremble. Visibility was no more than about thirty yards. He looked down at Anne and she gave him a weak smile.

'I took a fall, Angus, and now I think the baby is coming. Something happened when I fell, and it hurts a lot.' She winced as a spasm of pain hit her. Angus tried to console her by putting his arm around her shoulders.

'Hang on there, old girl. We'll soon have you in hospital. I'll change you over to the car when we get to Inverlochy, which will be a lot more comfortable for you. You'll soon be in good shape.'

Anne wanted to believe him but she had her doubts. 'Andy won't know what's happened to me,' she said. 'He's on his way home from Forbes.'

'Don't you worry about that. We'll leave a message for him at the Federal. He'll find you,' Angus said.

There was water spreading across the road below Inverlochy. The dip below the house was filled with water. It formed a cowal like a mini-billabong in flush times. Angus wondered how much more water was across the road on the way to town. If this rain kept up, nobody would be able to get to town. He debated whether to take Jane in with them. She was a couple of months behind Anne in her pregnancy, but Angus didn't want to risk her having a similar sort of fall. What's more, there was no time for her to pack.

He backed the big truck alongside the garage and looked down at Anne. 'Can you make it inside or would you prefer to wait here while I run and talk to Jane?' he asked anxiously.

She saw the concern on his face, even through her pain. 'I think I'll stay here, thank you, Angus. You won't be long, will you?'

'No, I'll just tell Jane to call the ambulance and then we'll get you into the car,' he said, and raced off towards the homestead.

As he came into the house without waiting to remove his dripping oilskins, Jane asked, 'Where have you been, Angus? What's happened?'

'Anne is in the truck,' he replied. 'She's had a fall and the baby is on the way. Will you ring the ambulance and get them to meet us on the road?'

'Oh, Angus,' she said with alarm in her eyes. 'Will you get Anne to the hospital in time?'

'How should I know? I'm not a doctor. I'm more worried about getting her there at all. You should have seen the creek. And our cowal is overflowing. I'm inclined to think you should come with us. Andy's out of town and I think Anne could use some support. No – on second thoughts, it could be a tough trip. I want you to stay here. Don't want you going into labour, too. I'll get back somehow.'

Andy was in trouble. The faithful Chev utility that had transported him to sheds all over Queensland had finally rolled to a stop in Bathurst. The nearest garage had towed it under cover and he had been assured that they could fit a new carbie.

'It's like this, mate,' the garage foreman said. 'There's this cocky who's a bit of a nut on Chevs. He's got a bloody great stack of Chev spare parts. I reckon he'd probably have fifty carbies out there.'

'Has he got one to fit my ute?' Andy asked, trying to keep his temper in check.

'Haven't a clue. He's out looking at his stock. Shifting them, his missus said.'

'I don't want to pressure you, but my wife is due to have a baby any tick of the clock and I can't get through to her by phone. She could be in big trouble.'

'That's tough, mate. Look, I'll send the young fella out straightaway. If Joe's got a carbie, we can fit it real quick. No sweat. You go and have a feed so you're ready to hit the track. Will your dog be right in the back?' Ring was sitting in the mesh crate with canvas roof and sides which Andy used for carrying his dogs around in.

'He'll be okay.'

Andy tried to call High Peaks again, but the phone was still dead. The Inverlochy phone sounded okay and he was relieved when Jane answered. But not for long. When she gave him the news about Anne, he was left temporarily speechless.

'Had a fall? And the baby's on the way? Hell. Look, I'll ring the ambulance.'

The ambulance station answered his call at the third ring. He knew all the staff there and recognised Tom Stratton's voice.

'It's Andy MacLeod here, Tom. I'm stuck in Bathurst with car trouble. Do you know what's happened with my wife?'

'Sure, Andy. We've already picked Mrs MacLeod up. She's in the hospital at the moment. She made it in time.'

'Thank heavens. I'll ring the hospital now.'

The hospital receptionist was not very informative. 'Mrs MacLeod was operated on not long after she was brought in,' she said. Andy had a job hearing her through the rain beating on the iron roof.

'Is she all right?'

'I believe so, but you would have to talk to Dr Ramsay yourself.'

'Look, I'm stuck in Bathurst and I can't get there yet. I'm Mrs MacLeod's husband. Surely I have a right to know what's going on.'

'Mrs MacLeod is in a satisfactory condition and the baby is doing fine,' the woman said almost grudgingly.

'God Almighty, you could have told me that five minutes ago!' Andy exploded. 'If it would not be too much trouble, would you mind telling my wife that I have had a breakdown in Bathurst and I hope to be back some time late this afternoon.'

'Very well, I will pass that message on.'

The line went dead and Andy put the phone down with his heart still beating wildly. Anne had had the baby and they were all right. A huge wave of relief swept over him. It was only then that he realised he had not enquired whether he had a son or a daughter. He swore under his breath and re-dialled the hospital.

'This is Andrew MacLeod again. Did my wife have a boy or a girl?'

'A boy, Mr MacLeod,' the receptionist said.

'A boy. Thank you. Thank you very much,' he said in something of a daze. Anne had had a boy. A boy. That was terrific. He walked down the street to the first cafe he came to. It was still raining cats and dogs. What did that matter? He had a son.

Andy MacLeod was a very relieved man when he finally parked his ute outside Merriwa Hospital. All he had been able to think about on the long drive over was Anne and the baby. The Chev hummed along through the rain and crossed every water-filled dip on the road back to Merriwa. He could have been stopped several times but he put the old canvas screen over the front and ploughed on through.

Anne was asleep when he entered her room. He looked down at her as she lay there, the woman who had transformed his life. He asked himself for the hundredth time why on earth Anne had chosen him. She looked tired and there were dark smudges under her eyes that he'd never seen before. For all that, he thought she'd never looked so beautiful. He stood gazing at her for some time before sitting down beside her bed. He lost track of how long he sat watching her before she eventually opened her eyes. They lit up when she saw him and she opened her arms out wide. He kissed her and buried his face in her hair.

'I'm sorry, Anne. I was a fool to go to Forbes. A damned fool. They say you've been operated on. Are you all right? What about the baby?'

Anne had never seen her husband so concerned. What would he think when she gave him the news?

'Oh, Andy, I am afraid there is both good and bad news. The good news is that we have a ten-pound son, and he is just beautiful. You'll love him.'

'A son. That's terrific, Anne. Can I see him? Where is he? Ten pounds. Isn't that rather heavy?'

'Heavy enough, dear, and you'll see for yourself in just a minute. But I'm afraid the bad news is that there aren't going to be any more babies. Something went wrong, and I'm sorry to say that the factory has been closed down.'

Andy bent and kissed her again. 'We couldn't want for any more than the two of us together and a child of our own. The main thing is that you're all right and so is the baby. Nothing else matters.'

'Oh, Andy.' She knew he must have been as dis-appointed as she was. They had both been so keen to have more children. She was determined not to cry in front of him, but his calm acceptance of her news broke down her resolution. He really was a man and a half.

'Please don't cry,' he said, taking her hands in his. 'It doesn't matter that we can't have more children. I've got you and I've got a son, so I'm a long way ahead of where I was a couple of years ago. But, tell me, how did you fall?'

'I slipped on the verandah, dear – top-heavy,' she told him, not wanting to let on what she'd really done. 'I had to have a Caesarean.'

'Oh, my poor Anne. I'm so sorry I was stuck in Bathurst.'

A young nurse came into the room and Anne whispered in her ear. She nodded and left the room, returning soon after carrying a bundle swathed in a blue and white blanket. A pudgy red face and some dark hair was all that could be discerned through the wrappings. The nurse handed the bundle to Anne and she placed her baby beside her. 'Say hello to your son, Andy.'

Andy gazed with wonderment at the small figure cradled against his wife's body. He didn't know what to say. Never before had he had anything to do with a day-old baby.

'You can nurse him, Daddy,' Anne said with her eyes shining.

Andy reached down and picked up the next-generation MacLeod. 'Ten pounds, eh? Reckon he might end up a big fella,' Andy said proudly.

'I reckon he might, if he's anything like his father.'

'And if he's got his mother's looks, the girls will drive him mad,' Andy said.

And the minutes passed into hours as together Anne and Andy sat staring in delight at the miracle in their arms.

The rain began to ease during the night and Andy decided to head out to High Peaks. First he had to call in at Inverlochy to thank Angus for everything he had done. Andy always felt uncomfortable about being beholden to Angus, but he never took anything for nothing. If a fellow did him a good turn, he always tried to reciprocate. It was hard to do that with Angus because he was so well-off financially. And despite the fact that he knew Angus respected him for his ability with dogs and horses, he did not accept Andy socially. Likewise, Andy didn't have much time for some of Angus's friends, who were out and out snobs. Angus fitted in with them well enough, but he did believe himself to be public-minded, a district benefactor. The thing was that whenever Angus did anything to help the community, it was always front-page news in the local paper. There were others who did good things but never got any publicity, and never looked for it.

Then there were the little incidents that had built up between Angus and Andrew over the years. Once, Andy had called in to collect a cheque from Angus, who had come out of his office with Rob Cartwright beside him. Rob had a glass of whisky in his hand but Andrew had not been asked into the office to join them. A similar thing had happened at the local show, on more than one occasion. Angus would be drinking with some of his cronies and would never ask Andrew over with them.

So it was with a little reservation that Andy approached Inverlochy. Angus came out on to the front verandah when he heard Andy's utility pull up on the drive. 'G'day, Andy. Going to try the bridge?'

'Have a look anyway, Angus. It usually falls pretty fast. What a season we should have after this rain. You'll have fat cattle for miles.'

Angus allowed a faint smile to cross his rather bleak countenance. 'Well, you need a few good seasons to make up for the ordinary ones. How is Anne?'

'That's why I've dropped over. I want to thank you for what you did.'

'Well, it's a bad show if neighbours can't help each other out in times like that. You'll help me next time, not that you haven't done so in the past,' he added.

'I'm obliged, anyway, Angus. You need any help, you just ask me.'

Angus nodded. He knew the calibre of Andy MacLeod. 'How did the trial go?'

'It wasn't worth the trip, but Ring did win the Maiden. Hugh reckons I should take him to Canberra, but it's damned hard for me to get away. There'll be other trials, and other dogs.'

Angus was a little resentful about the easy way Andy tossed off the news that he had won the Maiden. Winning trials all the time seemed to come so easily to Andy. The closest Angus had ever come to winning a trial was obtaining a third place. He wondered whether he should try for another imported dog. Perhaps a broken-in Wilson dog, if he could still get one out of him.

'You didn't tell me how Anne is doing,' Angus said.

'She's doing quite well, thanks again to you, Angus,' Andy said as he walked back to his utility. 'And I hope things work out well for you and Jane, too.'

Things did work out for the Campbells.

Two months later, Jane gave birth to a baby daughter, Catriona. If Anne felt any jealousy at seeing Jane with a daughter, she didn't let on to anyone. She was totally immersed in caring for her baby son, who had been given the name of David, or Davie for short.

When Andy went to collect Anne and David from the hospital to bring them home, his heart beat a shade faster than usual. And when he handed the baby up to Anne on their front verandah, he felt like a king coming home to his kingdom. The kingdom was High Peaks and David MacLeod was its prince.

Chapter Six

David MacLeod was indeed a great joy to his parents. If Andy MacLeod was the provider, manager and general factotum of High Peaks and Anne was the calm, capable homemaker – and, when required, stockperson – David was the heart and soul of the property. There was never a boy who loved his home more than David loved High Peaks. He had ridden over every inch of it before he was five years of age, and could crack his first whip some time before that.

Anne realised quite early on that her son was somehow different from other boys. He never sought the company of others and was perfectly content to roam the hills on his own, with a kelpie or two running beside his pony. For another thing, David was never going to be dux of the school as she had been before going to teachers' college. The genes that David had inherited from his father seemed to have swamped her own. Although he was as smart as paint,

David had no interest in anything but the bush and his animals. In the beginning it was all animals, but as he grew towards his teens, David's major passions became kelpies and stock horses. And his dogs loved him in return. There was a rapport between them that amazed many people. This was no surprise, since Andy was by far the best local dog man.

Anne was smart enough to be grateful that she had a fine boy. If she could not make her son a great student, she could at least make him a decent human being.

There were times, such as horse sports days, when David's activities caused her great anxiety. From a very early age David had exhibited a fanatical desire to ride horses with his father. When he was only two years old he had been given a rather rare red roan pony by a neighbour, Pat Metcalfe, in return for a week of Andy's shearing. For a while Andy led this pony from his own mount, until, at his small son's urging, he dispensed with the lead and together they rode the highest peaks of the land. But the lead was always clipped on again before they came in sight of the homestead. Andy knew full well what Anne would say about her son being let loose in wallaby country. It took a fair rider to handle a horse in the high country. To some extent you had to rely on your horse, but you couldn't go to sleep on the job. There were steep upthrusts of rock with deep gullies and shifty stones. Yet David's pony had the agility of a goat and never once came to grief. Moreover, his small rider could cling to him like a monkey as he rode the most dangerous places on High Peaks on his own.

Anne never ceased to worry about her son. When he was absent in the hills she would make many trips to the back gate to watch for the first sight of him emerging from the top country. She had a pair of field glasses, which hung on a hook at the back step. Anxious eyes scanned the high slopes until the pony came into view. Yet she never let on to David about her concerns. She had to be careful not to coddle her son. This would never do for Big Andy's boy.

The red roan pony was replaced by a Welsh pony gelding called Chips when David was six years old. He was a grey with lovely manners but with a pony's tricks. David soon had him under his spell. The pony used to follow its small owner up the path to the homestead where he would wait patiently until given bread or sugar. Once, David even rode Chips into the house – but he never made that mistake again.

The most important development in David's animal training happened when Tim Sparkes, the old horsebreaker mate of his father's, came to the district. Andy had reduced his own horsebreaking and recommended Tim take over these clients. When work was over for the day, Tim would head up to High Peaks for a drink and a yarn with Andy. He sometimes even stayed for a day or two between jobs. Tim was a horseman through and through, and could not help but be impressed with young David. He had never seen a child of his age so proficient with dogs and horses. In no time at all he had David performing even more sophisticated tricks with his pony. And from that time on Tim kept his eye open for David's next horse – a bigger horse.

It was Tim, too, who gave David his first lessons in self-defence. At school, David had gone for a bigger boy who had kicked a dog seeking titbits from sympathetic children – only some had not been so sympathetic. Tim noticed David's black eye and, when told that David had lost the fight, he set about training him in self-defence. Tim was no slouch. He had spent a season with Jimmy Sharman's troupe and knew his way round a boxing ring all right. It was grounding that would stand David in good stead.

The MacLeod name was famous throughout Australia, but this fame mostly concerned another branch of the family. There had been a famous partnership of kelpie breeders by the name of King and McLeod. The King brothers had been two of the original breeders of the kelpie. Indeed, King's Kelpie was universally regarded as the bitch from which the breed took its name. They later merged with McLeod to breed some of the greatest sheepdogs ever seen in Australia. The legendary Coil, who won the Sydney trials in 1898 with two faultless scores of 100 in each round, was passed from John Quinn's ownership to King and McLeod. The name 'King and McLeod' was held in such high repute that the owners kept on selling dogs for many years after their best days had passed.

Andrew MacLeod was not an immediate member of that McLeod family, though he was descended from the same clan in western Scotland, but his success with kelpies more or less ensured him of association with *the* McLeod of King and McLeod. Andrew began to trial dogs with the progeny of the first two kelpies presented to him by his mother's old manager, Paddy Covers. The proceeds of some of these trials, as with the campdraft events, helped Andy to pay off some of his debts. He was also able to sell quite a few pups and started dogs for good prices.

When Andrew took over High Peaks, he was so preoccupied with getting the property in order and reducing its debt burden that he was seldom able to travel very far to compete in the bigger sheepdog trials and campdrafts. His attendance at trials was virtually limited to the local ones, with a very occasional foray farther afield. Deep down, however, he had one great ambition, and that was to win the National Trials with one of his kelpies. These trials had only ever once been won by a kelpie, but that dog had won it five times.

Although Andy no longer journeyed away to trial dogs, he was not forgotten among breeding circles. Dog men, mostly kelpie enthusiasts, came from all over the country to meet and talk with him. Some stayed the night and talked dogs until the small hours, while others worked their dogs for Andy to pass judgement on. All of this was pure heaven to young David. The wisdom that flowed from Andy and his visitors penetrated David's young brain and was stored there for future reference. He carried this knowledge like an extra sense, with information stacking up, always available when he required it.

David soon learned the importance of 'eye' in a dog and the power this exerted over sheep. Some dogs had too much eye. They were called 'hard-eyed' or 'sticky-eyed'. Their 'eye' tied them up so much that they were either ineffective in moving sheep or they took too much time to do it. Dogs who had no eye were fairly useless in some situations, like when it came to mustering stragglers in the high country. Yet dogs with the right amount of eye could handle wild, fast-breaking sheep.

David also learned the value of natural casting dogs. His father always rammed home the importance of cast; he would not breed from a dog who was not a naturally good caster. David learned of the folly of teaching a dog to cast 'blind' when there were no sheep for it to locate. Andy never cast a dog blind unless he knew there were sheep over the hill.

David understood why his father preferred kelpies to border collies where many handlers did not. It was, his father averred, because of the way a top kelpie worked its sheep. The legendary old kelpies like Coil, Wallace, Biddy Blue and Blue King had wonderful anticipation and could judge when sheep were going to move. They were always ready in position before the sheep were. These dogs had the power to drive and hold, often only needing to move a few inches to cover and move sheep, so they didn't swing sheep all over the place. It was this attribute that Andy prized so highly in the best kelpies, and it was a characteristic of the best of the MacLeod dogs.

Andy did not worry too greatly about the colour of his dogs; this was secondary to the way they worked. King was a blue and tan, Ben was a solid blue, Bess and Lottie were blue and tan, Queen was jet black with just a tiny spot of white on her chest, and Dawn was a red and tan, or two-tone. Young David soon learned that although there had been some very great blue dogs like Coil and Wallace, some blues were poor-coated dogs and as they got older they were liable to suffer from kidney trouble. This was because they had little or no hair over the loins. Such dogs also had problems in the heat, because with so little coat, their skins heated up too much.

Occasionally, there was a pale, light-coloured or creamy pup. These dogs resembled dingoes and many bushmen claimed there was in fact dingo blood in the kelpie. Andy told David that the dingo story was just nonsense: people might have used the dingo, but it had never helped 'make' the kelpie. Angus Campbell had told him there were cream or lemon-coloured collies in Scotland and that they were the source of the light-coloured kelpies, not the dingo. David learned, most importantly, that the light-coloured dogs 'drew' sheep to them. This could be a good or a bad thing, depending on the sheep being worked. If sheep were a bit wild and 'stirry', the light-coloured dogs sometimes calmed them down, but if sheep were bold and aggressive, they would often take on a light-coloured dog more than they would a darker one.

All of these things were absorbed by David so that before he went to high school he knew as much about sheepdogs and the handling of them as most sheep-dog handlers three times his age.

Then there was the rearing of the pups. This was a time of pure joy for young David. He would sit on the wood heap with his father while the latest litter of pups played with their mother. Together they would look for the boldest pup, the shyest pup (shyness not being a positive trait) and the smartest pup, but most importantly, the pup they might keep to carry on the line.

Queen was David's favourite bitch. She was big and black and shiny and always produced top pups. They were the best coloured of the MacLeod dogs and were marginally better natured. David was nine years old when his father presented him with his first very own kelpie. They had picked him out of Queen's litter as the one who stood right out from his mates. He was a big black and tan who David came to call Glen. He now owned two ponies and a dog – well, a pup – and life was wonderful.

Glen was bred down from many of the great kelpies past. He was bred to cast and to hold wild sheep, and that is just what he did. Before Glen was twelve months of age, David could rely on him to muster the highest parts of the property and to retrieve all but the most cunning sheep. Glen was not yet in King's class, and might never be, but he was still a class dog and a very good one for his age. David was given plenty of advice by all and sundry about the best way to handle his first dog, but when he won the Novice event at the local sheepdog trial – he was the youngest person by several years ever to achieve such a win – there was general agreement that young David was a chip off the old block. After all, who had ever heard of a ten-year-old boy winning a sheep-dog trial?

In this event David worked against Angus Campbell, who entered two dogs and didn't make the final with either. Andy won the Open Trial, so father and son had joint reason to be happy. Everyone who knew Angus Campbell reckoned he would slip away before the presentation of prizes, but Angus was not too proud to come across and shake hands with Andy and David. Yet the defeat rankled. It was surely something to be beaten by Andy MacLeod, who could win anywhere, but to be beaten by his young son was pretty shattering for a fellow like Angus.

David took the win in his stride and listened carefully while his father pointed out where he had lost points. (Glen had scored 89 points from the possible 100.)

'If you work at a big trial, the gun handlers will

beat you if you lose that many points. You must keep your dog on a tighter course and not let him veer sheep to the left. And Glen still comes on to them a bit quick. Keep him back more,' Andy said.

David nodded. He knew Glen wasn't perfect, but he would get him right. And he did. Glen became so good that Andy said he was ready to win an Open Trial. He also thought they might try a litter or two by him. The MacLeod sires were getting on in years because Andy had had to sell the good young ones to help with their debt. They now had to look to keeping some top-class younger dogs. Glen was especially attractive as a potential sire because he carried two strains of the Blue King blood that was now virtually unattainable anywhere else. So Glen was mated with the red and tan bitch, Dawn.

Then tragedy struck. Three weeks later a big brown snake bit Glen as he was working sheep between two massive rocks in the high country. David knew there was little chance of saving him; he'd seen others die the same way. Tears coursed down his face as he savagely smashed his whip across the snake. It was a long ride back to the homestead and Glen was already in a bad way by the time he got there. Andy and David took him in to the vet but there was no anti-venom at that time and Glen died a couple of hours later.

David was completely shattered. Glen had been his very first dog, his first trial winner, and he had been a beauty. Anne had always been able to nurse her son through bad periods, but this time David was inconsolable. He lay on his bed with his face pressed into the pillow and refused to come out for meals.

The following day David saddled his pony and rode to the top of Yellow Rock. Well, almost to the top of Yellow Rock. It was impossible to ride to the very top; the last section had to be climbed by foot. This was the highest point of the range, next to Mount Oxley, and from its vantage point he could look down over a huge stretch of country. He could see both Half Moon and Jimmy's Creeks stretching like silvery snakes towards Merriwa, while high above him a brown falcon soared in majestic flight.

David could understand why his father had worked so hard to retain High Peaks. It was not really for the money, for the promise that once clear of debt the property would provide a good living. There was no great fortune to be made from the wool industry – which had slumped in 1970 and barely recovered – nor from the small herd of cattle they ran on the bottom country. What made High Peaks so special was that it was theirs and theirs alone. They knew every rock and tree on the property. David was sure he could never be happy away from there. Where else could a sheepdog so convincingly demonstrate its mastery over sheep as on the range country? And where else was there country so exhilarating to ride over?

And so David sat and mourned the loss of Glen, trying to adjust to the fact that he was gone. Finally, hunger drove him down off Yellow Rock. David was a boy with a very good appetite, and he had already missed two meals. He also knew that his mother would be particularly anxious about his return. Yellow Rock was a very dangerous place for the unwary rider. It was where his grandfather had died, as his mother never ceased to remind him.

It was late afternoon when he finally rode back into the horse yard at the homestead. He unsaddled his pony and hosed him down before walking slowly across to the house. His father was sitting on the front steps.

'Feeling pretty bad about Glen, eh, Davie?' he asked.

'Pretty bad, Dad.'

'Been up to Yellow Rock, I suppose?'

'Yes.'

'I think it's time you and I had a talk.'

'What about, Dad?'

'There's one thing you're going to have to come to grips with, Davie. While there's live dogs, there's going to be dead dogs. Things happen to dogs. You can look after them real well and things can still go wrong. Nobody can prevent that because you can't wrap a working dog up in cotton wool.

'Look, I know Glen was your first dog and you did a great job with him. But Glen won't be the last dog you'll lose. I've lost a lot, and some of them were better dogs than Glen. Never give your heart to a dog. Not completely. You understand me? If you like a dog too much, you'll be heartbroken every time you lose one. You hear me?'

'I hear you, but it doesn't make me feel any better.'

'Son, when you're an animal person you've got to understand that there are always going to be highs and lows in your life. Dogs don't live all that long and some have shorter lives than others. If you can't handle the fact that you're going to lose some, you'd be better to forget about them. The same goes for horses. The one you like best is the one that stakes itself or gets ripped up in barbed wire. You have to be big enough to forget the losses and keep going. The important thing is to have enough good breeding stock on hand so you can carry on.'

'Yes, Dad, you've told me that before.'

'Then remember it. Now, I'll tell you what we'll do. When Dawn whelps you can have the pick of her male pups. He won't be the same as Glen but he will be his son. How's that?'

'That's great, Dad. I'd really like a Glen pup,' David said with something like his usual enthusiasm.

'Good. Feeling like something to eat?'

'I reckon I am.'

'Your mother has kept your lunch. One other thing – if you ever ride off again without telling us where you're going, I'll wallop the daylights out of you. Is that understood?'

'Real clear, Dad,' he replied, heading up the steps in slightly better spirits. He was going to get a new dog. He had already decided that he would call him

Lad. Short names were best for sheepdogs. As soon as the pups' eyes were opened, he would start watching them. When they were about three weeks old his father would fire several shots close by so they would learn not to be whip-shy. His father hated whip-shy dogs.

It had looked like being a very bleak Christmas without Glen, but at least now there was a pup to look forward to.

Chapter Seven

It was high summer and the Christmas holidays. Up on High Peaks, Andrew and David MacLeod rode the hills looking for flyblown sheep. There had been a succession of storms and the muggy conditions were proving ideal for blowflies.

At the foot of the high country, Catriona Campbell was putting her new pony through its paces. It had been a Christmas present from her father, schooled by a top horseman and costing a great deal of money. Not that money meant much to Angus Campbell where his daughter was concerned. Catriona had been born three years after her brother, Stuart, and she was the apple of Angus's eye. Catriona was a few months younger than David, but in some ways a hundred years older in the head.

By the time she was ten years of age, Catriona, daughter of the district's leading grazier, was a very assured young lady. She was also remarkably pretty;

the prettiest girl for miles around. Her hair was golden and naturally wavy and her eyes were soft and brown, just like her mother's. Yet they could flash fire and often did. Catriona was the kind of girl who drew every eye. Fortunately, both Angus and Jane Campbell were sensible people who did not spoil her too much. Angus spent a lot of money on her horses and riding equipment, but for all that, Catriona had to toe the line.

One of the few boys who was not affected by Catriona's looks was David MacLeod. He, it seemed, always had more important things to do. The two children had begun school the same day. It was a small school at the foot of the range and was staffed by two teachers. Although they sat in the same classroom and played in the same playground, David would seldom acknowledge Catriona's presence.

Catriona had visited High Peaks many times before starting at school. Coming from very different social circles, Jane Campbell and Anne MacLeod shared an odd kind of friendship. Jane could be rather superior in her ways but she did like Anne. Everybody liked Anne MacLeod. Jane had known her before she married Andrew and valued her obvious intelligence and commonsense. Angus Campbell had never had to do the kind of manual labour Andy was used to – and could never beat him at a sheepdog trial. Both men helped each other out when it was needed, but neither man thought of the other as a real friend.

Like a lot of young station-reared girls, Catriona

was very fond of horses and riding, and she had been told many times how good at it she was – her pony club triumphs attested to that. David would never go to a pony club meet and was only ever seen at gymkhanas and the local show. It semed to Catriona that David was by far the best young rider she had ever encountered. He could do things that she had never seen anyone do before, like standing bareback on his pony and cracking a whip. He could also ride over country that she was not even allowed to attempt. What's more, he was beginning to develop into a very handsome young man. Tall for his age, with wavy brown hair that never seemed to blow about or look untidy, David had inherited his father's captivating grey eyes, although Catriona had once heard her mother remark that David would be much better looking than his father.

Throughout Catriona's childhood, David had always been there. This was not just because the MacLeods were the Campbells' closest neighbours, but because David's exceptional ability with ponies and stockwhips was becoming known across the high country. But he lived his life oblivious to Catriona, consumed as he was with his dogs and horses. Although Angus was practically unbeatable with beef cattle, sheep and wool, David had beaten him with a dog. This turn of events caused David's popularity to skyrocket, particularly in the eyes of Catriona.

It was a three-mile ride from the Campbell homestead up the road to High Peaks and, in company with Stuart, Catriona began making more regular trips, ostensibly to exercise her ponies and visit Anne MacLeod. Catriona already possessed the curiosity of most girls where boys were concerned, although her attraction towards David was more stirred by his disregard for her than for anything physical she might have felt. The ride to High Peaks was a safe one, because for the first half of the distance the road was visible from Inverlochy and for the second half it was visible from High Peaks homestead.

Catriona had her new grey show pony which she wanted David to see, so she told her mother she would ride to High Peaks to see Mrs MacLeod.

'Very well, Catriona. I'll call Anne and ask her if it's convenient,' Jane Campbell said. 'I know she likes to give you lunch when you visit.'

'I can take something to eat in a saddlebag,' Catriona said.

'Not in this hot weather you can't. Anyway, Anne looks after you very well.'

'But David goes out all day in the hills with what he carries in his saddlebag,' Catriona said.

'David is David. You are not. I know you're a good enough rider to get to High Peaks, but what will you do when you get there?' Jane was beginning to get suspicious of Catriona's constant desire to visit the MacLeods.

'I talk to Mrs MacLeod about lots of things. I help her make scones and cakes and other things David likes. And sometimes she rides with me up to the high places to meet David. I've been to most places except Yellow Rock. Why did they call it Yellow Rock anyway?' Catriona asked.

'I understand that it was because of all the broken yellow rock on the slopes. The big rocks have become eroded and cracked and when the sun shines on them they appear very bright,' Jane explained.

'Mr MacLeod says it's too dangerous for me to ride up there.'

'Very sensible of him, too. David's grandfather was killed there,' Jane reminded her.

'Yes, I know. It's funny it isn't too dangerous for David. He has been going up Yellow Rock for years and he's the same age as me,' Catriona said petulantly.

'If the MacLeods choose to risk their only child, that's their business. However, they are absolutely right not to let *you* ride up it,' Jane said with some asperity.

'Which only goes to show how much better a rider they consider David to be,' Catriona said.

'Catriona, don't be tiresome. There's more to it than you imagine. The MacLeod horses have all been reared in that kind of country. They're very sure-footed and they are also used to carpet snakes. There are quite a lot of those up there. Horses bred on flat country don't handle the rough country as well. I've heard your father say so on several occasions. The track up to Yellow Rock is only three feet wide in places. Have some sense, Catriona.'

Catriona was delighted that her mother was letting her visit High Peaks, so she was content to let the argument rest there – for the time being anyway.

Catriona set off on her journey after breakfast next morning. Jane watched her until she was out of sight. The grey pony had a good walking pace and handled the rise to High Peaks very comfortably. It was just on ten a.m. when Catriona rode into the house yard. Anne was standing on the front verandah with a pair of binoculars in her hand.

'Hello, Catriona. Is this the new pony?'

'Good morning, Mrs MacLeod. Yes, this is Princess. Do you like her?'

'She is very pretty,' Anne said diplomatically. 'Very pretty indeed.' Anne had learned a lot about horses since her marriage to Andrew. The first thing she had learned was that the best-looking horses were not necessarily the best horses overall. Not that she doubted the quality of the grey pony. Angus Campbell wouldn't waste money on inferior stock.

'I'm sure you're ready for some morning tea. I've some fresh cake and scones inside. And what about a cold orange drink?'

'That would be lovely, thank you,' Catriona said with her usual impeccable manners, and in the next breath: 'Is David close by?'

'No, I'm afraid he isn't. He went to look at sheep on Yellow Rock. And Andy is up on Jimmy's Mountain. They saw a couple of flyblown sheep yesterday and missed them. I doubt that either will be home

122

before late afternoon,' Anne explained.

'Oh,' Catriona sighed. 'I did want David to see Princess. Do you think I could ride up towards Yellow Rock?'

'Well, I don't know. How far would you go?'

'Up to the first big rocks. Mr MacLeod has never let me go beyond there.'

'I know. I have ridden right up Yellow Rock a few times and I always have my heart in my mouth. It's a very dangerous ride, but if you only go as far as the big rocks, that should be all right. David may see you crossing the creek and come down to you. If you don't meet up with him, you must come back here.'

'Very well, Mrs Mac,' Catriona agreed.

So after morning tea Catriona rode out of the house yard and down past the kennels that housed the MacLeod kelpies to the first gate. This opened into what the MacLeods called their holding paddock. Here sheep were turned in while waiting to be crutched or shorn or before being taken back to the old paddocks. This paddock opened into the first hill paddock, which was well grassed and not as steep as on the range proper. The further slope ran down to the creek, which she crossed before ascending into higher country. Half Moon Creek bisected the hills on either side of her. It was a favourite place for picnics and she had been there several times. A few wethers and some horned Hereford cows grazed along the creek. The peak of Yellow Rock towered majestically above her, dominating the rest of the countryside. From the creek it was a long, slow climb to the first big rocks. These were a collection of rocks of many different shapes and sizes which were scattered about over perhaps half an acre of hillside. Anne once said the rocks had probably been distributed as the result of some monstrous disturbance, like an earthquake. David, more romantically, had said that it looked as if a giant with a bad temper had flung them about.

This part of the climb, though steep, was not too rough, but from the big rocks on, the going became increasingly tough. Catriona dismounted and let her pony have a breather. Princess had been watered down at the creek and she was still quite fresh. She immediately began to crop the short grass between the rocks. Her small owner climbed up on top of one of the big rocks to get a better look at the mountain. There was no sign of David or his horse. That settled it – if David could ride up Yellow Rock, so could she! What a surprise he would get when she appeared near the top of the mountain.

Having made up her mind, Catriona remounted and pointed her pony up the track that led through the scattered rocks up one side of the mountain. The going got more difficult as the gradient grew steeper and the short grass gave way to crumbled rock and dead timber. The track grew narrower; in places it was no more than three or four feet wide. On her left the mountainside plunged away steeply. Slowly, very slowly, Catriona let her pony pick her way up the mountain. They came to one particularly narrow section which showed obvious evidence of past landslides. Water rushing off the mountain had scoured out rock and shale and pushed it into a ravine below the track. There was a great mound of soil, sand and fine rock that had built up over countless years. It was at that moment that she saw David silhouetted against the skyline. He was not on horseback and she remembered that Anne had told her it was impossible for anyone to ride right to the top of Yellow Rock. The last section of the mountain had to be climbed on foot.

David caught sight of the small rider on the grey pony just as Catriona saw him appear at the rim of the plateau that was the peak of Yellow Rock. His surprise was great, but it did not last long.

'Cat, don't come any higher! Get off and back your pony,' he shouted at the top of his voice. 'Don't try and turn her. The track's too narrow.'

Catriona had been on the verge of doing exactly what David had screamed at her. It was just that, having come so far, she couldn't bear to turn back and miss the chance to really surprise David.

Catriona took up the reins and gave the command to back. Princess took one obedient step backwards, but right at that critical moment she saw, smelt or sensed the big carpet snake in the small cave above the track. The side of the mountain was so steep that the cave was just above her head. Perfectly mannered and tutored though she was, Princess, like most horses, had an innate fear of snakes. She reacted to the snake's presence by taking one step sideways. Her near side front and back feet went over the ledge and she fell away down the slope.

David heard Catriona's scream as pony and rider fell over the ledge. He watched in horror as they hit the rubble and slid down the gully, finally coming to rest on the mound of sand and shale. Catriona had been thrown clear of Princess, who had somehow managed to get back onto her feet. Her legs had sunk several inches deep in the mound, which had halted the pony's descent down the mountain. But Catriona was lying prostrate.

David rushed down off the peak, leading his own pony as fast as he could, until he came to a section of track wide enough for him to tether it. He then lay on his stomach and looked down to where Catriona and her pony had fallen.

Catriona was trying to get up but there seemed to be something wrong with one of her legs. Her blouse had ripped away from one shoulder and a leg of her jodhpurs was hanging loose. Blood was running down one side of her face and dripping on-to the front of her blouse. The pony seemed to have fared better than her rider. She had hair missing from two large areas, a shoulder and just below her rump. A small trickle of blood dropped onto the sand.

'Cat, are you okay?' David called anxiously.

'I don't think so. My leg hurts awfully and so does

my shoulder.' He heard her voice weakly, as if it were coming from a great distance.

'Can you stand up?' he asked.

'I don't know. I'm too sore and everything hurts. Everything.' Catriona was crying and in deep shock. Her tears were flowing in little runnels through the dirt on her face. It was the most terrifying thing that had ever happened in her short life.

She had been temporarily stunned by the fall, though partly cushioned from full impact with the ground by the pony's body. One leg and shoulder had taken the weight of the landing. Now that the impact of the fall was wearing off, Catriona became aware of pain in several places. David was the only person within miles of her, and she realised instinctively that he could do very little to help her.

David squatted on his heels and examined the crying girl and her pony. He studied the slide and the position of the sun and came to a quick decision. Taking his handkerchief from his pocket, he knotted it around the neck of the blue kelpie at his side. Ben was one of Andy's old dogs, but David had worked him up until he'd been given Glen. Since Glen's death, David had gone back to using Ben. 'Here, Ben, get down.'

He pushed the dog over the ledge and watched him slide down the gully to where Catriona lay on the heap of rubble. The dog looked up at the boy and wagged his tail gently.

'Cat, untie the handkerchief from around Ben's

neck and lay it on the ground. Can you do that?'

He watched as Catriona untied the knot and spread the hankie out beside her.

'Stay, Ben. Stay,' he called down to the dog. Ben lay down on the square of cloth with his head pointing up to the ledge. The boy knew that his dog would not move from the handkerchief until commanded to do so. Ben would guard a saddle, a bridle, a stockwhip or any item of clothing. 'Watch it, Ben.'

'What are we going to do?' Catriona wailed. She was hurting, and very, very frightened.

'Cat, I'm going to have to leave you and go for help. Ben will stay with you until we get back. Is your watch still working?'

She looked down at her wrist and nodded. 'It seems to be.'

'What time is it?' he asked.

'Ten past one,' she called through her sobs.

'We'll be back here between two and three. I'll have to ride one of Dad's horses to make it quicker. Don't be scared. I'll bring ropes and a blanket for the other fellas to use. We'll have you up in no time. You thirsty?'

'A little bit,' Catriona sobbed. The prospect of David leaving her brought renewed misery.

David went back to his pony and unstrapped his water bottle. It was an unbreakable ex-army bottle which he threw down beside her.

'See you soon, Cat,' he called over his shoulder.

And then he was gone, leaving Catriona and Ben alone on the mountain.

Anne MacLeod was standing on the verandah with the binoculars glued to her eyes when she saw her son appear through the opening that led up into the steeper part of the property. He was alone and pushing his pony hard. David would never ride his pony in such a fashion unless something was wrong. She walked down the steps and stood by the gate, holding it open so David would not have to stop.

The pony was lathered and heaving and David was off in a flash. He took the bridle and saddle across to the stables that housed the working horses. Anne closed the gate and hurried after him, sure now that something awful had happened.

'David, stop. What's the matter?' she asked anxiously.

'Can't stop, Mum. Catriona is hurt. Maybe real bad. She and her pony went over the track on Yellow Rock. They landed on the sand pile. The pony is missing a bit of skin but doesn't look too bad. Cat doesn't seem to be able to get up. There's something wrong with one of her legs, and her shoulder is hurt, too.' He was panting as he threw the saddle on his father's mare, Jess.

'Oh, my God. What are you doing with that horse?'

'I'm going back to her. I'll take some throwing ropes, a blanket and another bottle of water. Mum, put the sheet out for Dad. When he gets here tell him we're near the place where he found Grandfather. Just a bit this side. He knows the spot. You'll have to ring Mr Campbell and get him and Stuart up here. They'd better bring saddled horses on their truck. Dad will need to show them the way. And, Mum, you'd better ring for the ambulance.'

'David, you aren't going on Jess?'

Jess was one of Andy's camp horses and much bigger than David's ponies. Unbeknown to Anne, Andy had let David try her out during their mustering trips.

'I've ridden her in the yard and I know I can manage her,' he fibbed. 'I need to get back to Cat in a hurry. She's crying a lot.'

Anne looked at her son in astonishment. He was only ten, yet here he was taking charge of a very serious situation and telling her what to do into the bargain. He was for all the world like a seasoned campaigner.

'Mum, tell Dad I've taken three throwing ropes. He had better bring his rifle in case we have to destroy Cat's pony. I don't think we can get her up the slope.'

'I thought you said the pony seemed all right,' Anne said with a frown.

'It would need a lot of men to get her up, and she might go crazy.'

'David, you must wait up top until Andy arrives. Don't try and do anything on your own. Promise me.'

'Cat is hurt, Mum. Hurt and scared. I have to get down to her. Don't worry. If Dad asks about Ben, tell him I left him with Cat.'

He rolled a blanket into a tight bundle and tied it neatly to the cantle of the saddle. He then used a piece of doubled binder twine to tie the throwing ropes through the saddle Ds. The last item to be added was a water canteen, which he filled from a tap in the horse yard.

'Put the sheet out quick, Mum,' he said as he climbed into the saddle.

With her heart in her mouth, Anne watched David lean over the mare's neck and send her racing up the track into the hills. He rode that horse as if he had been born on her back. It was only after Anne had lost sight of him that she hurried to the house for the sheet. There had been a longstanding arrangement between Anne and her husband that in an emergency a white sheet would be hung over the back fence or the fence into the holding paddock. This could be seen from most vantage points about the property.

Anne knew that Andy was up on Jimmy's Mountain and would have no trouble seeing the signal. She just prayed he would see it soon enough. It sounded as if Catriona were seriously injured. That was the only reason Anne had not raised stronger objections to David's rescue plans. In Andy's absence, David was the only person able to get back to Catriona in a hurry.

131

The sheet in place, she hurried back to the house and rang the Inverlochy number.

'Is that you, Jane? It's Anne MacLeod. Is Angus there?'

'He's in the study going over his books. Is something wrong?' There was a sharp edge to Jane's voice.

'Please get Angus, Jane. Get him quickly,' she said urgently.

'There *is* something wrong. Oh, Angus. Quickly. It's Anne.'

Angus came on the phone almost immediately.

'What is it, Anne?'

'There's been an accident. Catriona and her pony have gone over the ledge at Yellow Rock. She is conscious, but there's something wrong with her leg or ankle. David said she can't stand up. He's taken ropes and a blanket back with him, but he won't be able to get her up on his own. I've put out a signal for Andy. Can you bring a saddled horse on your truck? I'll ring the ambulance to save time.'

'Anything else?'

'I don't think so. Oh, it might be an idea to bring another man with you in case Andy doesn't turn up. I can take you up there, but you might need some more muscle.'

'I'll bring Stuart. Be there soon.'

Anne put the phone down with relief and hurried down to the horse yard to saddle a fresh horse for Andy as well as her own mare. That would save some time. As much as she was concerned for Catriona and her parents, Anne's mind was consumed with concern for her small son.

Her eyes searched the heights above her for the first sign of her husband. Please, God, let him see the sheet quickly.

Chapter Eight

Up on Jimmy's Mountain, Andy MacLeod finished his sandwiches and downed the last dregs of tea from his enamel mug. He scuffed earth over the small fire he had lit to boil his billy and then stretched out with his back against a log. From where he lay he had a clear view down the mountain. The homestead was at its base. It was the centre of Andy's life more than ever with Anne and David there.

Suddenly, he jumped to his feet in one movement. Something was wrong: there was a white sheet laid over the back fence. There must be an emergency.

Andy turned and strode to where the brown gelding was hitched to a sapling. He tightened the saddle girth and was in the saddle and moving down the mountain in a matter of seconds. If there was an emergency, it was likely to involve David.

On her umpteenth trip to the back gate Anne saw her husband coming down the mountain as fast as his horse could handle the slope. She went round to the horse yard where David's pony stood munching the hay she had fed it.

Andy approached and leapt off his horse in a flash. 'What's wrong, Anne? Is it David?'

She shook her head and as briefly as possible explained how Catriona had come to be stuck up on Yellow Rock.

Andy looked across at the two saddled horses and Anne responded to his unspoken question. 'A fresh horse for you and one for me so I can either go with you or guide Angus up.'

'Yes,' he said. He looked down the road past the homestead and saw a cream utility tearing up the road towards High Peaks. It was Jane Campbell at the wheel with Stuart sitting beside her.

'Dad's not far behind,' Stuart said as soon as he got out of the car. 'We'd turned the horses out into another paddock and they took a while to collect.'

Anne went to Jane and put an arm around her shoulders. 'It'll be all right, Jane. They'll get her up.'

A few minutes later the red International truck came up the road as fast as it could. Angus nodded a quick greeting and without further discussion he and Stuart had the ramp of the truck down and their two horses on the ground. Anne noted how much Stuart had grown since she'd last seen him. He was a big boy for thirteen.

Anne and Jane watched them as they mounted. There was a rifle in the scabbard of Andy's saddle and he had added an extra coil of rope.

'Time to go,' he said. Angus and Stuart followed him out of the horse yard and down to the first gate. Then they were through and riding fast for the hills and Yellow Rock.

Jane was crying as she watched the men leave. She had heard terrible stories about Yellow Rock and how dangerous it was. It was the very same mountain that had claimed the life of Andrew's father. Now her small daughter was lying injured somewhere up there.

'Don't worry, Jane, Andy will know what to do,' Anne said as she took Jane's hand, at the same time trying to keep her eyes trained on the three riders.

'She's only a little girl and that would have been a terrible fall. She could be hurt internally.'

'She wasn't knocked out, so she couldn't have hit her head too badly,' Anne said in as confident a voice as she could muster.

'How long do you think they'll be?'

'If they don't have any trouble, they should be back here within, say, two and a half hours. While we're waiting, I'll make some fresh scones and sandwiches. Perhaps the ambulancemen would like something while they wait. Why don't you come and help me?' Anne wanted to get Jane involved and keep her mind off what was happening on the mountain as much as possible.

Andy pushed his horse hard on the lower hill country. He made fair pace until he reached Yellow Rock and from then on it was all hard slogging. Stuart

136

Campbell had ridden over some of High Peaks, while Angus had not been up the mountain since the day they had recovered the body of Andy's father. When they came out of the valley and began to climb, the horses could not travel faster than a walk.

The steepness of Yellow Rock shook Angus up a little. That last time he had accompanied his father and had been anxious to prove his mettle. He'd had the notion that the danger posed by Yellow Rock was overrated. That first ride up the mountain had disabused him of that idea. Now older and wiser, he fully appreciated the danger of the place. He found it hard to understand why his small daughter would have tried to climb the mountain in the first place, especially on her own. What motivation could Catriona have had to attempt such a ride on her new pony, a pony that had not been reared in this country?

The going got steeper and rougher before they came to a small grassy clearing. It was not much more than five or six yards across and there were kurrajong trees growing quite thickly on the slopes above the clearing. The mare David had ridden was tethered to a gum sapling. She nickered softly when the other horses came into view.

'We'll leave the horses here and go the last bit on foot,' Andrew said as he dismounted. He took the rope and rifle from the saddle and tethered his horse alongside Jess. The Campbells followed his example and then they all set off up the slope. The track narrowed quickly and became much steeper, and Angus had to push himself to keep up with the others.

'There's the spot!' Andy said suddenly as they came up over a small rise. Here they had an almost clear view of the mountain's side. And there below them were the two children, the grey pony and Ben.

Andrew took in the scene at a quick glance. David had tied the throwing ropes together and one end was anchored to a half-grown kurrajong on the slope above the track. He had gone down hand over hand and he was standing beside a prostrate Catriona. David had made a pillow from a blanket and had placed it under her head. It looked as if he had given her a drink of water and washed her face, too, because there were two canteens on the ground beside her. David waved and called out when he spotted his father on the ledge above.

Andrew did not waste any time. He turned towards Angus and Stuart and proceeded to tell them what had to be done. The big rope had to be tied to the tree around which David had anchored his rope. The blanket under Catriona's head would be passed beneath her so it acted as a kind of sled. A loop of rope, protected by the blanket, would have to go under her armpits so that Angus and Stuart could pull her back up the slope. When they had done that, he would come back hand over hand with David on his back.

'What's to be done with the pony, Andy?' Angus asked.

'I'll have a look at her when I get down there.

I don't think there's a hope in hell of getting her back up the slope without equipment, and there's no room to use it anyway. Maybe a dozen men could pull her up, but we haven't got that sort of manpower.'

'Do what you think is best, Andy,' Angus said grimly.

Andrew nodded and, taking up the rope, he went down over the side. It did not take long for his mind to flash back to the day he had done the same thing to recover his father's body. When he reached the mound of rubble, he put one big hand on his son's head. 'You should have waited up top, Davie,' he said.

'Cat was crying and it was hot so I came down and washed her face and gave her a drink. I couldn't leave her down here, Dad,' he replied.

'Well, no point worrying about that now. Miss Catriona, how are you feeling? Where do you hurt?'

'Everywhere,' she wailed.

'Anywhere in particular?'

'My ankle hurts a lot and my shoulder. Everywhere.' Her shirt and riding breeches were torn and there were some nasty patches of scraped skin.

'Have you tried to stand up?' Andy asked.

'Mmm,' she mumbled through her tears. 'Once. My left ankle hurts a lot. Does Mummy know?'

'Your mother is with David's mother back at the house. You'll be with her before long. Your daddy and Stuart are up on the ledge, too.'

'Yes, I can see them.'

'Good. You can't have concussion. Looks like your shoulder and left side took most of the shock.'

He examined Catriona's left ankle and frowned. It was very swollen and, if not broken, severely bruised.

Andy realised that he could not proceed with his original plan of putting a loop under the girl's shoulders. That would put too much strain on the damaged shoulder. He would have to double the blanket and cut holes through it for the rope and he would put a second rope around her waist as a pre-cautionary measure in case the blanket tore.

'I'll tell you what we are going to do, young lady. I'm going to use this blanket as a sled and your daddy and Stuart will pull you up the slope. When they pull you up the slide, you must keep very still and not struggle. If you do that, it won't take very long to get you up to your dad. You can do that, can't you?'

'I think so.'

'Good girl. Remember, keep very still.'

Andrew spread the blanket and then doubled it before cutting two holes to take the rope. A loop of his own big rope was then knotted about the girl's waist.

'Keep your arms close to your sides, on the blanket, and keep your legs dead straight. That way you won't get rubbed. Do you understand?'

Catriona nodded in reply.

'Okay, away we go.' He looked up to the ledge where Angus and Stuart were anxiously waiting for instructions.

'Righto, up top. You can start pulling. Easy does it, no jerks, just keep a steady strain on the big rope.'

Angus and Stuart began pulling. Andrew watched critically as Catriona was pulled closer and closer to the track above. Then she was there and he saw Angus bend over and pick her up.

Now that Catriona was safe enough, she thought about her pony.

'You won't shoot Princess, will you, Daddy? It wasn't her fault. It was the snake that frightened her over the edge.'

'I don't know, sweetheart. We are not sure we can get her up the slope.'

'Oh, you mustn't shoot her, Daddy, you mustn't,' she cried.

'It's up to Mr MacLeod, Catriona. He will do what's best. Here, you sit with me for a little while until we're ready to go back.'

Andrew was looking over the grey pony. Except for the missing areas of skin, he could not find anything seriously wrong with her. She was standing fetlock-deep in the rubble and waiting very patiently, like the lovely mannered thing she was, for someone to guide her away.

'Right, that's one down, or up, Davie. Now it's your turn. You could go up on my back, or we could put a loop round you and pull you up.'

Neither suggestion found any favour with David. He had other ideas. Catriona had pleaded with him not to let them destroy her pony and he was not going to have that happen if he could help it. He had a lot of time to think about the pony and he reckoned he knew how to save her.

'What about the pony, Dad?' he asked.

'I think we'll have to put her down, I'm afraid. We can't get her up that slope on our own.'

'Dad, there's no need to shoot her. I think I can ride her out.'

Andy looked at his son in amazement. 'Ride her out? No way. You'd kill yourself.'

'No I won't. I worked it out while I was waiting for you. There's a ledge under this rubble that runs away to the left. We could push some more rubble down to make a better slide down to it. If I lead the pony by the reins and you push her, she'll slide down to the next ledge. I can lead her for a bit and then ride her down the mountain and meet you at the bottom.'

'Davie, it's just too dangerous. I can't let you do it.'

'Dad, Cat doesn't want her pony to die. It was a present and she thinks the world of her. I promised her I would get her pony down off here. I can do it. I know I can.'

'What do you reckon, Andy?' Angus called down from above.

'Angus, you take Catriona back to the house. Stuart had better stay where he is. We're going to try and save the pony. Tell the women you came on ahead. Just get Catriona back to the house. Can you manage it?'

'I reckon so.'

'If you can't manage her on your horse, stop and wait for us.'

'Okay. Thanks, Andy. I'll be seeing you,' Angus called down.

Andy MacLeod knew he had made a decision he might live to regret, but David had made a promise to Catriona and he couldn't let her down. If anyone could get the pony off the mountain, David could. Commonsense told him that it would be wiser to put the pony down, but he had to admit that what David suggested might just work.

Andy looked over the edge of the rubble pile and noted that it might be possible to get the pony down to that secondary ledge and from there find a way across the face of the mountain. But would the pony be up to it? She'd had a bad shaking-up and would get another fright when they pushed her down the side.

'We'll give it a go, Davie. Let's start shoving some of this rubble.'

They sat down and began pushing with their legs. Andrew marvelled at his son's spirit. The sand started to run and then the flow increased so it poured down the slope to the ledge below. In half an hour they had a ramp made of the rubble and a fairly substantial heap on the bottom ledge.

'Davie, you slide down on to that mound and I'll see if I can get the pony down to you. You'll have to be quick and try to catch the reins so she can't swing about and go overboard. Understand?'

'I understand, Dad.'

'Be careful.'

David slid on his bottom down the slope. Andrew took up the pony's bridle and she followed him like a dog. But she did not like the ramp and backed away.

'Stuart,' Andrew called up to the young man who had waited patiently on the track above him, 'pull those throwing ropes up and undo them. Then throw one down to me.'

When the rope came thudding down, Andrew put a loop under the pony's back legs. He was going to pull the legs from under her so that she would come down on her rump and slide down the makeshift slide to the next mound. It took a bit of doing, but at last Andy managed it and the grey pony slid down to where David stood waiting for her. She landed beside him and he grabbed her bridle and held it fast. He rubbed the pony's forehead and talked softly to her until she settled down. She had lost some more skin but it was a miracle she was still alive. David now had to persuade her to jump off the mound on to the solid ground of the slope, which, though grassy, was very steep.

'Give her a whack with the end of the rope when I jump across, Dad,' David called to his father. He took the bridle in his right hand and slid, then jumped to the slope. His father gave the rope a big overhead swing and brought it down across the pony's rump. Princess took off. She half stumbled and almost went down before recovering her footing. Finally she stood upright beside David on the steep slope of the face of Yellow Rock.

David's grin almost split his face in half. 'See you down the track, Dad.'

'You be careful, Davie. Don't try and ride her yet, just lead her until you get down a bit further. I'll wait for you.'

Wait? He'd wait forever. What David had done was madness, but it was magnificent. Yet he knew that Anne would have a very different view. There would be fireworks when she found out.

Ben had stood patiently beside them all the while they worked on getting Princess down. Now he looked up at Andrew with a knowing expression in his big brown eyes. He seemed to know it was time to go. 'I haven't forgotten you, old fellow,' Andrew said to the dog, and stroked him lightly on his head.

Andrew and Stuart made their way down the mountain to where their horses were tethered and then rode to the base of Yellow Rock. There was still no sign of David, but Andrew did not expect him for some time. They had a track to come down, whereas David would have to pick his way carefully across that steep face.

'I wouldn't like to be riding down there,' Stuart said and shivered. 'It would have been better to put the pony down. No horse is worth a person's life.'

Andrew had a very good idea that his wife would

agree. He appreciated what Stuart was saying but Davie was an extraordinary boy. He was a bugger of a boy in some ways, self-willed, sometimes disobedient and overconfident of his talents, but, for all that, he was a bottler.

'He's only a kid ... ten years old,' Stuart said.

'Almost eleven. And that's David,' Andrew said.

They sat their horses for a few minutes and then dismounted.

Time continued to pass slowly. After a while Andrew began to worry. Really worry. And then at last he saw boy and pony come into view away to their left. The first thing Andy noticed was that David was holding the pony with a very short rein, and with his right hand – something David never did. As they drew closer, Andrew's keen eyes picked up the blood running down the boy's face.

'I think,' he said very slowly, 'he has come a cropper.'

But David still managed a grin as he came up to them.

'You came off?' Andrew asked, not able to recall the last time that had happened.

'It wasn't the pony's fault, Dad. Even Jess would have had a job to stay on her feet back there. She's a good pony, not just a pretty one. She's done really well.'

'What about you? Your face is a mess. We'll have to clean that up when we get to the creek or your mother will have a fit. I reckon that pony must be

146

busting for a drink, too. And why are you riding with your right hand?'

'Oh, it's nothing much, Dad.' He wasn't going to let on about his shoulder in front of Stuart Campbell, the schoolboy football star.

'Do you want to rest for a while?' Andrew asked.

'No, but you could let me ride Jess and you could lead the pony,' David suggested.

Andrew nodded. He watched critically as the boy mounted the bigger horse. It was obvious that there was something wrong with his left shoulder: he had trouble pulling himself into the saddle.

When they got to the creek, the water tasted wonderful but it stung David's face. 'You'll have a nasty cut there,' Andrew observed.

'It'll be okay,' David said. 'It couldn't be as bad as the one I had on my leg.'

'Maybe not, but it's more visible. All right, let's go and face the music.'

They rode back to the homestead just as the sun was going down behind the range. Surprisingly, Angus Campbell was standing with Anne at the gate of the horse yard. Anne's eyes were on her son and they widened when she noted the raw wound on his face.

'David, are you all right? What happened? How come you have Catriona's pony?' Anne turned to her husband. 'Andrew MacLeod, you didn't allow David to ride down that face?'

'There's jobs to do, Anne. We'll talk about it later,' Andrew said. He was watching David closely. If his suspicions were correct, the boy would not be able to unsaddle and carry Jess's gear. He wanted Anne out of the way so that she would not notice it, too. He turned to Angus. 'What's the news on Catriona?'

'The ambulance men said she has a broken ankle and could have a broken rib or two. She has severe bruising, but they don't know yet whether there is any internal damage. I'll go to town when we get the horses back. I wanted to be sure everything turned out okay with you people.'

'Yes, everything is fine and Catriona still has her pony. In a few weeks, when the skin grows, she'll be right as rain.'

'Andy, you go and feed the dogs, and David and I will look after the horses,' Anne said. 'Dinner is ready and I am sure David, at least, is ready for it after the day he has had.'

David stood and looked appealingly towards his father.

Angus looked on, an unwilling spectator. He realised Anne was about ready to explode. It was an awkward situation and he felt rotten about it.

Anne was very smart. When David did not immediately reach to unsaddle Jess, she realised there was something amiss. 'What is it, David? Is there something else wrong with you? Something you haven't told me?'

David shrugged. He knew it would come out sooner or later so he might as well get it over with. There was no way he could carry the big saddle and that's all there was to it. 'I hurt my shoulder, Mum. I can't carry the saddle.'

'My God. How bad is it?'

'It's not too bad. I just can't use it.'

'You just can't use it? Right, I'm taking you straight into town. It's the doctor for you, young man.'

'There's no need for that, Mum. If we have to go, tomorrow will do. Can't you just put my arm in a sling?'

'Is it hurting much?'

'Not too much.'

Anne turned around and glared at her husband. 'Andrew, you ought to be ashamed of yourself. How could you risk your son's life for a horse?'

'I asked Dad to let me do it. Cat begged me not to let them put the pony down. Mr Campbell, please tell her that her pony is okay.'

'Go straight inside, David. I'll have a look at you in a moment. Andrew, you fix the horses.'

'Can we do anything, Anne?' Angus asked.

'No, Angus, thanks all the same. You and Stuart get your horses loaded and head off. That pony looks as if she needs some treatment. And no doubt Jane will be expecting you at the hospital. If there's any news on Catriona, please ring us.'

Angus nodded. 'Thank you, Andrew and David, for what you did. I don't know how Catriona got herself into that mess but I plan to find out. I can assure you that she won't do it again.'

'I wouldn't be too hard on her, Angus,' Anne said with a knowing smile.

Angus held out his hand. 'A man couldn't have better neighbours. Thank you all. I'll find a way to thank you.'

'No call for that,' Andrew said. 'Neighbours ought to help each other. That's the way it's always been.'

'Hmph. Anne, if there are any medical costs with young David, you let me know. Can't have you people out of pocket.'

Andrew helped them load the three horses and then went off to feed his dogs. Anne went back to the house.

David was inside lying on the sofa. He looked all in. Anne unbuttoned his shirt, took it off and then began to slip his singlet over his head. She noted that his mouth was clamped shut. There was a large red mark on the point of his left shoulder and he could not raise his arm. He would have a huge bruise in the morning.

'Commonsense tells me I should take you in to town tonight but perhaps you are more in need of some food and a sleep. I'll take you in first thing tomorrow. Are you hungry?'

'Too right,' he said.

'Good. I'll give you a wash-down since I can't get that singlet off. Then we'll have dinner.'

She didn't say much through the meal and David knew that she was very angry with his father. She had told him many times that he was a hard bushman who expected too much of his son. David always felt that his mother made too much of a fuss about such things. A fellow had to take some risks. Living on High Peaks wasn't the same as living in a back yard in town. Having a buster off a horse wasn't really much different to being bashed up playing footy. But he knew that as soon as he was asleep his mother would argue with his father. Such arguments didn't occur very often, nearly always concerned him and, though fiery, were usually over in a day or so.

David's aunt Kate had explained to him once why his mother got so uptight about his 'adventures'.

'You see, David, your parents really wanted three or four children, but just before you were born, your mum had an accident. What it meant was that she couldn't have any more children. So, Davie, you're it. That's why you're so precious. Don't be too hard on your mum. If you were my son, I would feel exactly the same way she does.'

That evening, while the three of them were eating dessert, the telephone rang. Anne took the call and listened carefully. When she came back to the dinner table she spoke directly to David and wouldn't so much as look at her husband.

'That was Mrs Campbell. Catriona is spending a little time in hospital. She would like you to go and see her tomorrow. I told her I would be taking you in to the doctor first thing in the morning.'

'Aw, Mum, do I have to? I hate hospitals and I wouldn't know what to say to Cat. Couldn't you go on and see her on your own?'

David looked pleadingly towards his father but got no help there. Andy knew that the best and quickest way to bring one of these rare domestic arguments to an end was to let Anne have her way.

'No. I'm sure that Catriona intends to thank you for what you did. If you choose to play the hero, you must be gracious when people offer their thanks.'

'Fool of a girl,' David muttered under his breath.

'What did you say?' Anne asked sharply.

'I said she's a fool of a girl,' David answered sulkily.

'Really. What makes you say that?'

'She should never have tried to ride up that mountain. She was told not to but, no, she had to try and show off her new pony and prove it was as good as ours, and that she could ride wherever we ride. That's just like the Campbells. They hate to think that anyone owns anything better than they do. Everyone knows what they are like. It's common knowledge, even at school, that Mr Campbell has a burr in his pants because he can't beat Dad at the dog trials.'

'I don't approve of that remark, David,' Anne replied. 'I think that there was more to Catriona riding up Yellow Rock than you imagine. I think perhaps she rather likes you, David. I know she is only young, but she is a very grown-up little miss for her age.'

David groaned. 'I don't want to have anything to do with girls, thank you very much.'

'But it is nice to have good friends – boys and

girls. I'm actually thinking of inviting Catriona up here for your eleventh birthday.'

David screwed up his face and groaned again. 'Aw, Mum, you wouldn't? It would spoil the whole day. I rode up to Yellow Rock to get away from her. I saw her coming through the gate of Creek Paddock and shot off. Jeez . . .'

'David, mind your language, please. I happen to think it's time you mixed a bit more with children your own age. There is more to growing up than training dogs, riding horses and cracking whips.'

David realised it was no good trying to argue with his mother while she was in that frame of mind. There were times when he could get her thinking his way but this wasn't one of them. She was crooked on his father for letting him rescue the pony and she wasn't going to let up.

Later that night Anne gave David an aspirin for the pain in his shoulder and he fell asleep almost immediately.

The next morning his shoulder was very stiff and sore and his mother had to help him to dress. They had an early breakfast, which was a silent affair as his mother and father were still hardly speaking to each other. As David got into the car his father gave him a secret wink and he knew he had him onside.

At the surgery, Dr Fuller examined David's shoulder closely then turned to him and said, 'You are a very lucky boy from all accounts. There is nothing serious to worry about, but there is a good deal of bruising and your shoulder will be sore for a few days. It will help if you keep it in a sling, and your mother can make up some ice packs.'

David was extremely accommodating with Dr Fuller, in an attempt to get out of the surgery as quickly as possible.

At the hospital, a very subdued Catriona was lying quietly in bed with her mother sitting by her side. Her eyes brightened when she saw Anne and David enter the room.

Anne had warned David to be especially nice to Catriona as she was feeling down. She had some skin off her face, although David's face was in far worse shape.

'How are you feeling, Cat?' he asked.

'Better, thank you,' she replied. 'Still sore in some places. I hear you had a buster getting Princess down the mountain.'

'Aw, it was nothing much,' he said.

'Then why have you got your arm in a sling and such an awful bruise on your face?' she asked.

'The shoulder is just a bit sore,' he said. He hated being sick in any shape or form.

'You were very brave to rescue me and even braver to get Princess down. Daddy says it was very bad of me to ask you to try and save her, but I knew they would shoot her if you didn't try something.'

'The pony's okay, Cat. You would have been proud of her.'

'Daddy has had the vet out to look at her. He says she's going to be fine and the hair will grow again. I am so pleased you like her. I won't be able to ride her for a little while, but when I'm well again, I'd like to bring Princess up and show you what she can do.'

'Aw, well, we'll see,' he stuttered. Jeez, was there no getting away from her any more? Couldn't they leave now?

'David is just a little bit shy with girls,' Anne explained. 'What he didn't say was that he would like you to come up for his birthday,' she said sweetly.

David groaned inwardly.

'Anne, how sweet of you,' Jane Campbell said quickly. 'Catriona, you'd like that, wouldn't you? And you should be back to your old self by then.'

'We mustn't tire Catriona, David,' Anne said. 'Your mother will let me know when you are back home and perhaps we could come and see you there.'

'Will you, David?' Catriona asked.

'Mmm,' David muttered. He was furious with his mother for suggesting another visit.

'Goodbye, Cat,' he said as he made for the door, and as soon as he was outside he muttered, 'Thank goodness that's over.'

'Really, David, you do go on. It wasn't so hard, was it?'

'Mum, I hate talking to girls. You had to go and bring me in here when Susan Cartwright broke her leg. She and Cat have got all their snobby friends. They don't need me.'

'You will have to learn that you can't always do exactly as you like. Now, would you like me to buy you something special? What about some of that three-coloured ice-cream?' Anne asked as they got in the car.

'It's okay, thanks. Can't we just go back home? I want to talk to Dad about letting me have a bigger horse. Jess is so much better than my pony.'

Anne threw up her hands in disgust. 'You come off one horse yesterday and want another today. I give up.'

'Does that mean I *can* have a bigger horse?'

'It seems that nothing I say makes any difference. By the way, I understand that Mr Campbell is going to recommend you for a bravery award.'

'Why would he do that?'

'For what you did on the mountain, silly boy.'

'Why should I get a bravery award for that? Dad was the one who went down the rope and got Cat up.'

'He had two other men up top. You were on your own, and what you did must have meant a great deal to Catriona at the time. You kept her company until help arrived. I am going to ride up and look at that slide so I can see for myself how foolhardy you were.'

'Well, it's over and done with now. There's more to think about than that – like Dawn's pups, for instance. Dad says I can have the male pick of the litter. I'll have to study those pups very carefully.'

Anne sighed. 'There are more things to life than dogs and horses.'

'Not for me, Mum. Dad says you can spend your

whole life and never know all there is to know about those animals, so it looks like I'll be busy for a long time.'

Anne sighed again as she ruffled his hair. 'It looks like you will.'

Chapter Nine

The long Christmas holidays were over and David had gone back to school. This would be the last year he would spend at the little school at the foot of the range. The following year he would travel by bus each day to the high school in town. David had recovered from his injury after a couple of weeks of enforced idleness. The most his mother had allowed him to do was crack a whip using his good arm.

During this time Dawn had her pups. There were six in all, three of each sex. They were now over six weeks of age and had reached the mischievous stage. Two of the male pups were black and tan and one was red and tan. Of the females, two were blue and tan and one was black and tan.

The pups had grown a lot in the last week. David had not had much time to watch them after school because he had been so busy with his other chores. He fed the chooks, fed and watered the horses and then let the dogs off for a run before feeding them, too. Andy seldom arrived home before dark and he was often away for days at a time, either shearing or breaking in horses. His mother milked a cow in the morning so the calf had to be penned each night. His mother also spent days, sometimes weeks, back teaching, which augmented the family income.

It was Saturday morning and David had wolfed down his breakfast so he could get out to the pups as fast as he could. Also, today was his eleventh birthday and his worst fears were about to be realised: Catriona would be arriving for lunch. He could not understand why his mother seemed so pleased about Catriona's visit. She was humming and singing a treat.

The truth was that Anne loved her son to distraction, but at times it was a relief for her to turn to another female for companionship; and, lately, Catriona had come to be like a daughter to her.

David's concern was not just about the few tedious hours he would have to spend with her at lunchtime, but also about the strong possibility that the Campbells would reciprocate the invitation and that he would have to attend Catriona's birthday party. He had seen some of Catriona's girlfriends at the show and they were a silly, giggly lot who chattered on about nothing. He simply had to think up some excuse to get out of that.

The day was very special in more ways than one. Not only was it David's birthday, but his father, who usually had only the weekends to do stock work, would be close by. On days such as this, Andy repaired things about the house and sheds and even, to David's greatest delight, worked on a whip. Andy MacLeod had quite a name as a whip-maker, so it was no wonder young David had learned to crack one almost as soon as he could walk.

David sat down on a big block of box timber beside the wood heap and watched the pups. He was particularly taken with the bigger black and tan male. He was the first pup to negotiate the woodpile and now sat on the uppermost block of wood with his head cocked to one side as he watched the other pups. He had an old-dog way about him, or, as his father would say, he had 'dogality' written all over him.

David knew he had to make his choice soon because two male pups had already been booked. He knew his father intended to keep one of the bitches, probably the blue and tan with the peculiar rosette of hair on her forehead.

Time flew by as he watched the pups. He was mostly looking for early evidence of 'eye'. One pup would crouch down behind a block of wood and 'eye' off a mate. Some pups would show this eye at a very early age. It didn't necessarily mean they were the best pups, but it did often indicate that they were more focused than those which wandered aimlessly about. David was so engrossed in watching their antics that he didn't even notice his father approach.

'Made your selection yet, Davie?'

'I like the big black and tan male best. He reminds me of Glen but he's even bigger than Glen was at the same age. What do you think, Dad?'

'It's a gamble, but I prefer the biggest pups. I thought I would keep that blue and tan bitch,' he said, pointing to the pup David had suspected he would choose.

David nodded sagely. He could have bet his last-year's pocketknife that his father would have chosen her. He was getting to know the way Andy's mind worked.

Father and son sat side by side on blocks of wood, watching the pups contentedly. Presently, the pup David had had his eye on climbed down off the top of the woodheap and began 'eyeing' the other pups. He ran from one block of wood to the other and crouched down like an old dog.

'That pup has got something,' Andrew said at last.

'Yes, he's the one I want. Can I have him today so he's a real birthday present?'

'Okay. We'll let the others go,' Andrew said as he noticed the sudden arrival of Angus Campbell's red truck. It made its way down the track and stopped just near the horse yard.

'Now, what on earth is Angus doing up here?'

They went down to the horse yard and were surprised to find that there was a very large Hereford bull on the back of the truck.

''Day, Angus, what brings you up here?' Andrew

asked. He thought Angus might have been delivering Catriona on his way to taking the bull to a client, but Catriona was not with her father and was not due to arrive until midday. 'And what's that you've got there?'

'G'day, Andy, David. It's a bull.'

'I can see it's a bull, Angus. What are you doing with it?'

'I thought you might be able to use it. I've been using it myself, but he's past the age I sell working bulls. Got a fair bit of Vern blood in him. I know you're trying to get a decent little herd together and, begging your pardon, that bull you're using leaves a lot to be desired.'

'Now, look here, Angus, if you're doing this because of what happened with Catriona, forget it. I told you that any man worth his salt would have done just the same as we did. I can't afford a bull as good as that fellow, and until I can, I'll get by with what I can afford.'

'I'm not asking you to buy the bull. You can use him for a couple of seasons to upgrade your females and then put another good bull over them,' Angus suggested in a conciliatory tone. He was aware how thin-skinned Andy was when it came to money matters.

'I don't like taking things for nothing. It's very decent of you to offer me the bull, but I like to pay my way.'

'Don't be so stiff-necked, Andy. If you want to

pay for the bull, you can either help me out with breaking in some of my horses or you can swap me a horse or shear some of my rams. Tim seems to be too busy to handle our horses any longer.'

'How many horses have you got to handle?' Andrew asked.

'Six or seven. The best of the crop,' Angus answered.

'How much is the bull worth?'

'Well, now, that's hard to say. He's an old fella.'

'How much, Angus?' Andrew persisted. 'A thousand, two thousand, three?'

'Somewhere about that,' Angus said airily. The bull was actually worth three times that amount, but he wasn't going to tell Andy that.

'I'd still be in your debt. I don't like being in debt. The bank was bad enough.'

'If you would take a horse on and draft it, maybe win a Maiden draft, that would suit me,' Angus suggested. It was what he'd had in mind all along. He had been trying to build a name for his horses for years, but not being the horseman Andrew was – or that a lot of other stockmen were – he hadn't achieved the status he'd been looking for.

Andrew looked up at the bull and considered the proposition with his usual care. There was no doubt that the bull was a clinker, worth a lot of money. Angus only ever used the best bulls in his stud herd. The Inverlochy herd was by far the best in the district. It was full of Colly Creek and South Boorook blood with some extra Vern blood tossed in. On the one hand, Angus had made a very neighbourly gesture and Andy would look small if he refused it. On the other hand, he did not want to owe Angus any favours.

David listened to this interplay between his father and Angus Campbell with great interest. He was well aware how fiercely independent Andy was, and for one long, horrible moment he thought his father might refuse Mr Campbell's offer of this wonderful bull. And it *was* a wonderful bull: as long as a wet week with terrific hindquarters and a great bull's head. David could picture it standing among the cows down on their bottom country, and he knew it would sire great calves.

'All right, I'll accept your offer,' Andrew said. 'But I'll work the bull out to my value. Agreed?'

'If that's what you want,' Angus said as they shook hands on it. 'Can we take him off?'

'Back your truck up to the ramp. Will he lead?'

'Oh, yes. We taught him to lead as a calf. He's been to the shows,' Angus said.

Andrew nodded. He thought he had seen the bull before today and he was definitely worth more than Angus had suggested. The only factor that pulled his price back a bit was his age. Still, Angus must be going soft.

They walked the bull off the truck and Andrew put a headstall on him. Close up, the bull was even bigger than he had appeared on the truck.

'Colly Creek would have been proud to offer this fellow,' Andrew said. It was a compliment that he knew would impress Angus. Colly Creek had been a famous name in the Hereford world before its dispersal.

Angus nodded. 'He's a fair bull and we've got some good young stock by him. He should do the job for you. Now I must be going, but I'll be back with Catriona in a little while.'

'Wow,' David exclaimed excitedly, as soon as Angus had driven away. 'Can I tell Mum?'

'Tell away.'

David shot off to give his mother the news about the bull and to urge her to inspect it immediately.

'My God, it's a monster,' she exclaimed when she laid eyes on the animal at the end of the halter.

'He's been to the shows, that's why he's so quiet,' David explained. He walked up to the bull's head and began scratching the short white hair in the dish of his head.

'David, get away from him,' Anne yelled. 'If that bull wanted to, it could toss you to kingdom come. Those horns would go right through you.'

'He's as quiet as a lamb, Mum,' David said as he went on scratching the great head.

'Famous last words, David. You are not to go near it. You can't trust bulls. Isn't that right, Andy?'

'Mum's right, Davie. Never take a bull or a stallion for granted and never turn your back on them. This fellow is too big to meddle with. Quiet he may be, but a bull can do anything.'

165

'Andy, you surely didn't buy him?' Anne asked.

'No, Anne. It seems that Angus feels he is in debt to us, so I told him I would work off the bull's cost. He makes our old bull look very ordinary.'

After a somewhat closer, albeit cautious, examination of the bull, Anne retreated to the house with a reminder that smoko would be ready in a few minutes. 'You should have asked Angus to stay for it,' she said.

'He was in a hurry, Anne. He had something else to do before he brings Catriona back.'

There was a very good reason why Angus had had to leave in a hurry, and that reason was contained in a large cardboard box which had been delivered from Tamworth that morning.

This box was on the back seat of Angus's car when he delivered Catriona to High Peaks just after midday. Angus managed to carry it into the house unseen by David and his father, who were out taking the bull down to his new paddock. Angus left Catriona with Anne and drove back to Inverlochy. He was well pleased with his efforts that morning.

'I must say, you've made a remarkable recovery, Catriona,' Anne said as she inspected her.

'I did have a little mark on my face but thankfully it has healed up now.'

Anne never looked at Catriona without regretting the fact that she had been unable to have a daughter. Catriona really was an enchanting child, with her beautiful golden curls and brown eyes. Her clothes were always of lovely quality and seemed as if they were made for her. That day, she was wearing a cotton frock of tartan pattern in soft blues and her hair was set off with a matching tartan ribbon.

'And how is your pony?'

'She's very well, thank you. Her hair has grown again and you wouldn't know anything had happened to her,' Catriona said.

'You must be pleased about that. David told me she is a very nice pony.'

'I am pleased, yes. Where *is* David, Mrs Mac?'

'Oh, he and his father took their horses and have gone off with the new bull. But of course you would know about the new bull.'

'Daddy did say something about it. Will they be long?'

'They were warned not to be, and they knew you would be here at twelve. They'd better not be late. How is school?'

'School is school. This is my last year at home. I'll be going to school in Sydney next year.'

'What do you think about that?'

'I'm not too keen on the idea, but Stuart goes to Scots and I have to go to PLC. It's expected of me,' Catriona said.

'Oh, dear,' Anne said with reserve, holding her tongue about what she really thought of sending children away to boarding school.

'There isn't a suitable school in town, you see,' Catriona added.

Anne understood why Jane Campbell might have given her daughter this message. Although government schools provided a good education, they did not provide the polish that the Campbells demanded for their children. Anne believed, however, that children paid a price for their years away, their very important formative years. She certainly wouldn't like to lose David for six years. He was too much of a free spirit to transplant into what would be a totally foreign environment for him. There were people who said the MacLeods were ruining their son by not making him do other things, such as taking him to sports practice on weekends, but Anne knew that her son was not cast in the mould of other boys. He was immensely gifted with animals, and one day he would inherit High Peaks, which was his whole life. True, she would like David to mix more with other children, something he had always shied away from doing. At least today was a start, with Catriona coming to his birthday.

As if reading Anne's mind, Catriona asked, 'Why doesn't David have other boys here for his birthday? I have several girls over for my parties.'

'David doesn't make many friends. He gets on well enough with most children, but there's nobody very special. You see, Catriona, David spends most of his time here on the property. I just can't tear him away.'

'It's a wonder that he bothers with me,' Catriona said in her curious young grown-up way.

'Well, you have a common interest of horses. And

168

your father is keen on sheepdogs, so that's something else you share.'

'I see,' Catriona replied, stealing glances around the room to see if David was on his way. 'Why have you set the table for five people, Mrs Mac? Shouldn't there only be four places?'

'My younger sister is due here any minute. She was leaving Sydney early this morning. Katie always tries to be here for David's birthdays as he is her only nephew and she is very fond of him.'

'Have I met her before?'

'Not for some years, since the very bad bushfire that went through part of Inverlochy. You were all evacuated to the school. I think it may have been the year you began school. You may not remember Katie, but you probably remember the fire.'

'My word I do. Thankfully, the wind changed or we would have lost the house. But no, I don't remember your sister. Is she like you?'

'Katie is a little like me, although more of a tomboy. She has been all over the world and done some extraordinary things, like hiking through the Himalayas and climbing the Swiss Alps. When she comes to High Peaks she spends more time outdoors with Andy and David than she does inside with me.'

'Is she a teacher like you were?' Catriona asked.

'No, she's a theatre sister at one of Sydney's biggest hospitals. And a very good one, too.'

'Is she married?'

'No, she has never married. She came very close

169

to it once, but the young man she liked married someone else. She has never found the right person since.'

One thing Catriona liked about David's mother was the fact that she treated her more like a grown-up than a little girl.

'Every couple of years Katie goes overseas to see some new place, and every other year she comes and stays with us.'

'What does David think of her?' Catriona asked with real interest.

'He likes her a lot. She's such a down-to-earth person and she doesn't make a fuss of him. They get on famously.'

'Mummy says that David is just like Mr MacLeod, or at least he will be when he gets older. Do you think so too, Mrs Mac?'

'I don't know what Andy was like as a boy. His father was in the army for five years and Andy only had his mother to depend on. He grew up a very quiet, self-sufficient young man. David takes after him in a lot of ways. I've tried to show David that there are other things in life outside High Peaks, although so far I haven't made much headway. David is rather keen on reading, though, whereas Andy only reads the rural papers.'

At that moment they were interrupted by the sound of a car approaching outside. Katie Gilmour had arrived. She was driving a new red Falcon and although she had wanted to announce her arrival by blowing the horn several times, she knew better. A few years earlier she had been given a dressing-down by Andy. He had been breaking in a young horse and the sound of the horn nearly put the colt over the top of the horse yard.

'Kate!' Anne screamed with delight as she flew down the path to greet her sister.

'Anne!' Kate shrieked in reply and threw her arms around her older sister.

'You look wonderful,' Anne said as she inspected her.

Kate Gilmour was taller than her sister (as a child she had often been described as gawky) but she did not have Anne's striking looks. She was not unattrac-tive, except that she had a rather long nose in a longish face. Her eyes were a shade lighter brown than her sister's and full of mischief. They alternately flashed and glowed. Her hair was dark and lustrous like Anne's, and when out riding she often tied it in a ponytail with a piece of string or baler twine Dressed now in yellow slacks and a cream silk blouse, Kate looked anything but the tomboy Anne knew she would become before the day was out.

'Come on in – lunch is ready. You always arrive on time. I'll ring the bell for the others.'

Andy and David were cantering up the horse paddock, having delivered the new bull to his harem. They had inspected him with approval for a final time. Their old bull had been cut out and turned into another paddock for the time being. They had seen the red vehicle arrive and, from a distance, thought at first it was Wilf White's utility. Kate had driven a green car on her last trip.

David's face lit up when he saw his aunt and his smile made Kate feel warm inside. If there was any person outside her parents and Anne for whom she had a special love, it was her nephew.

'Hello, Andy. Hi, David,' she called to them as they rode into the house yard. Both riders dismounted with the ease born of long practice.

Kate envied them their closeness with horses. She wanted to get on a horse right now and canter away down to the creek and then up into the hills.

'My, you have grown so much since I saw you last,' Kate said as she hugged David and kissed him. 'And I've been hearing some wonderful things about you ... rescuing a damsel in distress and saving her pony.'

'Aw, Dad did the rescuing,' David muttered, 'I just rode her pony.'

'Yes, I heard all about that, too. I mean to go and look at that spot. How are you, Andy?' She gave her brother-in-law a kiss on his cheek and a pat on the arm. She admired Andrew for what he had done on High Peaks. He had worked himself into the ground and it showed in the lines of his face and the grey streaks in his hair.

'Not too bad, Kate. The season is fair and prices are reasonable. Looks like the Vietnam business has fizzled out. Don't see why we had to be involved anyway. It's their business, not ours. It didn't help our wool prices. Not like the Korean show. Got yourself a new Ford?'

'Yes, I thought I would invest in a new car, and maybe do a few longer trips around Australia.'

'Come on, you lot. Let's talk inside. We're keeping our other guest waiting,' Anne said.

David rolled his eyes and Kate caught his gesture. She waited until Anne had turned away and then bent and whispered in David's ear, 'Who is it, Davie?'

'Catriona Campbell,' he growled.

'So this is the girl you and Andy rescued, is it?'

'That's her. I don't know why Mum had to invite her here for my birthday. I asked her not to.'

But when Kate got an eyeful of Catriona she had a very good idea why Anne had invited the little girl. Catriona was very well spoken with lovely manners, and she was quite at ease in the presence of three adults. She was still a little in awe of Andy, but after that day on the mountain he had assumed an almost god-like stature in her mind and, unlike David, he even talked to her.

This day was turning out to be no different in that regard. David virtually ignored her. He had more important things to concentrate on, like doing justice to the lunch his mother had set out, and after lunch there would be presents. That was always exciting.

Because of the hot summer weather, Anne had settled for a salad lunch rather than a hot meal. The only concession to this was a dish of small potatoes baked in their jackets, which both Andy and David liked a lot, especially with butter and cream. There was cold turkey, fowl and ham, and their own home-grown tomatoes and lettuce in a special tossed salad with Anne's own mayonnaise. This was followed by a dessert of fruit salad and ice-cream, small slices of cold watermelon, and nuts, and the special treat of jellied sweets.

In the centre of the big table stood David's birthday cake, complete with eleven candles. It was a double-decker cake filled with jam and cream. All in all it was a meal calculated to satisfy even David's appetite.

Throughout the meal Anne noticed that Andy's eyes kept flicking to the clock on the mantelpiece. Her husband's preoccupation with the clock began to get on her nerves, and at last she could restrain herself no longer.

'Andy, are you in a hurry to go somewhere, somewhere more important than your son's birthday lunch?'

'Not at all. What makes you think that?' Andy asked pleasantly.

'Because you can't keep your eyes off the clock. Are you expecting someone?'

'Now, why would you ask that?'

'You can't fool me, Andy, you've got –'

Anne's words were halted in mid-sentence by the sound of a vehicle outside. She went to the front door and looked out. 'Who do we know who owns a green truck and a yellow horse float?' she asked.

'Wow, it's Tim Sparkes,' David yelled.

'David, we aren't in the paddock and none of us is deaf,' Anne scolded. 'Sit where you are, please. If Tim hasn't eaten, he can have lunch with us.'

Tim hadn't. The tall, lean Queenslander explained that he should have arrived earlier but he had been held up by a puncture.

'Hi, everyone. Hi, Kate,' he said. 'How are you, young lady?' he added to Catriona. Tim had known Catriona since she was a baby, as he had been breaking in the Inverlochy horses for years.

'What are you doing down this way, Tim?' Anne asked. 'We heard you were busy running the big station with your uncle so sick.'

'I was. I am. Uncle Bob died and left the place to me. I've been flat-out trying to round up micky bulls and cleanskins. The place had been going backwards for years, but Uncle was making enough money not to worry about it. When he got crook, the place really went downhill. I've been trying to pull it back into shape.'

'So what are you doing here?' Anne persisted.

'Delivering a horse, actually,' Tim said, giving a wink to Andy.

'I wouldn't have thought you'd have time for that,' Anne said. 'Now, please sit down and help yourself to whatever you fancy, Tim. David, I can see that you're bursting to ask questions but they can wait until after lunch. I think that while Tim is eating we can start giving out your presents.'

'Wow, what a day,' David said excitedly. Tim's arrival had put a whole new perspective on things. He was sure to stay at least a day and they would be able to have a long yarn about his property and its horses. His father had told him a lot about the Sparkes horses.

The first present David opened was a roo-hide whip made by his father. It was plaited in black and tan leather with a six-foot thong. The whip was an absolute work of art and fell beautifully.

'Gee, thanks, Dad. It's a beauty,' David said as he ran his fingers down it.

'If you look after it, that whip should last you for years,' Andy said.

'Yeah, I've got one of your father's whips and it must be twelve years old,' Tim said. 'Could have sold it over and over again but money wouldn't buy it.'

There was a new pair of riding boots from Anne, who liked to give practical presents, and a wide-brimmed hat from Kate. Kate also presented him with two books on sheepdogs that she had picked up in Britain and put by for this day. And there were even more surprises in store.

Anne went into her bedroom and came back with the big box Angus Campbell had deposited earlier. 'This is a present from the Campbell family, David,' Catriona said. 'Daddy said you more than earned it.'

David's excitement level rose several notches. What could be in that big box? What would the Campbells give him?

176

He took out his penknife and cut the adhesive tape that bound the box together. When the flaps fell open, he could not believe what he saw inside – a fully mounted saddle.

He lifted it out and placed it over the arm of the sofa. Embossed quite clearly on both saddle flaps were the words *David MacLeod Poley Special*.

There was absolute silence in the room while everyone but Catriona stared at the saddle.

'It was handmade in Tamworth,' Catriona explained. 'Daddy ordered it some time ago and it was delivered just this morning. He says that one day people will be ordering saddles in your name. This is the first. It has a fifteen-inch seat so it should be big enough for a few years to come.'

The enormity of the gift left even David speechless. His very own brand of saddle. It was too much, and all for riding a pony down Yellow Rock.

'It's too much, Cat, far too much. I don't deserve a present like this,' David said with surprising maturity.

'Well, Daddy says you do and so do I. My pony is worth a lot more than that saddle.'

David shook his head. 'It is too much,' he repeated.

The adults inspected the saddle with clinical thoroughness.

'It's a lovely job,' Andrew said at last.

'A real beaut,' Tim agreed. 'Seems to me you need a bigger horse than your pony to do this saddle justice.'

'David would be the first to agree with you,' Anne said. 'He drives us mad about it.'

'Hmmm,' Tim sat back in his chair. 'After that great lunch I'd better go and walk about for a while. Andy, do ya reckon I could let the mare off for a bit?'

'Not at all. She won't come to any harm in the horse yard,' Andy said, smiling quickly in Kate's direction.

Outside, Tim let down the ramp, unhooked the horse inside and led her out. She was a beautifully put together bay with a white strip on her nose and two white stockings on her hind legs. David climbed up on a post of the horse yard and inspected the new arrival. He reckoned she was a shade under fourteen point two hands and a very impressive mare.

'What is she, Tim?' Anne asked, trying to keep her voice under control. It was all clear to her now. Andy had been watching the clock because his old mate was overdue with the mare. The pair of them had hatched up this second surprise.

'Well, now, Anne,' Tim drawled, 'she's a cross of stock horse and quarter horse. She's a mite small for most stockmen up our way because they like a horse about fifteen hands or a bit taller. Our cattle go like blazes and you need a real fast horse to catch them. Not that this mare isn't fast. She's a good one, terrific on her feet and lovely tempered. She's a winner in the show ring, too.'

'Where are you taking her, Tim?' David asked.

'Where am I taking her? I'm not taking her any-where. I'm leaving her here,' Tim said with a grin.

Andy took hold of the mare's halter and led her across to his son.

'Happy birthday, Davie. I reckon you're up to this mare now.'

David nearly fell of his post. He couldn't believe his ears. First, his very own brand of saddle, and now his first big horse, his very own big horse. And what a ripper.

'Do you mean it, Dad?' he asked in a kind of daze.

'Of course he means it, Davie. We worked it out between us,' Tim said. 'I didn't bring the mare all this way just to be looked at. Now, it seems to me that if I was a young fellow and had just been given my own saddle and a new horse, I'd be putting the two together real quick. I'd be charging back to the house for that saddle and I would have it on this mare as quick as I could. Hell, Davie, I want to see what you think of her.'

'Wow,' David yelled as he fell off the post and raced back to the house for the new saddle.

Andy had a bridle on the mare when his son returned with the saddle. Miraculously, there was now a new blue and white saddle blanket with the letters D.M. enscribed on it sitting on the mare's back. Andy and Tim watched critically as David saddled the mare. The leather was still stiff and it took a little longer than usual. David led the mare round the yard before pulling the girth up a notch. Then he was in the saddle, and in heaven. A touch on the rein and ribs and the mare spun to one side.

'Take her up the paddock, David,' Tim said. 'If you can get her down to a real slow canter you will find she's like a rocking horse.'

David did as he was instructed and found that the mare was absolutely foursquare and smooth as silk. She was like a cat on her feet and very quick to respond to any signal. When David brought her back to the others, there was a huge smile on his face.

'She's terrific, Tim, just terrific. Thank you.'

Tim nodded. 'Yeah, she's not bad. She'll be big enough for you for a few years. If you put a bigger horse over her later on, she'll breed ya good-sized stock horses.'

'She is just fantastic, and so is the saddle,' David said, looking up at Catriona who was now sitting on his post.

'Thank goodness,' Anne said under her breath to Kate. She had wondered if the enormity of the gift of the horse would override the gift of the saddle.

'You had better whack some oil onto the saddle. Those buckles are pretty stiff. New saddlery always needs plenty of dressing,' Andrew said.

'I'll do it, Dad. Gee, what can I say? Thanks again, Dad, and Tim. What a birthday.'

'I reckon you're worth it, Davie. If you don't win a junior draft or two on that mare, I'll be very surprised,' Tim said.

'I reckon he's just about ready to handle a junior draft,' Andy agreed.

Anne didn't know whether to feel pleased or

angry. Admittedly, Andy was a very deep fellow who did not always confide in her. Perhaps he had decided to keep Tim's gift of a bigger horse secret so they didn't argue about it. She felt that there shouldn't be any need for secrets between husband and wife. After fourteen years of marriage Andy still kept some things to himself, and it did rankle a little.

Just then David said something that surprised and pleased her very much. 'Mum, when you take Cat back to Inverlochy, I'd like to go with you so I can thank Mr and Mrs Campbell for the saddle in person.'

Anne nodded. 'I think that's a splendid idea. Now, what about a cuppa, everyone? I believe I could use one.'

'Good idea,' Andy replied. 'Leave your mare here with a slab of hay, Davie. We'll probably put her in the old stallion stable later on.'

Inside, Catriona informed everyone that her father was importing a new border collie by the name of Toss. If the dog was as good as it was supposed to be, Angus proposed to work him in the local trial.

When Catriona said this, David had just taken a gulp of tea and he almost choked on it. He looked across to where his father sat and noted the gleam in his eye. He was about to make a comment but the tiny shake of his father's head stopped him dead. David was quite confident that no matter how good this Toss was – and that remained to be seen – he would not be as good as their dogs, especially on merino sheep. But Mr Campbell had to try and beat them.

After he had finished his tea, David, at Anne's whispered entreaty, took Catriona to show her the pups. More specifically, to show her his new pup.

On his way out the door, Kate asked him what he would do if Catriona tried to kiss him goodbye. He blushed but said that he reckoned he could put up with it as it was a pretty small price to pay for a fantastic new saddle. After all, what was a kiss? It might mean something to a girl but it didn't mean much to him. He was more interested in whether a pup tried to kiss him when he blew into its nose. If a pup didn't try to kiss you, it was a safe bet that it would have a bad nature. His father had read that in a dog training book and it had proved to be correct.

But when they left Catriona at Inverlochy, she didn't try to kiss him. She merely said goodbye to him in her well-mannered way. She was very pleased he liked the new saddle and was happy to see how good it looked on his new horse.

As they were driving back to High Peaks after dropping Catriona home, David said to Anne, 'That was a great birthday, Mum. The best ever.'

'Well, there's still a hot dinner to come tonight,' she said. 'And I know you'll want to sit up and listen to Tim tell his yarns.'

'You bet,' he agreed.

'You can stay up an hour later but not one minute

longer. And by the way, I think you behaved quite well with Catriona. I know you're not mad on girls right now, but I'm sure you'll change your mind in a few years. Catriona is a lovely child. If boarding school doesn't turn her into a snob, she might grow up into a very nice young woman.'

'Dad says that she will marry some rich grazier.'

'You do have some interesting discussions with your father, don't you? Let me tell you that I predict nobody will tell Catriona who she is to marry. Your father might be good at a lot of things, but he is no authority on ladies.'

'He sure knew the right one to marry, though,' David said calmly.

This remark so stunned Anne that she was left speechless all the way back to High Peaks.

But nothing could keep David quiet. 'Mum, you know very well that the Campbells are snobs. They never invite you and Dad to their parties. When Catriona is older, she won't even want to look at me.'

'What a profound young man you are today,' Anne said.

David sighed. 'I listen to what other people say. And I am sure that once Catriona goes away to school next year and mixes with all the other snob girls and their brothers she will be a completely different person. There are a lot more important things to think about than her, like winning sheepdog trials and campdrafts, and taking a team of kelpies to the National.'

'We'll see, young man. At least you behaved well today. I was very proud of you.'

'How long will Aunty Kate be staying, Mum?' he asked. Kate's visit was of very real interest to him. Last time she came, he and his father had begun to initiate her into flag and barrel races. She did everything with such wonderful enthusiasm that it was sheer fun to be with her. David reckoned that he now had a horse who would be competitive anywhere, but it wasn't the same racing on your own. Kate's visit promised a lot.

'A couple of weeks. I thought she would be a help while we're crutching. You know how Kate loves to help.'

Andrew MacLeod did not employ crutchers, but did the lot over about a week and half. David and Anne would muster the sheep and bring them to the shed. One of them would work inside the shed while the other would take the sheep away. When Kate stayed with them, she often shared their jobs. David much preferred the outside work because crutching meant mustering – and that meant dog work. Dog work was his major passion in life. For this up-coming crutching, mustering also meant a lot of riding on his new horse.

David had had the perfect day. Sure, his mum had gone on a bit, but she was a great mum really. At times, like when his mother went riding with him, she was as good as any mate. The best of all times was when they had a picnic or barbecue at the creek on summer evenings and his mother took her guitar and sang. Sometimes she played and sang on the front verandah.

David did not speak again for the remainder of the short trip back to High Peaks. There were several important matters to consider, not the least of which was a name for his new horse. It needed to be a short, clear name because he taught his horses to come to name. There had once been a great drafting mare called Gleam, which his father told him had been one of the best he had seen. David was half inclined to call his mare by that same name.

'You've gone very quiet, David,' Anne said as they came into sight of the homestead.

'Just thinking about a name for my new horse. I think I'll call her Gift. What do you think, Mum?'

'I think that would be very appropriate,' Anne agreed.

'And I'll name my new pup Lad.'

Chapter Ten

Now that he had a new pup and a new horse, a proper-sized horse, David was happier than he had ever been. School days seemed to drag intolerably because he yearned to be home with Gift and Lad. His father had promised that he could begin in junior drafts, so there was cattle work in plenty to get Gift ready. Because she had done a fair bit of cattle work after Tim Sparkes broke her in, Gift was well on her way to becoming a top drafter, but she wasn't there yet. He would need to work with his father in the big cattle yard where they drafted up sale cattle. There he could gauge Gift's strength against cattle and see how fast she was when a beast was lifted from the camp.

David also had the urgent need to find some excuse not to attend Catriona's birthday party. He knew he would have to go unless he had a foolproof excuse, so he went to his father with the problem.

Andrew had the choice of attending two camp-drafts that weekend, so he decided they would nominate for the event that included a junior draft. Fortuitously, this was the date of Catriona's party. The plan was that, when invited, David would be able to tell his mother honestly that his father had entered him for his first draft. Anne would have to get on the phone to Jane and explain why her son couldn't attend. David's strategy worked this time, although Anne was furious because she rightly guessed that Andy and David had colluded. She expected the Campbells to be miffed about David's late withdrawal, and though Jane seemed a bit offhand about it, Angus displayed genuine interest in David's entree into campdrafting. There were not many eleven-year-old boys good enough to compete in drafts.

Kate extended her stay by a week so she could be on hand for the last of the crutching. She wore a pair of faded blue jeans patched on both knees and a man's checked shirt, and with her grey, wide-brimmed hat she looked a real ringer. On Saturday nights she and David went eel-bashing. Kate had discovered a new recipe for cooking eels and wanted to try it out. Despite her long experience with surgical instruments, she could not match David's skill with the pieces of flat iron they used to whack the eels. But once they were in the sugar bag, Kate could skin them quick sticks.

In the shearing shed, Kate swept the board of crutchings, and if David was not present to pen up, she did that, too. There was little to do beyond opening the gates, because old Ben knew the shed routine so well he could have done the job on his own, had he been able to open the gates. He would go to the back of a pen of sheep and then climb over their backs to get the leaders moving. The pens filled once more, Ben would retire to a spot under the wool table where he could watch his boss crutch and wig the sheep.

The MacLeods ran over 4000 sheep, of which there were about 1000 ewes. The ewes were run with the Herefords on the richer bottom country, while the wethers were run exclusively in the hills. They also had about 100 Hereford cows. Andrew had borrowed money from a local agent to buy most of these, and had then gone away and shorn extra sheep to earn the money to pay for them. He was supposed to sell what he bred from them through the agent who loaned him the money. Now the cows were paid for and beginning to show a return on his investment.

Andrew said it was important not to have all his eggs in one basket. In their country, only cattle could be considered an alternative to sheep. Andrew did have plans to purchase a few more good mares and also invest in a top-class stallion, but those plans would have to wait until he had the cash in hand. Currently they sent half a dozen mares away to good stock horse stallions, and broke in and handled the young horses. Andrew's horses, like his dogs, were always in great demand because he bred from only a few high-class animals.

During her stay at High Peaks, Kate insisted on being taken up to the infamous ledge on Yellow Rock. Andy was high up in the hills ringing green timber and would not be home before dark, so Anne, Kate and David decided to make a day of it. They took sandwiches and a billy for a lunch in the hills.

At the bottom of the mountain Kate looked towards David and said, 'Righto, young man, you lead the way,' and turned her horse towards the narrow track up Yellow Rock.

'Okay,' he replied. 'There's a whopper carpet snake that lives in a cave up near where Cat went over, and your horse might spook. A horse can smell a snake a fair way off. We'll get off this side of the ledge and leave the horses there.'

'Lead on, Macduff,' Kate said, winking at Anne.

There was no sign of the snake this day, so they tied the three horses to trees and saplings and from there they made their way on foot to the narrow ledge above the rubble slide. Kate got down on her hands and knees and peered over the edge. 'No wonder you couldn't get the pony up this way. And is that the slide where you jumped her down?'

'That's it.'

Kate stood up and rolled her eyes at her sister. She patted her nephew on the head. 'Don't ever join the army and go to war, David.'

'Why not?'

'Because you're the sort of boy who would run at a machine gun or try some other ridiculous feat and be awarded the Victoria Cross for it. Whew, this place makes me feel funny. You don't mean you actually ride up this track?'

'Oh, yes. I haven't ridden Gift up this far before, but my ponies never had any trouble. Sometimes there are wethers right on top.'

'Since we've come this far, why don't we walk up the rest of the way?' Anne suggested. 'It's about the only spot on High Peaks you haven't seen, Kate. There is the most marvellous view from up there.'

'If you're game, I am,' Kate said and clapped David on his back. 'Up you go, captain.'

David grinned. He led off up the mountain with the others labouring behind him. When at last they stood at the very top of the mountain, Kate drew in a deep breath and then exhaled.

'Oh, this air. You could eat it. What a view. Anne, why have you never brought me up here before?'

'Perhaps because the ride is so dangerous. I always steer clear of it. Also, it has some rather special memories. Andy proposed to me up here.'

'What a perfectly wonderful place for it,' Kate said.

'Sheep come up here because they think they're safe,' David said. 'Some sheep never leave these high places. They drink water from rock pools and springs and they don't mix with other sheep. As soon as they see a horse or dog, they bolt for the roughest place they can find. It takes a really good dog to get them

190

down and can take a week to get every last one. Dad said that when he started mustering up here it was common to find sheep with three or four years' growth of wool. Sheep like high places more than flat places. They always head for the higher places at night,' David explained.

'Thank you, professor,' Kate said. 'I can assure you that I won't be coming up here at night.'

Anne pointed out several landmarks. Far below them they could follow the course of Half Moon Creek as it snaked its way towards Inverlochy and then on towards the Cassilis Road. In the other direction they could see the township of Willow Tree.

'Once upon a time the tops of these ranges and the fall of the water used to be the boundary lines for the first big stations,' David recited, memorising word for word the story that had been passed down from generation to generation of MacLeods.

'Didn't Grandfather MacLeod come to grief on this mountain?' Kate asked suddenly.

Anne nodded. 'Yes. Andy found him, but unfortunately not in time.'

'I can see now why the Campbells were so appreciative of what you did, David. It was a miracle that Catriona landed where she did.'

'Mum told her not to come up here and she should have had enough sense not to attempt it. It was her own fault. She was trying to show off.'

'Ah, well, I can understand that. She had a lovely new pony and she fancies herself as a rider, pony club champion and all that. She wanted to impress you.'

'She did not,' David said gruffly. He wished people wouldn't keep harking back to Cat and that day on the mountain.

They stood for several minutes and tried to absorb the vast panorama exposed from the peak of Yellow Rock. Although a fairly warm day on the lower country, it was deliciously, refreshingly cool on the peak. A few white clouds in the intensely blue sky cast shadows across the side of the mountain. Far above them, floating in the thermals, was a wedge-tailed eagle.

'There's an eagle's nest in the big old tree on the next hill,' David said and pointed. 'You can't see it from here because it's on the other side of the hill. Sshh, look down below us. There.' He pointed to a patch of scrub and rock on the opposite side of the mountain. Kate followed his finger and picked up two wallabies squatting on a ledge of rock. 'Plenty of them up here,' David informed her. 'Also some roos and wombats. You need to be careful of wombat holes. If a horse puts its foot in one, it can do itself a lot of damage, maybe break a leg. Horses bred and worked here look for that sort of thing.'

Kate smiled inwardly. David was a real chip off the old block. He had ridden at his father's knee since he was two years of age and he had as much bush lore and wisdom at his disposal as most people collected in a lifetime.

Sated of the view, they made their way back down

the crest, collected their horses and rode to the creek. It was lined with she-oaks, and when the wind blew, the oaks sighed and moaned. The sound emanated in the hills and traversed the length of the creek almost to Merriwa. Andy said it was because the creek was in a kind of funnel.

'Dad says that when you hear the she-oaks sighing, it's a sure sign there will be rain to follow,' David told his aunt.

'Is that right?'

'Almost never fails,' he said.

David would have preferred to stay out longer and have afternoon smoko beside the creek but they had finished off all the tucker at lunchtime so they rode back to the homestead and had smoko there.

Kate always helped David collect the cow and calf and feed the horses. She would then leave him and go to help Anne prepare the evening meal. David would let all the dogs off and take them down the paddock for a run before feeding them. When he had the time, Andrew would kill sheep to feed his dogs. There were always several bags of dog biscuits in the feed shed as these were a great standby. In winter – mostly on weekends when there was more time – they boiled up meat and vegetables and made a broth to pour over the biscuits. The pups were given milk two or three times a day, depending on their age.

There was only one hiccup to mark the perfection of this period for David. One morning soon after Kate arrived, Anne announced that, as Kate was with them, it would be a good opportunity to teach David to dance.

David went hot and cold. Dance! Did he hear his mother say *dance*?

'You will be going to parties, David, and you must know how to dance. Later, there will be balls. If you learn to dance now, with us, you won't have to learn later on. Kate and I will dance and you can watch. Then, while one of us plays, the other will partner you.'

'Gee, Mum, do I have to? I don't want to dance, now or ever.'

'Nonsense. Even your father knows how to dance. That was how we met. If he hadn't been able to dance, you wouldn't be here.'

David had no reply.

'You should be a very good dancer,' Kate chipped in. 'You have natural agility. Look at the way you get on and off a horse.'

David could see that it was one of those times when his mother's mind was made up. She insisted that he spend at least half an hour two or three times a week while she and Kate instilled into him the technique required for several dance steps. Both Anne and Kate were accomplished pianists and dancers so the lessons he received were both thorough and professional. David appealed to his father for relief but for once received no help. Andrew approved completely of the dancing lessons. They would have been a real pain except that his aunt made a fun thing out of just about everything.

On top of the dance lessons, David had yet another unpleasant surprise in store. He knew that his father had been plaiting a bridle. It was a beautiful job, worth a lot of money, and he imagined that his father could only be making it for him. His face fell when he was informed that the bridle was to be the MacLeods' present for Catriona's eleventh birthday. As Anne pointed out, 'If you aren't going, the least we can do is send a worthwhile present. It would look very paltry of us not to do so after the Campbells' gift of your lovely saddle. Furthermore, you are going to deliver the bridle yourself the day before the party.'

David took it in good part because anything at all was better than having to attend the party with a lot of silly, chattering girls. The thought of it made him shudder. While they were carrying on in their idle, stupid fashion, he would be at the campdraft – and this time he would be competing.

The day before Kate was due to return to Sydney she sat with David under the big pepperina tree in the back yard and watched him as he handled his new pup. He had been training the pup by attaching a long piece of cord to its collar and every now and then he would call the pup to him as he pulled on the cord. By the last week of her stay, he had the little fellow coming to him quite quickly and had even begun teaching him to sit. Lad was only a baby but he seemed to grasp what was required of him very quickly.

During the previous weeks, Kate had ridden – mostly with David – over nearly all of High Peaks and had come to admire her small nephew's wonderful horsemanship and stock sense. She had watched him with her heart in her mouth as he had practised drafting Hereford steers both in the open and in the cattle yard. She reckoned that if God happened to speak to her out of the clouds above High Peaks and offer to grant her one wish, she would ask for a son in David's mould. She had wanted to be truly loved by a man and to have children, but this had not happened. David was the closest thing she had to her own child. It was not that he was a perfect child – far from it. He was at times headstrong, impulsive and very intolerant of people outside his sphere of interests, and the interests he did have were, at that stage, all associated with livestock. Andy was his role model and instructor and David was his willing disciple.

'What do you hope to achieve with your dogs, David?' Kate asked at last.

David looked at his aunt but did not answer for a little while. He was used to people slinging off at him, even making fun of his interest in sheepdogs, and although he knew that his aunt was not that sort of person, he still had doubts about admitting his innermost thoughts to her.

'I want to breed and work the best kelpies in Australia and I want to win the National Trials with one of them,' he said at last.

'The National Trials. Are they the biggest?' she asked.

'Yes. The biggest and the most important. Only one kelpie has ever won the National. His name was Johnny, and he won five of them. Dad says he had a lot of collie in him, but he was always called a kelpie because he looked like one and worked like one. Dad says he was a freaky dog and his handler was a genius. No other kelpie has won at Canberra since Johnny's last win in 1952. Two kelpies dead-heated for second in 1953. They lost by only one point. An old blue kelpie probably should have won that year and some say would have won if they had finished working the final that afternoon. Instead, they ran two next morning when the weather and sheep were miles better.'

'Why is winning the National so important to you?' Kate asked.

'It's like winning the big campdraft at Warwick. It would be the best thing a fella's dogs could do,' he said simply. 'Also, it would be the best present I could give Dad for all the years he's tried to keep the dogs so good. Dad was never able to take his dogs away to places like the National because he couldn't afford the break. I'd like to win the National for him.'

'What did people think when you won the local trial? They couldn't have been very happy about being beaten by a ten-year-old boy.'

'I think they were pretty pleased for me. Sheepdog people are mostly fairly decent. All but one came up and shook hands with me. Even Mr Campbell said I did very well, and he'd had a dog in the trial. There was a fourteen-year-old girl working at the same trial and she came fourth.'

'Four years older than you. Four years is a fair difference in age,' Kate pointed out.

'She doesn't have a father like mine,' David said. 'That made the difference. And she didn't have a dog as good as Glen.'

'So now you have to try and produce another dog like Glen. Is Lad a son of his?'

He nodded. 'Breeding sheepdogs is all about trying to produce better dogs,' he said very patiently. 'If you lose a good dog you just have to forget about that and get on with the job of trying to produce another good one.'

'Which is what you are doing with Lad.'

'Yep. If not with Lad, some other dog or bitch. The main thing is to know what you're looking for and then be able to handle a dog when you have it.'

My God, he's like an old man, Kate thought. Surely there isn't another boy like him in the whole country. She stretched her legs towards the sun. She had put on a pair of shorts so she could get a suntan on her legs before she went back to Sydney.

'When will you know if Lad is good enough to go on with for trials?' she asked.

David considered the question and tried to work out how he could explain. Some dogs matured very early while others did not come really good until they were three to four years old. It was all a matter of temperament and breeding.

'I'll have a very good idea what Lad has in him by this time next year. He won't be ready by then but we'll know if he has the things in him that we want in a dog. Some dogs can't be rushed along. Dad says a lot of people spoil kelpies by trying to push them into trials too soon. He says the great Scottish handlers don't make that mistake. They let a dog mature. There was a Scottish trainer by the name of James Wilson who won nine international trials and some of his dogs were four years old when he brought them to a trial. They were real mature dogs. A lot of good young dogs are ruined because people won't let them mature.'

David spoke in the quiet, assured manner of a middle-aged man, and Kate had no doubt that every word he said made good sense. She could not help but feel that at some stage down the track her nephew would achieve his ambition. He had the ability, and he would move towards achieving his goal just as surely as the water in Half Moon Creek eventually merged with the river that carried the water on to the ocean.

'I hope you achieve your ambition before you get tangled up with girls,' she said. 'You're going to be a very handsome young man.'

'Girls.' David spoke the word with utter scorn. 'I won't be going near any girls.'

'David, just about every boy your age says the

199

same thing. They nearly all change their tune. It's called growing up.' She ruffled his hair affectionately. 'I hope you win your National Trial, David, and I'd like to be there to see you do it.'

David picked up his pup and made his way over to the dog yards.

Kate went and joined Anne in the house. 'That son of yours is so serious about what he wants to do,' she said.

'I know. It worries me, Katie. His idea of having fun is to muster Yellow Rock or Jimmy's Mountain. David lost interest in toys years ago. His whips are his toys. One of the only times I've seen him laugh was when you fell in the creek that time we went eel-bashing. He's much too serious for a boy of his age. I don't want him old before his time, but you can't change him. Dogs and horses are serious business with him. Some of the other boys call him "Barky", but he doesn't even care about that.'

'Yes, David does need to lighten up, but there is something very special in that boy. And his confidence is amazing. He is absolutely committed to winning the National Trials. I'm sure there isn't another boy in the country who has that same ambition.'

'That's all he thinks about,' Anne sighed. 'School is simply an impediment to his goal. He does just enough to pass everything, yet the little rascal could do a whole lot better. His school reports all say the same thing. You see, Kate, David knows he's going to inherit High Peaks so he feels there's no need for him to worry about working too hard at school.'

'I appreciate all that you're saying, but I wouldn't worry too much. I have the feeling that David will go a long way and make a wonderful man. I'm very fond of him.'

'I know that in his own way David is very fond of you too, Katie. I am glad of the time you spend with him on your visits here to guide him through adolescence so he does not become a recluse up here. If anything happened to Andy and me, that is what he would become. He loves this place and the animals just too much. That was why I made you executrix. I knew that you would take over here and look after David.'

'I can see that I shall have to try and visit here more often,' Kate said. 'Would you mind that, Anne? Would Andy mind?'

'Please, come as as often as you like. You know you're always welcome here.'

Kate felt a surge of affection for her sister. They had always been fairly close, but were probably closer now than they had ever been.

Kate left for Sydney the next day with the greatest reluctance. She would have liked to stay forever because she so loved High Peaks and the three people who lived there.

In the following weeks, as Sister Kate Gilmour scrubbed up for another operating session each day, her thoughts invariably flew to High Peaks as she pondered what each member of the MacLeod family might be doing. If only she were there with them ...

Chapter Eleven

Catriona was very disappointed to learn that David MacLeod would not be coming to her birthday party. The tale of his feat on Yellow Rock had been magnified in the telling so that it had become almost legendary, like *The Man from Snowy River*. There was doubt about whether the Snowy River story had ever actually happened, but there was no such doubt about what David had done. The local newspaper had written up the story on its front page with a big picture of David included. That was the third time he had been featured in the local rag. The first was when he was guest whip-cracker for a visiting 'Wild West' show; the second, after he had won the Novice event at the local sheepdog trials. So it would have been a feather in Catriona's cap to have him attend her party. She had told Susan Cartwright and some of her other girlfriends that he would be attending.

When Catriona asked David why he wasn't

coming, he had passed it off very casually by saying that his father had entered him for his first junior campdraft on that very day, and that he could not possibly disappoint him by pulling out. He did say that he would be coming to see her the day before the party as he had a present for her. This pleased Catriona a little, but did not make up for David missing the party itself.

David did not win the junior draft, although he did run a very creditable second. He was disappointed with the result, and it was small consolation to him that the boy who won was several years his senior. Andy told him after the event that no boy of his age could possibly know all there was to know about cattle and drafting, but David, with his innate stockmanship, realised quite clearly where he had lost the points that relegated him to second place.

Andy was delighted with his son's performance. David was by far the youngest competitor and he had only come two points below the winning score. In Andy's book that was a great first-up performance.

There were no sheepdog trials for David that year because Lad was too young for competition work. The MacLeods had heard that Angus Campbell's imported border collie, Toss, had come out of quarantine and was due to enter the next local trial.

Shortly after Toss arrived at Inverlochy, Andrew received a phone call from Angus. 'I'm wondering if I could bring my new dog up for you to have a look at, Andy. I'd value your opinion of him.'

'Okay, Angus. Make it a Sunday, if you don't mind. Let me know beforehand and I'll have some sheep ready for you.'

Andrew put the phone down with a thoughtful look on his face. 'That was Angus,' he said to Anne. 'He wants to bring his dog up here for me to look at. It sounds like he has some doubts about him.'

'You may well be right,' Anne agreed. 'I happen to know that Angus has great respect for your judgement where dogs and horses are concerned.'

'Ah, well, I suppose we must be thankful for small mercies. My whole outlook on life would be shattered if Angus Campbell considered me good for nothing.'

Anne smiled at his sarcasm. 'Jane has also told me that Angus considers David to be the best horseman for his age he has ever seen.'

'Does he now? Things are looking better and better.'

'Don't be cynical, Andy. Angus can't help the way he is. Deep down he is quite a good man. You know he does a lot for the district.'

'He can afford to. It's easy to be benevolent when you're in his position.'

Anne sighed. She had tried very hard to cultivate a harmonious relationship with Angus and Jane, yet feelings between them were strange. Angus would not invite them to social functions but he had no compunction in calling on Andy for advice about his animals.

'David will be interested to see this imported dog,' Andy said.

And David was. He found it hard to concentrate on his lessons for the remainder of the week, but that was nothing new. He always found it hard to concentrate because when he looked out of the window he could see the high country of High Peaks looming above the school. The splendour of that vista and the feelings it evoked completely overshadowed maths and English. He had read a great deal about the working-dogs of Britain and about the wizards who handled them, and the prospect of seeing one of these dogs excited him greatly. He had also seen border collies bred from imported stock but he had not yet seen a direct importation.

David was at his father's elbow when Angus arrived that Sunday morning. To David's dismay, Catriona was accompanying her father. She was sure to want to chatter on about something stupid and spoil the whole morning. He knew for a fact that Cat wasn't the slightest bit interested in sheepdogs, so why did she have to tag along with her father? He looked appealingly towards his father, who caught the gesture and nodded.

'Catriona, I think Anne would like to see you,' Andrew said. 'She has some idea for the school concert.'

Catriona looked long and hard at David, whose gaze was directed at the hill above the house where his father had placed three lively four-tooth wethers not much more than half an hour earlier. Years ago, Andrew had cleared the lower part of that hill, which was part of what they referred to as Jimmy's Mountain, and had built a couple of trial obstacles, a bridge and a race. It was a good paddock in which to teach a dog to cast and not far from the house.

As Catriona disappeared into the house, Angus jumped his new dog from the back seat of the car.

David reckoned Toss was a fairly typical collie with a medium-length black and white coat and a fair bit of hair on his tail. One ear stood straight up and the other drooped.

Andrew pointed up the hill towards the sheep. They were about 400 yards distant, which was a fair enough cast for a flat-country dog but nothing for a real hill-country dog. Andrew knew that any decent border collie bred in Scotland should cast that distance without any trouble.

Angus cast Toss out on his right and the dog swept well out, ran up the hill and eventually came in right behind the three wethers. Toss stopped as he was supposed to, and the sheep turned and looked at him. He crept slowly towards them and they turned and bolted down the slope towards the trio of watchers. Angus left them and took up a position beside the race. After a little bit of trouble getting the wethers to the front of the obstacle, Toss positioned them a few yards out from the mouth of the race. The wethers broke and Toss gave them too much clearance. And no matter how many times the dog placed them outside the race, he could not hold them there; they always beat him round one side. This went on for several minutes before Angus walked across to the next obstacle, which was the bridge. Here again Toss had great trouble holding the lively wethers. He always seemed to be fractionally slow to anticipate and block them. Finally, with Toss puffing and blowing, Angus gave it away and called the dog to him. He walked back to where Andy and David were sitting on a log.

'Well, Andy, what do you reckon?'

Andrew hesitated before answering, because no decent sheepdog person likes to be overly critical of another person's dog, especially when that dog had been imported at great cost from the old country.

'I reckon they don't have merinos in Scotland, Angus. Toss casts well, and you would expect him to, coming from Scotland. The problem is that he's not used to working lively sheep. Toss is what I would describe as a "late mover". He moves after the sheep do. With really lively sheep, a dog needs to have good anticipation and block movement before it happens. I reckon that Toss has been worked on quiet, doughy sheep that probably fought a dog more than ran from it. You can see that he's a strong dog, but he hasn't got the idea of being in position quickly enough. He can't drive and hold. Not many dogs can, only the very good ones.'

'Can I do anything about it?' Angus asked with a frown.

'I am sorry to say that I doubt it. The dog is probably too set now. He'll be a fair dog anywhere but on the obstacles. If you take my advice, you won't work him in trials. Just try him as a sire. I suggest you mate him to a couple of lively bitches and see how his pups shape. Will he work a mob?'

'He's not too bad,' Angus replied. 'He's better on a small mob than a big one.'

'The dog may never have seen a big mob. I don't like late-moving dogs, but in his favour there's a big difference working merinos after Scotch blackface. Toss would probably handle them quite well.'

'I made a lot of enquiries,' Angus said. 'The dog was highly recommended.'

'That may be so, but what we've got here is a different kettle of fish. The Brits set great store on walk-up strength; the American handlers refer to it as power. It's important for a dog to be strong, but when you're working merinos, especially in this range country, it's also very important that they don't get away from you and head back into the rough country. That can mean a lot of extra work. So a dog needs real good anticipation. The same thing applies to working lively sheep at a trial. I know that collie handlers like to give a lot of orders but I prefer a dog that has control of its sheep, knows what the sheep are going to do and is in position before they move. The great old kelpies worked like that and I have tried to keep that trait in my dogs. You've seen my dogs work so you know what I'm talking about.'

This was a long speech for Andy, who was known as a man of few words.

The advice was not wasted on Angus. He knew MacLeod better than most people. 'I see what you mean. You've actually confirmed my own opinion. He's a nice dog in himself, but it's a big disappointment to bring a dog from the other side of the world, for a big outlay, and find he isn't what you want,' Campbell said.

'That's the risk you take when you import stock you haven't seen. Don't forget that a lot of border collies before Toss didn't suit our conditions but some of them sired good dogs.'

Andy knew full well that he could have sold Angus a better dog than Toss for probably a third of what it cost to land the dog in Australia. The thing was that Angus would never buy a kelpie from him.

They went down the hill to the house for tea and freshly baked scones.

Across the table from David, Catriona sat with a look in her eyes that had been there since her accident. Anne caught a glance of it and a small smile passed over her lips.

'I think you ought to take a little more notice of Catriona when she comes up here,' Anne said to her son after Angus and Catriona had left.

'Why, Mum? I see Catriona at school every day. She's in my class. Besides, she's a girl.'

'I should remind you that your Aunt Kate and I were once girls. You don't have any problem getting on with us.'

'That's different. You're not silly and giggly like the girls at school.'

'Catriona has never struck me as being silly. I think she's very mature,' Anne said.

'You should see her when she's with the other girls. She's just as bad as the rest of them.'

'You must confess that she is very pretty, though.'

'So? Mum, I don't want to talk about girls any more. I wish Mr Campbell wouldn't bring her here.'

Later, Andrew took up the subject with Anne. 'I don't think you should try and push David towards Catriona. Not even now. The Campbells are nice enough people, but they move in another circle to us and I'm sure neither Angus nor Jane would wish to see Catriona keen on David. If he did get to like Catriona, it could cause a whole heap of trouble. Get the idea out of your head, Anne. David will find his own girl when the time comes, or she will find David.'

'I don't agree with you on this occasion, Andy. Even now you can see that Catriona has feelings for David.'

'Rubbish. She's only a kid. She thinks he is wonderful for saving her pony, that's all. She is going off to school next year and she'll come back a different girl. I say leave David be. He knows what he wants.'

For all his professed indifference to Catriona, David did have a soft spot for the little blonde girl from next door. The problem was that he had been reared by a tough bushman and he had grown up in the company of other hill-country horsemen and bushmen, all of whom were fairly hard characters.

David realised from a very early age that it was not the thing to be seen in the company of girls, or even to discuss them. To gain the respect of these men, a fella had to stay close to the things that really mattered, like land and dogs and horses. But that did not blind him to the fact that Catriona was by far the prettiest girl at their school and probably in the whole district. Susan Cartwright had lovely dark hair and flashing eyes, but Catriona was a league above her. And there was something to be said for having the most beautiful girl in the district keen on you. Well, wanting to be mates, anyway.

Somehow, fate kept bringing the pair together. In the last month before Catriona and David were to leave the little school at the foot of the range, Catriona had a run-in with a boy in their class by the name of Stanley Masters. Stanley's father was overseer of a big property on the Cassilis side of Inverlochy. Jack Masters was not a bad sort of fellow, except when he drank too much, and then he became quite obnoxious. He also fancied himself with women. Stanley was an obnoxious little boy, and David hated the sight of him. Stanley had a dirty mind and had been caught trying to peek on girls in the toilets. That episode earned him six of the best, and he was lucky not to have been expelled. However, his punishment did not deter him.

David realised from the outset that Stanley was different from the rest of the boys at school. He had taken off his trousers and exposed himself to a sixth-class girl who had made some comment about the physical differences between boys and girls. The girl in question never reported the incident, and, much as David disliked Stanley, he wasn't going to dob him in.

There was only one boy who had any time for Stanley, and that was Wade Missen. All the other boys were more or less from farms and stations in the area, and most of them rode horses and played cricket and football for fun. But Stanley and Wade would sit together and watch the girls when they played. David had heard them discussing the girls' legs and their budding breasts. Stanley was the stronger personality and Wade seemed to be dominated by him.

David was in a toilet cubicle one day when he heard Stanley and Wade come in. Stanley laughed and said quite clearly, 'Catriona and Susan are down under the willow tree. I'm going to ask Catriona if I can have a look under her blouse.'

'Jeez, Stanley. Maybe you're taking a big risk. Catriona and Susan aren't like Alice. What if they report you?'

'I'll say she started it. If you back me up, it would be our word against hers.'

'What about Susan?'

'I reckon she'll be jake. I've seen her and Gladys giggling when I sit near them.'

Stanley and Wade left the toilet and David rushed to the door to watch them. Most of the children were sitting eating their lunches under the trees beside the schoolhouse. At the lower end of the school grounds there were some big kurrajong trees and a very large willow. The willow had its roots in a small creek that flowed into Half Moon Creek. The branches of the willow were so long and dense that anyone sitting on the bench under the tree could not be seen from the school building. It was a favourite place for secret games and discussions.

David watched Stanley and Wade walk quickly down towards the willow tree and then disappear. A strange feeling came over him and he felt his senses quicken. Then a surge of anger possessed him. Nobody, least of all a creep like Stanley Masters, was going to insult Catriona or lay a finger on her.

The willow tree was about fifty yards down a gentle slope from the toilets and David was behind it in a matter of seconds. He arrived in time to hear almost all of Stanley's opening conversation.

'... with you and Susan.'

'I suppose so,' Catriona answered. 'What do you want, Stanley?'

'Before school breaks up, I just thought I would tell you how pretty you are,' Stanley said. 'You, too, Susan.'

'Are you after something, Stanley?' Catriona asked.

'You've got a great figure as well. Can I have a look at it?'

'What did you say?'

'I said, "Can I have a look at your figure?" Just

undo your top buttons. Here, give me a go.'

David looked through the branches of the willow and saw that Stanley had actually undone the top button of Catriona's blouse and had started on the next one. Catriona let out a strangled scream, and when she tried to get up, Stanley pushed her back and thrust his hand down inside her blouse. Catriona screamed again and David waited no longer.

There would have been no argument among the children about David MacLeod being the strongest boy at school. His arms and shoulders had been toughened by axe work, as he had helped his father ring hundreds of acres of green timber. And his wrists, arms and shoulders had been further developed by years of practice with his whips. If this was not enough, David had been well schooled in boxing by Tim Sparkes. David remembered Tim's advice very clearly: 'Davie, if you have to fight, don't mess around. Give the fellow a hard one in the breadbasket to soften him up. That should double him over and then you can whack him again.'

David followed Tim's instructions to the letter. He arrived on the scene like a miniature express train and jerked Stanley around to face him. His first punch doubled the boy over and his second made his nose bleed. Wade's jaw dropped open and then, seeing his mate in trouble, he jumped in to help. David's first punch split Wade's lip and his second was sure to give him a black eye. Wade was a coward at heart and he had no wish to end up like Stanley. He retreated through the willow and then ran as fast as he could for the principal's office.

'Sir, David MacLeod is belting up Stanley Masters. He hit me, too. Sir, you've got to come quick. He's gone mad.'

Mr Carruthers guessed that Masters was probably getting his just desserts, but he could not tolerate fighting at school. He dropped what he was doing and followed Wade back to the willow. There he found David, unmarked, standing over Stanley, who looked in rather a bad way. Blood was streaming from the boy's nose and one eye was beginning to close. Catriona and Susan were standing close by with white faces.

'What on earth is going on here? David, stop that at once. Catriona, tell me what caused this fight.'

The two children refrained from answering. David's anger was still simmering. He looked at the damage he had caused Stanley with no small amount of satisfaction. He reckoned the creep wouldn't lay a finger on Catriona again in a hurry.

'Very well, I will see you children in my office. Stanley and Wade, we are going to see Mrs Carruthers. She will attend to you.'

The three children walked back up the slope, with every child in the school looking on, until they stood side by side outside the principal's office.

When Mr Carruthers returned, he took David inside and left the two girls outside. 'Now, tell me, what caused the fight?'

'I would rather not say, sir.'

'You would rather not say. You half kill another boy in my schoolyard and you would rather not say. You know that I do not tolerate fighting. You gave Stanley a real hiding and I want to know why. I must know, David.'

David did not want to dob Stanley in, creep though he was, but he was mostly concerned that Catriona did not get into trouble. If he told Mr Carruthers that Stanley had undone Catriona's blouse, he might somehow imagine that she had done it willingly.

'I think you're hiding something and I mean to find out what it is. Go back to class and send Catriona in.'

'I didn't tell him anything, Cat. Not a word,' David managed to whisper in her ear before she went into the office and the door closed behind her.

'Now, Catriona, I want you to tell me what happened down there. You are a very sensible girl and David has never given me an ounce of trouble so there has to be a very good reason for all this. I want you to tell me about it. Did Stanley say or do something to upset you?'

He saw by the way the girl's face flamed that he was on the right track.

Catriona was not her normal self. She was, in fact, in a state of shock. Her mother had warned her about incidents like this, but Catriona had never expected it could happen in the school grounds. But, out of fear that she might be blamed, Catriona, like David, said nothing. And when Mr Carruthers pressed her harder, she burst into tears.

After several minutes of fruitless questioning, Carruthers gave up and sent her along to Miss Warne. He decided to try a different approach with Susan.

'Now, Susan, Catriona has given me her version of what happened and I want to check the details with you. Tell me in your words what happened.'

Susan told the whole story. Mr Carruthers listened carefully until she had finished. 'So David intervened when Catriona screamed. Is that right?'

'Yes, sir.'

'He actually got his hand inside Catriona's blouse?'

'Yes, sir.'

'You are absolutely certain that Catriona did nothing to entice Stanley?'

'Oh, no, Mr Carruthers. Catriona and I were just talking when Stanley and Wade came over.'

'Is David a special friend to Catriona?'

'I wouldn't say he is a special friend. Catriona likes David a lot. He helped her last Christmas holidays. It was in the paper.'

'I am aware of what David did. You may go now, and thank you. Please ask David to come back here.'

'Sit down, David,' Mr Carruthers said when the boy returned to his office.

'Yes, sir.'

'Susan has told me what actually happened down at the willow tree today and I have no doubt that what she told me was the truth. If it had been an ordinary fight, you would be in serious trouble. However, it seems that you acted from the best possible motives.'

'Yes, sir. Stanley has a dirty mind. Wade is almost as bad. When I heard Catriona scream, I let him have it.'

'You certainly did. Stanley is in quite a mess. Did your father teach you to box?' Like most other people in the district, Mr Carruthers knew of Andrew MacLeod's reputation as a tough man.

'Actually, sir, it was Tim Sparkes. He was with Sharman's boxing troupe for a season. He taught me.'

'I see.'

'But I was told that I should only fight when there's no other way to settle an argument. I couldn't very well have asked Stanley to leave Catriona alone. He would have just laughed at me. That's the kind of boy he is. I had to teach him a lesson, sir.'

There was a gleam in the principal's eye and he could not refrain from smiling. 'You may go back to class. I shall give you a note to take home to your mother. I should like to see her before school breaks up. Please do not discuss any of this with the other children. Understand?'

'Yes, sir.'

There was a kind of hush as David took his place in the classroom. Catriona still looked white and strained. She looked across at him and gave him a weak smile. He nodded in reply.

Stanley Masters did not come back to school that afternoon, nor for the rest of the term. David eventually heard that the Masters family had left the district. Apparently Jack Masters had taken up a position on a property in southern New South Wales.

Wade Missen did not finish the term either, and from that day on he began to hate David MacLeod, not just because of what he had done to him, but because he knew that he would never be able to beat him.

Mr Carruthers did not take the senior classes that afternoon. Instead he took Catriona and Susan to their homes and explained what had occurred. Neither girl came back to class that day.

David never said a word to anyone. His mother learned of the fracas from Mr Carruthers in the first instance and from Jane Campbell shortly after. Anne complied with the principal's request that she come and see him.

'Has David said anything to you about what happened here the other day?' Mr Carruthers asked.

'I was not aware that *anything* had happened,' Anne said rather tersely. 'Did it involve David?'

'Oh, yes, it certainly involved David,' he said, and then related the full story, including the second interview with her son.

'Oh, dear. Was the boy badly hurt?'

'He wasn't in first-class condition. Between the two of us, I think Stanley got what he deserved. I did not punish David because any boy worth his salt would have reacted in similar fashion. David also tried to defend Catriona by keeping quiet. That boy of yours is really something, Mrs MacLeod.'

'I suppose the Campbells know all about this?' Anne asked.

'Oh, yes. I took Catriona and Susan home that afternoon. I also told them what other action I would be taking. I had to do that in case there is further trouble. I doubt that there will be because there is prior evidence of Stanley's unseemly conduct.'

'How did Angus and Jane react to your news?'

'Naturally they were shocked. You don't expect to find such behaviour in a primary school.'

'Goodness, I've heard nothing at all,' Anne said.

'It's David I really wanted to discuss with you today. I am afraid to say that in many ways David has disappointed me because his heart is not in his work. He is a very bright boy and he could be at the top of the class, but he only ever does the bare minimum. Many times I have caught him gazing out the windows, lost in his own world. He really needs to concentrate on his lessons.'

Anne sighed. How could she make Mr Carruthers understand how passionately David loved High Peaks and his animals?

'I understand what you're saying. Believe me, I know how difficult it is to motivate David. He feels that going to school is a penance he must live with until he's old enough to leave and look after High Peaks.'

Mr Carruthers shook his head. 'The land is very risky, Mrs MacLeod. Your husband has nearly killed himself to free your property from debt. Is that what you want for David?'

'Did you advise Stuart Campbell in this same fashion?' Anne asked bluntly.

'Well, no,' the principal said and coloured slightly. 'But the Campbells have a large property. Stuart's future is assured.'

'So it's fine for the Campbells to be landowners but not the MacLeods?' Anne asked, raising her eyebrows.

'Well, in all strictest confidence, Stuart was not nearly as bright as your David, although he did try harder. I am just saying that it could be worth him learning something else in case things don't turn out so well on the property. To do that he would have to work harder at high school than he has done here.'

'David will probably learn to shear like his father, and that brings in good money. We hope to buy another property and we could pay that off if two incomes were coming in.'

'If you don't mind me saying, Mrs MacLeod, David could set his sights higher than shearing. He is very bright.'

'Shearing helped to pay off the debt on High Peaks, Mr Carruthers. Right now we don't owe anybody a brass farthing. I know you mean well and I appreciate you talking to me about David, but as you know, I was a teacher myself. I know David better than anyone. He is a unique child, and to try to change him too much would do more harm than good.'

'As you say, you know David best and I'm sure you're right. I think he's too bright not to be pushed a little harder, but having said that, let me also say that I would be very proud to have David for my son. He is a splendid boy.'

'Thank you, Mr Carruthers. I'm pleased that we both agree on that point. And I am very sorry if David's fight caused you problems,' Anne said.

'Well, just between you and me, I do not regret the departure of Stanley Masters from this school. And Wade Missen, too. It is a fact that children seem to be maturing faster these days.'

'I am sure David will not be unduly affected by what goes on at high school or anywhere else. He knows what he wants out of life and Andy and I will do all we can to see that he achieves it.'

So that was that. But as Anne drove back to High Peaks she wondered what Angus and Jane thought of the Stanley Masters affair. Twice during the current year David had come to Catriona's rescue. How would Angus take that?

'He told you about it, didn't he, Mum?' David asked. He was having afternoon tea a few minutes after getting off the school bus. He had seen his mother through the classroom window and had sensed trouble.

'Who told me what?' Anne answered.

David knew he was right. There was trouble looming. It was probably a lecture. His mother was never formal unless a lecture was to follow.

'Mr Carruthers told you about me fighting with that creep Masters.'

'Was there a fight? I gained the impression it was all one-sided. Did Stanley hit you at all?'

'Well, no, I didn't give him the chance to hit me.'

'And I suppose we can thank Tim Sparkes for your new-found prowess?'

'Too right.'

'I am going to have a serious talk with you, David. You need to know some things before you go to high school. It's important that I talk to you about the facts of life in case the Campbells should ring or come and see us about what happened.'

'Why should they?' David asked as he reached for another piece of chocolate cake. If he had to sit through a lecture, he might as well take advantage of what was in the cake tin.

'You'll make yourself sick if you eat too much of that. Have a piece of fruit instead. Now, you may not appreciate the fact, but the Campbells are once again in our debt – well, your debt, really. If you hadn't intervened, Stanley might have taken things even further.'

'What do you mean?'

Anne sighed. It was a great pity that children had to grow up. But the first shadow of what lay ahead for her son had crossed his path and now she would have to try to explain it.

So for the next hour, Anne gave David his first major lesson in the facts of life. It was an ordeal for her, and she sensed it was an ordeal for David, too.

'Are you clear about everything now?' she asked finally.

'Yes, Mum. Can I go now?'

'Yes, you can. And in case you think I'm cross with you, I'm not. I'm proud of what you did, but I hope it is the first and last time you have to do it.'

'Me, too. Thanks, Mum.' He ran for the back door and she heard it bang loudly behind him. She had absolutely no idea how much of her words he had absorbed, and a brief feeling of sympathy for Mr Carruthers passed over her.

That night Jane Campbell rang with an invitation for Anne and David to come to Inverlochy for afternoon tea on Saturday. David, as usual, resisted.

'You are going, David. That's all there is to it. This invitation requires common courtesy,' his mother said.

David appealed to his father, who was engrossed in the latest issue of *The Land* newspaper.

'It's only one afternoon, Davie, and if I know the Campbells, and if Mrs Rogers is still housekeeper, they'll bung on a big spread,' he said.

David tried to assess the appeal of a big spread against a ride up Jimmy's Mountain with Lad behind him. Inverlochy lost hands down. He was about to protest again when his father stopped him.

'I'll tell you what I'll do. You get this thing at the Campbells' out of the way and Sunday morning I'll give you your first shearing lesson. How does that strike you?'

'Wow, will you, Dad?' David had been busting to learn how to shear. His dad's promise silenced his protests about going to Inverlochy and he resolved to put on the best face he could for the blasted smoko.

So it was that in a very fair mood he accompanied his mother to Inverlochy. They were welcomed by Jane Campbell, who stood at the front steps of the big homestead as Anne's car pulled up. Catriona was standing beside her mother and looked prettier than Anne had ever seen her. She had grown a lot in the year since her accident on Yellow Rock. Today, her long golden hair was tied in two plaits with blue and white check ribbons, and she was wearing a blue and white dress to match. Catriona coloured slightly when David came up the steps. He had been a witness to what had happened to her under the willow tree and that indignity was still fresh in her mind.

'Hi, Cat,' he growled.

'Hello, David,' she replied softly.

They were taken into the very large lounge room, which Anne had come to know well from her visits over the years. The room was furnished with huge leather chairs and an enormous matching sofa. The Campbells sometimes used this room for formal dinner parties and other gatherings. There were two original paintings on the walls, one a Gruner and the other a McCubbin. Anne was keen on art and had once studied it, not that she had ever been able to afford paintings like those. The other main point of interest in the room was the fireplace. This was recessed about five feet and would take a very big log or stump.

Anne and Jane sat in the lounge chairs facing each other and David and Catriona sat at each end of the sofa. The children listened while their mothers spoke of many things – Christmas, the holidays, Catriona's clothes for boarding school ... it went on and on ... and David was bored stiff. He hoped that Stuart Campbell would make an appearance so that he could escape with him to the stables where the in-feed horses were kept. But both Stuart and his father were nowhere to be seen.

Presently Jane looked across at her daughter and nodded. 'Catriona has something to say to David,' she said with a half-smile. Anne thought it rather a forced smile, one of someone trying to be pleasant in a difficult situation.

'Thank you, Mummy. I want to say that Mummy invited you over today so that I could thank you again, David, for what you did at school.'

Catriona said her piece like a well-drilled child actress. But she had not finished. 'Mummy has told me what might have happened,' – and here her face went quite pink – 'if you hadn't followed those awful boys down to where Susan and I were sitting. It was two against one and you could have been hurt, David. It was very brave of you to tackle them the way you did.'

Catriona, like David, had also had a lecture from her mother, though in her case it had not been her first. The emphasis this time was on the biological consequences of being handled by boys and men, and the fact that, as she grew older, more and more males would look at her.

Catriona was more advanced physically and mentally than David and she had thought a great deal about what her mother said. She really liked David MacLeod, and she would lie awake at night thinking about him before she went to sleep. Her mother's words kept coming back to her: 'It's a woman's prerogative to decide who you will allow to take such liberties.'

She had discussed the idea of boyfriends with Susan and they had agreed that Catriona couldn't tell her mother about all her feelings for David.

'Aw, it was nothing, Cat,' David said. 'I never liked Stanley. I wasn't going to let him get away with frightening you.'

'It was very gallant of you, David,' Jane said graciously. 'I know you don't want to talk about it, so I think we should go out on the back verandah for afternoon tea.'

That was the best suggestion David had heard all day and he got up smartly and followed the others outside. Spread out on one long table was about the biggest array of food David had ever seen in his young life. There were several large cakes, including one chocolate and one double-cream cake, and plates galore of other delicacies. There was also a selection of soft drinks in a big copper of crushed ice.

Poor Mrs Rogers, Anne thought as she surveyed the spread in front of her. She must have been up since dawn putting all this together.

'You weren't here for Catriona's birthday party and she will be away at school next year, so we have to make the most of today. It is also a kind of thank-you for being such a good friend to Catriona over the last year,' Jane said.

David's eyes widened. He didn't know what to say under the circumstances but finally blurted out, 'It's very good of you, Mrs Campbell, but there was no need to make such a fuss. Any other boy would have done just the same as I did.'

'I doubt that very much, David. And I should also add that this is a kind of farewell party because Catriona will be going away to Sydney for a few years,' Jane added.

'She will be coming home for her holidays, though, won't she?' David asked.

'Oh, yes, we shall have her home for most holidays,' Jane said.

'Go easy on the chocolate cake,' Anne whispered in David's ear as he went to pile his plate. David had once eaten half a chocolate cake and been mightily sick, and his mother would never let him forget it. He sampled a fair proportion of what was on the table and washed it down with several glasses of fruit drink. Catriona did not eat very much but stayed close to him.

'Do you want to go away to school?' he whispered in her ear when her mother left them to get a pot of tea.

'I have to,' Catriona whispered back. 'It's something that can't be avoided. Why, will you miss me?'

David had not meant the question in that light. 'Aw, I just think it's rotten of your people to send you away for six years. I wouldn't go. No way. And Mum wouldn't send me.'

Catriona struggled to find words to answer him. It was very difficult to explain that a boarding-school education was an essential part of life for a Campbell.

'Who will look after your horses?' he asked.

'We have a stud groom, and he will exercise them. I shall be home to ride them at the camps because they are usually held in school holidays.'

'Gosh, Cat – weeks and weeks, maybe months, without a horse to ride. What will you do with yourself on weekends?' he asked.

'There will be plenty to do. There are concerts and other outings, church and social gatherings. Then there is homework and we also learn dancing.'

David groaned. 'Jeez, Cat, I feel sorry for you. I really do.'

'Don't feel sorry for me, David. Mummy says I will come home a very polished young woman.'

'You're polished enough now,' he said gruffly.

Catriona looked pleased. 'Thank you. That was a sweet thing to say.'

David let the topic rest. As his father often said,

what the Campbells did was their own business.

Just when Anne had decided that David had eaten enough afternoon tea for two boys his age, Jane produced a large cardboard box which she began packing cakes and other goodies into. 'You must take these back with you, Anne. I know what kind of appetite David has, and it may save you some cooking for a few days.'

David, urged on by his mother's whispered entreaty, thanked Mrs Campbell for the box of goodies and for the afternoon tea. He even went so far as to say it had been 'fantastic'.

That night Anne sat down and wrote to her sister. She knew that Katie would want to know all the details of David's latest exploit.

Kate Gilmour's eyes misted as she read her sister's letter several days later. She was realising how much she loved and missed the MacLeod family at High Peaks. She had already determined that she would not go ahead with her planned motoring holiday; other forces were pulling at her. She had come back from High Peaks with the knowledge that she had a fierce love for her sister's son. He had really wound his way into her affections during her last stay. The realisation that it was unlikely she would ever marry had altered her outlook on life. The fact was that there wasn't a man in sight who meant anything to her. Her parents were in good health for their age and did not actually need her. How lovely it would be to up sticks and move to High Peaks permanently. But she would have to find a job at the hospital.

The more Kate thought about the idea, the more it made sense to her. She had excellent references and was a triple-certificate nurse. Even if she had to live in Merriwa, she felt it would be preferable to living and working in the Sydney rat-race. She decided to talk to Anne about the possibility of moving to Merriwa. She could then be with the family almost every weekend. She could buy her own horse and ride it all over High Peaks. Andy would let her have a good horse, a horse that was tried and tested in the hills. He could take her with him when he and David competed in campdrafts. Maybe she could even compete herself.

Kate realised time was passing her by. David was at such an interesting age right now, and Christmas was nearly upon them again. Next year David would be going to high school, and she wondered how he would face up to that. He would be like a square peg in a round hole. Yet she was sure she could help him through. It was not that Anne wasn't the best mother a boy could have, but she so wanted to be there to lend an extra hand and help David out when he ventured into the hills.

Kate's head raced with excitement about how her new life might be. All she had to do was talk to Anne and make enquiries at Merriwa Hospital. It wouldn't take much for her dream to be made true.

Chapter Twelve

'Don't push the machine too hard, David. Speed doesn't matter yet. Concentrate on filling the comb and making your strokes clean.'

It was the week following Christmas and Andy was giving David another shearing lesson. There were three lambs in the pen – wriggly devils, but nowhere near as big and hard to hold as a wether for a learner shearer. Kate Gilmour was sitting on a butt of crutchings and watching her nephew with great interest. She had come up from Sydney for Christmas and was staying on another week.

The MacLeods bred merino lambs on their lower country where the cattle grazed. Sheep that were bred in the area thrived better than sheep brought in from other districts. There was a lot more work involved in running merino ewes, but the wether portion of their drop replaced the older wethers and any excess or cull ewes could be sold for cash. The pick of the ewe portion was retained for breeding.

David finished the lamb and straightened up. He watched the lamb run into the counting-out pen and reckoned he had made a fair job of shearing it.

'How's the back, Davie?' Kate asked.

'Not bad,' he said.

Kate knew he would never say otherwise, never admit weakness. He and his father were a good pair. They could be dead on their feet but still 'okay' by them.

'Have a few minutes' spell before you do another one,' Andrew advised.

'All right,' David agreed. He put some oil in the handpiece and then leant up against a post and inspected the other two lambs. He was just about to go into the catching pen for another lamb when they heard a vehicle pull up outside the shed.

Kate got off the butt and went to the door of the wool room to check out who the visitor was. They didn't get a lot of visitors at the end of the road. The wool rep called a couple of times a year but most of their visitors were dog and horse enthusiasts.

'There is a very large man with a grey pointed beard getting out of a red utility,' Kate informed them.

There was only one man in the district who answered that description. Andy and David knew at once that it had to be Wilfred White, their next-door neighbour. His property's side boundary adjoined their back boundary and, lower down, the White property adjoined Inverlochy.

Wilf was one of the district's genuine characters. He used to have an identical twin brother called Wesley. The White twins were huge; no taller than Andrew but carrying far more weight and not anywhere near so lean and hard. They had been big, fat boys right from the start. Wilf had thighs as thick as strainer posts and walked with a distinctive rolling gait, more like that of a sailor than an old bushman. Both Wilf and Wesley had copied their late father's peculiar habits of speech. The old chap had had very little schooling because he had worked his guts out since he was twelve. He was a disciple of Henry Lawson and his Bible was *The Bulletin*, which he read laboriously from cover to cover. Most of his sentences began or finished with the words 'by gum', as did Wilf and Wesley's. Wilf also used English in a convoluted way. It sometimes took a while to work out what he meant, although Andy and Anne didn't have any trouble.

When the twins' father died, the two boys and their sister, Gertrude, inherited the 3300-acre property, Poitrel. It had been surveyed and divided into three equal portions so they could each do as they liked with their blocks. Gertrude had then married, moved away, and left her portion for the two boys to look after. Wilf and Wesley were bachelors at the time Japan bombed Pearl Harbor, overran Malaya and then bombed Darwin. The boys had not paid much attention to what the Germans did because it was all so far away, but when Japan entered the war it was a different matter entirely. However, only one brother could join up as the other would have to stay and look after Poitrel. It was Wesley who joined the AIF and, tragically, was killed in New Guinea.

Wilf took his brother's death very badly. He became almost a recluse. He never married, he seldom left the property and, until Gertie came back to look after him, the mailman delivered his groceries.

Wilf's major interest in life was horses. He had a wonderful collection of thoroughbreds, some of which had won classic races. He was a walking, talking authority on the subject. He also bred an amazing range of poultry, including pheasants and peacocks.

Wilf spent a great deal of his time studying equine pedigrees and race performances. The shelves on his office walls were lined with thoroughbred journals from Europe and the United States. Angus Campbell raced a few horses and considered himself something of an authority on thoroughbreds, but his knowledge was nothing compared with that of Wilf White. Wilf also had a reasonably good knowledge of stock-horse pedigrees. Although he could not handle a horse anywhere near as well as Andy MacLeod could, he probably had a better theoretical knowledge of the background of most stock horses than Andy.

Andy shore and crutched Wilf's sheep, and took his payment in sheep. It seemed that Wilf never had any spare cash. Nobody could work out why this was, because Wilf was not a fellow to throw his money around, not locally anyway. Andrew knew that Wilf sent a lot of his money to his widowed sister. He also knew that a fair slice of Wilf's money went into training fees for his horses. Wilf lived for his horses and his dream was to breed and own a Melbourne Cup winner. Andrew had handled a lot of horses for him and probably knew him better than anyone else in the district. One thing he did know for certain was that Wilf had never bet on a horse.

The MacLeods had a soft spot for Wilf. During the war, when Andy's mother ran High Peaks, Wilf had been very helpful. He would come and help Paddy Covers put the shearing through, and many times he had helped muster the high country. He never came empty-handed, but always brought a gift of some kind, usually a box of chocolates for Anne and a large bag of sweets for David.

'Wilf White,' Andy said to David.

'I wonder what he wants,' David said with a grin. 'Probably got some horses for you to break in, Dad.'

'We'd better go and find out,' Andy said.

Wilf was on his way up to the house when they came out of the shearing shed. 'Hey, Wilf, over here,' Andy called.

The big man's rolling walk came to a stop. He turned and his face lit up when he saw the three of them standing outside the shearing shed.

'By gum, it's a good morning to you, Andy and David, and this must be Sister Kate.' He nodded to Kate, whom he had never met.

'Yeah, Wilf, this is Anne's sister, Kate. Kate, meet Wilfred White.'

'By gum, Sister, I am very pleased to meet you. A fine large day, Andy. Just look at young David here. You've grown a foot since I last saw you. What are you doing in the shed, David? You tell me.'

'I'm learning to shear, Mr White. Dad is teaching me.'

'You're learning to shear? You're starting early. I bet you'll be a gun shearer just like your father. Your Dad's the best I ever did see.'

'Maybe I will be and maybe I won't,' David said, doubting that he would ever be able to shear as well as his father.

'You got time for a drink o' tea, Wilf?' Andy asked. He knew that Wilf had never been known to knock back a cuppa, because that meant he got to sample Anne's cooking. This had reached new heights since she had begun competing in local shows. Wilf had a sweet tooth, and because of his predilection for cream and other rich things, he was very overweight. Gertie had read the riot act to him and put him on a diet. But he always had a big feed when he came to High Peaks.

'I should think very much so. I might be here a while, Andy. I've got to talk to you real hard.'

Andrew repressed a smile. He was aware that Wilf used peculiar language, but his meaning was never in doubt. 'That sounds serious, Wilf. Let's go inside.'

Anne always made a fuss of Wilf, and she was

delighted to see him. He had been unfailingly kind to her from the very first time she had met him as a new bride. Several times she had sent him samples of her cooking, and Wilf was one of those people who never forgot a kindness and always repaid it. The pure Jersey cow she had milked that morning had been a gift from Wilf. And of course Andy never charged him for breaking in his horses, which Wilf repaid with loads of lucerne hay.

'How have you been keeping, Wilf?' Anne asked when they were all seated in the big lounge room.

'Not the best, Mrs Mac. Not the very best,' he replied, looking a bit downcast.

'That's no good. What's the problem?' she asked.

'Well, you see, Mrs Mac, it's my heart. I had a heart attack. Gertie came up and took me to the doctor. They put me in the hospital. They frightened me, Mrs Mac. Told me my heart is no good, no good at all. Gertie is over home now.'

'Oh, Wilf. I am sorry. You kept that very quiet didn't you? Why didn't you tell us sooner? And you should have brought Gertie with you,' Anne scolded. 'I haven't seen her for years.'

'You will. I promise. Gert wanted to come but said she had too much work to do.' Here the old chap looked a bit sheepish. 'The house got in a bit of a mess with me not feeling so good and Gert is cleaning up. Packing up things, too.'

Wilf put his hand in his coat pocket, brought out a packet of jubes and placed them in front of David.

'I think you are getting too big for lollies, young fellow. Mrs Mac, don't let me leave without giving you something that is in the old ute. Gert says I'm getting a bit forgetful.'

'You really shouldn't bring me things, Wilf,' Anne protested.

'Like doing it, Mrs Mac. You're a bonzer woman. Best woman I know of in these parts.'

Anne blushed as she put the morning tea on the small table within easy reach of the old man. Andy could see that there was something on Wilf's mind. He had never seen him so agitated.

'David, perhaps you could go and chop some wood for your mother?' Andrew said.

'Good idea. I'll go with you,' Kate suggested.

'I'd rather you didn't, Kate. David, do as I asked,' Andy said firmly. David could see his father's mind was made up.

Wilf watched the boy leave the room. 'By gum, you've got a great boy there. I've been hearing wonderful things about him. I wish he were my son. Too late for that now. I never did meet a woman like you anyway, Mrs Mac.'

'I'm sure you did, Wilf,' Anne said and smiled. 'I heard tell that you and Wesley were the two most handsome boys in the district.'

'You always say kind things, Mrs Mac. Never known you not to.'

'What's the problem, Wilf?' Andy cut in on the small talk. 'Is there anything we can do to help?'

'I want to sell Poitrel,' Wilf said.

There was total silence in the room while Andy and Anne digested this startling announcement. Kate, not so aware of the importance of Wilf's declaration and what it entailed, nevertheless sensed that something big was in the wind.

'The whole place?' Andy asked at last.

'The whole place. All three blocks.'

'What are you going to do without it?' Anne asked.

'Gert and the doctors aren't going to let me do much, Mrs Mac. I reckon I might do a bit of fishing. Always wanted to do a bit of fishing in the ocean. Gert and I are going to live on the north coast. She's sold her house in Sydney. I couldn't abide to live down there.'

'But your horses, Wilf. Your lovely horses,' Anne said. She saw his face soften and knew that she had targeted his most vulnerable spot.

'How are you going to sell the place, Wilf? Privately or by auction?' Andy asked.

'Neither. I want you to have it. You and Mrs Mac and young David.'

'We couldn't afford to buy your land, Wilf. I haven't long cleared the debt on this place. I don't have much cash right now. If it was just one block I would have a lash at it, but three would be too much for us to handle. How much have you got on it, Wilf?'

'You can have it for ten dollars an acre under the going price, but I want to sell it as a whole, and I want you to keep my horses. If I die before I sell it, what will become of my horses? I want them all to end their days on Poitrel.'

'Wilf, I've got to be honest with you and say that I'm not a thoroughbred man. You know that. If – and it's a mighty big if – we could handle Poitrel, what would I do with your horses?'

'You could use some of the mares to breed stock horses. You won't find better bred mares anywhere. Put them to top stock horse sires and you'll breed the best. Andy, you're the only man I know who would keep his word once he gave it. You always have and I know you always will. There's no other man I would trust my horses to and know they'll be looked after.'

Andrew shook his head. The ten-dollars-an-acre discount amounted to over $33 000, which was not to be sneezed at, but it was a small sum compared with the true value of Poitrel. He would have to see the bank about mortgaging High Peaks. If they bought the land it would put them back in debt again and he would probably have to go back shearing for the extra income. Certainly there would be added revenue from Poitrel, but Andy knew that the place was badly run-down. The sheep flock had been let slip and was in a right old mess, and the cattle were a hotchpotch of poor-quality Shorthorns and Herefords. It would take some years to pull the place back into shape.

But Wilf's offer excited him. The purchase of more land had always been a dream since Anne came to High Peaks. The beauty of Poitrel was that at least half of it was first-class grazing country. There was also a splendid valley where Wilf grew his lucerne. The two places would give them over 7000 acres, which was a very creditable spread of country. And the best thing of all was that Poitrel adjoined High Peaks.

'What financial arrangements do you have in mind?' Andy asked after a break in the conversation.

'Andy, if you can give me the deposit, I'll carry the finance. That way you won't have to ask the bank for so much. You pay me something every six months and I'll be happy.'

'How much deposit do you want?'

'Enough to buy a good house on the coast and enough money to live on until your next payment.'

'How many sheep have you got up there?' Andy asked.

'I reckon about eighteen hundred, and perhaps a bit over one hundred cows.'

'And how many mares?'

'About forty, and the young stuff. I'll throw the stock in with the price of the place.'

'Cattle, too?'

'Yes, the lot.'

Andy breathed a little faster. Wilf's terms were unbelievable. Nobody in their right mind could turn down his offer. It was his horses the old chap was worrying about. Wilf could not bear to see them sold.

'Wilf, you know that Angus Campbell could give

a better deal than you're offering,' Andy suggested.

'Appreciate that. Honest of you to say so. I don't want Angus to have Poitrel. Never cared whether I lived or died, or his father before him. Never came near me when Wesley was killed. Know who came first, Andy? Your mother. Damned fine woman, your mother. None better outside Mrs Mac here. That's where you get it from, Andy, you and young David. No, Gert and me want you people to have Poitrel. And pretty damned quick in case I keel over.'

Andy glanced across at Anne. 'When do you need an answer, Wilf?'

'Can see it's a bit of a shock to you. You'll have to see the bank. Say a week. You can have the offer for a week. Is that fair enough?'

'It's more than fair, Wilf. Your offer is extremely generous.'

The old chap put his hand in his shirt pocket and pulled out a piece of dog-eared notepaper. 'I've written the whole deal down on paper. Gert and me have signed it. If anything should happen to me during the week, the deal still stands. You can show that to the bank. If your bank won't handle it, mine will. Seen them already. Tell your bank that.'

'That's very decent of you, Wilf,' Andy said.

'Got to look out for my horses, Andy.'

'Will you stay for lunch?' Anne asked.

'I would love to, but only if I can ring Gert and tell her I'm here and all right. She worries about me when I get out of her sight. She also says I've got to lose weight. Got me on this low-fat diet. Great way to finish up, eh, Andy?'

Andy, who knew how prodigiously Wilf had eaten over the years, reckoned Gertie was about twenty years late in instituting a diet for Wilf.

Later, after Wilf had left, the three adults and David – who had been told of Wilf's offer over lunch – sat in a kind of stunned silence. Kate had quickly grasped the significance of the offer, and the glimmer of an idea was growing in her brain. The acquisition of land was a tremendously important matter in the life of a farmer or grazier. More land meant greater productivity and, therefore, a greater financial return. If they could pay it off, Poitrel would give the MacLeod family financial security. It would more or less guarantee David's future.

Anne sat at the table and wrote down the figures Andy had given her. Despite the more than generous offer Wilf had made them, the purchase of Poitrel entailed a big parcel of money. The deposit alone would amount to a year's income off High Peaks and that would have to be loaned by the bank. There would not be a wool clip off Poitrel for nearly twelve months and, what's more, the sheep had been neglected and did not cut much wool. There would be some cattle to sell, but the money from that would only pay some of the running costs of the property, like shire rates, chemicals, and so on. Andrew reckoned that the only way they could possibly meet Wilf's terms was by asking the bank for more than the amount of the deposit Wilf required – and by himself going back to the big shearing runs. This would mean he would be away for weeks, even months, at a time. How could he look after two properties and shear as well? And was it fair to leave Anne and David for such long periods?

Slowly and carefully he explained all of this to Anne and Kate. Anne, who knew how much he wanted Poitrel, appreciated all that Andy was telling them. She was a smart woman and she didn't have to be told a thing twice. 'The long and the short of it is that it means going back into debt again,' Andy said, 'and I can't look after over seven thousand acres of country from a shed in Queensland. Also, it would mean we would have very little spending money.'

'Well, I don't have a problem with any of that – except you going back to shearing,' Anne said.

'But you know I can make a fair bit of money from it,' Andy said.

'And half kill yourself in the process,' Anne protested.

'I know a way out of your predicament,' Kate said.

'Please tell me,' Andy said with a weak smile.

'First off, I could let you have several thousand dollars –'

'Kate, we couldn't borrow from you,' Anne protested.

'Wait a sec and listen to what I have to say. It seems that now is the right time to let you know what's been on my mind for a very long time now.

The fact is that my job and Sydney in general have been getting me down. Oh, the job is all right, but I'm not getting anywhere. Sydney's such a rat-race, and I miss you all so much that I've been wondering whether I could get a position at the Merriwa Hospital. Now it's occurred to me that if you purchase Poitrel, I could live there myself. I would have to live somewhere, so why not next door? I could be a kind of caretaker into the bargain. And I could help in other ways. If I had a rent-free home I wouldn't need any cash so I could loan you some money towards the deposit. If you had to go away, Andy, I'm sure that the three of us could handle things. If I do say so myself, I think I have become quite handy lately,' Kate said. She was so excited about the argument she had just put forward that she could hardly wait for the others to respond.

'Kate, it would be terrific if you could move up here,' Anne said excitedly. 'It really would. I didn't realise you were so serious about the idea. Apart from my own feelings, I am sure David would love to have you here. What do Mum and Dad think of it?'

'Oh, they manage quite all right when I am overseas. And it's not far back to Sydney if they need me.'

'Then I'm all for it, Kate. It would be perfectly splendid to have you here under any circumstances, but with Andy going off to his old sheds for weeks and months at a time, it will be even more fantastic. My only reservation is you living alone at Poitrel,' Anne said.

247

'That is a minor issue that shouldn't concern us right now,' Kate said. 'There are more important considerations. You've been presented with a wonderful opportunity to expand, and to secure your future. You should grab it with both hands.'

'I appreciate all that,' Anne put in quickly, 'and so does Andy. But he's talking about going back to shearing more or less full time. It isn't much of a life for him, breaking his back over sheep in terribly hot sheds, and if I know Andy, he'll push himself to the limit. I thought he'd finished with that kind of slaving. Besides, I would miss the big lug. The prospect of having to go through all that again doesn't fill me with great joy,' Anne said vehemently.

'This time David is older and I would be close by. I could even stay here, if that would help,' Kate said.

'You can't live at two places, Kate. And you would probably be on shift work at the hospital, and that's all hoping that you *do* get a position there. On top of that, David will be travelling long distances to high school. There's a lot to think about.'

'If the price of wool goes up, we could probably pay back the money much quicker,' Andy suggested.

'If, if, if. We can't rely on that happening, Andy. If wool goes up, then all well and good. I know it's a great opportunity but there is a trade-off, isn't there? The heaviest burden falls on you, and we'll have to do your work between us, mainly on weekends when David is home to help.'

Kate glanced at her nephew, who was sitting

through all of this conversation without uttering a word. He was stunned. Wilfred's offer filled him with such joy that he could barely contain himself, but he had enough commonsense to realise his parents and Kate were talking serious stuff.

'David would love that,' Kate said.

'Perhaps, but it would mean a lot of work for a young boy. It would be like Andy all over again – a boy grown up too soon,' Anne said with a sigh.

'Well, I don't see why the three of us can't handle it,' Kate said. 'There are good yards here and I am sure there are yards at Poitrel. You have the dogs and the horses to do the job. A bit of jetting is nothing. And we can always employ someone for a day or two if we need an extra hand.'

'There's a bit more to it than jetting, Katie. There is drenching and crutching and lamb- and calf-marking. Who is going to crutch them? Do you expect a twelve-year-old boy to crutch over 5000 sheep?'

'I'll learn to crutch and we can both do them,' Kate said with enthusiasm.

Anne threw her hands in the air. 'Katie, you're as bad as David. If only it were all so easy.'

'Look, sister dear, I want to make this place and this district my life from now on. If I can do anything to help David, and you two, I will. So it's going to be a bit tough for a few years. So what? You can't expect three thousand three hundred acres to come tumbling into your laps without a few sacrifices.'

'Kate's right, Anne,' Andy said. 'I appreciate your argument. I know it isn't going to be easy for any of us. At least David is older now and very useful. If Kate is going to be close by, that should make a difference. If we don't take on Poitrel, I reckon Angus Campbell would buy it. We'd be landlocked by him and we'd have to look further afield for extra country. I think we should sleep on it. In the morning we'll go over to Poitrel and let Kate see it at close quarters.'

'That's a good idea,' Kate agreed enthusiastically. Her eyes were shining at the prospect before her. It was just what she had been waiting for.

Her enthusiasm was more than matched by David's. 'Are we really going to buy Poitrel, Dad?' he asked when he got his father on his own.

'There's a good chance we will, Davie. But Wilf's let the place run down a fair bit. That would mean a lot more work for you and Mum, and Kate, if she comes into the deal.'

'Don't worry about the work, Dad. We can do it.'

'Good on you, son. Your support means a lot to us. We'll have to agree to keep Mr White's horses and look after them until they die. If we buy Poitrel, we keep the horses, and if anything happens to me, you would have to honour that agreement. A man is not worth a spit if he doesn't keep his word. And Mr White is trusting us to do the right thing with his horses.'

David nodded. 'Whatever you say, Dad.'

'Good man. We'll go over in the morning and inspect the place. If we do end up buying it – and I'm not saying that we definitely will – it would be very handy to have Kate over there. It might also be better for management purposes to cut our boundary fence and put in gates so we can move stock around a bit easier. We could bring all the sheep from the Poitrel high country through our place and shear them here. There's a fair bit of work in looking after more than seven thousand acres, but we've got good dogs and good horses and we know the country. It mightn't be so bad.'

David nodded. His father had gone to great lengths to explain things. 'We can do it, Dad. I know we can.'

'I reckon you'd try your heart out, son.'

'How many years would you be away for, Dad?' David asked with real concern in his voice. His father was his best mate and the major source of all the knowledge he had acquired.

'I really don't know, mate. It depends on a lot of things. Like how soon we can get Poitrel producing more wool and vealers, and how the wool market goes.'

'In three years' time I could leave school and work here full time,' David said in a voice of great maturity for his age.

'Your mother might have something to say to that. I think she has plans for you to go through to fifth year. I know that Mr Carruthers has been at her to

251

make you do a course so you could have a trade to fall back on.'

David was horrified by this suggestion. Six years at high school and a course as well? He couldn't believe it.

'Dad, I don't need to stay at school that long, or do a course either. If we got Poitrel paid off, wouldn't we be in a good position to buy more country?'

'Whoa, David. We haven't even bought Poitrel yet, let alone paid for it. Let's not jump any more fences. We'll see what happens about school in three years' time. Tomorrow morning you get the horses in and saddle and bridle them. We'll have early breakfast and leave straight after.'

'Righto, Dad. Are we taking dogs?'

'Not this trip. I know what Wilf's sheep are like.'

David's head was in a daze. The prospect of acquiring more land and stock to add to High Peaks induced a kind of euphoria far more intense than anything he had ever experienced. What made it even more wonderful was the possibility of him doing a lot more of the stock work himself.

Chapter Thirteen

Next morning Kate was out of bed as soon as she heard David leave his room. She was just as excited as he was. They had the horses saddled and their legs padded, ready to board the old truck straight after breakfast. It was not long after seven when the utility and truck left High Peaks. There was a drive of about three miles down to the crossroads close by Inverlochy homestead. One road snaked its way towards the Merriwa–Cassilis road while the spur road that led on to Poitrel and four other properties turned left. It was about four miles from the crossroads to the Poitrel gate, a total drive of about seven miles from High Peaks. This took ten or twelve minutes in the ute (depending on who was driving); the gravel road twisted and turned, making fast driving fairly risky. A few town hoons had come to grief on the Poitrel road.

The truck took twenty minutes, so Anne and

Kate – who'd arrived first – were sitting on the verandah of Poitrel homestead talking with Wilf and his
sister Gertie when the others arrived.

'By gum, you're all prepared, Andy. No doubt
about you,' Wilf roared in his booming voice. 'G'day,
young fellow, what's this I hear about you having a
top Sparkes mare?'

'Yeah, she's okay, Mr White,' David answered.

'More than just okay, from what I hear. Second
in your first draft with her. Get her off, lad. I want
to see what she can do.'

'Hello, Gertie. Long time no see,' Andy said to
the big woman who followed Wilf down the steps.

'Long time, all right, Andy. This is never David?'

'It is, Gertie,' Anne answered.

David could just remember the big red-haired
woman who used to give him piggyback rides on the
lawn at High Peaks.

'Lordy, he's going to be as big as his father, Anne.
And nice-looking, too. The girls will be after him
good and early.'

'I hope not,' Anne laughed.

David suffered Gertie to kiss him and then he and
his father let down the truck's ramp and led the
horses off. They tethered them to a tie rail beneath a
big yellow jack tree.

'Now, look, young fellow. I want to see what this
mare can do. Can't hide your light under a bushel,
not with old Wilf. I'll be going away soon and I want
to remember you. You get on that mare for me.'

David looked across to his father, who nodded. 'All right, Mr White,' he said.

He looked about the big grassy area outside the tall netted fence which enclosed the homestead and its lawns. There was a truly amazing array of poultry spread out in all directions. Parading through scores of game and guineafowl and Indian runner ducks were several magnificent peacocks which were fanning their gorgeous tail feathers and making an unholy racket. 'One of them will do,' David muttered to himself. He vaulted into the saddle and turned Gift towards the nearest peacock. The cock took immediate umbrage to the mare's proximity and began to retreat towards the nearest of his hens. But Gift was in between them in a matter of seconds. When he turned to run the other way, she was there, too. For five minutes the big old man and his sister stood with the High Peaks trio and watched Gift work the peacock away from all the other birds until David at last delivered it almost to Wilf's feet.

There was a faraway look on Wilf's face as he watched the bay mare spin and slide to keep the peacock coming towards him in a straight line. It occurred to Anne that he was witnessing something he had never expected to see, nor would ever see again.

'Is that enough, Mr White?' David asked.

'By gum, that was terrific, young fellow. What footwork she's got. Just like a cat on her feet.'

'She's not too bad,' David said modestly as he

dismounted. Gift rubbed her head up and down David's back and it was obvious the pair were mates.

Wilf patted the boy's shoulder and winked at Anne. 'I don't know that I've got a mare as good on her feet as you have, but I do have one with a lot of speed. She won three races in Sydney. I reckon she's the best-looking mare I've ever had. Come along and I'll show her to you – to all of you, I mean.'

So they all followed Wilf out to the next paddock, which was what he called his 'young horse handling paddock'. There was a set of yards for breaking in, and a couple of rows of stables with a paved courtyard between them. The stables were a much grander concern than would be seen on most properties, and it was obvious where Wilf had spent his money. By comparison, the adjacent shearing shed looked very second-rate.

There were several yearlings running about in the paddock. David thought they looked a treat. Wilf walked on to the yards where there stood a solitary bright-chestnut mare with a broad splash of white on her face and three white stockings. Andy recognised her immediately as one he had broken in three or four years earlier.

'What do you think of Ajana, young fellow?' Wilf asked.

David wasn't sure what to say. He knew enough about horses to be able to tell what was and was not a good type. David recognised that the mare before him now was an even bigger, grander version of Gift.

'She's a real beaut, Mr White. The best-looking mare I've ever seen. Big, too. She should have a fair stride.'

'No flies on this boy, Andy. Chip off the old block. You've picked it straight off. She *has* got a big stride. She's by a son of Ajax. Same colour as Magnificent. Could be his sister, to look at her. And she's got terrific speed.'

David had never heard of Ajax or Magnificent, but he thought they were probably long dead, knowing how Wilf raved on about past champions.

'Have you bred from her yet?' David asked.

'Not yet. Not sure if I would send her back for another season of racing. Not going to now. Refused a six-figure offer for her. Got another use for her.'

'What's that?' David asked.

'Do you like her, son?'

'Well, she seems a terrific mare from what I've seen. I would like to be on her when she's galloping.'

'Glad you like her – she's yours! Now, Mrs Mac,' he said, turning abruptly to Anne, 'you listen to me. This is to be David's mare. He can use her any way he likes. If he wants to breed a few good thoroughbreds, she would be a great foundation mare. By gum, she would. She is never to be sold. Only condition that goes with her. None of my mares are ever to be sold.'

'Wow, do you mean it, Mr White?' David asked.

'Of course I mean it. Never meant anything more in my life. I heard what you did up there on Yellow

Rock. Saved that pony and took a buster doing it. Only a true horseman would have done that. Plenty round here would have put that pony down. You're going to be something, David. Maybe one day you'll even be a legend. My days are done with horses, but I reckon I can help you. Mind you, I'll be coming back here while I'm able, and I'll want to see what you're doing with Ajana.'

'What if we don't buy Poitrel?' David asked with his heart in his mouth.

'The deal stands. This is between you and me, young fellow. It's got nothing to do with your parents. The mare is yours. I've just given her to you. Her papers will be transferred to you, too. You could even race her up here if your Dad says it's okay. Now, here's my hand on it.'

David took the big hand that was thrust at him, and his own hand was engulfed completely.

'Can we take her back today?'

The big man's laughter boomed out like a cannon. 'Course you can. No good Ajana here and you over there thinking about her.'

'Looks like we'll be taking five horses back today, then,' Andy said. 'Thank you so much, Wilf. I'm not sure if David really appreciates just what he's got and what this mare is worth. He's a very lucky boy.'

'No, Andy, you're the lucky fellow to have a boy like him. I wish I had a son of my own, then I wouldn't be selling Poitrel. No, by gum. Now, I reckon you will all want to look through the house.'

The homestead was a timber construction, painted white, with a green galvanised-iron roof. It was a very large house with a verandah on three sides. Bulk electricity had only recently reached Poitrel, and the old generator was still in place. Gertie had installed a new electric stove in the big kitchen. The rooms were large with high ceilings and most of the walls were adorned with paintings or framed photographs of horses. Some of these pictures were positively spectacular. One that caught David's eye was a colour picture of Ajana winning a Randwick race by three lengths. 'Wow,' he breathed as his eyes dwelt on it.

On the far side of the house there were steps that led down to a quite extensive vegetable garden. There were tomatoes, lettuces, cucumbers and pumpkins galore. At the lower end of the garden, where the land was flat beside the creek, several half-sheets of galvanised iron were set in the ground and held there with steel posts.

'What you reckon about my irrigation set-up, Andy? Just remove the iron and it waters that whole flat. Grow anything there, you can.'

'No wonder you don't go to town,' Kate suggested. 'You have plenty to do here.'

Yes, including studying pedigrees and race form, Andrew thought.

'Keeps me busy, Sister Gilmour,' Wilf replied.

'Kate, please,' she said.

They went back into the house, where Gertie was waiting for them with some freshly brewed tea. She

259

put her head to one side and studied David intently. 'Oh, yes, he is going to be very nice looking, Anne. I can see his grandmother in him. Of course I can see both of you in him, but one could never forget David's grandmother. This young man is going to break hearts before long.'

'Mine first, Gertie, if he's to ride that big mare,' she replied.

Wilf's laughter filled the room. 'I reckon this young fellow could handle Ajana in his sleep.'

'He doesn't need any more encouragement, Wilf, thank you. His father is bad enough. No wonder I have grey hairs.'

'One day this son of yours will be a household name, Anne. You remember what I say.'

'Don't give him a big head,' Anne laughed. 'He's hard enough to handle as it is. Now, Wilf, we have brought some tucker. We thought we'd lunch up on the peak.'

'Great idea. Would you mind if I poked along with you?'

'Course not,' Andy replied.

'You know the place and could show us the short cuts.'

'Might be the last time for me,' Wilf said.

'Can I saddle you a horse?' David asked.

'You can, young David. Damned good of you to make the offer.'

Later that afternoon, when they had seen as much of Poitrel as could be seen in one day, Wilf insisted that they stay for afternoon tea. It was obvious that he wanted to talk about the sale of the property. When they had finished their smoko he looked directly at Andrew and said, 'Well, Andy, you've had a good look at the old place, warts and all. What do you reckon? Do you want Poitrel?'

'Sure I want it, Wilf. We all want it. I'll go and see the bank tomorrow. What worries me most is that we might have trouble meeting the six-monthly payments. As you know, our wool clip is our main income, and we won't be paid for that until the end of the year. I can't make enough, even if I ring every shed, to make all that much difference. The first year or two will be the worst, until we get the stock built up here. Poitrel could handle another thousand sheep. If we could run near three thousand sheep plus cattle, we would be in better shape. I think I'd prefer to ask the bank for a bigger initial loan to give you your first two payments. That way you could buy your house and have enough to live on for twelve months and by then the two wool clips will be paid for. How does that strike you?'

'I tell you what we'll do, Andy. You get your solicitor to draw up a contract that suits you money-wise and then bring it back and let me see it. I want you people to have Poitrel and my horses. Don't see why we can't do as you suggest.'

'We're very grateful to you, Wilf,' Andy said gravely.

'Well, Sister Kate,' Wilf said, turning his attention,

'now that you've seen the old place, would you like to live here?'

'I'd absolutely love to,' she replied.

'Well, the foxes are a menace. They get a few stragglers that will perch outside the pens. There's a few good Jerseys here for milk and cream. Do you milk, Sister?'

'I do now,' she said.

Finally, laden with vegetables, the MacLeod family, including Kate, left Poitrel. The new mare went with them, and David watched her with his eyes glued to the back window of the truck.

'You'd better let me handle her for a while, Davie,' Andy said. 'Most racehorses have only two paces – walk and gallop. She'll need a bit of education. That is, if you plan to ride her. We'll have to see how she handles the hill country. She's a big mare and I doubt she would be as good on her feet as our horses. Your mother will worry like hell if I don't try her out first.'

'I haven't thought what I'll do with her, Dad. You know best. It would be handy to be able to ride her. Perhaps we could put a good stock horse or quarter horse over her.'

'That would be my way of thinking. We certainly won't have any spare money to play about with thoroughbreds for the next few years. They cost a mint. But she's a bonzer mare and a proven winner. She could breed anything, and her stock should be worth a fair bit.'

David's face was all smiles. It seemed to him that

the day had been almost perfect. They had ridden all over Poitrel, with the entertaining Wilf in tow, lunched on the highest part of the property, and brought back with them to High Peaks the fastest mare in northern New South Wales – and she belonged to him. To him. The fastest mare in the north and one of the fastest in all Australia belonged to him.

That night at dinner Andrew and Kate discussed the logistics of taking on Poitrel.

'A man would be an idiot not to take it on Wilf's terms. I just wish David was a few years older,' Andrew said.

'Andy, I've said I will help all I can. Coming up here has given me a whole new outlook on life. There is a real challenge here. There's something elemental about these hills. I need this change just as much as you need Poitrel,' Kate replied.

'And we can't wait to have you, Kate. You must treat both places as your home. If this Poitrel deal goes through – and I can't see why it won't – and you decide to live there, there would be no rent and the power and phone bills would be paid out of the station account. We will make you a legal share-holder, but don't expect any return on your money for some time.'

Kate couldn't wish for more than that.

The next morning, Anne decided that she would accompany Andy to see the bank manager. David hated going to town so he opted to stay at home with

Kate. Together they stood at the front steps and watched the utility head off down the road, carrying both their hopes with it. They knew they were on the threshold of a new and exciting development.

'I hope there aren't any problems with the money,' David said.

Kate put an arm about his shoulders. 'You and me both, Davie. I sure do want to move up here. I'm busting to have a go at those campdrafts, and I want to buy a horse I can call my own.'

'Dad says that Angus Campbell will be fit to be tied when he learns about us buying Poitrel. He'll never believe we could afford it. He's made no secret of the fact that he wants the place. He'll be nearly as mad about me getting Ajana. He's never had a horse as good as her.'

'You and I are going to have a lot of fun over the next few years. Maybe I'll even learn to work a sheepdog. I couldn't have two better teachers. Now, what are you going to do today?'

'Aw, not much. Mum said I have to hang about the house while she and Dad are away. I might give Lad a lesson and I might trim Ajana's feet. Save Dad a job.'

'Right, then. I'll see you back in the house when you're ready.'

Later, they did all the chores earlier than usual so there would be nothing left to do but run the cow and calf in when Anne and Andrew arrived back from town. Kate could sense the excitement building up in David.

Aunt and nephew stood together when at last the utility came up the road and through the front entrance of High Peaks. There was no smile on his father's face and David's spirits slumped dramatically. Kate gave his arm a squeeze and they went down the steps of the verandah to help carry in the groceries.

Beyond his usual greeting Andy said nothing.

'Have a good day, David?' Anne asked.

'Mmm. Kate made me a chocolate cake,' he replied.

'She will spoil you rotten,' Anne said.

'Well, I'd better go and get changed and do a few jobs,' Andy said.

'They're all done, Dad,' David said. He was dying to ask what had happened at the bank, but he couldn't bear to be told that they had been turned down. Behind his back Anne winked at Kate.

Andy walked away a few steps and then turned and looked at his son.

'I can see that you're busting to know how we went at the bank,' he said.

David just stared up at his father, his eyes wide open in anticipation.

'We got the loan,' Andy said quietly.

David let out a whoop. 'Does that mean we own Poitrel now?'

'I reckon it does. I've already rung Mr White from town and given him the news. Our solicitor is drawing up the contract right now. We have a lot to do, Davie boy.'

'You beauty! Just as well it's school holidays. What's first?'

'I'll have to ring Gil Henderson tonight and see if he'll give me a pen for his Queensland run. He used to kick off early February, so we've got about a month to get things sorted out. I've asked Wilf if we can go ahead and put in some gates on the back fence, and that's a goer. I'll have to draw up a programme for you three to work to. By the way, Davie, your Aunty Kate is now a shareholder in High Peaks Pastoral Company.'

'What does that mean?'

'It means she's a part owner. It also means she can give you orders until you're old enough to take over.'

'You mean it?'

'I mean it. If you do silly things while I'm away, she can whomp you, too.'

Kate winked at him and David knew that everything was going to be all right.

Gil Henderson was very pleased to hear from Big Andy MacLeod that night. 'There's a pen for you whenever you want one,' he said. 'I thought you had everything worked out over there.'

'We've bought the next-door property, Gil, and I'll have to find some extra money to keep things going. I don't know how many two-hundreds are in me these days, but I'll keep your fellows honest.'

'I reckon you will,' Henderson said. He had seen Andy shear 260 in a day at Blackall.

The month sped up, and when the MacLeods took delivery of Poitrel on February second, Andy, although the calmest of men, found it hard to maintain his composure. They had almost doubled their land with this acquisition.

They all went over to farewell Wilf and Gertie and to install Kate in her new home. By an amazing coincidence, not just one but two vacancies had cropped up at the local hospital and Kate and a young woman who had been a student nurse with Kate in Sydney got the positions. Sister Jean Courteney was looking for a place to live, so Kate suggested that she stay with her at Poitrel for the time being.

'You know you'll be welcome to come back any time, Wilf,' Andy said. 'You can stay with us at High Peaks, or with Kate. Kate is one of the family and of the same mind.'

'Thank you, Andy,' Wilf muttered. It seemed that for once he found it difficult to say much more.

'Thank you for Poitrel and for Ajana, Mr White. We'll look after them both,' David said.

'I know you will, young fellow. And I'll be thinking of you a lot. You write to me and tell me every time you win a dog trial or a draft. Promise?'

'I promise.'

'I'm not a man to say much, Wilf, but believe me when I say we all appreciate what you've done for us. Nobody here will ever forget it,' Andy said.

'The bush needs people like you and yours, Andy. I am pleased to help you on your way. Yes, by gum.'

All eyes followed the red utility as it turned out of the gate and on to the road to town. Anne couldn't help but shed a tear as she wondered if she would ever see that kind man again. When the ute disappeared from view, they made their way back inside the homestead.

Jean Courteney was waiting for them. The MacLeods had taken an instant liking to her, and she was glad to have such a warm family around her. She had had an unsatisfactory marriage and was now divorced. Like Kate, she was keen on animals and prepared to help out on the property wherever she could. Jean was fair-haired with hazel eyes, and she had a willowy figure that never seemed to show fatigue.

The day before Andy was to leave for the Queensland shearing run, he took David aside for a serious talk. 'Davie, I don't have to tell you that I wouldn't be leaving here unless I had to. It's not something I'd planned on doing. You'll have to do a lot more work with me away. That includes always keeping your eyes open. Watch the stock at all times. You'll have to do a fair bit of riding at weekends and in the holiday periods. Pay strict attention to troughs and windmills. Never go out without fly-dressing and shears. Now, ten to one something will go wrong sooner or later. That can't be helped, because you can't be home here and at school, too. You'll have to cut back on the dog trials and drafts while I'm away.'

'Can I work Lad at the local trial?'

'You'll have to sort that out with Mum and Kate. I'll give you a tip. They both love you a lot, but don't take either of them for granted. Know what I mean?'

'I think so, Dad.'

'That's the ticket. In a few years you'll be able to drive yourself, and then you can trial and draft to your heart's content. What we've got here is a matter of priorities. The dogs and horses will be here when we've paid for Poitrel and you'll also be in a far better position to go away . . . Follow me?'

'Sure. I'll be just as happy looking after the two places anyway.'

'That's the boy. And there's something else. I don't want you killing yourself with work while I'm away. With what Kate has given us and some extra money from the bank, we can afford to pay for a bit more labour. I don't want you busting yourself trying to crutch at weekends and then going back to school completely stuffed. If we need a man to help us, or a couple of crutchers, we'll employ them. Okay?'

'Dad, I'll only crutch and shear anything that really needs it.'

'Good. I've drawn up a programme for you to follow. The main things to watch are water, drenching, lambing and calving. And, of course, the flies. If you've got any doubts about the stock, call the stock inspector. I've had a word with him and he knows the set-up. I think you'll find that he'll drop in every now and again. Don't hesitate to get Mum or Kate to call him if you think anything is wrong with the stock. Don't do anything silly with the horses. Stick to the ones you know you can handle. Don't ride the big chestnut mare in the hills. She's okay for poking about the cows, and you could ride her from here to Poitrel by road but not up Yellow Rock. Now, about high school – how are you finding it?'

'Aw, all right, I guess. There's more kids and more teachers, and a lot more sport.'

'Do your best, Davie. I know you will.'

'Don't worry about us. We'll manage.'

'I know. I have a lot of faith in you.'

'Thanks, Dad. I wish you didn't have to go, but I know you do.'

There were tears in Anne's eyes when she kissed her husband goodbye. 'I'll miss you an awful lot, you know,' she said as he held her close.

Andrew nodded. 'I hate like hell to have to go but there's no other way.'

'Promise me you won't overdo things trying to ring every shed. Let the younger shearers do that.'

Anne and David stood together at the bottom of the steps as Andy MacLeod drove away for the Queensland shearing sheds. Andy's departure would leave a big hole in Anne's life: they had lived and worked together as closely as any couple could. Anne knew that Andy had never looked at another woman from the day he had met her, and she was sure he never would.

Although David wished that his father did not

have to go away, he welcomed the extra responsibility that had come his way. If he didn't have to go to school during the week, he would be the happiest boy in the country. The teachers and some of the kids took a lot of putting up with, as they had no idea of what his life entailed.

He sighed and then put one arm around his mother's waist. Anne's eyes were still fixed on the road down which her husband had driven.

'We'll be right, Mum. You've got me now.'

She bent over and gently kissed the top of his head. 'Thank God for that,' she said.

In town, the cat was out of the bag. The news that the MacLeods had bought Poitrel had spread. Angus Campbell was ropable, not just because he had missed out on the land but because Wilf White had chosen Andy MacLeod over him. What's more, the MacLeods now had under their control the best lot of thoroughbred mares in the district. He was under no illusions about that. That old fool White did know thoroughbreds. And he had also given his top mare to young David. Angus appreciated that he had never bred a mare as good as Ajana, and he knew for a fact that a six-figure offer had been made for her. If the MacLeods wanted to race her locally, she would wipe the floor with everything else. And what was David doing with her? Riding her about to look at cows? A mare worth six figures being used as a stock horse. It was incredible.

The whole set-up was unbelievable. The question was on everybody's lips: How could a kid and two women run over 7000 acres of range country? It was ridiculous.

Chapter Fourteen

The next few years were very tough for the MacLeods. They were years of constant effort for Andrew, Anne and David, and Kate threw her weight behind the others, too. They were years that saw David develop from a boy to a young man, the transition beginning the day his father drove out of the driveway at High Peaks away to the shearing sheds of Queensland. David followed his father's example every way he could in the management of the two properties. He revelled in the extra responsibility and in the extra stock work, which was meat and drink to him.

At sixteen, David was as big as his father – perhaps three inches over six feet, and with shoulders the width of a door. He was, according to all the local girls – and especially Catriona Campbell's bosom friend, Susan Cartwright – the best-looking boy in the district. But David still showed little interest in girls. He was diffident about saying much at all, but no boy at the high school took him lightly.

Despite preoccupation with weekend work at High Peaks and Poitrel, David had worked Lad in two local trials and broken in one of his sons. This son David considered to be the best dog of all three that he had owned. His name was Nap.

At the first of the two local sheepdog trials he had entered while his father was away, David won the Novice with Lad and ran second in the Open, beaten by a point by an experienced border collie. Although his father had always taught him to cast a dog to the head of sheep, in the Open Trial he hadn't done that. The sheep were walking into a westerly wind and he thought Lad might stop short and thereby lose casting points. So David cast Lad around to the right, and by the time the dog got around, the sheep were well off course and he had lost several points for it. He learned that day that he simply had to have more confidence in his dog.

The following year he did win the Open with Lad, but, tragically, a fortnight later the dog was killed. Lad used to love to sit with his head through the horse yard while David educated a young horse. The tragedy happened when one of these horses kicked backwards and split Lad's head open. David looked down at his faithful friend, whom he knew was dying, and felt as if his heart would burst. Lad was the first dog he had won an Open Trial with and he'd been his loyal companion for the past five years. He remembered his father's admonition about losing his heart to a dog, so he kept his grief locked up inside. Even Anne was not aware that Lad had died until several days later. David laid him to rest alongside the dog's father and carried on his training with Lad's son, Nap.

High school was just as much of a trial for David as primary school had been, only more so because he was away from home longer each day. Sport was compulsory, and although he had asked his mother several times if he could be excused, she always turned him down. She felt that David should have a normal education. He had more to do at home than any other boy in the district, and she did not consider it fair that he should have to work while other children were playing. She knew that David wasn't keen on sport, but it was an important part of his education. He had his own sport, whip-cracking, at which he was now considered to be without equal. He appeared as a guest turn at almost every travelling 'Wild West' show staged in the district.

David had developed a reputation as a young man not to be trifled with on any account. He could crack two whips simultaneously and could cut leaves in two with both. By the time he was fourteen, he was able to use a ten-foot whip with ease, although he preferred shorter whips for exhibition work. One feat was to cut a single leaf from a tree. His twice daily exhibitions at the local show always pulled in a big crowd. And when he asked for volunteers to hold things for him, there was usually a rush of girls anxious to be noticed by him. David practised constantly and was always adding new things to his routine.

School subjects bored him to tears. He hated mathematics and loathed algebra. He found them totally irrelevant and a complete waste of time. The only lesson he really liked was Australian bush poetry. He came to memorise every bush poem he read, but, to his regret, there was not much time devoted to the likes of Henry Lawson and Banjo Paterson.

There was continuing argument between himself and his mother over what he should do after Year 10. Anne – and Kate, too, for that matter – felt that he should stay the extra two years so he could get into a course such as agricultural science – just in case things didn't work out for them on the land. But David said that it was silly for him to stay another two years when there was so much to do at home.

During the four years since Catriona Campbell had finished primary school, she continued her schooling in Sydney. David saw her very seldom, perhaps only four or five times while he was at high school. After one of her rare visits home, Anne remarked that Catriona grew 'prettier and prettier', but David was still indifferent to Catriona, and her looks.

Despite her enforced absence from David, Catriona still seemed to be anything but indifferent to him. She was also aware that she faced competition from Susan Cartwright. Not that the Cartwright family was any more keen on a liaison between their daughter and David MacLeod than the Campbell family was. Both families had much grander matrimonial plans for their daughters.

One Sunday morning towards the end of David's final week of Year 10, he was driving some cows and calves along the road from High Peaks to Poitrel. They were still building cattle numbers at Poitrel, having culled some of the poorer quality beasts they had inherited with the property.

A grey utility was coming down the other side of the road. It was travelling very fast, too fast by far for the gravel surface, and much too fast in the presence of stock. David immediately recognised the vehicle and the two men in it. The one driving was Bill Missen, and the other was his younger brother, Wade.

The ute made no attempt to slow down as it drew closer to the little bunch of cows and vealers. A white-faced steer vealer plunged sideways from the mob and the ute slammed into it and didn't even try to stop. There was no way that the driver could have failed to realise he had hit the vealer. David cantered his horse to where the poor vealer lay injured on the road. He realised with desperation that there was no way he could save it.

David pulled the dying calf off the road and saw the mob into the nearest paddock. It was only half a mile or so on to the Poitrel homestead which was his destination. Kate was working in the vegetable garden and she rested one foot on her spade when she saw David riding up the driveway.

'Can you drive me down to the Missen place, please? And would you also bring me the .410 from the house?'

'David, what's the matter?'

'You'll see,' he said.

'Do I need to change my clothes?' Kate asked.

'No, I just want you to drive.'

'Pull up here for a moment,' he said when they reached the stricken calf. He took the gun and shot the animal in the head, then cut its throat with his stock knife so that it would be bled by the time they returned. He hated losing good calves, whatever the reason, but to lose one to two hoons like the Missen boys was simply not on.

'Right,' he said. 'On to the Missen place.'

The Missen property was a few miles past Inverlochy on the road to Merriwa. David knew Roy Missen slightly, as he had accompanied Andy to the Missens' property on horse business on a couple of occasions. Roy was acknowledged to be a decent fellow and a good worker on his place, but his two boys were wild. They had been in trouble with the police, and many people thought that it was because Roy had been too easy on them. Bessie Missen thought her boys could do no wrong, and because Roy loved his wife he went along with her.

Kate parked the Falcon at the front steps of the homestead and David picked up his whip and got out. 'You want any help?' Kate asked, pointing to the gun.

David gave her a tight grin. 'I hope not. Roy's a decent fellow. He won't want to see his boys cut about.'

'Is that what you're going to do?' she asked anxiously.

'Only if Roy doesn't pay for the vealer,' David said.

He turned and walked up the steps. The butt of the whip applied to the front door made a fair enough clatter to rouse anyone.

When Roy appeared, David said pleasantly enough, 'Good morning, Mr Missen.'

'Hello, David. What can I do for you?'

'I've come to get a cheque from you for a steer calf.'

'What did you say?' Missen replied sharply.

David repeated his request and Missen frowned. 'Would you mind explaining that?'

'About half an hour ago, Bill and Wade drove past me on the Poitrel road where I was shifting a mob of cattle. Bill was driving like a maniac and he hit one of our vealers, which I had to destroy. They didn't stop, although they knew what they had done, so I want you to pay for the vealer.'

'You do, eh? Well, what if I don't?'

'Then I'll flog your two boys until they can't stand up any more. We aren't busting our guts to pay off a property so your boys can get away with killing one of our animals.'

'Now, hang on there. You can't go about the

country threatening that sort of thing. I won't have it,' Missen said heatedly.

'Then you should teach your boys to respect other people's property. If you don't believe what I'm telling you, get them out here and ask them yourself.'

'Bill, Wade, get out here,' Missen thundered.

The boys emerged from the house looking anxiously towards their father and the grim-faced young giant holding a coiled whip. David MacLeod had a fearsome reputation with his fists, but an even more fearsome reputation with stockwhips. Their eyes dropped to the roo-hide whip which he held loosely in his right hand. Then their glances took in Kate leaning against her red car.

'Did you fellas drive past David while he was driving cattle this morning?' he asked.

Bill and Wade dropped their eyes and Wade licked his lips nervously.

'Well, did you?' his father demanded.

'Yes, Pa,' Bill answered.

'Did you hit one of his vealers?'

'Well, we weren't sure, Pa,' Bill said.

'You weren't sure? Did you stop to make sure?'

'No, Pa,' Bill said for both boys. Wade couldn't tear his eyes away from the whip in David's hand.

'David says you were driving too fast, hit a vealer and kept going. If that's what happened, there'll be some evidence of it on the utility. We'll go and have a look,' Missen said.

David followed the three Missens down the front

steps and around to the back of the house where the grey Holden utility was parked under a big old gum tree. Blind Freddie could have seen the smashed front light and the red hair adhering to it. Roy looked from his sons to the tall figure of David MacLeod. His mind went back to the last district show when he had seen this young man do things with stockwhips that he had not imagined possible. There was little doubt that David was quite capable of giving Bill and Wade a flogging. The MacLeods were like that: nobody ever messed with Big Andy, and from what Roy had heard, David was going to be even tougher.

'How much are you wanting for the vealer?'

'Market value for a steer vealer. Same as you'd get for one of yours. No more, no less.'

'Come up to the house and I'll give you a cheque. Bill, Wade, wait here. I'll be back to talk to you shortly.'

Roy went into his office and wrote out a cheque for the dead calf. David glanced at the figure, nodded and put the cheque in his pocket. Missen held out his hand and David shook it.

'I'm sorry about your calf, David,' he said, sounding genuine.

'So am I, Mr Missen.'

'You're a hard young fella, David. Anyone ever tell you that?' Missen said, looking up into David's serious face.

'No, but nobody has ever killed a calf on me before. I hope for your sake that Bill and Wade never do anything like that again. Good morning.'

Roy watched the tall young man as he walked down the front steps and out to the red Falcon. You had to hand it to him – he was only a boy in age yet he was more of a man than most.

Later that day, Kate took enormous pride in recounting the details of her morning to Anne. David had only given her the bare details when he had handed over the cheque. Anne decided to let the matter drop. But a week or so later there was an even more dramatic confrontation involving her son, and this time Anne was a spectator. School had finished for the year and Anne was taking David to town to have him fitted out with new clothes. He had virtually grown out of his others. They were driving along the main Merriwa–Cassilis road when they came upon a droving plant. There was a long line of sheep feeding out down the road and a droving plant stationary in the shade of a few box trees. David's eyes flicked across the scene and locked on to something that made his blood run cold. 'Quick, Mum, drive over there. See, where those men are.'

'David, what is it?' Anne asked in alarm as she spun the car off the road towards the plant.

'Don't you see?' he said grimly.

He bent to the tool box on the floor and took from it a pair of fencing pliers. There were two whips on the seat beside him and he snatched them up and was out of the vehicle before it had even stopped moving completely. He was half conscious that

282

another vehicle had pulled up behind them. Just then, Anne gasped as she saw what had attracted her son's attention. Her breath caught in her throat.

Hanging from the branch of a tree by a length of fencing wire was a thin black and tan kelpie. A noose of wire was around the dog's neck and it was slowly choking to death. The dog's tongue was abnormally swollen and it was making terrible gasping sounds as it fought for breath. As if this was not enough for the dog to endure, one of the three men near the plant was belting it with a piece of stick. Anne felt physically sick.

David shouldered the dog's tormentor to one side and, holding the dog up with one arm, he cut the wire just above its head. It was a good kelpie head, despite its fearfully distorted eyes.

'Hey, you, what the hell do ya think ya doin' with that dog?' the drover yelled at him. The man advanced towards David with his stick. The next moment he stopped dead in his tracks as his right ear exploded in white-hot agony. David recoiled the right-hand whip and looked across at the three men. One was a boy, perhaps his own age but nowhere near his size. David didn't reckon he would interfere. The head drover, the one who had yelled at David, was of medium height and thick build and had a very red face. He had been wearing an old wide-brimmed hat which now lay on the ground while he nursed his ear. The man was very bowed in the legs and looked as if he had never done anything but ride horses. The third man was younger, probably in his mid-thirties. His skin was very brown and he looked capable enough, although not formidable.

David glanced down at the choking dog at his feet and then across to the other dogs lying nearby. They were all pathetically thin, with hipbones jutting out sharply from their skinny frames. Their coats were turned up and they looked as if they had never had a decent feed in their lives. Cold anger ran right through David. He had never felt such fury in his life.

'You mongrels don't deserve to own dogs. What the hell do you mean by treating a dog like that?' he asked venomously, provoking the men to try something.

He was aware that some bushmen killed cull dogs by strangling them with wire, and that some even used hanging to get control of 'hard' dogs. Such methods horrified him and filled him with contempt.

'What would you know about dogs, sonny?' the head drover said sarcastically. 'You're still wet behind the ears. I've had dogs all my life and I know how to handle the buggers. If a dog won't do as he's told, you've got to show it who's boss.'

'Most of the time it's morons like you who are at fault. You're not a dog man's bootlace. The condition of these animals is a disgrace.' He could see the gasping dog out of the corner of one eye and thought that there was a chance the kelpie might survive if he could get it to the vet's in a hurry. He sure as hell wasn't going to leave it with these creeps, but he did have to be careful how he extricated himself from the situation.

The younger man stepped towards him with a menacing look in his eye and David let him have it with his left-hand whip. The man howled blue murder but was only aggravated even more, so David let him have one on the other ear. They were the softest blows he could deliver, and were designed to intimidate rather than cause real injury.

David's assailant collapsed on a log, gripping his agonising ears. He was down but not out.

'Listen to smart arse here telling me how to handle my own dogs. What would you know?' he continued.

'More than you ever will,' said a quiet voice appearing from behind.

David turned and saw Roger Cartwright standing at his side. His sister, Susan, was back next to Anne by the car. But this was a different Roger Cartwright to the boy who had been a couple of years above him at primary school. In those days Roger had been the school wimp. The children had nicknamed him Blub because he broke into tears so easily when picked on for being overweight. The Roger who stood before David now was several inches shorter than him but very powerfully built.

'David MacLeod is the best handler of dogs this district has ever seen. You wouldn't be fit to be spoken of in the same breath,' Roger said. 'David, you need any help?'

Roger's powerful figure beside him was immensely

reassuring. He turned back to the three men at the plant. 'That all depends on these apologies for stockmen,' he said caustically. 'I'm taking this dog with me. I'm going to report you to the police, the RSPCA and the Pastures Protection Board, so you'd better get some decent tucker into those other dogs. I hope they fine the tripe out of you. If I ever run into you again and find your dogs in the condition they are now, I'll flog the daylights out of you. If you think I'm talking through my hat, ask this man beside me,' David said. Then he bent down and picked up the kelpie and carried it across to the utility, where he laid it on a bag in the back. When he turned around, Susan was beside him.

'You were terrific, David,' she said and gave him a dazzling smile.

'I'm sorry, Susan, I haven't got time to talk now. The vet's – quick, Mum! Thanks for your support, Roger. I hope I'll see you later.'

Anne had stood transfixed while all this was going on. If she had not seen it for herself she would never have believed it. It seemed only yesterday that David was just a little boy, but she knew that she could not have stopped him today.

'David, I can't believe what you just did,' she said as she started up the motor.

'Mongrels, that's all they are. Fancy treating a kelpie like that. They're earning their living from animals and they know nothing about them. You see their other dogs? People who use animals ought to be licensed and have their animals subject to inspection.'

He looked through the back window and noted that the dog was still lying as he had placed it but now seemed to be breathing a little easier.

As David and Anne drove away, Roger took out his notebook and wrote down the number of the drover's truck.

'What are ya doin' that for?' the head drover asked.

'My father's on the local PP Board. I'm going to report you for cruelty and neglect of your animals.'

'Aaah.' The sound that came out of the drover's throat was not something that could be interpreted.

'Clean up your act here,' Roger continued. 'Those dogs are a disgrace. They don't have to be in that condition to work sheep.' And with that advice, he turned and left.

Roger had a soft spot for David MacLeod. David had been one of the only boys who had never made fun of him at school, and on a couple of occasions he had actually defended him.

When David and Anne arrived at the vet's, David explained what had happened and stood by while the kelpie was being examined. Eric Chalmers was recognised as a good vet and he had known David since he was a small boy.

'He looked at last gasp when I cut him down,' David said.

'You got him just in time. I think he'll be okay but his throat has been damaged and he may not bark normally for some time, if ever.'

'We'll call in and see you before we go out, Mr Chalmers. If the dog can be taken away, we'll take him. Don't let anyone else touch him.'

'What will you do with him, David?' Anne asked as they drove up the main street to the clothing store.

'I think I'll give him to Kate. She wants a companion dog. Should have had one before now. After what he's been through, that dog should appreciate a bit of love and attention in a good home. He'll look a new animal with some decent tucker in him.'

So that was how Lucky came to live at Poitrel. Kate said he had to be named Lucky because he was so damned lucky to be alive. After a few lessons from David, Kate soon had Lucky under control. The dog's biggest drawback was his bark – or, rather, lack of it. It was more of a high-pitched yip than a bark, but he became a very good guard dog and always warned Kate and Jean when a vehicle turned in at the front gate.

Kate and Jean had settled in very well at Poitrel. They shared the jobs, and after Jean learned to ride, either one or both of them would ride out and inspect the sheep and cows. This took some of the load off David's shoulders. The long-neglected flower garden became Jean's responsibility, while Kate concentrated on the vegetables. Kate taught Jean to milk, too. Jean told Anne that living at Poitrel gave her a kind of freedom and happiness she had never previously experienced. She said it was as if she belonged to something worthwhile.

Chapter Fifteen

The day after David had brought Lucky to Poitrel, Andy arrived home from New England. The shearing run had started way out in western Queensland and finished in the cooler northern tableland area. Andy sat and listened in growing admiration as Anne recounted David's exploits. But Andy's obvious interest in his son's achievements did not disguise the fact that he had aged a lot during the past year. His once dark-brown hair was now almost totally grey, and he had lost a lot of weight.

'Are you all right, love?' Anne asked.

'Just a bit tired, old girl,' he said. 'It's been a long year.'

'You'd better take it easy for a while. We're managing well.'

'Maybe I will,' he said. 'Maybe I will.'

That admission was in itself a source of concern for Anne because Andy had never taken it easy. But after a couple of days of riding about the properties with David, he seemed a little brighter.

There followed a week of stormy, humid weather and the flies became very troublesome. They began striking the ewe lambs and Andrew suggested to David that the best course of action would be to shear them.

'No need for you to touch them, Dad. I can whack the wool off them.' David had become a reasonably proficient shearer over the past few years and could manage eighty to ninety sheep a day quite comfortably. It was still a long way below Andy's tallies, but David had never been away to the sheds to develop.

'We'll do them together, mate,' Andy said. 'I don't want you busting yourself all the time.'

So the next day the pair of them yarded the ewe lambs and began to shear them while Kate swept the board and picked up the wool.

About halfway through the next run David looked up and saw that his father had not emerged from the catching pen. He carried on with the lamb he had started and then crossed the board for another sheep. What he saw in the pen made his heart stop dead.

His father was down on his back with a strange, twisted look on his face.

'Kate,' David called at the top of his voice.

She was in the wool room putting a wool pack in the press.

'Kate, in here, quick,' he called again.

'What is it, David? What's the matter?'

'It's Dad,' he said, pointing at the catching pen.

Kate ran into the pen and dropped to her knees beside her brother-in-law. 'Where does it hurt, Andy?' she asked.

Andy tried to answer her but no words came out of his mouth. One hand crept towards his heart and then flopped back. Kate looked at his face and felt alarm race through her.

'What is it?' David asked. Kate saw the worry in his eyes. This was a new experience for him. He had never seen his father stricken with any kind of sickness. Andy had always seemed to be built of iron.

'I think your dad has had a stroke,' she said. 'We need to get him to hospital very quickly. First we'll have to get him onto a bed of some kind. Is there an old door or something in the shed?'

'There's a camp bed in the feed shed,' he answered quickly.

'Go and get it, but first run and tell Anne I need her. Don't tell her why. I don't want to panic her.'

David charged out of the shed, told his mother that Kate needed to see her, and raced back to the feed shed for the old wire-mesh camp stretcher. By the time he returned to the catching pen – now emptied of lambs – his mother was kneeling with Kate beside his father. He noted the concern on the women's faces, especially Anne's, as she held on to Andy's hand.

David put the camp bed down on the grating floor

and, between the three of them, they lifted his father onto it. They carried the makeshift stretcher out through the wool room and down the back steps of the shed before they laid it down. 'Wait here and I'll back the ute across,' Kate said. 'We'll put a mattress in the back and, Anne, you'll have to ride with Andy and keep the sun off his face.'

Anne took David's hand and pressed it. 'You stay here, darling. I'll ring you at two o'clock,' she said.

David nodded. 'Is it very bad?'

'We won't know until we get Dad to hospital.'

After the women had left, David began to think about the implications of what life would be like if his father had had a stroke. If Andy could not work, he could not go away shearing, and if he could not shear, that would mean a lot less money coming in. That was a real concern.

Before she left, Kate had asked him to ring the hospital and warn them that they were coming.

'Don't look so alarmed, David. Andy will be in good hands,' Kate had said as she left.

But David was alarmed. After he had rung the hospital he tried to carry on shearing, but it didn't seem to be the same place without his father alongside him. Andy's presence back on High Peaks had reminded David just how much he had missed him over the past three years. Would things ever be the same again?

David continued shearing until nearly one o'clock, at which time he returned to the house for lunch. He made a meal of cold meat and salad and boiled the jug for tea. Just after two o'clock, exactly as expected, the phone shrilled beside him.

'Is everything all right?' he asked straightaway.

'Not exactly. I'm sorry to say that your father has had a stroke, a severe stroke.'

David's heart stopped. How could this be? Sickness was something that happened to other people, he thought. He had hardly had a sick day in his life, and neither had his father. He just could not envisage Andy laid low. There was nothing he hated so much as visiting people in hospital, and to know that his father was lying there now was shattering.

David didn't know how to reply, but finally managed to utter the words, 'Oh no. Should I ring anyone and let them know?'

'No, dear. We'll wait a day or two before we do that. Kate is coming back to get you and bring you to the hospital. She'll probably stay with you tonight as I won't be coming home.'

'Righto, Mum.'

David didn't like the sound of things at all. His mother wouldn't call him to the hospital unless his father was real crook. Maybe he was going to die and had asked to see him one last time. What a thing to happen. His father had always seemed indestructible, yet there was no doubt he had looked a lot older and wearier since he'd arrived back this time. Andy had worked like hell to stay the top shearer, but look what it had cost him.

David went across to the dog yards and let Nap off his chain. The shorn lambs went back into their old paddock and the woolly sheep were let out into a small holding paddock. The other dogs had a run before they were fed. It was a bit early to run the calf off the cow so he brought them up to the horse yard and fed them some hay. He could take the calf off when he got back home later. Then he fed the fowls and collected the eggs. There were some broken egg-shells in one pen and he reckoned a goanna was on the go again.

Kate arrived back at four o'clock.

'How is he?' David asked as soon as she came into the house.

'He's not well, I'm afraid, Davie. He could be worse, but he's bad enough. He's had a major stroke and his right arm and leg are affected, and his voice is just a croak at this stage.'

'Why would Dad have had a stroke? He's not old and he's as strong as a bull.'

'Even bulls break down, you know, and they aren't subject to stress like we humans are. Andy has pushed himself hard all his life,' Kate explained. 'He's also had his fair share of worry. It gets you down in the end. Now, I must tell you, there is a fair chance that your dad will return home a semi-invalid. He could also have another stroke, or a series of strokes, which could finish him. It's no good me trying to pull the wool over your eyes. You need to know the complete picture.'

'We're lucky to have you, Kate,' he said.

Kate knew David was being sincere. He always was.

'I consider myself lucky to be here,' she said, putting an arm around his shoulders.

The drive back into town was probably the most miserable trip David had ever made along the familiar road, and the sight of his father in intensive care did nothing to improve his state of mind; it just depressed him even more. He had never before seen anyone connected to so many tubes. Surely it couldn't be his father lying there so quietly.

Andy's eyes were open and they flickered momentarily when David came into the room and stood beside the bed.

'Hi, Dad,' he said.

There seemed to be the vestige of a smile on his father's face but no sound came from his mouth. David did not know what to do next; everyone around him was speaking in whispers. The place seemed unnaturally quiet. He couldn't just stand and look at his father as his mother was doing. All he could think of was his father on the back of Jess or Gloss or Cecil Miss, or working Ben and King.

Presently Kate took Anne's place beside the bed and Anne led David outside.

'I wanted Andy to see you, David,' she said. 'I thought it might help to keep him going. There's nothing more you can do here. Kate will take you back shortly. Jean will look after things at Poitrel. She's on duty here and Kate has spoken to her about it. I shall probably be staying here for some days, at least until we see what happens. If Dad improves we'll be able to bring him home. Until then, you and Kate need to look after each other. You will be all right, won't you?'

'You know I will, Mum. Don't worry about me. You stay with Dad and let me know how things are going. I can look after things at home. If I had my licence I could come in each day, but that's not far away now.'

After dinner that night, David and Kate sat together on the wide verandah and looked out across the moonlit countryside. Away in the distance they could hear a fox yapping and the mournful cry of a mopoke.

'We are going to have to look at where we're going, Kate,' David said after a long spell of silence.

Kate looked across at him. It seemed to her that just as he had grown up so rapidly when Andy went away shearing, he had within these last few hours matured just as much again.

'What do you mean?' she asked.

'Now that Dad is sick he won't be able to shear. He's going to be right out of the picture, work-wise. I could probably get a bit of local shearing and crutching but I'm not a fast enough shearer for the big runs and, in any case, I can't leave here for long spells. There's too much to do. If the wool price was higher, things might be a bit different, but as things are, we are going to be a fair bit down on money.'

'I've been thinking about that, too,' Kate said. 'If I put my wages into the kitty and you did a bit of local work, I think we could manage.'

David shook his head. 'We wouldn't expect you to do that, Kate. What would you live on?'

'I don't need much, not here. I have meat, milk and vegetables, and the station pays the bills.'

'Well, if we went that way, we would have to increase your share in the company. But let's wait until Mum comes home and thrash it around then.'

Kate nodded her agreement.

'I'll bet things liven up around here when the word gets about that Dad's sick,' David said.

And he was right. As soon as the news flashed around the district that Andy MacLeod had had a stroke and was in hospital, the phone started to ring. The wives of near neighbours sent cooked meat, cakes and biscuits. It was a job getting away from the house for the callers, and Kate, who was staying at High Peaks, said that she had a full-time job keeping the kettle boiled.

The most significant of these visitors was Angus Campbell, who arrived unexpectedly with Catriona in tow. The Campbells, especially Angus, had been rather cool towards the MacLeods ever since they received word that Wilf White had sold them Poitrel. But Angus could never forget what David had done for Catriona in the past.

'Is David home?' Catriona asked as soon as she made her way up the front steps.

'Yes, but he's on the phone,' Kate replied.

A look of relief swept over Catriona's face with the news that David was actually in the house. So many times he hadn't been.

'Will you come in?' Kate asked. She noted the basket Catriona was carrying.

Angus nodded. 'Can't stay too long. Just wanted to deliver this basket of things. Thought it might come in handy, what with Anne spending so much time at the hospital. And if there is anything at all we can do to help, please just let us know.'

'How thoughtful of you, Angus,' Kate said. She was still trying to come to terms with the extent of the goodwill flowing into High Peaks. It was quite incredible.

At that moment, David came through to the lounge from the office. Kate noted the quick glance Catriona threw in his direction. If she had been expecting any special welcome, she would have been disappointed because David did not oblige.

'Hello, Mr Campbell. How are you, Cat?'

Catriona was surprised by the change in David's appearance. He was now taller than her brother Stuart and he moved more athletically.

'I've come to offer our help, if you need it,' Angus said without preamble.

'That's very good of you, We've been over-whelmed with kindness. It really means a lot to us. I think we'll be okay. Kate and Mum and I can manage things at the moment.'

'How's Andy?' Angus asked.

'It's too early to say. The doctors say he could come out of the stroke with either marginal or permanent damage, and there is also the serious concern that he could have another stroke.'

'Never thought Andy would go down like that,' Angus said. 'He seemed so indestructible. Makes a man think about things.'

'When you've worked as hard and for as long as Andy has without a break, I would say that a stroke is not too unexpected. Now he's paid the price.'

'Quite so, Kate. Well, David, and how are things going with your animals?'

'I've been too busy to do much competition work outside the local trials. I'm sorry to say I lost Lad and now I have a son of his called Nap. I think he's the best dog I've handled. Quite the best. Very brainy. Some of the big kelpie studs have been trying to buy him. The money they're offering is fairly staggering. We've also got a very good, young blue bitch, and she's the best we've had for years. She has a short tail like a lot of Dad's good old dogs of the past. Both these dogs could win good trials if I could just get the time to work on them. How are yours these days?'

'Not too bad. I did breed a few fair dogs by the imported fellow. But if I ever decide to import another dog, I'll go over and select it myself.'

'Good idea,' David agreed.

'What about the horses? Did you do anything with Ajana?'

'We mated her to an Abbey horse and got a very nice filly foal. She looks a beauty. We missed her the following year and then mated her to a Bobby Bruce horse. She's carrying that foal now.'

'Hmm, it's a pity you haven't mated her to a top thoroughbred, David. She's too good a mare not to get a thoroughbred from.'

'We aren't racing people, Mr Campbell. Even if we were, the fee for a real top stallion would be out of our reach right now. We can sell all the good stock horses we can breed and handle on Dad's name alone – and for far less outlay.'

'Look here, David, I would be prepared to come to some agreement with you on Ajana. I'll pay the service fee for a half-share in any foals. If they were good enough, I'd race them in Sydney.'

'I'll think about it. I know that Mr White would like to see Ajana bred to thoroughbreds. I wouldn't mind trying to breed something that could run.'

'Do you ever see Wilf these days?'

'Once a year or so. He seems to be keeping quite well. Gertie watches him like a hawk and she's got a fair bit of weight off him.'

Catriona wished her father would stop talking and let her speak with David. He had changed so much over the past few years. Apart from his size, he had a very confident manner. He was also extremely handsome, and she was frustrated that he didn't show any interest in her. He was about the only boy she had met who didn't. She was also concerned about

Susan's interest in him. Susan was very keen on him, and Catriona knew what some girls would do to get the boy they wanted. Catriona was really worried that Susan would ask David to take her to the next ball. Catriona had her heart set on David escorting her to the ball, but did not feel she could mention it while his father was so sick. But he was such a good catch, especially now he had two properties behind him. She knew what her father's plans for her were, but Catriona knew that the boy of her choice was in the room with her right then.

'Have you got the Ajana filly close by?' Angus asked. 'I'm looking for another horse for Catriona and she might fill the bill. Can I have a look at her?'

'I haven't broken her in yet. We were late getting Ajana bred the first year, so she isn't two years old yet.'

'That's all right. I'd still like to see her. The cross of bloods sounds interesting, and if you say she is a beauty, she must be up to show type.'

'The filly is with her mother in the paddock below where you drove in. It's not far. Will you come, Kate?'

'No, I think I'll stay here, thanks. I'll put the kettle on and have smoko ready for you when you get back,' she said.

Angus glanced across at Catriona, who nodded almost imperceptibly. 'Thanks, Kate.'

They walked past the shearing shed and down to what David called the foal paddock. It was fenced with wooden posts and split timber rails rather than barbed wire, and must have involved an enormous amount of hard work to build it.

There were half a dozen mares and three younger horses running in the paddock. Ajana stood out for her colour and markings but there wasn't much in it. Every mare was of a wonderful type. Perhaps the best of the lot was a bright bay filly with as sweet a head as Angus had ever seen on a horse.

'Is that the Ajana filly?' he asked, pointing towards the bay.

David nodded. He slipped through the fence and walked towards the little mob of horses. Ajana and the filly came right up to him and he put his hand in the mane of the younger horse and led her back to where Angus and Catriona were sitting on the fence.

'She won't take much breaking-in. I can catch her anywhere. Mind you, I've handled her since she was foaled. And her mother is a great-natured thing.'

Catriona stroked the filly's silky neck while Ajana rubbed her head up and down David's back.

'These your shop-window lot?' Angus queried in his peremptory way.

'Not really. We don't breed from many mares and only keep the very best. We picked a few mares from the lot Mr White left and mated them to stock-horse stallions. They were good types with nice natures and it seemed a pity to waste them. We can't supply all the enquiries we get.'

'Is that so?'

'We could sell ten good broken-in horses right now and, frankly, I wish we had them to sell. The problem is getting the time to handle them. But dogs are my main interest. I'd like to spend more time on them. I'd like to have a spell at trialling, but it looks as if I'll have to put that off for a while. If Dad doesn't come good, I shall be tied here for some time.'

Catriona had the perfect solution. In her mind, she fantasised that if she and David were married, she could handle the horses while he concentrated on the dogs. The only problem was that David didn't appear to be the slightest bit interested.

'Can we come back and have a look at this filly when you break her in? And I'd be interested in looking at anything else you have for sale. I need a good horse myself,' Angus said.

David pondered this change in attitude. Angus had never before shown more than lukewarm interest in their horses. He wondered if Cat had had anything to do with it.

'Sure. I don't know that I'd be keen to sell this filly, and she'd need a fair bit of work before I could tell if she'd make a show horse. There are some others that are fairly good. I particularly like a black colt running over at Poitrel. He has the size to make a good show horse. He moves like a dream. There was a chap here from Moree who took a great liking to him. There's also a liver chestnut which could be a likely type, but you really don't know what a horse will be like until you've handled it.'

'Will you let me know when you have the black colt handled?' Angus asked. 'And the chestnut?'

'Certainly. I haven't made a commitment to anyone, but the Moree chap did like him,' David said.

Angus and Catriona found it hard to believe that David was still only a boy. He certainly didn't look it any longer and he didn't speak like it either. What he said always made very good sense.

'So are you actively breeding horses to sell?' Angus asked.

'Yes, we are. We need the money. Some day I'd like to keep my own stallion, but a top entire costs big money.'

'Have you got one in mind?' Angus asked.

'There's a really good stallion up Rockhampton way. Tim Sparkes owns him. The horse is a legend up there. He's a freak sire,' David explained.

'Very interesting. Please don't forget that I'm interested in the black colt, and what I said about breeding Ajana to a thoroughbred.'

'I won't forget. What are you riding these days, Cat?' David asked.

'I've outgrown all my ponies and have been riding a polo mare of Stuart's. Dad's always said I should leave getting a new horse until I finish school. I wouldn't mind having a go at dressage but it takes up a lot of time and you need a really good-tempered horse.'

'Yes, dressage is time-consuming,' David agreed.

'I would never have time for it. Any time I get goes into the dogs. Kate's doing more horse work, and she loves it. We can't afford to employ anyone full-time at the moment,' he added, as they walked back up to the house. 'Dad used to break in all our horses. We're all putting in as much as we can right now.'

Inside, Catriona took up her usual position at the table next to David, a place she had reserved ever since she'd first started coming to High Peaks. David was polite enough but not overly friendly. It seemed to Kate that he was keeping Catriona at arm's length. Still, he was only a young man and maybe in a year or two it would be a different story. She couldn't bear to watch him neglecting Catriona. A girl like that wouldn't wait around forever.

Kate often wondered about David. He was a lot deeper than he appeared on the surface. Most people regarded him as the dead spit of his father because of his quiet demeanour, hard work and talent, but Kate knew that David was deeper than Andrew; she knew that he studied books on animal breeding and read bush poetry in his room late at night, even if he didn't talk about it. The stable upbringing that Andy had been deprived of was evident in David's character.

Catriona was furious with David. Her feelings for him were fluctuating almost daily. His seeming indifference to her presence brought tears to her eyes, and she was extremely frustrated to be ignored. She knew that she could bring most adoring young men to heel by ignoring *them* for a period, but how could she handle a young man who ignored *her*?

There had been a time when Catriona was able to confide her innermost thoughts to Susan Cartwright, but this was no longer the case since Susan had become a competitor for David's affections. Catriona had another close friend from Cassilis, Amanda Nelson. The two often came together at social gatherings, especially because Amanda had her eye on Catriona's brother, Stuart.

'Amanda, I must say that David MacLeod is the most maddening person I have ever met,' Catriona told her last time they met. 'He walks around like some kind of guru instead of a sixteen-year-old boy. Even Daddy thinks he is simply wonderful. Can you imagine him talking man-to-man with any other boy David's age? Well, he may be a genius with animals but he is a dumbcluck when it comes to girls. But the thing is, I just can't seem to forget him. I have always had this feeling for David. He has always been there for me.'

'I wonder what your parents would have to say about all this,' Amanda said.

'I wouldn't let them stop me. I know what I feel for him, and nothing is going to change my mind.'

'Catriona! Do you know what you're saying?' Amanda asked, shocked.

'Of course I do. And I happen to know that Susan Cartwright has the same idea. Oh, Daddy would kick and fight right to the end, but if he saw that he couldn't win, I'm sure he would give in and make the best of it.'

'You really think so?' Amanda doubted that Angus Campbell would ever give in.

'I know Daddy very well. If I made him see that I would much rather be with David than any other boy I have met so far, I'm sure he would come around. David is such a divinely genuine person. I am sure he would never play around. Not like some of the boys I know. David and his father are one-woman men. That is what I want, a man who is going to be for me and me alone. It's no good me thinking I can simply forget David. I tell you, Amanda, one way or another, I mean to have him. Oh, he makes me so mad. He talks to me as if I'm his sister. I was going to ask him if he would take me to the ball, but I can't very well do that now with his father so sick.'

'And after that you will be back at school,' Amanda reminded her.

'Yes, another year away from David. I have thought about getting him to write to me. If I write first, surely he'd reply. That might help keep his mind on me.'

Amanda considered Catriona's suggestion. 'That might be a very good idea. You could write and ask David about the horses you looked at. If he answers, you could keep the correspondence going.'

'Quite so. And, you know, his mother, Anne, likes me very much. I think I'd have her support. I can't wait to have my licence and a car of my own so I can drive up to High Peaks without Daddy. All I hope is that while I'm away some other girl doesn't grab David.'

'What other girl would want to live in the hills and take second place to dogs and horses?' Amanda said with a laugh.

'Amanda, I don't think David would be like that. I would be quite happy to forego the social merry-go-round to be Mrs David MacLeod.'

If David was aware of Catriona's interest in him, he said nothing of it. But Kate was aware of exactly what was going on in Catriona's mind. She thought that an outing or two for David would do him the world of good.

But David continued on his way, oblivious to what was going on around him. When Catriona wrote to him from school some weeks later, he replied: *The horses are going well, as I am. Your father saw the black colt and liked him a lot. David.*

Catriona read the two sparse sentences and burst into tears. It was as if David was deliberately going out of his way to be indifferent to her. He had even delayed contacting Angus about the horses until Catriona was back at school. It was Stuart who accompanied his father up to High Peaks to inspect them.

Anne had come home for the day, although Andy was still in hospital and far from out of danger. He had passed through another period of crisis following a second, though less severe, stroke just as they were

308

preparing to take him home. He was now being held in hospital with no news of his homecoming confirmed.

David had the two colts in separate yards when Angus and Stuart arrived. David thought that the black colt gave promise of being something exceptional, but he was quick to point out that it was too soon to assess his full potential.

'He moves very well and has a nice nature, but he needs more time to develop. I reckon he needs another year here.'

'Would you sell him, David?' Angus asked.

'You mean now?'

'Either now or I'll make a down payment on him as a deposit and pay the balance when you reckon he's right,' Angus said.

David shook his head. 'I won't sell him now. It wouldn't be the right thing to do. I'll finish breaking him in and then let him go for a while before I start on him again. Maybe by next Christmas I'll be able to tell you what's in him.'

'Does the same apply to the other colt?'

'I'd say so. Right now we're only guessing what's in them. They're just not ready for you to take away.'

Angus was disappointed that he had not been able to close the deal, but he was respectful of David's decision. He knew that David could use the money, but he wouldn't sell the horse until he really believed it was ready. Angus appreciated that if David gave him the offer of either horse, it would be an offer too good to refuse.

Angus had been right in thinking that the MacLeods' money problems were far from over. They had put virtually every penny they'd made on High Peaks and Poitrel over the past three years into paying off the money they owed Wilf White. The only money they had taken out was for taxation purposes. All of Andy's earnings from shearing before his stroke had also been used to help pay Wilf. The two families depended a great deal on Kate's nursing salary and Anne's occasional teaching. It had been three years of tough, unrelenting grind, during which money was only outlayed for real necessities.

Meanwhile, Andy had come home to High Peaks. He had been weeks and weeks in hospital and was now but a shadow of what he was. It tore at Anne's heart to see him. He was on medication, and always would be, and although the doctors had told her he would improve, Andy would never be able to do some of the things he had taken for granted. Anne felt like crying when she saw him sitting quietly beside the fire in the lounge room or, if the day was sunny, out in one of the easy chairs on the verandah. At first Andy seemed very tired, but gradually his old spirit reasserted itself and he looked to Anne and David to keep him informed about what was happening on the place. Within a fortnight he was taking short walks, mostly to and from the horse yards where he could watch David working.

Anne watched him like a hawk and never allowed him to overexert himself.

Andy's stroke had affected David greatly because he felt partly responsible: Andy had wanted Poitrel so that David could have a better future. For the first time since he was a very small boy, David did not know how to behave around his father. Whereas his mother adjusted with sensitivity to his father's condition, he found it very difficult. Without a response from his father, David could no longer discuss with him the many things they used to. He was both frustrated and remorseful at the sight of his father sitting around for hours, but that was before Anne and Kate began working on him with massages and warm salt baths. They gave him simple exercises, which they kept up until he was able to walk the distance of the horse yards to the gate of the first paddock beyond the dog yards.

David took heart at this small improvement in his father's condition, but it still hurt like hell to know that he would never be the man he once was. They owned, or as good as owned, two properties, but his father was now only half a man. It was a hell of a price to pay for an extra lump of ground. David was more pessimistic about his father's recovery than Anne and Kate were. Anne, buoyed up by Kate's insistence that Andy would improve, threw herself heart and soul into improving her husband's condition, both mentally and physically. She gave him all the news of the area and outlined what David

was doing each day. So gradually some of Andy's fire came back. To begin with it was more like a spark than a fire, but Andy was too good a man to be laid low for long.

Not long after David's altercation with the drovers, he obtained his driving licence, and with it the independence of driving himself about. As soon as he had the licence, he began looking for local crutching and shearing work to help the family out financially. He was mostly well liked in the area, and people who knew his father's reputation were keen to give David a go, too. David tried not to resent the time he spent away from home working, but he was always aware of what he would rather be doing with his dogs and horses, and he was always disappointed by the fact that no matter how hard he worked, there was never enough money coming in. The problem was how they could get more.

And then, out of the blue, a solution presented itself, but David would have to make the toughest decision of his life.

Chapter Sixteen

David MacLeod, like his father, always had supreme faith in the working kelpie. And David, like his father, also regarded the kelpie as heaven-sent for Australia's wool industry. David dreamed from his early years that he would one day win the National, Australia's greatest sheepdog trial, with a kelpie. He sought this prize not only because it would set the seal on the quality of the MacLeod kelpies, but also in honour of his father, who had never been able to work at the National Trials himself. Through all his family's trials and setbacks, the dream of working great kelpies at the National was never far from David's mind.

Bush dogs have anything but easy lives. The mortality rate is high. David had the misfortune to lose some very good dogs over the years, each loss tearing at his heart a little more, as well as affecting his breeding endeavours. By the time he was seventeen

years old, the best dog David had ever bred was
Nap. Nap, a red and tan male, was a brilliant dog
with a great cast and a lovely way of shifting sheep.
He would work anywhere, and every sheepdog
handler who saw the dog said that without a doubt
he was as good as they come. David had won the
last local trial with Nap, and a couple of visiting
dog handlers had spread the word about the dog's
ability.

Just after David had turned seventeen, he received
the following letter in the mail.

'Jimbawarra'
Deniliquin NSW 2710

Dear Mr MacLeod,

*You may be aware that I have a large kelpie
stud and send dogs all over Australia. I also
export a large number of dogs. The perpetuation
of my stud depends on my ability to maintain
the highest possible standards, and from time to
time I have purchased several top-quality dogs
and bitches. I believe that money is no object for
the right dog.*

*I am writing to you because I have received
several highly complimentary reports about your
kelpie Nap.*

I would be very interested in seeing this dog,
and if he is as good as I have been told,
I would like to purchase him for use in
my stud.

I would appreciate it if you would contact me
at your earliest convenience regarding this
matter.

Yours sincerely,

Bruce McClymont

David read the letter through twice and then folded it and placed it in his shirt pocket. He was not a person who made snap decisions where the sale of animals was concerned, and this offer was too important to take lightly. David had never considered selling Nap – the dog was simply too good to part with and too important for David's future plans. He and Nap operated on the same wavelength. Nap would never understand if he were sent away. The more David thought about Bruce McClymont's offer, the more he felt that he shouldn't sell Nap for any price.

That night, he showed Mr McClymont's letter to his mother. 'Why, David, what a name Nap has made. You wouldn't be thinking seriously of selling him, would you?'

'Under normal conditions, no. There wouldn't be enough money in the world to buy him. But you know how tight things are right now. Of course it depends on just what McClymont is willing to pay. When I think of what Dad did so we could get Poitrel, I feel ashamed of trying to hold on to Nap. I'm wondering if I could lease him for a certain period, so that I could still get him back later on.'

'That's a good idea, but you'd need to have it done legally. I haven't any idea what this man is like, although I do know that some dog people are anything but honest,' Anne said.

'You're right, Mum. I'll make some enquiries, and if people say McClymont is to be trusted, I might put a proposition to him.'

'That's very wise, Davie, but I want you to know that neither Andy nor I would push you into selling Nap. We know how much he means to you. We'll manage without you having to let him go.'

'I know, thanks. We do have pups on the ground by Nap so I can go on with them. I did want to mate him to Belle but she was too young last time. Nap is important to me, but if I have to wait a bit longer to get to the National, so be it.'

David talked with several of his father's old mates and established that Bruce McClymont, though a big seller of dogs, was an honest man who could be trusted. A few nights later David sat down and penned a note to the Riverina breeder.

Dear Mr McClymont,

Thank you for your letter and kind remarks
about Nap. We think he is a very good dog and
almost up to the top kelpies of the past.

I have considered your offer very carefully and
have decided that I would not consider selling
Nap outright as I have big plans for him.
However, I would lease him to you for three
years for the sum of $3000.

I wouldn't let Nap go sight unseen, so you
would have to come and inspect him. If he
is what you want, you could take him away
with you.

Nap is to be returned by you, in good condition,
three years to the day on which you take him.
Knowing the dog as I do, I believe you could
breed a lot of very good dogs by him over a
three-year period. If these conditions are
satisfactory, I expect I will hear from you
soon.

Yours sincerely,

David MacLeod

317

David had composed the letter after consultation with his mother. Anne doubted that McClymont would come at the $3000, but, as David pointed out, if they didn't get a worthwhile lease fee, why let the dog go? They could earn more than that from the pups Nap would sire over the next three years.

A week later they received a phone call to advise them that Bruce McClymont would be driving up to High Peaks to inspect Nap, and if he was as good as he was supposed to be, he would accept the conditions set out in David's letter.

'I'll bet McClymont hasn't owned a dog as good as Nap,' David said to his mother when she told him about the call.

'Your father won't know what to say if this deal comes off,' Anne said. 'He never got anything like that money for the best of his dogs.'

'That was then and this is now,' David said. 'People seem to have a lot more money these days. Trials are bigger affairs now, too,' he said.

'You had better get an agreement drafted up before McClymont arrives,' Anne advised. 'You can't be too careful. I shall tell Andy all about it. It might cheer him up a bit.'

Andy had not been able to speak properly since his stroke but he could hear perfectly well. Anne spent several hours each day relating all the news to her husband. David still felt uncomfortable conducting a one-way conversation with his father. What he wanted was his father's opinion, and he would get frustrated when he could not obtain it.

Anne had taken him aside and had a few words with him. 'David, it would be a big help if you told your father what you proposed to do each day, and gave him an account of the day's activities. Just because he's had a stroke doesn't mean he's not interested in whether there's feed in the hills or how the sheep look.'

'Okay, Mum. I guess I've been a bit shy of talking to Dad.'

'I know, son. It's difficult for us all, adjusting to this new situation. But don't forget that on the inside Dad is just the same as he ever was.'

The year that had led up to his seventeenth birthday had been a traumatic one for David. Now this letter from the Riverina was yet another complex consideration.

'I haven't given up my dream of winning the National,' David told his mother. 'It will just have to wait a bit longer, that's all. We need the three thousand dollars. It's as simple as that.'

'David, that's a very tall order. No kelpie has won the National since Athol Butler won it with Johnny, and Dad always said that Butler was a genius.'

'Yes, and Johnny won it five times. That's proof that a kelpie can do it.'

'But wasn't it Butler's handling that won those trials?' Anne asked.

'No matter how good a handler is, you can't win a trial like that without a very good dog that has been well schooled. I know our dogs can do it. What they

319

have to do here is far tougher than anything they'd face in Canberra.'

'But there are so many good handlers at those big trials. You can put up a brilliant score and still not make it to the final heat,' Anne said.

'If a fella has top dogs and can handle them, he will win good trials sooner or later. I'll know when a dog is ready to take to Canberra. Right now our first priority is paying our way, and if I have to put off big-time trialling for a few years in order to do that, it isn't such a high price to pay for what we have now.'

'I admire your outlook tremendously, David, and I want you to know that Dad and Kate and I all think it's very mature of you to let Nap go.'

Bruce McClymont came to inspect Nap a few days later. It was a very steamy morning with the threat of a storm in the air. David had been up since daylight checking sheep. Flies were a problem and he had ridden the bottom country looking at the ewes. After breakfast he put a few wethers in the paddock above the house and then cut off a mob and ran them down to the yards. He reckoned McClymont would want to see Nap work in the yards as well as outside.

The new Ford utility came up the road at about nine-thirty a.m.; McClymont had spent the night at the Federal in Merriwa. The utility was complete with a very substantial mesh crate which was covered by a double roof. In between, there was a layer of some kind of material to cut down the heat, and the front of the crate was closed in so the dogs were protected from the cold air. There was also a thick chain and a padlock on the crate's mesh door. It was a very professional set-up. David was impressed.

Bruce McClymont was a man of medium height with sandy hair and bright, hazel-grey eyes. He had a restless manner that had caused some of his neighbours to dub him Mr Perpetual Motion.

'I'm looking for David MacLeod,' he said as he got out of the Ford. 'Am I in the right place?'

'Yes, this is the right place, and I am David MacLeod,' David said, holding out his hand.

'You surprise me. I expected an older person,' McClymont said.

'I started very young, Mr McClymont,' David replied. 'Come with me and I'll show you Nap.'

They walked down the track to where the dogs were housed. Most of them were in their logs under the shady trees. David walked over to where the big red and tan dog was lying on top of his log. His head was between his paws and his eyes never left David's face.

'This is Nap,' David said as he unclipped the dog. 'Come on, Nap, jump down. Sit.' The dog obeyed immediately.

'I've put some sheep on the hill behind the house. Dad reckons that when a dog can cast either way up this hill it's ready to take to a trial. Being hill-country sheep, their natural inclination is to get back to the hills after they've had a drink,' David explained.

'Those six wethers have been grazed in the paddock through that far fence. They want to get back to it. I thought that would give you an idea of Nap's strength and holding ability because they'll want to keep breaking back up the hill.'

'Will he cast that far?' McClymont asked. 'It must be a quarter-mile or more.'

David's smile was fleeting. 'Nap will cast a lot further than that. All our dogs will run out of sight.'

David sat Nap about twenty yards behind him and then sent him away to the right. Nap raced up the fence, cleared the six wethers by about fifty yards and finished right behind them. He stopped there and waited while the wethers stamped their feet and milled about. David leant against the fence and watched proceedings with what seemed only casual interest.

Then Nap edged forward a little and the wethers turned away. One sheep broke out to the side and Nap gathered him in neatly. In under five minutes, Nap had the six wethers directly in front of them. David had not given Nap a single command after he had cast him away. Instead, he had sat on the log seat his father had constructed years earlier and watched Bruce McClymont's reaction.

'Can you move him around?' McClymont asked.

'Sure. Nap, back.' Nap moved from right to left and stopped.

'Nap, behind.' This time Nap moved from where he was back to the right, his original position.

'Is he as good in the yard as he is in the paddock?'

'Oh, I think so. He'll back all day but he's too good to make a welter of that sort of work. All our dogs will work in the yard and the shed. Our main priority is outside work. Up here we often ride for a week to pick up the last of our sheep. If our dogs couldn't cast, and if they didn't have the right field work, we would never get them. I've put some wethers in the yard so you can see what he'll do.'

They walked down the hill to the wool shed and its yards. David opened some gates and clicked to his dog. Nap speared over the nearest fence and went in behind the sheep in one of the forcing pens.

'Speak, Nap,' David commanded.

Nap let out a big bark which galvanised the wethers into action. They shot down the long drafting race and David sent Nap over their backs.

'Speak, Nap.' Nap barked again to push the wethers tightly into the race and then came back over the top of them. David then opened the gate of the race and sent Nap up the side. He barked through the race as he ran along the side. 'Up, Nap.' Nap jumped onto the side of the race and balanced himself on the rail. 'Speak. Stay, Nap.' Nap stayed where he was but barked to urge the sheep down the race.

'Anything else?' David asked, after Nap had dutifully completed all his tasks.

'I've seen enough,' McClymont said. 'He's a lovely dog.'

'He's not bad. I've taught him a few tricks, like carrying a stockwhip in his mouth and jumping on my back. I'll show you.'

He bent over and Nap jumped on his back and sat there. 'Off, Nap.'

Nap jumped down and stood looking up at his owner.

'Is there anything he can't do?' McClymont asked.

'Not too much. The thing is that Nap is a really brainy dog. He uses his head. That's what I like in a dog.'

'If I can breed dogs as good as he is, I'll be even happier. Are all your dogs as good as he is?'

'Some of Dad's old dogs were better than Nap.'

'What about your bitches?'

'No difference. If they aren't good, we don't use them,' David said simply.

'Will you work one for me?' McClymont asked.

'Sure. There's a young bitch here that hasn't done much work yet. She wouldn't be twelve months old. Her name's Belle. I think she'll be a good one.'

They walked back to the dog yard and David clipped Nap up to his log. He walked down the line to where a young blue bitch was tied to another log.

'This is Belle,' David said.

'She has a very short tail,' McClymont commented. 'And what is that funny mark on her forehead?'

'You get both of those characteristics in our dogs. They came in from the Quinn and King and McLeod dogs. There seems to be more of both of those traits in our dogs than in anyone else's.'

'I'll put her on those same six sheep that Nap worked. They should be okay for her,' David said.

Belle moved over the ground like a wraith. She made no sound at all and she seemed to have the sheep mesmerised. David moved away about six feet and Belle moved about the same distance to bring herself into line with him.

'Belle had perfect balance from the first day she started working,' David explained. 'She's a real good bitch in the making.'

'She looks a beauty,' McClymont agreed. 'As good as Nap.'

'Better, in some ways, although she doesn't have his strength and push. She is all class and would be a great bitch on fast-breaking western Queensland-type sheep.'

'Would you sell her to me?' McClymont asked.

David shook his head. 'I'm sorry, no. Not to you nor to anyone else. Belle is not for sale.'

'Put a price on her.'

'No, Mr McClymont, I won't. When you bring Nap back to me I'm going to mate him to Belle and breed a kelpie to win the National.'

McClymont looked at MacLeod in amazement. Was this young fellow for real? Certainly MacLeod had shown him the two best kelpies he had seen in a long while, but surely he was having himself on now.

'No kelpie has won the National since Johnny's

last win in 1952,' McClymont pointed out.

'I'm aware of that,' David said. 'However, we have the dogs here that can do it. You've seen two of them. Have you ever seen any border collies any better than Nap and Belle?'

'Now you put it that way, I haven't. The problem is that kelpies don't seem to perform as well at trials as they do at home. They get too stirry.'

'Mine won't,' David said calmly.

'One thing I can promise you – if you ever win the National, I'll be there to see it. And I'll be offering you more money for your winning dog than any kelpie has ever been sold for and then some. Can I order a pup from Belle?' he asked.

'You might have to wait a while. We may not breed from her without Nap here, and I'd like to run her at our local trial.'

McClymont had a sudden thought. 'Tell me, why do you think you can breed your National winner from Belle by Nap?'

David smiled enigmatically. 'Practical reasons, to begin with, and my own intuition. Now, you'll have lunch with us, won't you?'

'If it's no trouble,' McClymont replied.

'It's no trouble. My aunt Kate is with Mum today. She's a director of the partnership and she's also a nursing sister. She's been a big help with Dad.'

McClymont nodded in sympathy. 'It was tough him getting hit like that. I was looking forward to talking to your dad. I've heard the MacLeod name mentioned ever since I started in this business. You must have learnt a lot from him.'

'Everything I know,' David said. 'Dad is the best dog and horse man in the district, and a fair way beyond that, but I doubt he'll ever work a dog again. Come on, let's go down to the house.'

When they had finished lunch, McClymont took out his cheque book and wrote out a cheque for $3000. David looked at it and then handed it straight to his mother. Andy was sitting nearby, propped up in a big lounge chair.

'This is the cheque for Nap, Andy,' she said.

Andrew looked at the cheque and his eyes widened. He made a valiant effort to speak and, after several unsuccessful croaks, they all heard him speak the words, 'Good dog, Nap.' They were the first decipherable words he had spoken since his stroke.

'Andy!' Anne said with a lovely smile. David had not seen her smile much at all these past few months.

'Look here, David, I won't hold you up any longer,' McClymont said. 'I want to be home in the morning. We've got crutching coming up and there's a South Australian chap coming to look at a dog.'

David and Mr McClymont walked back to the kennels and David unhooked Nap to let him have a quick run around before jumping him up into the utility. He patted him on the head and then stood back while McClymont closed and locked the door of the crate.

'I'll look after him, David. When I bring him back

here he'll look just as he does now, barring accidents, of course. You can never tell what will go wrong but I'll sure do my best by him and watch him closely. I've got plenty of dogs, as you know, so I won't work the tripe out of him. I want Nap for a sire and to show off to my clients. Have you any special advice?'

'Show him off in the open on a few wild sheep. Nap should cast out of sight in your country,' David said.

'Any hints on the breeding side?' McClymont knew that for all his money and the name he had built up for himself, what he lacked was MacLeod's innate ability.

'It would be worth putting Nap back over his best daughter before you bring him back. You could put a son of that mating with a bitch from Belle and that should give you a top breeding family. But don't sell the inbred pups to anyone else. If the mating works, you could get anything. You should keep them and use them to stay on top.'

'I might try it. Never done a close mating like that before. Never had a dog as good as Nap before.'

David handed him an envelope. 'This is Nap's pedigree.'

'Thanks, David, I'll have him back here three years to the day.'

'I'll expect you to. If you have any trouble with him, give us a ring. Have a safe trip and good luck with him. You might let me know how you get on with him and how his pups are shaping.'

'I'll do that. It's been a real pleasure meeting you.' He waved to Anne and Kate, who were standing beside Andrew's chair on the front verandah.

'I sure hope your father improves. I would like to have a yarn to him one day,' McClymont said as he got into his car.

David watched him pull away. Nap was standing at the back of the crate with his nose pressed through the wire. He watched the dog until he could no longer see him, a deep ache burning inside his chest. He felt terrible about letting the dog go. Nap wouldn't understand why he'd been sent away. And what David feared most was that Nap would never return. Snakes were deadly on dogs. Yet when he thought again of how his father had sacrificed himself so that the MacLeod family could have a more secure future, it was small of him to feel guilty about Nap. A bloke had to be a man about these things. His decision had been made, and that was that. At least McClymont would promote the hell out of Nap, and his owner.

'He was a nice man, David,' Anne said as he walked back up the steps to the house.

'Yeah, he seemed all right. Dad say anything more?' he asked.

'Just a word or two,' Anne said. 'It's a start.'

David sat on a chair beside his father and told him what he had done and where Nap was headed. When he had finished, David distinctly heard his father say, 'Good boy.'

Those words cheered him up a little. Andrew had never been known to hand out praise lightly. Although people always said that his father was a hard man, they also said he was a fair one. David did not want to be known as a hard man. A fair man and an honest man, yes. But sometimes you had to be hard to survive. He knew he had not done the right thing by Nap. The dog loved him and he had sent him away. Animals often suffered for humans; they were regarded as expendable. Nap had trusted him and he had let him down. It was as simple as that.

His father had once told him that he should never lose his heart to a dog, but the problem was that Nap was alive, and tonight – and every other night – that good, brainy dog would be wondering why he wasn't back at his log kennel. Life was damned hard.

Chapter Seventeen

Life at High Peaks and Poitrel went on in much the same way as it had always done. There were good seasons, fair seasons and poor seasons, and High Peaks Pastoral Company weathered the troughs and moved closer to financial independence. The wool market climbed out of its lethargy, the cattle market picked up, and the governor-general kicked out Gough Whitlam in favour of Victorian grazier–politician Malcolm Fraser. For people on the land, it was a time of rejoicing.

David had sowed fifty additional acres of lucerne and was now able to make hay on both High Peaks and Poitrel. Angus Campbell had the equipment for haymaking, and his men cut and baled David's lucerne. In return, David had taken the place of his father in breaking-in the Campbell horses. Having a shedful of good hay had been a real bonus: there were always horses in feed, and in the poor seasons they were able to utilise some of the hay to feed their cows.

Andrew had made a remarkable, although partial, recovery. His speech had developed so that he could speak in halting sentences, which often took some understanding. He had also gained some mobility and could even do odd light jobs, like feeding the fowls and the dogs, but he did tire easily and he could not use his right arm well. Still, as Anne said, he was improving.

David seemed to take everything in his stride. Andy's stroke put the kybosh on David staying at school. He left at the end of Year 11. He never wanted to leave the two properties, and except for local shearing and crutching jobs – and the local show and sheepdog trials – he almost never did. He had worked Belle at the local trial and had won both the Maiden and the Open Trials with her at her first outing. His father had performed this feat three times and David was the first person since his father to take out the double.

The following year, David again won the Open with Belle and scored 99 with her in the final – the highest score anyone could remember being awarded at that venue. When he came off the ground, his father, who had been watching quietly from the side-lines, clapped him on the back with his good left hand. This was the first gesture of its kind from Andy, and David felt that he was beginning to get somewhere.

Bruce McClymont had written to David and

informed him that Nap had settled down quite well and was receiving positive comment from anyone who saw him work. One of Nap's sons had won a trial at Narrandera, and several other of his pups had been exported. Needless to say, Bruce McClymont was over the moon when David told him how Belle had done in the local trial.

Catriona Campbell had finally come home from boarding school. She was now eighteen and an extremely beautiful young woman.

One day not long after she had arrived back at Inverlochy, she took a drive to High Peaks in the new car her father had promised her. It was a yellow Holden and she was very proud of it.

'Hello, Mrs Mac, Mr Mac,' she said as she pulled up in the driveway. She greeted them warmly and then kissed them both.

'Catriona, it's lovely to see you,' Anne replied. 'I heard that you were home. Finished with boarding school at long last?'

'At long last. It seemed to go on forever,' Catriona said.

'What are you going to do with yourself now?' Anne asked as she scrutinised the girl. Catriona now spoke, walked and behaved quite beautifully.

'I'm not sure. Daddy is keen for me to go to university, but I don't fancy going just for the sake of it. I should go because I really want to. I once thought about doing vet science but my marks weren't high enough. I may take a trip overseas and see how I feel when I get back. Daddy suggested that as an option, and I think it's a good idea to go before I have too many other commitments.'

'I see. Where would you go?'

'Oh, Britain and Europe, I think. Daddy has relatives in Scotland and I could stay with them for a while. I'd like to have a look at the Western Isles and the Scottish Highlands. Daddy said that he and Mummy might come over and join me for a little while. I believe Daddy is thinking of importing another border collie and he wants to see a trial or two. By the way, where is David?'

'Out looking at sheep. He'll be here for lunch, though. Can you stay? Would you like to come inside?'

'I told Mummy I might. I thought David might show me the black horse. I understand he's been gelded. If I like him, Daddy will buy him for me for a show horse,' Catriona said, looking out towards the horse yard. 'Does he still think the black will make a show horse?'

'You'll have to talk to David about his plans for the horse. I don't interfere at all with that side of things. David is more than capable. He hasn't put a foot wrong since his father's been laid low.'

'Mrs Mac, I think Mr Mac is trying to say something,' Catriona said.

Anne saw her husband signalling to her from his big leather chair which had been placed on the front verandah with a perfect view over High Peaks.

'What is it, Andy?' she asked.

'David . . . black horse . . . bottom paddock,' he croaked.

'David has taken the black gelding down to the bottom paddock where the breeding ewes are,' Anne translated. 'What do you say we take a little walk and see if we can catch him coming up the slope? Andy, will you be all right here?'

Andrew gave a slow nod and a wise little smile.

'Okay, I'll go and get my hat,' Anne said.

Together Anne and Catriona walked out past the horse yard and down the track that led to the front gate. The track forked there and the left path led down past the foal paddock to the bottom country. It was a downhill slope all the way to the Inverlochy–Poitrel road. Once past the foal paddock there was an uninterrupted view where a rider could be seen for well over a mile.

'David shouldn't be long,' Anne said. 'He told me he would be back for early lunch.'

'It's all right, Mrs Mac. I don't mind waiting.' Catriona would have waited forever if she had thought he was interested in her. What made it worse was that somewhere, deep down, she felt that David did like her – if only he would let on to her. There had to be some reason for David's indifference and she meant to find out what it was.

Anne took Catriona's arm and pointed down the slope. She could just pick out a small black speck that grew marginally larger as she watched.

'David's on his way. You'll see a great sight very shortly. That black horse is really an eye-catcher.'

Catriona watched horse and rider as they came up the slope.

'Did you ever see anything like the canter on that?' Anne asked. The black horse was on a fairly loose rein but moving with a slow, rocking canter just as if he were parading for a judge in the show ring. He had grown a lot since Catriona had seen him last, and now looked magnificent. By the way the horse was moving, David must have put in a lot of work on him. She had never seen a finer combination.

'Isn't he splendid?' Catriona said with her eyes aglow.

'Splendid,' Anne agreed, but it seemed to her that Catriona's eyes were focused more on David than the black gelding. And then in one easy movement David was on the ground and standing beside them. Catriona hardly recognised him.

'Hello, Cat,' he said casually.

'Hello yourself,' she replied. 'Do you know you are still the only person who calls me Cat, mountain man?'

'You will always be Cat to me,' he said. 'Why aren't you in riding clobber?'

'What, you want to go riding? I thought you were far too busy to devote any time to me,' she said and nudged Anne.

'Do they teach sarcasm at boarding school along with a swanky voice?'

'Sorry, David, but you never once asked me to go riding with you.'

'Since when have I had to?'

'I don't go anywhere unless I am asked,' Catriona said very firmly. 'Besides, as you may have noticed, I am not a little girl any more.'

'I'm not blind, and I'm not asking you to go riding with me. I asked why you weren't dressed to go riding. I thought you wanted to try the black horse. Your father has pestered the daylight out of me about him. Anyway, to what do we owe the pleasure of your company?'

'Who is being sarcastic now? And condescending?'

'Hey, you two,' Anne cut in sharply. 'You haven't seen each other for months and you're sparring like Kilkenny cats. David, when you've finished with your horse, would you come up to the house? Catriona is staying for lunch. Please don't be long.'

'Righto.' David walked off leading the black horse, and the two women watched him all the way to the horse yard.

'My goodness, David has grown since I saw him last, and he certainly has his wits about him,' Catriona said.

'Never underestimate him, Catriona. He is very much his own man. He's had to be. Come on, let's go eat.'

After lunch – during which David had shown more interest in what was on his plate than on who was sitting beside him – Catriona asked if she could have another look at the horse.

'Having second thoughts, Cat?' David asked. 'Something about him you don't like?'

'Not at all. I'd just like to see him unsaddled,' Catriona said.

Anne looked at her from across the table and then at her son. She was sure Catriona didn't want to look at the horse – she wanted to get David on his own.

As they walked down to the horse yard, Catriona turned and walked past the stables and on to the wool shed.

'You won't find the black horse there, Cat,' David said.

'I don't want to see the horse, David. I don't have to. He's magnificent. I want to ask you something else. It's a favour.'

'All this doubletalk to ask me a favour. What is it?' he asked bluntly.

'David, would you escort me to the Debutantes' Ball?'

David looked at her as if she had asked him to destroy one of his dogs. 'Why ever would you ask *me* to escort *you* to that kind of function?'

'Because I have known you longer than almost any other boy. And, besides, I thought you might like to.'

'Is there something particularly important about this ball? I mean, other than the fact that you and some other girls will be coming out, or whatever the term is?'

'It's a very big occasion for a girl. Why do you ask?'

'Susan Cartwright has also asked me,' he said.

'You're escorting Susan?' Catriona asked. She couldn't believe it.

'No, I'm not. And I won't escort you either.'

'Why not? I don't have two heads, do I?'

'Don't fish for compliments, Cat. Your appearance has nothing to do with it. I've no doubt you'll be the best-looking girl on show. Susan won't be far behind.'

'Then why won't you escort me?'

'Have you discussed this with your family?' David asked.

'No, not yet.'

'I thought not. Beats me what you learned at that fancy boarding school. Let's get a few things straight. You people – and that includes the Cartwrights – move in a different social circle to us. That doesn't mean I think we're inferior. The thing is, your parents didn't send you away to boarding school for years so that you would come home and ask David MacLeod to escort you to the Debs' Ball. They would hit the roof. Now, I understand that making your debut is important for you, and it should be a very happy occasion, but it wouldn't be if I was insensitive enough to say yes to your invitation. So I am sorry, Cat, but I must decline.'

'It's a pretty poor show when a girl can't have who she wants as her escort,' Catriona said.

'I'm sorry, but the only way I would ever agree is if your father invited me on your behalf – and that he would never do.'

'David, I've always got on very well with your

339

family, especially your mother. I do not consider myself to be a snob. You were the first boy I thought of to escort me to the ball. No doubt Susan had the same idea.'

David shook his head. 'What you and Susan want and what your parents will want will be very different.'

'I am so disappointed. I had set my heart on you escorting me.'

'Discuss it with your parents, Cat. We will, of course, be there to see you make your debut,' David said with a grin.

'Who will?' Catriona asked.

'Mum, Dad, Kate, Jean and me.'

'You are going?'

'Oh, yes. I'll be looking after Dad. He'll want to be there but he tires easily these days.'

'You are *beastly*, David! You'll be there large as life and yet you won't escort me.'

'There will be more than you to look at, Cat. Quite a few pretty girls, I'm told.'

'If I had something in my hand, I would throw it at you,' Catriona said. It was clear that David was not going to escort her to the ball. Why does everything have to be so difficult? she thought. At least he wasn't going to escort Susan either, which was something of a relief. And then she remembered the second reason for her visit to High Peaks.

'Will you let me ride your black horse?' she asked.

'You mean now? In that dress?'

'Of course not, you ninny. I could come back tomorrow.'

'I suppose I could stretch a point and let you ride him.'

'Ha, very decent of you. Can I bring Daddy with me?'

'You can bring anyone you like. What time tomorrow?'

'In the morning, if that suits you. Say about ten,' she suggested.

'Ten is fine. You going back to the house?'

'Yes, I want to talk to your mother.'

'Then I'll see you tomorrow, Cat. There's things I've got to do here now.'

Catriona ran back to the house in high dudgeon. Anne could tell that something was amiss. The usually serene Catriona was close to tears.

'Catriona, what is it? Surely you and David haven't been arguing again. Has he said something to upset you?'

'I asked him to escort me to the Debutantes' Ball and he refused. He said I should have asked my parents.'

'Oh, you too,' Anne said sympathetically.

'So you know that Susan also asked David?'

'Yes, dear. David gave her the same answer he gave you.'

'I suppose I have to be thankful for that. It would have been the end if he had agreed to take Susan. She would never let me forget it. Oh, Mrs Mac, I

341

had set my heart on David escorting me.'

'Did he explain why he won't escort you?' Anne asked.

'Yes. But it's my night and I can't see why I can't have the boy of my choice.'

'I'm sorry to see you so disappointed, but I must say that I agree with him. Not because he's my son but because I think he's right. Angus and Jane will be expecting you to choose a boy they approve of.'

'It's ridiculous.'

'I understand what you must be feeling, Catriona. I was a girl once and I recognise that your feelings can override your commonsense. Either you and Susan are engaged in some private feud over David or you both like him more than you are letting on.'

'Oh, Mrs Mac, Susan is my best friend. I wouldn't feud with her. I know she likes David a whole lot, and that's that.'

'What about you, Catriona? Do you like him a lot, too?'

'More than a lot. I think I'm in love with him.'

'Does David have any idea about this?'

'I'm never sure where I stand with him. He either ignores me or does something madly heroic on my behalf. I've had at least a dozen boys try to kiss me and two proposals of marriage, yet David has never so much as touched me.'

'Or, I should add, any other girl,' Anne pointed out.

'How long can that go on? You know what men

are like and you must know what some girls will do.'

'Would you do anything for David?' Anne asked.

'If I knew he loved me, wanted me, yes I would,' Catriona said.

'Oh, dear. I don't know what to say. But I do know that David doesn't want to get married for some time. He wants to work his dogs at the National. It's as if he wants to get that out of the way before he begins the next stage of his life. You see, Catriona, he really wants to win the National for Andy. That means a lot to him.'

'You know him best, Mrs Mac. Do you think he likes me at all?'

'Of course he does, dear. It's just that David isn't ready to tell you. I realise it must be infuriating for you, but I can only suggest that if you love David, you must be prepared to wait for him. Do your parents have any idea of your feelings for him?' Anne asked.

'I suspect Mummy might have some inclination, but Daddy has other things in mind for me.'

'So if it comes to the crunch, what would you do?'

'If David ever told me that he loved me and wanted to marry me, there would be no decision to make.'

'You'd marry David against your parents' wishes?'

'I certainly would.'

'Do you think you'll feel the same way in a year's time or even three years' time? You might have to wait that long.'

'I'm sure this is not just a crush, Mrs Mac. I've

always had feelings for David, ever since I was a child, but what I feel for him now is something quite different. But, please, you won't mention it to anyone, will you? I don't want David to know about it.'

'It will be a secret between the two of us,' Anne said, putting her arm around Catriona's shoulders. 'I must tell you that nothing would give me greater pleasure than to see you marry David.'

'Really? That means a lot to me. Thank you.'

'There is one other thing, Catriona.'

'What is it, Mrs Mac?'

'I think it's about time you started calling me Anne.'

'Very well, Anne. I'll see you tomorrow. I'm coming back to ride the black horse,' Catriona said as she turned to leave.

'Good. I'm sure you'll like him.'

As Anne and Catriona walked out to the verandah, Catriona stopped and said, 'Anne, you seem to know a lot about the MacLeods' background. Would you mind telling me more about it some time?'

'Not at all. Actually, I have it all written down. I managed to get quite a bit out of Andy and I found some records his mother had kept. I think it's important to keep a family record, especially when the history of that family can be traced back over a thousand years. You must come to dinner one night and I'll tell you everything I know.'

Anne stood thoughtfully on the front verandah for a long while after Catriona had driven off. She cherished the hope that David and Catriona would one day come to love each other and marry, despite opposition from Angus and Jane. She resolved to speak to David about Catriona's visit for the following day.

That evening, as soon as dinner was over, she tackled him about his attitude. 'David, having delivered one brickbat to Catriona today, I do hope you'll be more friendly to her tomorrow, especially with Angus in tow. You know you have disappointed her deeply,' she said.

'Yes, I'll be nice to her. Angus, too. No brickbats, perhaps a bouquet,' David said with a laugh.

Anne gave him a quick, critical glance. 'I'm not sure that I like the sound of that. I do hope you're not plotting some mischief.'

'I wouldn't call it mischief, Mum.'

'Hmm. Now you have got me worried. Please don't do anything to get Angus off side, David.'

'I'm going to serve him up some of his own medicine, Mum.'

'Oh, David, please believe me when I tell you that it is not in your best interests to offend him.'

'He won't be offended by what I do tomorrow, but he might be when Catriona tells him I knocked her back for the Debs' Ball.'

'You should get the cheque from him before she gives him that bit of news.'

'I'm sure I will. Cat won't tell him before tomorrow. She wants that black horse.'

Chapter Eighteen

The following morning, Catriona arrived with her father and she was fully decked out for riding.

'Morning, Mr Campbell, Cat,' David greeted them.

Catriona gave him a quick glance, noting that he seemed to be in high spirits today.

'Hello, David. How are you faring these days?' Angus asked.

'Getting there, Mr Campbell. Prices are on the up and the seasons are fair. The wool traveller told me they reckon wool might go up a bit more.'

'So I've heard,' Angus agreed. 'Now, where have you got this great horse?'

'In his stable. I didn't saddle him as I asked Cat to bring her own gear. I've got the liver chestnut saddled up for you to try, too, Mr Campbell.'

'Good heavens, I'd forgotten about him. What's he like?'

'He's a nice-going horse and good on his feet. No vices and you can cut out a beast with him. He hasn't got the same class as the black horse but he's as good as most going about. You don't have to take him if you don't want him. I could sell him tomorrow.'

'What do you want for him?'

'A thousand.'

'I'll try him, David.'

'Okay, I'll get him and King while Cat's getting her gear.'

'Is King what you've called the black horse?' Catriona asked.

'If I were going to ride him in the show ring, I would call him King o' the Night.'

'Where on earth did you dig up that name?' Catriona asked, arching her long eyebrows.

'If you read the history of England and its legends, you would find that the King of the Night is mentioned before the Romans invaded Britain. I thought King o' the Night would be a real good name for a black horse.'

Angus and Catriona looked at him in surprise. 'I had no idea you were interested in that sort of thing, David,' Catriona remarked.

'I'm pretty keen on a lot of English poetry.'

David went down to the stables and came back with the two geldings. The liver chestnut was a nice stock horse and would have taken a few eyes if paraded on his own, but he was very much over-shadowed by King.

Angus walked around both horses while David was saddling King with Catriona's gear.

'What is he, David? Sixteen hands?' Angus asked.

'A touch over, Mr Campbell.'

When the horse was saddled, David handed the reins to Catriona and stepped away from the horse. 'King is very light in the mouth and ribs, Cat. So is the chestnut, Angus. Take them out through the gate to Creek Paddock and work them there. You'll find a cleared ring where I work the horses. I'll open the gate.'

The two horses stood stock-still as Catriona and Angus mounted. 'Just a touch, Cat, and he'll go,' David said. He walked alongside the horses and opened the gate that gave them access to the first of the hill country paddocks. Beyond this were the foothills below Yellow Rock. There was not a cloud in the sky and the rugged, scrub-covered peak stood out starkly against the sky. It was a warm day, although not as warm as it would be later.

David watched the two riders as they walked their horses down to his work circle. Catriona was dressed in grey riding trousers, a cream silk blouse and long leather riding boots. Her brown eyes were sparkling beneath her wide-brimmed grey Akubra. He thought she looked a picture.

David sat down on a log and watched father and daughter work out his horses. Catriona put King through his paces, all of which he performed perfectly. David didn't pay much attention to Angus;

he just didn't have it as a rider, and the chestnut was really too good for him.

Catriona cantered back with a flushed face and a flashing smile. 'David, King is just great. What a canter he has. You could go to sleep on him. He's more horse than anything I've been on.'

'He's not bad for what he's done,' David said.

'You like him, Catriona?' Angus asked.

'I love him, Daddy. He's easily the best horse I've ever ridden.'

'How do you like the chestnut, Mr Campbell?' David asked.

'He's a good horse, David. I'd have to work him on cattle to get a really good idea of his ability, but he seems a smart horse.'

'I can soon run a few steers up. I'll show you what he can do and then you can try him out yourself.'

'No need for that, your word is good enough for me. If you say he'll cut out a beast, I know he will. He's better than anything I've got.'

David reckoned that was a safe bet. Angus was inclined to ride gentle horses and would let Stuart and his employees do the tough cattle work.

'So you'll take him?'

'Here's my hand on it,' Angus said, extending his hand.

'The chestnut is yours.'

'Right. How much for the black horse?' Angus asked.

'He's not for sale, Mr Campbell,' David said calmly.

Angus looked thunderstruck and he could see the disappointment on Catriona's face.

David had waited years for the chance to get even with the Campbells. They had presented his family with a stud bull they couldn't afford and a damned expensive saddle. He hadn't wanted a saddle for helping Cat. He knew it had been generous of the Campbells, but it just highlighted the fact that the Campbells had the money to give such presents and the MacLeods couldn't reciprocate. Well, now they could.

'I understood that the black horse was for sale. Look here, David, put a price on him. I promised Catriona that I would try and get her this horse ever since I first saw him.'

'I didn't ever tell you that King was for sale,' David said.

'You led us on to believe he was. Why else would Catriona have come up here to ride him?'

'Catriona came here to see if he suited her,' David said.

'And he does,' Angus replied heatedly. 'She wants him. I'll give you three thousand dollars for him. That would be the best price you've ever been offered for a horse.'

David shook his head. 'King isn't for sale. Not for three thousand or thirty thousand. I wouldn't sell a horse like this.'

Catriona looked stunned. It was as if she had seen a vision of paradise and been blinded in the very next

350

instant. She was even more astonished when she heard David's next words.

'The reason the horse is not for sale, Mr Campbell, is because I am giving him to Catriona.'

David looked with satisfaction at Catriona's disbelieving expression and Angus's look of puzzlement. Angus was a proud man who had the money to buy the best livestock in the country. On this occasion he had come up against a young man who could not be influenced by his power to purchase. Angus knew that if he accepted the black horse he would be beholden to David MacLeod, and if he didn't he would devastate his daughter.

'You're gi-giving me the black horse?' Catriona stuttered.

David nodded.

'Why?' she asked.

'You once gave us a very good bull that helped us a lot. He was a much better bull than we could afford. We've owed you for that.'

'Andy did a fair bit of work to pay for that bull,' Angus said.

'He was worth five times the value of the work Dad did for you. You also gave me a very expensive saddle. You didn't have to do that and I certainly did not expect it. This is my way of returning those favours.'

Angus and Catriona still looked stunned. Angus had been going to offer an even lower price for the chestnut, and now he was glad he hadn't. He would have looked damned small.

David went to the gate and opened it. 'You'd better bring your horse, Cat,' he said.

Catriona looked at him speculatively and then did as he suggested. Angus followed suit.

They walked down to the horse yard in silence.

'Have you got time for a drink of tea?' David asked.

Angus nodded. How could he refuse after what David had just done?

After greeting Anne and the silent Andrew, Angus and Catriona went into the bathroom for a wash. Anne raised her eyebrows and David winked. She thought he seemed very pleased with himself.

'Do you know what your son has just done?' Catriona said as they sat down at the table.

'No. Is it safe to ask?' Anne said with a smile.

'He has *given* me his black horse.'

'Has he indeed? What a pleasant surprise. I can honestly say I had no idea. What David does with his horses is his own business. Cake, Angus?'

'Thank you, Anne. How are you, Andy?'

Andy raised his arm to indicate that he had heard the question.

'Thankfully Andy is a shade better than he was,' Anne responded. 'Catriona, have you got your Deb dress yet?'

'Oh, yes. I've tried it on.'

'Who is escorting you to the ball, Cat?' David asked with a glint in his eye.

'I'm not sure yet. The first boy I asked knocked

me back. I was so shattered that I haven't had the heart to ask anyone else.'

'You've got a good horse to work now. That should lift your spirits,' David said.

'Who the devil knocked you back, Catriona?' Angus asked with his eyes flashing fire. 'Is he anyone I know?'

'Yes, Daddy, but I don't want you to worry about it.'

Angus appealed to Anne. 'Can you give me any good reason why a young fellow wouldn't want to escort my daughter?'

'No, I can't, Angus. Not unless he has his eye on another girl.'

There was the same hint of devilment in Anne's eyes as there was in David's as he sat eating his mother's cake.

'I've got a daughter who looks like a film star and she tells me a boy won't escort her! I've heard everything now,' Angus continued.

'We shall be there to see you, Catriona,' Anne said. 'And I am sure you will look marvellous and that the next boy you ask will escort you.'

'That's very sweet of you, Anne. It's just that I did so much want *this* boy.'

'Speaking of boys, did you know that Bill and Wade Missen are back?' Angus said. 'I was talking to Sergeant Hooper and he told me that they've been at Nimbin. They got into some trouble up there – drugs, I think. Wade was charged but let off with a caution.'

Anne looked across at her son. The spark in his eyes was gone and in its place was pure ice. She knew well what David thought of the Missen boys.

'They've got some other fellow with them,' Angus said. 'The three of them were drinking at the bottom pub and got into a fight. Beats me how two nice people like Roy and Bessie could produce two boys like Bill and Wade,' Angus said.

'They're no good,' David said. 'Neither of them. They're wild and there's a mean streak in Wade. They'll come to a bad end. Better they stay away. There's no telling what they might get up to.'

He got up and stormed out.

'Oh, dear,' Anne sighed. 'David sees red when you mention that pair. If they so much as look at him sideways, I am fearful of what he might do.'

'He would have a good ally in Stuart,' Angus said.

'Excuse me, Anne, Andy,' Catriona said and left the room. As she went down the steps she saw David leaning against the rails of the horse yard. His head was down and he didn't notice Catriona until she was standing right next to him.

When he looked up and saw her he gave a weak smile. 'Sorry about that, Cat. You ready to load the horses?'

'Ready,' she said.

'Good luck with King. He should keep you occupied for a while. I shall be very disappointed if you don't win a few Champion Hack awards with him,' David said.

Catriona looked at him and focused on what he had just said. Was there more to the gift of the horse than appeared on the surface? What did David mean by Catriona needing to be 'occupied'? Was he sign-posting something further down the track?

After they had loaded the horses, Angus drove up to the fence that surrounded the homestead. Anne had come down the steps to have a last look at the horses. Angus was at the wheel of the Fairlane and Catriona asked him to wait while she said goodbye. She kissed Anne on the cheek and then did the same to David, this time allowing her face to rest against his. As she looked past him she found Anne's eyes fixed on her. Anne winked, and Catriona knew she had an ally.

They had not driven as far as the bend in the road when Angus spoke his mind. 'That young fellow out-gunned me. I never imagined I would see anyone make a gesture like that. And Anne took it all in her stride . . . as if the loss of three thousand dollars didn't matter.'

Catriona pondered what she should say next. She realised that sooner or later her father would have to know how she felt about David. But she would have to tread warily and sow the seeds very gently.

'David is the boy I asked to escort me to the ball. He is the one who refused me,' she said.

Angus put his foot on the brake and brought the car to a stop. 'He what?' he roared.

'Steady, Daddy, we have valuable horses back there.'

'It was David you were referring to and you let me make a fool of myself in front of the MacLeods? Have you taken leave of your senses, girl? Why on earth did *he* refuse *you*?'

'He said I had to ask you first.'

'The devil he did.'

'Susan asked him before I did and she got the same answer,' Catriona said.

'Well, I'll be damned. Yet he's going to be there on the night.'

'Oh, yes, David is definitely going to be there. The whole family will be there, even Mr Mac.'

'You should have talked to Jane and me before you asked David to escort you. I don't know whether I should be more angry with you or with that young devil back there. David is a lot shrewder than I imagined. And to think he knocked you back, and did he use the gift of the horse to gain our favour? Not David. Not David MacLeod. He has told us exactly what he thinks of us. Damned if he isn't an infuriating fellow.'

Angus was still running hot and the car was still stationary. 'Did David elaborate on why he wouldn't take you to the ball?' he asked.

'He said that he didn't want to be the cause of a dispute between me and my parents. That and the fact that he considers us snobby,' Catriona threw in.

'What? Damned cheek of him. Pure insolence. If he hadn't given you that black horse, I'd go back and tell him exactly what I think.'

356

'I wouldn't advise that. Apart from the fact that David could handle you with one hand behind his back, he is absolutely right. We are snobs. So David isn't saying anything that's untrue.'

'Now, look here, young lady, there are people who have to set high standards. Why do you think we sent you and Stuart to private schools? I'll tell you why: it was so you would have the class to marry well. If you marry well, your children will have their futures assured. I suppose David realises there are dozens of boys who would fall over themselves to escort you.'

'I'm sure he does. That wouldn't worry him a bit. He's his own man and will always do things his way. You either accept him on his terms or you don't accept him at all.'

'Catriona, I get the feeling that there is more to this than meets the eye. Why are you defending him?'

'I've always been keen on David, Daddy. The problem is that I've never known whether David is keen on me. Not until I spoke with Anne yesterday, and now there's this gift of King.'

'Don't talk in riddles, Catriona. Are you saying that David is keen on you, too?'

'Not on the surface and not in so many words. He's not ready to get involved in a romance yet. A girl would have to be prepared to play the waiting game if she wanted David, and it just so happens that I think he is worth waiting for. I dare say that you and Mummy won't agree, but there it is.'

'Catriona, you can do much better than David

357

MacLeod. Anne's a damned fine woman, none better, and a smart woman, too, but she wouldn't entertain sending David away to a decent school. Probably couldn't afford to. That might have made a difference.'

'I know he's not perfect, but he is a real man. Straight and true. You should hear the stories I've been told about some of the men you make me mix with –'

'That's enough of that, Catriona,' Angus cut in sharply.

'Well, David would never be like that. A girl could trust him to the ends of the earth. No other boy comes near him.'

'I know some who are pretty decent,' Angus said.

'You *think* you know them. Anyway, time usually solves most problems. I propose to accept David's gift with thanks and to enjoy working him.'

'Your mother will want to know what we paid for him,' Angus said. 'What do we tell her?'

'We could tell her the truth, but that wouldn't be very wise. We could say that we have the horse on trial for a few months. Or you could bend the truth a little and tell her that you worked a deal on stock ... say cows or ewes,' Catriona said with an enchanting smile.

'That would be damned deceitful and very sensible,' Angus agreed. He gave her a grim sort of smile. But at least it was a smile.

'Of course, if Jane talked to Anne, our goose

would be cooked,' Angus said just before they arrived at Inverlochy.

'I'll have a word in Anne's ear,' Catriona said. 'Promptly.'

The idea of his daughter marrying David MacLeod was preposterous to Angus Campbell. If Catriona was serious about David, he would have to send her overseas. That would fix her crush. By then she would be ready to marry someone who could give her everything she deserved. Even when the MacLeods finished paying for Poitrel they wouldn't be top-bracket graziers, and David definitely didn't have what it would take to marry Catriona. Angus decided to say nothing to Jane about Catriona's disclosure regarding David. No sense stirring up an ants' nest when it was likely to blow over in a few months' time.

King was ensconced in the best stable on Inverlochy. Catriona rode him almost every day and soon started him on more demanding work. She was determined to win Champion Hack with him and so prove to David that she was worthy of his handsome gift.

She was still upset that David would not be escorting her to the ball. It would make so much difference to have David alongside her. Apart from simply wanting him as her escort, she wanted to try and get David out more. She had to get him to mix and talk with people who weren't only interested in dogs and horses. After much thought, Catriona decided to ask Roger Cartwright to escort her. She knew that Susan would be pleased, and Roger was a decent enough boy. He was nowhere near as handsome as David and was probably six inches shorter but still slightly taller than herself. One thing in Roger's favour was that he could be relied upon to behave reasonably throughout the evening. Between Roger and Stuart – who was escorting Amanda – she considered she would be well looked after. As for David – well, he was a free agent and would do as he pleased. But she would have to keep an eye on Susan. Oh, what a night it promised to be.

Chapter Nineteen

There was usually a capacity crowd for the Debutantes' Ball. For many people in the district it was the highlight of the year. Other people preferred the Show Ball, which was a more egalitarian affair. For those who preferred the Deb there was something infinitely splendid about the evening: the spectacle of the district's finest young women being officially presented to the world. The Deb was about as close to pomp as could be achieved in the bush, and parents of debutantes looked forward to the occasion.

Anne, Kate and Jean stood together and watched the ten white-gowned debutantes and their escorts come up to be presented to the town's mayor. It was a wonderful scene in the beautifully decorated hall. There were balloons, streamers and lattice arches entwined with crepe-paper roses and ivy. The pink and white theme transformed the hall so that one would never know that it was actually an old building.

Catriona and her mother had made several trips to find the ideal gown. They wanted something different from the usual taffeta, satin and tulle. They had chosen a filmy chiffon over a satin lining, with guipure lace for trimming. The gown was tight-waisted with a flowy, gathered skirt. A swathe of chiffon covered her back and shoulders, forming the cape sleeves and modestly dipping like butterfly wings to her bosom. Catriona's long blonde hair was caught back and hung in ringlets. A slender gold chain and locket around her neck and long white gloves were her only accessories.

Anne, Kate and Jean all agreed that Catriona was the belle of the ball. Although Susan Cartwright was very attractive with her dark hair and flashing eyes, Catriona really stood out.

David was sitting with his father and seemed to be taking little interest in the proceedings, although he was not ill at ease in what was such an alien environment for him. He had been assured by his mother that 'coming out' was an important happening for girls of Catriona's social class, but he felt it was just another piece of pomp and ceremony of the kind indulged in by the likes of Angus Campbell and his snobby set. He couldn't see any significance in a girl being presented to the mayor. She wasn't given anything or changed in any way by the procedure.

Catriona, while exuding glamour and a sparkling personality, was taking peeks in David's direction. He had never seen her in such a setting and she was keen to gauge his reaction. But, as always, Catriona was disappointed. David's eyes were occupied elsewhere, although not with anyone in particular. David was in fact paying very close attention to Bill and Wade Missen, whom he had noted in the crowd. Their behaviour this evening seemed very odd. Every now and again they would disappear outside and then reappear a few minutes later in worse shape.

There was another young man with them, not a local, and he was well dressed and seemed primed for mischief. His face was vaguely familiar and David tried to remember where he might have seen him. It was most likely to have been at the local show. He was making audible comments about the debutantes, and Bill and Wade were laughing almost hysterically. On one occasion Wade pointed towards Catriona and the other two young men nodded and laughed.

At that stage David suddenly remembered Angus talking about the Missen boys being mixed up with drugs. He felt the hairs on the back of his neck begin to tingle. He sensed trouble; it was in the air. He left his seat and collected another beer for his father.

'That fellow with the Missens, Dad, you ever see him before?' he whispered to his father.

Andy took a long, careful look at the bloke and shook his head.

David looked up and saw that the man in question was watching him. He was a fairly nice-looking young man, of slim build and about the same height as

Wade, who was a couple of inches under six feet.

David turned away from the Missen boys and their mate to dance. He was anything but an avid dancer, but on this occasion he couldn't very well get out of it. He partnered his mother first, then Kate and Jean in turn, and as Susan was looking in his direction he decided to ask her to dance with him, too. He reckoned that would put him in Catriona's bad books. David was just about to walk across to where Susan was sitting when Catriona appeared at his side. She was not backward in telling him just what she thought of him for ignoring her throughout the evening.

'Cat, you have plenty of admirers. They're all falling over themselves to dance with you. You can see me any old time.'

'That isn't the point, David. Tonight is special. I expected you to dance with me.'

'I am,' he said, taking her hand and leading her on to the dance floor with a mild grin.

'But I had to come and find you.'

'I would have looked you up, Cat. You had to give Roger his money's worth. He escorted you. By the way, who's the dark-haired fellow with the Missen boys?'

'I don't know, but I don't think much of him. He has been making some rather unseemly remarks about the girls. Don't you know him?'

'His face is familiar. I wondered if he'd been at the show.'

364

'Don't worry about those boys, David. They're simply enjoying themselves. I suppose you'll have to dance with Susan?' Catriona said.

'I suppose I will,' he agreed.

'One dance would be sufficient,' Catriona said. 'And then you could come back to me.'

David shook his head. There was some sort of power play going on between Catriona and Susan and he seemed to be stuck in the middle of it. It was the last place he wanted to be. 'I think you should go back to Roger, Cat.'

David turned away from her and went back to sit with his father for a while.

Later that night, David partnered Catriona through two full dances, just as he did with Susan. He wasn't going to have Catriona dictate to him, and by dancing twice with each girl he was not able to be accused of favouritism.

At midnight Anne said that she thought it was time to take Andy home, and that she and the others would go home in Kate's car. David wanted to stay on a little longer. He danced with a few of the girls he had gone to school with and drank a glass or two of punch, all the while keeping his eye on the Missens and their mate.

Finally, Catriona and Roger came across to where he was sitting and told him they were leaving. As they left the hall the Missen trio quickly followed them. David got to his feet and tailed them. He had thought all night that the Missens were primed for trouble. He was even surer now.

Roger Cartwright was driving a new Falcon and, from the top step of the hall, David watched the car head off for Inverlochy. David had seen Angus and Jane leave about an hour earlier and he knew that there was to be some kind of late supper at Inverlochy involving the Cartwrights and a couple of other families. Roger's car was followed almost immediately by a big dark car which accelerated sharply and almost side-slammed a mailbox. David hurried to where he had left his utility and in that instant he had a blinding realisation of who was with the Missens. It was none other than Stanley Masters, the boy he had fought back at primary school.

'Bloody hell,' he swore. 'God knows what they'll do if they get their hands on her.'

He started the utility and accelerated away as fast as the vehicle would respond. When he got out on the main road to Cassilis, he could see the lights of the two cars ahead of him, perhaps two miles away. He doubted very much that they would attempt anything on the main road because there would be people going home to Cassilis and Coolah from the dance. No, if they were going to try anything, it would be on the road to Inverlochy.

The two sets of lights were still ahead of him when he turned on to the Inverlochy–High Peaks road. And then as he came up out of a dip he could see them no longer. It was clear that the cars had turned off the road. The Missen trio had made their move. In that instant he wished he had his father, fit and well, beside him. The two of them could handle that rotten lot up ahead. But he would have to tackle them on his own. What on earth could they have in mind following Catriona home at this hour?

It took him only a few moments to discover what had happened. Roger's Falcon had been forced off the road and had slammed into a fence post. It was starkly illuminated in the lights of the dark car which lit up the whole horrifying scene. He heard a high-pitched scream that made his blood run cold, and an icy rage coursed through him. The Missens and their mate were going to pay dearly for this.

He slammed on the brakes, grabbed the whip from behind him and was out of the vehicle in one swift movement. Roger was sagged over the steering wheel with Bill keeping an eye on him. Wade and Stanley had dragged Catriona out of the car and pinned her to the ground. Wade was holding her by the legs while Stanley tried to tear off her beautiful white gown. Catriona was screaming so loudly and the three men were shouting and laughing so much they hadn't even noticed David's arrival.

He reversed his hold of the whip and hit Wade a mighty blow behind the ear. The handle was weighted with lead and Wade slumped to the ground within seconds. Masters had torn Catriona's dress off and she was naked to the waist and wearing just her underpants. He looked up and saw

David standing behind Wade just as David delivered his blow.

'You bastard, MacLeod. Hit my mate, would you?' He dropped the gown and rushed madly at Wade's attacker. David put out a leg and tripped him up, then hit him on the side of the head with the whip. It was not as clean a hit as the first one had been and Masters did not go down. David threw a punch in the best Sparkes tradition and Masters doubled over. Bill Missen attacked next with a piece of gum stick that he swung down at David. The stick struck David a fair blow on the side of the head just above the eye. It was enough to open up a cut and David could feel that it had drawn blood. He reached out and hit Bill with his left hand and then cracked him with the whip handle.

Out of the corner of his good eye David could see Roger staggering away from his car. He looked terrible and could barely walk. Meanwhile, Bill Missen was trying to get up, and when he was halfway there David transferred his whip to his left hand and hit him flush on the jaw with his right. Bill went down in a heap, and this time he stayed there. David dragged him over to the dark car and hauled him into the back. Wade and Stanley were groggy but still had some fight in them, and David accommodated them. He was just so angry. With his whip in one hand he threatened Stanley and Wade enough to get them into the back of the car with Bill. 'You move from that car and you'll wish you'd never been born,' he growled.

Now, at last, he was able to turn to Catriona. The girl who had not so long ago been the belle of the ball was now lying face down on the ground, sobbing in shock and fear.

He knelt beside her and pulled the white gown over her naked shoulders. 'Cat, it's me, David. Are you all right?'

Catriona turned her head sideways and looked up at him. 'Oh, David,' she cried, throwing her arms around his neck for comfort.

'Ssshh, it's all right now. Are you okay? Are you up to driving my ute?'

Catriona nodded bravely.

'Good. I want you to drive to Inverlochy, tell your father what's happened and where I am, and get him to ring the police and an ambulance.'

'Of course,' she sobbed. 'David, you're hurt. There's blood all down your face. Will you be all right if I leave you?'

'Yes, but hurry. I think Roger has concussion. He's out to it. Here, let me help you up.'

He averted his eyes from her top half and put his hand under her arm. 'Quickly now, Cat. The sooner the police get here the better. These cretins are not getting away with this stunt.'

Catriona tried to hold her gown together as she ran towards David's vehicle. She stood by the utility and looked back. She was a sorry figure compared with the proud, happy girl of an hour ago.

'David, will you be all right?' she asked again.

Her concern for him at this moment when she must have been feeling truly awful broke him up, and at that moment David realised her depth of feeling for him.

'You can't do anything here, Cat. For Christ's sake, go,' he said roughly.

Catriona turned away and a few moments later the utility pulled away and headed up the road for Inverlochy. He could hear it for a little while and then he was alone with all the silence of a bush night. He went and turned the lights off on Roger's car and then stooped and looked at its owner.

Roger was lying very still, and there was nothing David could do for him.

Suddenly, behind him, he heard the sound of breaking glass and he wheeled about and ran to the other vehicle. Wade had smashed a rear window with his fist and had managed to open the door. As Wade fell out of the car, David let fly with his whip and it chopped Wade's hand so hard he let out an unearthly screech.

'If you move again, I'll cut you to pieces,' David warned.

Wade was a pathetic figure as he pulled his body back into the car and closed the door behind him.

David took out his handkerchief and wiped his own face. The cloth came away covered in blood. He had very little vision out of his right eye, as it seemed to be closing. He was a little concerned that the three in the car might break out together, so he jammed two big dead branches against the door catches on the left side of the car and then took up station on the driver's side.

It was a very quiet night with a half-moon lighting up the tops of the trees. Away in the distance he could hear a dog barking. He did not expect he would have to wait long for Angus to arrive. Angus was a real pain at times but he could always be depended upon in an emergency.

David was right. Angus and Stuart arrived in not much more than half an hour, but it was the longest half-hour David had ever put in.

'God Almighty, are you all right, David?' Angus asked as soon as he arrived on the scene.

'I think so,' David said. 'My eye probably looks worse than it is. Did you get on to the police?'

'Jane did. They shouldn't be long. Catriona was screaming at me to get back here to you.'

'How is she?'

'I didn't stay long enough to find out. She's badly shocked. Tell me what happened. Did they give you much trouble?' Angus asked as he and Stuart peered into the car at its three sorry-looking occupants.

'Not too much.'

'What a nasty way to finish a splendid evening,' Angus said. 'Are those fellows stirring at all, Stuart?'

'I wish they would,' he replied grimly. The very thought of anyone trying to attack his sister was almost too much for him to bear.

'Look here, David, you'd better sit down. You've got blood all over you. We'll watch this lot.'

David had been walking up and down beside the big car, his whip still in his left hand.

'I'll be right. I hope Mum isn't too worried about all this.'

But it was Kate who arrived on the scene first. Unfortunately Jean was on night duty so Kate had to come on her own. Her car was the first of what seemed to be a procession of vehicles on the road that night. Kate strode straight over to David and threw her arms around him. When she saw the blood on his face and clothes she recoiled.

'Are you okay, David?' she asked, and began to examine him by torchlight. His cut was about three inches long and fairly deep.

'That will need stitching,' she said. 'You'll have to go to town. I don't have any local anaesthetic on me.'

'I believe an ambulance is on its way,' Angus said.

'Right. What sort of shape are they in?' Kate asked, looking towards the dark car.

'I don't know, Sister, but I should think they'll have considerable headaches tomorrow.'

The lights of another vehicle were approaching from the Inverlochy road.

'That will be Anne,' Kate said.

It was, and she was out of the car and running towards them almost before the car had stopped. 'Are you all right, David?' she asked anxiously.

'Yes, he is,' Kate answered for him, but she could see that he was suffering from some kind of reaction to the incident. Even David was vulnerable.

Anne looked into her son's eyes and he gave her a weak smile.

'I'm okay,' he said. 'It just looks a bit messy and it's aching a bit now.'

'A couple of aspirins for you right now,' Kate said, and dug into her bag for the pills.

'Angus,' Anne said, approaching him, 'what a terrible thing. I'm so sorry.'

'Thank you,' he replied. 'I shudder to think what would have happened if David hadn't come along when he did.'

'Can we take David to town now?' Anne asked.

'I'm afraid not,' Angus replied gently. 'We will have to wait for the police to arrive. I'm sure they'll want to question David, and they'll also need to inter-view Catriona and Roger.'

'Poor Roger,' Kate said as she knelt beside him. 'Two more vehicles are coming,' Stuart reported.

'Thank goodness for that,' Angus replied.

The police car was travelling very fast and the ambulance wasn't far behind it. They pulled up in a cloud of dust and gravel and Angus went across to meet the two police officers.

'Evening, Mr Campbell,' Sergeant Hooper greeted him. 'This is Constable Walker. He hasn't been with us very long. What is the situation?'

Angus summarised briefly what David and a shocked Catriona had told him, and then the police moved on to question the others.

David recounted the events of the night and how he had come to follow the three men from the ball.

'I see,' the big man said and nodded to his colleague. 'Right, I think it's time to get those three out.'

Constable Walker kicked away the branches David had placed against the car doors and shone his torch inside. 'A very sorry looking trio, Sergeant,' he said as he reached in and pulled them out one by one.

'I want some answers from you fellows and I want them quick,' Hooper said.

'Don't say anything,' Bill croaked.

'Shut up, Missen, and don't open your mouth until I ask you to. I think we'd better get you three down to the station. We'll be back later to interview Miss Campbell.'

The ambulance officer, Eric Wood, sat the trio down on a log and in the light of the car's headlights gave them a quick examination. 'There's nothing too serious here, but I'll need a few minutes with each to patch up some cuts and bruises. But there is one other thing, Sergeant,' Eric said. He whispered in the big man's ear and the sergeant raised his eyebrows.

'Constable, please come here a moment.'

He talked in a low voice to the young constable, who then went to the glove box of the dark car. When he emerged from the car, he nodded to his sergeant.

'Right, put them in the car, Constable. Are you finished with them, Eric?' he asked.

'Yes I am, but young MacLeod needs a few

stitches. I'd like to take him back with us, if you don't need him any longer.'

'No, you do that, Eric,' Hooper said.

'I'll follow the ambulance into town and bring David home, Sergeant,' Anne said. 'Will you need him again tonight?'

'No. We'll talk to him in the morning, Mrs MacLeod. You get David fixed up.'

'I'd better get back home and let Andy know what's happened,' Kate said. 'He'll be worried.'

'Good idea,' Anne agreed.

The group finally broke up. Three vehicles headed off for town while the other two turned left for Inverlochy and High Peaks.

An hour or so later, with the Missen boys and Stanley Masters in custody, Sergeant Hooper and Constable Walker arrived at Inverlochy. Angus and Stuart were standing by the front steps (their supper guests had made a very hasty departure when they had seen the state Catriona was in). The whole area was a blaze of light. Angus led the way into the big lounge room where Catriona, in a floral-patterned dressing-gown, was sitting with her mother. The once beautiful white gown she had been wearing earlier that evening was draped across the lounge-room table. Catriona had been told that the police would require it as evidence. Angus introduced the two police officers and they seated themselves in chairs at the table.

'Miss Campbell, I know you're distressed by what

happened tonight, but I'm afraid I need to record your version of events as soon as possible, while the incident is fresh in your mind. Do you understand?' Catriona nodded. 'Good. Now, we'll need to start from the very beginning.'

Catriona was asked all sorts of questions about the evening: who she had danced with, what she had been drinking, what time she had arrived and departed. She answered all the questions clearly and precisely, but when she was asked more intimate questions she began to show signs of distress.

'For the record, is that the gown you were wearing tonight?'

'Yes, Sergeant.'

Hooper reached for the gown and examined it.

'Is it true that the gown was ripped right off you, and your brassiere, as well?'

Catriona looked distraught at this question, but managed her reply. 'That's right, Sergeant. I was lying on my back on the ground and they had ripped my dress right off me. The next thing I knew one of them had fallen to the ground. I didn't know what was happening because I hadn't even heard David arrive.'

'And where was Roger while all this was going on?'

'I don't know. I didn't have time to look before I was grabbed and pulled out of the car. The next time I saw Roger was after David had thrown the others in their car. By then Roger was lying on the ground.'

'Okay. Now, please think very carefully and

answer me truthfully – did you hear any of those young men say anything that indicated what their intentions were?'

Catriona blushed and looked across at her father and brother.

'Do I have to tell you exactly what they said, Sergeant?' Catriona asked.

'Yes, and if a court case arises out of this matter, you could be questioned on this very point. Perhaps you would like a little privacy.'

'Yes, I would,' Catriona said.

Angus and Stuart got to their feet. 'We'll leave, Sergeant. Would you like me to get you something to eat or drink? It's going to be a long night,' Angus said.

'A cup of tea and a biscuit would be great. My mate is a coffee drinker, thank you.'

While Catriona recounted the sordid details of the night, her mother closed her eyes and shook her head. It seemed that she could hardly believe, let alone bear, what she was hearing. Catriona's evidence implicated all three of her assailants.

When all the questioning was over, Sergeant Hooper said, 'You had a very lucky escape, Catriona.'

'I know. David MacLeod seems to have made a habit of being on hand when I need him,' she said.

Angus came back into the room and listened carefully while Hooper summarised what would happen as a result of the assault.

'All parties will be questioned again. We'll need to

take a statement from your daughter, which she will have to sign. There are a number of charges against the young men, including attempted sexual assault. Their actions also resulted in an injury to Roger Cartwright, the extent of which we don't as yet know, and we found drugs in the glove box of their car. The charges will be very serious indeed,' Hooper said.

After the two police officers had departed, Angus took Catriona's hand in his and smiled rather grimly. 'I'm terribly sorry this had to happen to you, Catriona. It was a grand night and now it looks as if you'll be involved in court proceedings. I still can't believe those fellows would do such a thing.'

'It could have been worse, Daddy. Much worse. Poor David. He must be sick of playing guardian angel to me.'

'Catriona, if I know young David, I shouldn't think a cut eye would worry him greatly.'

'Still, I shall have to go and see him, to thank him. You do see that I must, don't you, Daddy?'

Angus nodded. 'Of course you must. Plain good manners. But you should wait and get the police interview over first. I'll talk to Anne and tell her that you'll be along after the interview.'

At this point, Jane burst into the conversation. 'David MacLeod. I am getting heartily tired of hearing that name,' she said. 'If I'm not being told how wonderful he is, I am hearing how he's rescued you from some terrible situation. It seems to me, Catriona, that you are much too friendly with that young man. I think you should stay right away from him in future.'

'That's very unfair, Mummy. You should be thankful that David is the kind of person he is. Think what might have happened if he hadn't turned up tonight. Your high and mighty friends wouldn't have wanted their sons to have anything to do with me then. I would have been spoiled goods if things had been taken any further.'

'Catriona, I forbid you to talk like that. I understand you are upset and tired. I think we should get you to bed. Of course I am grateful to David. I just think you are getting too friendly with him. I agree with your father that you should go away for a while, or do a university course.'

'Right now I can't think beyond getting a good night's sleep, making it through the police interview tomorrow, and going to thank David,' Catriona said.

It was a dejected Roy Missen who made his way to Inverlochy midmorning the next day.

'Angus, I don't know what to say. I'm just so terribly sorry for what happened. Where did we go wrong?'

'Roy, I sympathise with you and Bessie,' Angus said with genuine sorrow in his heart for this good man. 'I respect you for coming to see me.'

'Well, my boys got what they deserved from David MacLeod. I'm not worried about that, and I'll pay for any medical costs for David's eye. He and his father are a hard pair but they're straight as a die. Please let me know if there is anything I can do for Catriona.'

'You had better concentrate on what you can do to help Bill and Wade. I have to tell you, Roy, that I've asked the police to oppose bail. I don't want them wandering about anywhere near my family.'

'I understand how you feel, Angus, but it grieves Bessie and me to think of our boys in prison.'

'There is a high probability that prison is where they will be for the next few years,' Angus said bluntly.

'Granted it looks bad for them, Angus. I wanted you to know that I'm personally very sorry for what happened to Catriona. I'll head on to High Peaks now.'

Angus Campbell watched his neighbour walk down the driveway to his car, start the engine and drive off up the road. Clearly Roy Missen was a broken man.

Anne thought Roy looked pathetic as he stood at her front door. He gave a genuine nod of apology to Andy and then turned to talk to Anne.

'I came to say how sorry I am for what happened and to see if you would allow me to pay for any of David's medical expenses. Is he here, Mrs MacLeod?'

'My sister took him into town to give his statement to the police,' Anne said. She did not know Roy and Bessie Missen very well, although she knew that Angus had always spoken well of them.

'It's good of you to call so quickly with your boys in trouble,' Anne said with a smile.

'It's the least I can do in the circumstances,' he said.

'Would you like a cup of tea?' Anne asked. The poor man seemed lost.

'I wouldn't impose on your hospitality, Mrs MacLeod, not the way things are. You let me know what the costs are for David's eye.'

Roy Missen walked slowly back to his car and drove away. Anne rested one hand on her husband's shoulder and then heard him say, albeit croakily, 'Roy is in worse shape than me.'

Anne looked down at him in amazement. 'Andy, that was a full, coherent sentence. You've got your voice back!'

'Some of it,' he said with a grin. 'It just happened so suddenly. One moment there was nothing and the next the words just came out.'

Anne bent over and kissed the top of his head. 'Maybe this is the beginning of a complete, miraculous recovery,' she said with a glint in her eye.

'I sure hope so,' he said, smiling even more broadly.

David and Kate arrived back for lunch with the news that the Missen boys and Stanley Masters would be charged with a number of offences, and that the police were going to oppose bail.

'Angus rang me to find out if you would be here this afternoon. They're all coming up to see you, David,' Anne said.

David grimaced. 'I should ride out and look at some sheep,' he said lamely.

'You can't do that, Davie,' Andrew said firmly.

David stared at his father in disbelief. 'You've got your voice back! Mum, did you hear it?'

'Yes, it would appear so,' Anne said.

'Dad, that's fantastic,' David said, his face beaming. 'At least that's one good thing to come out of this rotten mess. For you, Dad, I suppose I can see the Campbell clan.'

'You must never throw gratitude in people's faces,' Anne said. 'And, besides, Angus is talking about sending Jane and Catriona overseas for a while. Catriona has had a very unpleasant experience so a change would do her good,' Anne said.

'I suppose so,' David said, but he couldn't really understand anyone's desire to leave the range country. 'Is Cat all right?' he asked.

'She has a few bruises but otherwise she's okay. You'll see her for yourself soon enough. I dare say she looks better than you do. You are going to have a bad eye for a while.'

'It's not too bad. I can still see out of it. What's a few stitches?'

Anne threw her hands in the air. 'What's a few stitches? They could have split your head open with that stick.'

'But they didn't, Mum,' David said calmly. He was sick of the whole episode.

Angus, Jane and Catriona arrived just before afternoon smoko, as Anne had expected they would.

Despite the trauma of the moment, Jane had brought a cake.

'Jane, you shouldn't have bothered. Not now,' Anne protested.

'It's nothing. Anyway, Mrs Rogers made it.'

Catriona looked around for David.

'He'll be back in a little while, Catriona. He went somewhere to look at a water trough.'

'Hello, you lot,' Andrew greeted them.

The three Campbells looked at him in amazement. They were aware of how badly the stroke had affected his voice and were now astonished to hear him speaking almost like the Andrew of old.

'Isn't that something?' Anne said. 'Andy's voice came back this morning. Properly, I mean. Ah, here comes David.'

David's tall figure came up the path in long, easy strides. The right side of his face surrounding his eye was black and blue and the stitches were covered in gauze.

Catriona looked across at her parents and then went to greet him. They met at the top of the steps and she put one hand against his left cheek while she kissed the other.

'Thank you once again,' she said very softly in his ear.

David thought she looked as beautiful as ever, if a shade more subdued. He could smell her perfume, and that combined with her closeness did strange things to him, made him feel light inside, in a way he had never felt before.

'Hello, Cat,' he said gravely.

'Hello, yourself,' Catriona said as brightly as she could manage. 'You aren't so handsome right now.'

'I ran into a branch,' he said.

'I know. I saw you do it.'

He inclined his head and looked at her. He could remember in every detail how she had looked last night. She was at her splendid best when presented at the ball, and later, by the light of the dark car's headlights, he had seen her as she lay helpless and vulnerable on the ground, at the mercy of those three awful men. Catriona did not doubt that he had seen her lying so exposed, but relief at being rescued over-rode any feelings of embarrassment she might have felt.

'You're looking much better now than when I last saw you,' he said, a little uncomfortably.

Catriona turned pink. 'I feel better, too. I don't know why, though, after the grilling the police gave me. They were very thorough.'

'They sure were,' David agreed.

'You know there will be a court case and you and I are the main witnesses,' Catriona said. 'I would like to think that will be the last time I ever see those characters.'

'You're not the only one,' David replied.

'I hate being looked at by creepy men. I want just one man to admire me, to want me,' Catriona said, and her eyes settled on David's battered face. 'One man who loves me.'

Anne interrupted at this point. 'I think it's time we had a nice cup of tea,' she said quickly.

'What a good idea,' Angus replied. 'What do you reckon Malcolm Fraser will do for us, Andy?'

Catriona didn't concentrate much on the conversation that afternoon. Anne watched her out of the corner of her eye and observed how her eyes kept straying back to David's face. The look in those eyes was that of a girl very much in love. Unfortunately she did not see the same intensity in David's eyes. But a change had come over him. She knew him too well not to recognise the slight difference in the way he responded to Catriona's conversation.

'You must come to dinner one night, Catriona,' Anne said as the Campbells were preparing to leave. 'You asked me about the MacLeod family history and I've put it all together. Kate wants to hear it, too. And it's about time David knew a bit more about his forebears. I declare he knows much more about the ancestors of his precious dogs than he does about his own family.'

'I would love to, Anne. I really would,' she said as she looked across at David standing with his father, but her mind was elsewhere. She wanted to get David right away from everyone else and have an honest talk with him. There were a few things she had to get settled in her mind. And if her father was going to insist on an overseas trip, she wanted to do it before she left. She had felt David's eyes on her throughout the entire afternoon, and she knew she had to speak now or never.

'You'll be mustering again, Andy,' Angus said as he got in the Fairlane. 'Harry Cameron had a stroke and he's back farming again. One arm was stiff just like yours, but it's amazing what he does now.'

'I sure hope so, Angus. David has a huge job on his hands here and I've been no help at all. If it hadn't been for Anne and Kate and Jean, I don't know how he'd have managed.'

'I would be happy to help out, if I'm about,' Catriona said. 'I could help with the mustering, anyway.'

Jane didn't like that suggestion. She could sense what was behind her daughter's motives. The sooner she got Catriona overseas the better she would feel. There she would find other attractions to take her mind off David. That was a liaison that had to be nipped in the bud.

Chapter Twenty

The best thing that could be said about the next few months was that Andrew MacLeod exhibited a remarkable improvement in his physical condition. He still walked with a slight limp and he did not regain the full use of his right arm, but he could now hold objects with it and was no longer one-handed. The return of his voice brought normality back to the household. Andrew could once again offer advice and, to a certain extent, direct activities. He was proud of the way David had looked after both properties and he told him so. The establishment of the lucerne block had been a very worthwhile initiative and had helped enormously with feed costs.

During the period of Andrew's convalescence, Kate's presence had never been more valuable. She had been a huge help to David work-wise, as she had developed into a first-class rider and all-round stock handler. She would come home from a long stint at the hospital, throw on her working clothes and sally out to look at sheep or cattle or do some other chore. Her energy was inexhaustible and she was interested in every aspect of rural life. Jean Courteney was an admirable partner for Kate. While she too had become quite a good rider and stock handler, she was a much more 'homey' person than Kate. Jean loved to cook and to paint and she kept the homestead spotless. Kate blessed her for this because it allowed Kate more time to spend outside and, particularly, with David. Jean would feed the poultry and collect the eggs and look after the chickens. As she told Anne, being with Kate at Poitrel kept her mind and body occupied. Her marriage had been a disaster. 'Once bitten, twice shy,' she said. Anne thought Jean was a sweet young woman who would make some man a really lovely wife, but for the time being Jean was dead scared of committing herself to anyone.

Kate reckoned that she and the MacLeods were lucky to have Jean at Poitrel. She had become like another member of the family. David, in his practical way, was grateful to have Jean at Poitrel for quite another reason. Like Kate, Jean had her certificate in obstetric nursing and this came in handy from time to time in the birth of horses, sheep and cattle. Once Jean had even stitched up a gaping wound in a young foal. Kate and Jean together were like a pair of sisters to David.

Apart from Andrew's incredible and unexpected return to health – although he was still not permitted to do any heavy work and was harassed by Anne if he tried – the MacLeods constantly thought of the ordeal that lay ahead when David would have to appear as a key witness in the trial of the Missen boys and Stanley Masters.

David hardly ever mentioned the trial, but Anne was aware that he was concerned about what he would have to go through. David was a bushman who hated fuss and procedure, and Anne realised that the atmosphere of a court would be anathema to him.

At the Campbell home, Jane had been pressing the subject of an overseas trip for Catriona. She knew that up until a few months ago Catriona had been excited about the prospect of such a trip, but she was much less enthusiastic now. Nevertheless, Jane went ahead and made all the necessary arrangements. She and Catriona would be leaving as soon as the trial was over.

Catriona visited High Peaks several times, and as the trial grew closer, Anne could tell that the spectre of what she would have to endure was having its effect on Catriona, too. Her evidence would be crucial to the outcome of the case. The defence lawyers would try and fault her story and make assertions to try to trap her.

When it came to the crunch on her big day in court, Catriona gave her evidence very clearly and could not be shaken at any stage. Her evidence, backed up by David's and Roger Cartwright's, left her assailants without a leg to stand on.

The jury was out for only a brief period and their verdict of guilty on all counts was received with enormous relief by the Campbell and MacLeod families. But across the row from where they sat in the courtroom, Roy and Bessie Missen sat with grief-stricken faces. They had aged years in the last few months.

The presiding judge sentenced the guilty trio to five years in jail, with a minimum parole period of three years. Angus reckoned they got off far too lightly, but he still took his family and the MacLeods to dinner to celebrate their victory.

A fortnight later, Jane and Catriona left for Europe, a trip which would take them several months. Catriona sent David numerous postcards from many of the places she visited. The part of the world that interested David most was Scotland. Firstly, because his ancestors had lived there and, secondly, because Scotland had supplied most, if not all, of the original dogs that formed the kelpie breed. The name kelpie was itself Gaelic and meant water spirit.

When Catriona returned, it appeared as if the trip had done her the world of good. She was back to her gorgeous best and entertained the MacLeods with a detailed account of her travels. She also informed them that she was going to university to do an Arts course. It would take three years. This, Anne decided, was the time to issue her long-delayed dinner invitation to get David and Catriona together.

Catriona was just as keen to spend time with

David before she had to go away again, so she suggested to Anne that King needed plenty of work, having been simply fed and not worked while she was overseas. She said that she would bring him up after lunch and give him a work-out and also let David see how the horse was shaping up. She would then stay on for dinner. Anne thought this was a splendid suggestion.

Jane, however, could not get Catriona away to Sydney quickly enough. She realised that anything could happen once Catriona got David to herself. But she was in no position to forbid Catriona to go to High Peaks after what David had done for her. So it was with great misgivings that she and Angus watched her ride away on King and eventually disappear round the bend of the road that led to High Peaks.

David met her as she came through the front gate. He was leading Ajana's beautiful bay filly, which he had recently broken in and was now educating. He reckoned she was the best horse he had ridden, including King, and that was saying something.

'King is too fat, Cat,' he said as they rode down the first paddock to the creek. Then, when Catriona rode straight past the exercise area where she had first ridden King, David said, 'I thought you wanted to show me what he could do.'

'I didn't come here to talk horses, David. I came here to talk about us.'

'What about us?' he asked.

'Wait until we get to the creek,' she said. She was

aware that David had a special place on a log beside the creek. Anne had told her that he went there when he needed to think things out. It was a really picturesque place, with big kurrajongs on either side and a yellow box tree hanging over it so that it was cool there, even on very hot days.

David took King's reins from Catriona and hitched the horses to separate trees. As he came back to her, she was untying the ribbon in her hair. She shook her head and her golden waves fell gloriously into place. Catriona watched for David's reaction. There was none. She sighed inwardly.

David thought that Catriona must have been steamed up about something, and he thought that it was going to be a heavy afternoon. He had never done anything to encourage her affections because he wasn't ready to settle down, but she always made him feel as if he owed her something.

'Look here, David, are you seeing Susan Cartwright?' Catriona burst out.

'No. Why?'

'Well, she implied that you were.'

'I escorted my Aunt Kate to the Hospital Ball and Susan happened to be there. I had a couple of dances with her, that's all. What's this all about, anyway?'

'David, have you got no idea at all about how I feel about you? Don't you care for me at all?'

'What gives you the idea I don't care for you? Of course I do. We've been friends for years.'

'I don't mean in terms of friendship. I'm talking

about genuine affection, something deeper than that. You have never shown any real enthusiasm for me; never tried to kiss me like other boys have. You've never asked me out. It seems to me that I've always been secondary to your dogs and horses,' she blurted out passionately.

'You have,' he replied calmly.

'There you are. That's what I mean.'

'I don't give horses like King to any old girl. You haven't seen me giving anything to Susan, have you?'

'Did you give me King for my sake or did you do it to get even with my father? I don't know. I have never known where you stand, David. Is there something about me that you find obnoxious? Are you looking for a different kind of girl?'

'What gives you the idea I am looking for any kind of girl?'

'If you aren't, I'm wasting my time even trying to figure you out. I want to get things settled between us before I go away to university for three years.'

'Cat, why would I be looking for a girl when the one I like is right next to me? I've never had eyes for anyone else.'

Catriona couldn't believe the words that were coming out of David's mouth.

'The problem isn't me; it's your parents. Your people have made it very clear that they're looking for a fellow with a big station and the right background. It's plain silly me thinking I could have you.'

Catriona looked at him with relief on her lovely

face. 'David, why didn't you say something? What does it matter what my people say? They would get used to the idea. They would have to.'

David shook his head. 'I doubt it. They have grander things in mind for you. But, Catriona, something else is just as important for me. You see, I don't want to settle down yet. I'm not ready. I can't think of getting married until we clear the debt on Poitrel, and once we've done that I want to have a go at winning the National Trial. I want to win that trial for Dad. He's never had the chance to show what his dogs can really do, but I know how much they mean to him. Nothing would please him more than to see one of his dogs win the National against the best dogs in Australia. I wouldn't care if I never worked another trial, if only I could win that one. I would come back here and be happy with what I've got. But I have to win that trial, Cat. It is my first and only dream.'

'Well, you are mine, David MacLeod,' Catriona replied, 'and you might never win that trial. There are scores of top dogs at Canberra.'

'Oh, I will win it, and when I do, then I'll come back here and see which way the wind blows.'

'If you want me, really want me, I will wait for you, David,' Catriona said, her eyes aglow with delight.

'If you insist on sticking it out for me, you'll cut yourself off from a lot of your friends. I'll never have the sort of money they have.'

'My God, I had no idea that sort of thing was

holding you back. Look, money isn't a problem. Stuart and I get a share from Inverlochy and Daddy has other investments in our names. I could put my money into a trust for our future.'

'Inverlochy is a fine property and I wouldn't want to contribute to it being cut up. That wouldn't be doing the right thing by Stuart. I'm not that sort of person. The land means a lot to me. Nobody likes to see acreage taken from them.'

'But don't you want me?' Catriona asked him honestly.

'Wanting and having are two very different things,' he said. 'Cat, I wouldn't want to be the cause of your unhappiness or to know that you got less than you could have. You could have anyone, Cat, anyone at all. You sure could do a lot better than me. Right now you might think I'm what you want, but will you feel that way in a few years' time? Wouldn't you be jealous if Susan married a rich guy who could give her everything?'

'David, I can't believe you would even ask that of me. You are the only man who could give me everything I want. I have even told Daddy as much.'

'You did? And what did he do?'

'He sent me overseas,' she said, laughing.

'Okay, so your father knows. That doesn't mean he approves, or ever will.'

'David, do you love me?' Catriona asked.

'I don't know. I'm very fond of you, I really am. I just don't think this is a good idea. You could never convince your people to accept me, and I wouldn't want you to have to try.'

'Yes, I could. If it's my parents that are holding you back, we can settle the matter right here. You can make love to me here and now and if I get pregnant, they will have to agree to you marrying me.'

'What a damned stupid suggestion, Cat. You must be off your head,' David said vehemently. 'You just said you thought you knew me. Hell, Cat, you don't know me at all if you think I would put you in that position. You go off and do your uni course. I need more time. See how you feel in a year's time.'

'David, I love you. You just think about that. The day you feel the same way and tell me that you do, we will become engaged. I don't care if it causes mayhem at Inverlochy. It's my life and I'm going to live the rest of it my way. I know you want it, too. I can see right through you.'

'Don't be so bossy, Cat. It doesn't suit you. Let's get going. Who knows what my folks will be thinking?'

'The mind boggles,' Catriona said, and laughed with real joy for the first time in years. She leant her head against David's shoulder and he responded by putting an arm around her waist. She sighed and closed her eyes. 'If you only knew how much I have wanted you to do that,' she said. 'You must believe me when I tell you that I'm sincere about waiting for you.'

'I'd like to think you are,' he said.

'I think you really do love me, David. What do I have to do to convince you that I'm serious about you?'

'You could learn to milk a cow,' he said.

'Milk a cow! Why would I need to milk a cow?' she asked.

'How else do we feed the pups?' David laughed.

Catriona made a face. 'David MacLeod, you'll be the death of me,' she said.

Catriona rode back to Inverlochy to have a shower and get changed before driving back up for dinner. Anne was waiting for David as he came up the steps from seeing her off.

'Have you and Catriona finally decided to get together?' she asked with ill-concealed impatience.

'Mum, can't a bloke get a bit of privacy around here? If you must know, Catriona told me that she loved me and I told her I liked her a lot but that I have some things to do before I settle down.'

'God help me. You put her off?' Anne gasped.

'Yes and no. I suggested she sees how she feels in a year or so.'

'You seem to be treating this as a big joke. I thought you must have told her something wonderful. She certainly had a glow on.'

'I told her I was fond of her. That was about halfway to what she wanted to hear. If Catriona is a really special girl, she'll wait for me. Otherwise, I'm better off without her. It's as simple as that. If I have to go up against her parents, I want to know she's behind me all the way.'

'Nothing is as simple as that,' Anne said.

'I'm not going to worry too much for the time being about what Catriona does. She's going off to do her course, and who knows what will happen down there? Catriona is a lovely girl and I'm just a hill country stockman.'

'You are an old hardhead for a boy of eighteen,' Anne said.

'You've also told me a million times that I am very practical. Aren't I being practical now?'

To that question, Anne could not find an answer.

Chapter Twenty-one

Catriona looked stunning when she arrived that evening for dinner in a plum-coloured dress which enhanced her lovely figure. She had changed her hair-style so that it was coiled up. She came bearing two bottles of white wine, which she knew both Kate and Jean enjoyed with their evening meal. Andy and David drank the occasional beer.

The first course of the meal was spinach in a pastry so light it almost melted in the mouth, and Catriona said she had tasted nothing nicer on her overseas trip. The main course was a piece of prime beef that had been sewn into a roll and then filled with herb and onion stuffing. And for dessert they had apple pie and cream.

'Wow,' David said as he finished off a big slice of the pie. 'That was some dinner. Cat, you should come more often.'

'I am sure she would if you asked her,' Anne got in quickly.

After they had cleared away the dishes and drunk some coffee, Anne took out her papers and put them on the table in front of her.

'The details I have here came principally from Andy and his mother,' she began. 'But I also wrote away and obtained some additional information on the MacLeod family. I intend to put this material into book form before I am too much older. Your family has their history properly recorded, Catriona. It traces back a very long way.

'There was, of course, a big difference between the Campbells and the MacLeods back in Scotland. The Campbells were Lowlanders while the MacLeods were Highlanders. Most of the Highland clans were enemies of the Campbells, who in turn considered the Highland clans to be mere cattle thieves.

'Andy's blood traces back to the MacLeods of Harris, Skye and Glenelg from the Western Isles of Scotland. Like many other Scots, the MacLeods were subject to eviction and were forced to leave their native country and make new lives in the United States, Canada and Australia, where their descendants can still be found to this day. Perhaps as many as thirty-five thousand people were evicted in all. The torment began after the Jacobite rebellion in 1745 to 1746 and continued for over one hundred years. Tenants were evicted to make way for sheep, and, after sporadic resistance, the western Highlanders were involved in what came to be known as the Crofters' War. This caused the British Parliament to despatch a committee of enquiry into the whole awful business. Some Scots returned home but most did not, because although conditions were hard in the colonies, they were not as hard as back on the hills of their native land.

'William MacLeod was one of these refugees. Along with his wife and small son he was destined for Canada but, because of his knowledge of cattle, he was offered a position on a developing cattle ranch in the United States.

'William was an excellent cattleman and much sought after for his knowledge of cattle husbandry. He took up land for a ranch of his own and, as fate would have it, he prospered. A descendant still owns this ranch today. One of William's grandsons, Angus MacLeod, migrated to Australia after the gold strikes of the 1850s, eventually struck it lucky and purchased land along the Lachlan River. Periodic floods drove him off this land and on to the New England district between Glen Innes and Armidale. There were many Scots in this region and, while the country was hard in winter, if you owned enough of it, you could make a fair living. Labour was cheap and there was a rising demand for wool.

'Angus MacLeod fathered six sons and three daughters. One son, Tormid, went as an officer to the Boer War. On his arrival back in Australia he became a landowner and politician through the acquisition of a large property near Scone in the Hunter district of New South Wales. Tormid married an actress of some repute and their only son, James, was Andy's father. James grew up to be very good-looking and women were attracted to him like bees to honey. He had a certain degree of irresponsibility, which set him apart from the previous males of the MacLeod lineage. But there was no doubt he was a courageous man, which he proved in the Second World War, coming out of the AIF with a chest full of medals – and a propensity for whisky.

'Now we come close to home,' Anne continued. 'Some years earlier, when the few large original properties in the Merriwa, Willow Tree and Quirindi districts were cut up for closer settlement, Tormid MacLeod purchased a hill property fairly cheaply. He had installed James on this property in 1939, but James didn't stay there long. When he joined the AIF he left his wife and young son on the property with only one old stockman to keep an eye on things. While James was overseas, the property went downhill as rabbits bred in thousands. Tormid died in 1945 and James came back from the war to find that he had inherited a run-down property and that he had to find a lot of money to pay the onerous death duties. The sale of the hill property, which is where we find ourselves sitting tonight, would not have realised enough money to pay those duties, so the property at Scone had to be sacrificed. There was still not enough money left over from the sale of that to clear the debt on High Peaks, and there was hardly a living in the place the way it was, especially for a person with James MacLeod's flamboyant tastes.

'Fortunately, Andy's mother, Alice, was made of good material, and she needed to be because High Peaks was not a place for the faint-hearted. The property was situated at the very end of the road and topped by high peaks. When the wind blew, the she-oaks along the creek would sigh all through the night. Going to town was a real adventure, as petrol was rationed and Alice and young Andrew sometimes had to come in by horse and buggy. For all that, Andrew had a very happy childhood and he was lucky to have a neighbour in that old Paddy Covers, who was a top bushman and stockman. He taught young Andrew all that he knows today. Thankfully, Andrew somehow reclaimed the industrious character of the earlier-generation MacLeods rather than that of his father.

'By the time Andrew's father came back from the war, Andy was in his early teens. He could do almost anything in the way of bush and stock work and had a real flair for handling sheepdogs and horses. There were several outstanding dog and horse men in the area, and Paddy himself was good with both. Paddy had acquired some very good kelpies and with these dogs he could do any kind of stock work. Andrew took an immediate liking to the kelpie, and Paddy let him have a pair for his own use.

'Andrew and his mother were very close but there was antipathy between Andy and his father. The property had a big mortgage on it and simply did not run to the extravagances his father was fond of. While Andy was tramping the hills ringing green timber and shooting foxes to earn pocket money, his father was away at social functions all around the country, wasting money that should have been going into the property. Moreover, he drank far too much. It was his father's drinking that set Andy against alcohol, which is why you rarely see him drinking to this day.

'The real crisis in Andy's life came when his father, returning to High Peaks late one night after a party, crashed his car into the creek below the bridge and killed Alice. Her death caused a big change in Andy. He became a silent, withdrawn teenager who would hardly speak to his father from morning to night. He looked after himself, took himself to school, washed his own clothes and prepared his own meals. Every spare moment was spent up in the hills.

'Unfortunately, Alice did not live to see the wool boom, which began in 1950 at the time of the Korean War. This brought in more money than the Mac-Leods had ever handled on the property, but the extra money was put into buying an expensive car, race-horses and more high living. James MacLeod did not concern himself with reducing the debt that still plagued the running of the property.

'Andrew grew into a large, powerful man, and when he left school at the age of fifteen, he began shearing and crutching at the local sheds. He was able to bank his money in a small account his mother had

404

started for him. After two seasons of shearing, Andy was putting out a lot of sheep and ringing sheds. He bought himself a Chevrolet utility and began going to sheepdog trials. He won most of them and established the reputation his dogs have today.

'But Andrew continued to consider that his father was very weak, despite all the medals he had received. He believed that plenty of other men had been to the war, had seen as much or more than his father had, had suffered more, yet hadn't become booze artists. But the booze was only part of it. The way his father wasted money was an even bigger problem. However, the fact remained that James was his father and Andrew couldn't disregard him completely.

'Towards the end of his life, James made a couple of half-hearted attempts to effect a reconciliation with Andy. It was as if he could see that Andy was everything he was not. James told Andrew that he was really proud of him, that he'd done a hell of a job on High Peaks, and that he appreciated Andy saving his money to help out with the debt on the place. He then went on to confess that his heart was not the best: he'd had some bad pains and had been to see the doctor. He knew his time was coming to an end and wanted Andy to know how he really felt about him. He told Andrew that the property had been willed to him, and he asked Andrew to make a strange promise; a promise that if he ever needed advice he was to go and see Angus Campbell. Angus had been made an executor, who would keep an eye on things until Andrew was old enough to take over. This was Old Angus Campbell he was referring to.

'It was also during this rare conversation that James asked Andrew how he was off for money. A bolt of dread ran through Andy as he hoped his father wasn't about to ask him for a loan. Thankfully he wasn't, but he did confess that he had discussed their financial woes with Old Angus.

'Andrew was appalled. It was bad enough to waste money as his father had done, but to have taken their problems to a neighbour was extremely embarrassing, especially knowing that old Campbell would never waste a penny of *his* money. It was at that moment that Andy swore to himself he would clear the debt on High Peaks, even if it killed him, and he would never run to a neighbour with details of his affairs.

'James MacLeod lived on for another seven months. Andy was shearing at a local shed and coming home every evening.

'One night Andy came home to find no sign of his father, and the house in complete darkness. He grabbed for a torch as quickly as he could and set about on a desperate search. In the stables he noticed his father's favourite horse, Rajah, was missing.

'He returned to the house in a real quandary. There was nothing he or anybody else could do that night. The hill country, especially the slopes of Yellow Rock and Jimmy's Mountain, was simply too dangerous to ride over at night. And on this particular night there was not even a moon to light his way.

'The next morning, the first thing Andy saw out of his window was his father's horse standing patiently at the gate beyond the dog yards and kennels. Its reins were trailing and one was broken short. He caught the horse and brought it back to the stables, where he went over it for injuries. There was none that he could see. He was reluctant to involve Angus Campbell at this stage, but he had a feeling the matter was serious and felt that he didn't have any choice. Old Angus said that he would come himself with Young Angus and their overseer, Buck Covers, a son of Andy's old mentor, Paddy. The three men and a horse for each arrived within the hour. Equipped with ropes, a blanket and a water bottle, the four men set off into the mountains.

'It was Andy who first saw the body in the gully to their left up on Yellow Rock. Below the track, the side of the cliff plunged away down a steep slope that was bisected by deeply cut gullys and ravines, and it was there, at the pit of one of those ravines, that James MacLeod's body was sprawled.

'Andy tied a rope to a rough-barked kurrajong, and without another word he dropped over the ledge. Hand over hand with his boots scuffing loose rocks and shale, he lowered himself down to his father's body. In Andy's mind he had not set himself a remarkable task: he was young, very strong and confident of his own ability. Of course if the rope had broken, that might have been the end of him then and there, but Andy never used faulty gear.

'Andy at last eased himself off the rope and saw the others, two rope lengths above him, peering anxiously down. He lifted his hand to signify that he was in good shape and then dropped to his knees to examine his father.

'When he turned him over he was momentarily shaken by the sight of the ruined face. He felt for signs of life. The body was cold and stiff. His father was dead.

'During the traumatic years following his father's death, Andy grew to depend on Old Angus. He had been there when Andrew found James's body, he had helped out with the police enquiries, and he had always been on hand to give Andy advice or help him out with special deals with stock and station agents. Andy returned his help by handling the Inverlochy horses and by shearing. The two men had a lot of respect for each other, despite their social differences. Old Angus gave off an outwardly cold impression to outsiders, but he was an eminently fair man. He was a hard taskmaster, but he acknowledged talent and excellence whether it was displayed by a horseman, a shearer or a stud breeder. There was no second-best for Old Angus, and Young Angus – your father, Catriona – followed closely in his father's footsteps. Old Angus was the first outsider to recognise Andy's talent and his capacity to work hard to make something of himself. Perhaps their common Scottish ancestry meant something to Old Angus.

'So you see, Catriona, our families trace back

together a very long way. There are ties that bind us together over many generations, and I dare say these bonds will only be strengthened in the future,' Anne said with a glimmer in her eye.

Later in the evening, when David saw Catriona to her car, she took his arm and held him close to her. 'I will wait for you, David,' she said. 'You are the only man in the world for me. You win that National Trial and I'll prove it.'

'Time will tell, Cat,' he said. He didn't want her to leave, yet he couldn't ask her to stay. There was a price to pay for everything. His father had almost paid the supreme price. Winning the National for his father might mean losing Catriona, but he had to take that risk. Time was running out for his father. He had to put everything he could into winning. No matter what, David wanted to be able to hand the big cup and sash over to his father, acknowledging Andy's outstanding expertise in kelpie breeding, for all the world to see.

Catriona kissed David on the cheek and gently touched the scar above his right eye.

'Get going, Cat. Get going to your old uni,' he said gruffly. It was all he could manage to say.

Chapter Twenty-two

While Catriona was away at university, David and High Peaks saw about as much of her as they had when she had been away at boarding school. Not that they had much time to lament her absence. There was always so much to do.

It was fortunate that after some years of low prices the wool market had risen considerably and cattle prices had also strengthened, allowing David to go out shearing and crutching a little less. And at this time the MacLeods were able, at last, to pay off the remaining money owing on Poitrel.

But what was most important in David's mind was the pending return of his splendid dog Nap. During the three years that Nap had been away begetting many fine pups, David had had to take a rather low-key role with his dogs. He had attended the local trial each year, enjoying great success every time. He had bred and kept a few young dogs from his father's old bitches, the best of which would have suited many people. Yet none of them had been exactly what David was looking for. They had not possessed the almost magical qualities that he knew should be present in a truly outstanding dog.

Bruce McClymont kept his word and David received a phone call to say that he would return Nap three years to the day from when he had left High Peaks. Anne, who realised what a wrench it had been for her son to let Nap go, sensed how excited David was about the dog's imminent return. She had hardly seen him so worked up as when he waited for Mr McClymont to arrive. This time it was a new green Ford utility that pulled up in the driveway, and its driver was marginally older and a little greyer than he had been three years earlier.

It was then that something quite remarkable happened, something that neither Bruce McClymont nor David would ever forget. McClymont unlocked the padlock on the dog crate and called Nap out. The big red and tan dog jumped down, sniffed the air and then raced across to where David was standing a little distance away. Nap stood before David, wagging his tail, and then turned and trotted across to his old log kennel. He jumped up on the log and then lay down with his eyes fixed on David. It was as if the intervening three years since his departure from High Peaks had never happened. For Nap, Bruce McClymont had ceased to exist.

'Well, I'll be damned,' McClymont said. 'Nap sure

knows where he is. It's as if he's never been away.'

David walked across and patted the dog's head before snapping the chain on his collar. Except for a slight greyness about his muzzle, it was the Nap he knew so well.

'Did he do the job for you?' David asked.

'Best sire dog I ever used,' McClymont said enthusiastically. 'I've got some very good dogs by him, thank you. I took your advice and put him over his best daughter, and there's a male that is Nap all over again for looks. Started real well, too.'

'That's great. I've got a pup for you. We mated Belle twice and this pup is from her latest litter.'

He took McClymont across to the concrete-floored shed beneath the giant pepperina tree where all the MacLeod pups were reared. There were six pups in the pen. David bent over and picked up a dark-blue and tan bitch pup and handed her to McClymont.

'This pup is very like Belle except that she hasn't got her short tail. If she's as good as her mother, you won't have any reason to complain.'

'Terrific, David. What do I owe you?'

'Nothing at all. You honoured our agreement and brought Nap back in good order. We should work together to keep these strains going. It's hard for one person to do it on his own.'

'I'm very grateful to you, David. Any time you want something from me, it's yours.'

David nodded his acknowledgement of the offer.

'So you're going to mate Nap to Belle and work on those pups?' McClymont asked.

'Yes, I am. We've paid off our debt, and now I can concentrate one hundred per cent on the dogs.'

'That's great, David. You've waited a long time for this. The day you go to Canberra, I want to be there, too.'

'I'll be sure to let you know. I don't expect to be working dogs there for another three years, though.'

'I guess not,' McClymont agreed. 'Belle has just had this litter so it will be some time before her pups develop. Your dogs will still be young 'uns in three years' time.'

'But old enough if good enough,' David said. 'And I'm going to take Belle, too.'

'She's a top dog, all right. I don't think there's been a real top kelpie bitch working in trials since Kanimbla Betty. They tell me she was a real eye-catcher.'

'I didn't see her so I wouldn't know. She was too lively early on, by all accounts, but when she won the Open at the Queensland Championships in '54, she was the only dog in the Open final to pen her sheep. Belle has the same cover and footwork that Betty was supposed to have had.'

'How is your father?' McClymont asked.

'Miles better. He has his voice back now and can even do odd jobs around the place. He'll enjoy talking to you.'

So Andy, David and Mr McClymont spent several

413

hours yarning about kelpies, and when McClymont left for his Riverina property, he was possessed of a great deal more knowledge than he had thought possible to acquire in one day.

Later that afternoon, once McClymont had left, David and Andy walked down to the dog yards to have a look at Nap. 'He knew the place straight off, Dad. Just trotted away and jumped up on his old kennel.'

'An intelligent dog like him would never forget where he came from. When you boil everything down, it's brains that really matters most in a stock dog. You can breed plenty of dogs with eye, and with eye and cast, but you need brains and heart to make a top dog. I know you realise that, and you were very wise not sell Nap outright. I wouldn't wait for Belle. Use Nap on the first bitch that comes on season. That way, if anything happens to Nap, you'll have some of his progeny to go on with. You could have dogs going before Belle's pups are old enough to assess. If you lose Nap before he has pups, then you've lost everything. You know what can happen to stock dogs,' Andy said.

'I suppose if Molly comes on, I could mate her to Nap.'

'That's the stuff. The sooner you get that trial out of your system, the sooner you can settle down.'

'You're as bad as Mum.'

'Life's short, Davie. That Catriona is a bonzer girl. Don't lose her for anything.'

414

'You've sure changed your tune. I still reckon Angus wouldn't want me for his son-in-law.'

'Times are changing, mate. I reckon Catriona will do whatever she wants to do. Sure, Angus is a hard, shrewd bloke. He'll play the game right to the final bell; but if Catriona puts her foot down, he won't risk losing her. You see if I'm not right.'

Catriona hadn't changed her feelings in the slightest. During her breaks from university she worked King intensively, and the year after she went away she won her first Champion Hack award with him. And in every holiday break she came to High Peaks and rode the hills with David. It seemed to Anne and Kate to be a strange sort of relationship, more like that of a brother and sister working together than a passionate love affair. David appeared to have no romantic interest in Catriona, but the girl still had stars in her eyes when she looked at him. The two women wondered how long Catriona would be prepared to play the waiting game. They were aware that she had several other suitors, and that Angus favoured at least two of them.

'If David loses her, it will be his own fault,' Anne complained to her sister one day.

'Damned right,' Kate agreed. 'If Catriona puts up with this state of affairs, she's a girl in a million.'

Even the matter of Susan Cartwright's wedding did not provide sufficient impetus to spur David into action. Susan had finally given up on David and had

415

become engaged to a young grazier from Coolah by the name of Michael Hunter.

Catriona was a bridesmaid at the wedding, and even the MacLeods were invited. This could have been because of Catriona's friendship with David, but was more likely due to what David had done the night Roger and Catriona were assaulted. David had little time for weddings but finally agreed to attend at Catriona's behest.

David was the biggest and best-looking young man there, and Anne took great pleasure in observing the attention he received. David thought it was a boring and wasteful afternoon. Most of the young men were only interested in getting plastered. He put up a cheerful front, though, and even danced with the bride.

'You look lovely,' he said as he danced Susan across the floor.

'Thank you,' she replied.

'I hope everything works out well for you,' he said.

'Thank you, David. So do I,' Susan said.

He was pleased when their dance came to an end because he could see Catriona watching them. She looked absolutely stunning. She always did.

'Poor Susan,' Catriona said when they were finally dancing together.

'Why do you say that?' he asked.

'You know she really wanted you,' Catriona said.

'Well, I never wanted her. Susan must love Michael enough to marry him,' David said.

'There's a lot more to it than that. Not everybody gets exactly what they want.'

'You're doing exactly what you want,' David said.

'No I'm not. I'm waiting for you to get this dog business out of your system.'

David didn't know what to say in reply to that, and was thankful when the music came to an end.

The next morning he was up in the hills very early. He was riding a young horse called Gilt, which he had bred from one of Wilf White's old brood mares. He had ridden better horses, but they weren't all cracker-jacks. It was exhilarating to ride across the top of the range country and feel the early morning breeze on his face. He sat with his leg thrown across the pommel of the saddle and drank in the vista that was spread out before him. Nap sat beside the horse and seemed to be enjoying the view just as much as David. There might be grander and more picturesque mountains in the south, but this range was David's country. One day he would be buried on the hill above High Peaks home-stead. His grandparents were buried there and his parents would be buried there, too. He did not think very often of the afterlife. He was more attracted to his father's practical philosophy of being honest and keeping your word. His mother had tried to teach him Christian values, and he understood that Christians believed the soul lived on forever, but he did not give the matter a great deal of his attention, although he did like to think that the souls of his parents would remain forever in those ancient hills.

When he returned from his ride, he found his father waiting for him by the horse yard.

'Tim Sparkes has sent us a message, David,' he said without preamble. 'Seems he is real crook in Rockhampton Hospital. He had a bad fall and he wants to see us both. He told us to bring a horse float.'

'Hell, that's terrible, Dad. I didn't think there was a horse that could throw Tim.'

'There's always a horse that can throw you, David.'

'Why the float?'

'I wouldn't be surprised if he had a horse for you. Trust Tim to think of horses even while he's on his back.'

'Dad, can you manage it? It's a long way.'

'I have to go, Davie. Can't let my old mate down. He wouldn't ask us up there without a good reason.'

'Okay, but take it easy. Let me do the driving. Can Mum handle things here?'

'Kate's going to take a few days off and stay with her. Jean'll stay on at Poitrel. The sheep are crutched so they should be right, and Lucky is a good watchdog.'

They left at five a.m. the next morning and made it to Toowoomba that night. David insisted that they stay at a motel, as his mother had laid down the law about not getting Andy over-tired. The next night they got as far as Biloela after crossing the palm-lined Dawson River. It was only a short run into Rock-hampton next morning, and they were at the hospital by nine o'clock. When they asked for Mr Sparkes they were introduced to one of the hospital's resident doctors, who took them into his office and asked them to sit down.

'I understand that you are very close friends of Mr Sparkes and have come up from New South Wales to see him. I should warn you that you're in for a shock. He was very badly hurt when the horse threw him. He has severe spinal injuries and will never walk again. And that is not his only injury. He is lucky to be alive. You will find him completely immobilised. Try not to look too surprised when you see him. He has great spirit and has been looking forward to your visit. Ready to see him now?'

They followed the doctor to the intensive care unit, which brought back unpleasant memories of Andy's stroke.

The unit Tim was in was larger than the one at their own hospital. A nurse was sitting beside a bed in which a man lay with a collar of some kind about his neck and a number of tubes attached to his body. They never would have recognised that man as Tim Sparkes. But then he spoke and there was no doubt. Although huskier, the voice was unmistakable.

'Hi ya, Andy, Davie. How's my old mates? Gee, it's good to see ya. When did ya leave?'

'The morning after we got your message,' Andrew answered.

'I just knew you'd drop everything to get here. Some blokes you can put your wallet on and some

419

you can't. I was talking to Anne some weeks ago and she said you'd made a terrific recovery, Andy. Hell, who'd have believed it, eh, mate? Jeez, look at the size of young Davie. You're a bloody giant. And I hear you've been handing out hidings.'

'Nah. Don't know what you're talking about,' David said.

'Don't try and bullshit me. Anne sent me up the bloody paper!'

David hadn't been aware that Tim and his mother had been swapping news regularly. Tim was no letter writer, but he had rung every few months to find out how things were going, even more frequently following Andrew's stroke.

'Should you be talking so much?' David asked and glanced at the nurse.

'You can have ten minutes with him now and another ten minutes this afternoon,' she said. 'I will be just outside the door.'

'Stuff ten minutes,' Tim said. 'These are my mates and they've come twelve hundred miles to see me. You come back when I ring for you.'

The nurse threw up her hands and left.

'Bloody Hitlers, these nurses. It's bad enough having them hold a man's dick in a bottle without them tellin' ya how long ya can talk to your mates. Listen. I'm real glad you could get up here. I want to lay something on the line now you're here. I'm done for. My spine is buggered and I'll never walk again, let alone ride a horse. I've got the station and plenty of

420

money in the bank, so I can afford the medical expenses . . . full-time nurse and all that crap. I asked you to bring a horse float because I want you fellas to have the stallion. He's the best stock-horse sire in Queensland and I know that you both want to breed. Take him, and a good mare with him.'

'Tim, that's very generous, but won't you need the stallion? You sell young horses,' Andy said.

'I've got several good colts by him, Andy. I don't need him any more. There's still plenty of years and foals in him. Look, there's a map in the drawer there. That's how you get to the station from here. My overseer knows all about it. Grab those horses and some feed and head off for the high country. It will be a big relief to know the horse is with you fellas. Say, how is that mother of yours, Davie? And Kate?'

Tim was more keen to hear what had happened at High Peaks since his last visit than to discuss the business of his stallion any further – and it took a lot longer than ten minutes to tell him! The nurse fluttered in and out, but she did not have the heart or the courage to ask Andy and David to leave. It was obvious how much her patient was enjoying the visit.

'Look, Tim, we mustn't stay too long. We'll have some lunch and come back later, eh?'

'Great, but don't hang about on my account. You grab those horses and clear out.'

'We aren't going to do that,' Andy said. 'There's a lot to talk about. We don't have to bolt back.'

Andrew and David stayed in Rockhampton for

two days before going out to Tim's station. It was about a hundred miles north of Rockhampton, and not difficult to locate using Tim's map.

After they had inspected the horses they were left in no doubt that Tim knew his business. The stallion was magnificent and as quiet as a lamb. He was a bay with a white star on his forehead and two white stockings on his hind legs. There were two lovely mares – bay in colour, like their sire – and chock-full of quality.

'Beats me how a fella could pick between those mares,' Andrew said. 'I hate having to try and pick the best.'

'The boss said that I was to run some cattle in if you want to try the mares,' the overseer said as Andy and David inspected the two mares in Tim's big horse yard.

Andrew shook his head. 'No need for that. If Tim picked these mares out for us, there's no need to try them. He's spot-on with horses and he knows what we're looking for. Either mare would be right.'

The overseer nodded. 'I reckon you're right. They're a bonzer pair. The stallion gets them like that year in, year out.'

Finally, Andrew let David make the selection. The mare he chose seemed to be a slightly freer mover than her mate but there was almost nothing between them. She had a peculiar-shaped blaze on her head, which he liked, and a great pair of eyes. David thought she looked to be clever. They loaded the horses, threw in some hay and chaff, and took off.

But they weren't heading home to High Peaks just yet. There was one more session at the hospital with Tim. It was hard to say goodbye, and tears were brought to the eyes of even those three hard nuts.

'What a way for a bloke like Tim to end up,' David said as they drove out of Rockhampton.

'If you mess about with young horses long enough, you're sure to get hurt, but it beats me how a horse by this stallion could be so mean,' Andrew said and scratched his jaw.

'It wasn't a horse by this stallion, Dad,' David corrected him. 'It was a mate's horse. Tim told me all about it while you were out of the room. I just don't know how Tim will handle being an invalid,' David said.

'Nor me,' Andrew agreed. 'I suppose you realise that this stallion could bring us in a fair bit of money if we stand him?'

'Gee, Dad, I haven't got time to mess about with a heap of outside mares. I think we should use the horse for our own mares and keep his progeny exclusive.'

'It's just that he isn't a young horse. If we were going to stand him, we should do it fairly soon,' Andrew said.

'I don't have the time for that sort of thing, and you can't go playing about with mares in your condition. I want to win that National before I do anything with horses. If we mate our best mares to this

423

old fellow, we'll have young horses ready for handling in about three years' time. That should be just about right for me.'

'More important right now is the question of where we are going tonight,' Andy said.

'Somewhere north of Toowoomba, I reckon.' They had packed their swags and cooking gear because they knew they would need to camp out on the way home with the horses.

It was almost dark before David spotted the creek he had seen on the upward trip. While David walked and fed and watered the two horses, Andrew collected kindling and branches for a fire. It was cool enough to enjoy the fire's warmth, and after they had cooked and eaten a rough but filling feed of steak and tomatoes, they climbed into their swags and lay back, well satisfied with the camp they had made.

'If we could get away real early, we could be home tomorrow evening,' Andrew suggested.

'That would be a big day for you, Dad. It's a good ten hours' drive from Toowoomba to home.'

'If we can get away by four, we could do it easily, even with a halfway stop to let the horses off,' Andrew said.

'We can give it a go, but if you're feeling tired, let me know and we'll camp. Mum said that I wasn't to push you in any way,' David said.

'I've got a very good idea what Mum would have told you,' Andrew said, grinning.

He was nearly back to what he was, David

thought. Andy couldn't work like he used to, but he had all his wits about him. It was just great to be able to talk to him again.

They were up at three a.m. and left just after four. David drove and made several stops so the trip was as easy as possible for Andrew and the horses. They stopped for lunch at a good-sized creek north of Glen Innes. The horses had a decent drink and nibbled some of the fresh grass along the creek.

'That should do them until we get home,' David said. 'You okay, Dad?'

'Never better, Davie.'

When they reached Tamworth, David rang to let his mother know where they were.

It was still light when they arrived back at High Peaks, and Anne and Kate were standing near the horse yards waiting for them. David embraced his mother and Kate, who were both obviously relieved to have them back.

'Is Dad all right?' Anne whispered in David's ear.

'Right as rain, Mum.'

The two men slept soundly that night, and David was up at six next morning. He had his usual toast and cup of tea and went out to give the dogs their early morning run. He was currently working on a dog from Belle, whom he had called Jack. Jack had been sired by a son of his father's great old dog, Ben. Jack looked like being a fair three-sheep dog, although he was not a world-beater. He was a dog to put some polish on while he waited for Nap's pups.

Andrew had suggested taking Jack to a Maiden Trial.

'You wouldn't be disgraced,' he said.

'I don't know, Dad. I don't think he's good enough to cart about. I can do a lot better.'

'Look here, David. Mum and I have been talking and we reckon it's about time you had a spell. Why don't you take a few days off and drive down to Canberra and just have a look at the National? You'll get a good idea of the standard of the dogs and the layout. You could learn a lot.'

David thought about his father's suggestion and decided that it was worth taking up. He rang the secretary of the Sheepdog Trials Association and booked a caravan on the ground. He wouldn't enter a dog, not even Belle, but would simply go as an onlooker.

When he finally took off, he left behind a very relieved family who had never before been able to persuade him to take time off.

He was full of trepidation about negotiating Sydney and handling its traffic, but he took his time, and with the aid of a meticulously marked map from Kate he finally made it to the southern outskirts of the city. He hadn't driven in such traffic before and wondered how people could endure it day in and day out. He drove at his leisure and tried to look at everything he passed. The variation in country amazed him; and none was more surprising than that around Gunning. He had heard about the high prices paid for Yass and Gunning wool and expected that it would be green and lush like New England. The hard, flinty nature of the country around Gunning surprised him, but he supposed that it was a factor in the production of the very clean wool for which Gunning was famous.

He drove to the Canberra Showground from Yass and did not have to negotiate Canberra itself, although his mother and Kate had instructed him not to come home without seeing the city. David decided to wait until the trials were over before becoming a tourist.

He arrived at the showground towards evening of the second day of competition and saw that most of the caravans seemed to be occupied by triallers. There were dogs everywhere; some were locked in small mesh crates or on the backs of utilities and some were staked out beside vehicles. He was disappointed not to bump into anyone he knew that first evening on the ground.

The next morning the first dogs were working quite early. He had stayed in bed an hour longer than usual, and had heard the first handlers and their dogs being called while he was cooking his breakfast. There had been a fog across the whole showground and some of it persisted as he saw a black and white dog being walked through the gate onto the ground. He was in no hurry, as he knew there would be plenty of dogs to watch over the next few days. It was ideal having a caravan on the ground because it was a snug place to get out of the wind, which could be very cold indeed.

After breakfast he found a seat in the stand behind the casting peg and settled down to watch the dogs. Some of the names of the handlers working these dogs were familiar to him. It was not until nearly lunchtime that he saw anyone he actually knew. The first was Harry Marchant, who had several times worked dogs at their local trials. Harry was working a young kelpie and border collie-cross he had trialled at their last local event. Unfortunately it wasn't doing very well at the National. It was short on its cast and came on to its sheep too quickly. David marked it down on his list and penned in some remarks for his father.

Most of the dogs were border collies, although a lot of them looked as if they had a splash of kelpie blood in them. There were not many of the heavy-coated Old Country-type border collies he had expected to see. The highest score for the day was 91 out of a possible 100, and while David felt that although most of the dogs were well handled, very few had exceptional holding ability at the obstacles. They seemed to be over-commanded, as if their handlers had either taken the initiative out of their dogs or they were not confident enough of their dogs' abilities to allow them to demonstrate natural cover and holding traits. Only two kelpies worked that first day of David's stay, and both of them overworked and consequently stirred their sheep too much. One kelpie scored 72 and the other 68. David knew he could do much better than this.

The next morning he bumped into Harry Marchant, who was walking a dog round the ground's perimeter.

'G'day, David. This is a surprise. Never seen you in these parts before. Where's your dogs?'

'At home. I'm here on a bit of a holiday, actually. First one I've had since I left school.'

'You should have your dogs here. I've told a lot of people about your kelpies.'

'I'll come back in a year or two and bring some dogs.'

'That's great. I'll look forward to it. Now I have to go and walk this dog, David. I'll look you up later on.'

Harry spread the word that David MacLeod was on the ground, and several kelpie handlers came and introduced themselves. Harry had told the southern triallers about David's exploits, like winning a trial at the age of ten. David and Andrew had been only names to most of the interstate kelpie men so they did not pass up the opportunity to meet the son of a legend.

Talking to these handlers filled in most of the morning so David did not see all the dogs work their rounds, but that afternoon he saw a familiar figure get out of a green Ford utility: Bruce McClymont. McClymont went straight across to where David was standing.

'You didn't tell me you were coming here, David,' he said. 'No dogs?'

'No, just come for a looksee. It was a last-minute decision.'

'It's great that you're here, anyway. Come and meet Mona. I've told her a lot about you, and she sure loved Nap.'

David was taken across to the McClymont caravan where he was introduced to a strapping, dark-haired woman who seemed to take an immediate liking to him. David was sat down and given a huge afternoon tea, and then found it hard to get away.

From that afternoon on, David hardly had a minute to himself. If he was not with someone watching dogs on the ground, he was in someone else's caravan drinking tea. His early nights had also come to an end, as he was expected to join Bruce or one of the other triallers for a yarn late into the night.

Despite the sidetracking hospitality, David did manage to see a lot of dogs, and these included dogs owned by nearly all of the major sheepdog figures of the time. He noted their techniques and the way their dogs worked, or were allowed to work, and stored all these observations away for the future. The scores crept up as the better dogs worked, and the top dog was on 96 when the Open Trial concluded. The top-scoring dogs had to work in the final and the cut-off score was 92. That meant that only four points separated the top-scoring dog from the lowest-scoring finalist. With so few points separating them, any of the eight finalists could have won the National.

A bitter wind began to blow as the first of the finalists came out to work. The first thing David noticed was that the sheep became more difficult to handle. They did not stand and wait for the dog as a lot of the sheep had done in the first round. They walked or trotted into the wind in the manner of sheep down through the centuries. This meant that a dog had either a short cast on one side or a long cast on the alternate side. This posed the most interesting trialling he had seen since he had arrived on the ground.

In between the first and second finalist, he ran back to the caravan for a warmer coat and then resumed his seat behind the casting peg. The wind blew all that afternoon and it became progressively colder as the other dogs worked. One dog crossed while casting to the short side and only two dogs scored above 90. The border collie that won the trial was, in David's opinion, a very good dog with a tonne of strength. It also had the ability to roll sheep in at the obstacles. The old chap who worked this dog gave it more leeway than most of the other handlers did. He seemed to have confidence in the dog's ability to do the job. David felt it was a pleasing result.

At the end of the day David took several pictures of the course. It was too cold to hang about for long, and he was on his way to the van when Bruce McClymont caught up with him.

'David, you must have dinner with us tonight.'

'That's very decent of you, Bruce, if you're sure it's not too much trouble.'

'I insist. I want to talk dogs with you. You'll probably be off in the morning.'

David shook his head. 'I promised Mum and Kate that I'd have a look at Canberra. I'm told it's a weird place to get about in but I'll give it a go.'

'I'll take you around myself. I've been several times and know my way about. Mona and I will take an extra day and show you the main places.'

'That's very kind of you, but you don't have to.'

'I want to. It's a very interesting place and I suspect a lot has changed since I was there last. You simply must see the War Museum. It's inspiring, absolutely inspiring.'

After dinner that night McClymont wanted to talk. He wanted to know what David thought of the dogs he had seen and how they compared with the MacLeod kelpies.

David, like his father, was loath to praise his dogs to other people. They were tough bushmen who believed in letting their dogs and horses speak for themselves by their performances. But McClymont kept pushing him to make a comparison.

'Bruce, what you've got here at this trial is a collection of the best trial handlers in the country; a lot of good handlers working a lot of well-educated dogs. It's a very professional operation. If you want my honest opinion, I don't think any of these dogs have any more natural ability than our dogs. I like a dog to work more naturally than a lot of these handlers allow their dogs to do. Some of them have taken a lot of the natural ability out of their dogs. They wouldn't be any use in our country where a dog has to think for itself. But you do win trials with push-button dogs, and that is what these handlers are after.'

'Do you still think you can win the National?'

'Yes,' David said very calmly. 'I will win it, or at least give it a big shake.'

He made this pronouncement without any trace of bravado, but in such a quietly confident manner that McClymont felt that perhaps the young fellow really could pull it off.

'But first I have to get another couple of good dogs and then take them around the country, getting them used to strange grounds.'

'My own view is that I wouldn't swap Nap and Belle for any dog I saw here, except maybe the winning dog. When they work, they take your breath away,' McClymont said.

'You're just a biased kelpie breeder,' David joked. 'What it boils down to is that talk is cheap. Anyone can talk up a dog. In my book, a dog has to do the job against other dogs to be considered a top dog. I came down here to have a look at the dogs and the course so that I would have a better idea of what's ahead of me. I know now. I've seen some good animals, but if my dogs could handle the strange conditions, they could do anything. So it's up to me to see that they get acclimatised.'

'You be sure to let me know when you'll be back here.'

'I'll let you know.'

The next day David had his tour of Canberra, with Bruce and Mona as tour guides, and the morning after that he headed for the Sydney suburb of Kogarah, where he stayed a night with his grandparents.

He arrived back home at High Peaks at lunchtime the next day. Most of that afternoon and evening was spent yarning with his father about the trial and what he had seen in Canberra. It had been an interesting trip and he felt all the better for having gone. Most importantly, he felt that his dream was one step closer to becoming a reality.

Chapter Twenty-three

The day Belle whelped her litter to Nap, David stayed close to the house and regularly checked to see how things were going. At the end of the day Belle had given birth to six pups. David knelt down and examined them one by one. The sexes were even: three males and three females. There were red and tans, blue and tans and one fawn and tan female. Fawns were not favoured, not only because of their usually poor coats but because sheep did not work as well for light-coloured dogs. Sheep were inclined to be more curious about these dogs and 'drew' on to them. This often meant that a light-coloured dog had to be very 'strong' to shift sheep. If this happened in a three-sheep trial, it could cause problems. Andrew had never retained a fawn or a fawn and tan pup and, because of the difficulties with their coat, David did not intend to either. He knew that Shaun Covers, who was working on a big property on the

Cassilis side, would take a Belle pup irrespective of colour, so that left him with five pups. He would keep all five and run them on to pick the top pups out of them.

By the time they were four weeks of age, the five pups were reduced to four when a huge wedge-tailed eagle snatched one up in its claws. Anne heard the dogs barking furiously and ran out of the house just as the pup was being taken skyward. If she'd had a rifle in her hand, she would have tried to shoot it, but the eagle would have dropped the pup, which would have killed it anyway. Two males and two females remained.

Anne hated to have to tell David that one of his precious pups had been taken, but it had to be done. They had never lost a pup to eagles before. Cursing his luck with dogs, David covered the pup yard with fine wire and did not allow the pups to leave it unless someone was there to watch them.

David started handling the pups when they were eight weeks old. They were fitted with light collars, to which he attached long lengths of cord. They were also tied up for brief periods each day. One of the males was a red and tan like its sire and the other was a blue and tan. From the outset the red and tan seemed to be the better pup of the two. The two bitch pups matched the colours of the males, but in their case it was the blue and tan that appeared to be the better pup. On the strength of these early impressions, David put in a lot more time with what he considered to be the two best pups of the litter. As the months went by, his first impressions were confirmed. The two pups he liked were so promising that he was beginning to feel quite excited. He called the red and tan male Clancy, and the blue and tan bitch Needle.

Often he would take the two pups to town on the back of the utility so that travelling became second nature to them. David wanted to get the dogs completely used to strange noises, such as loudspeakers, as well as unfamiliar grounds and their different surfaces. At first he took Belle along with her offspring, which initially helped to minimise their concern about being transported away from their familiar haunts. David was fairly committed to working Belle at the National and he reckoned it wouldn't hurt her – seasoned bitch though she was – to be carted about.

The two young dogs exhibited different natural tendencies. Clancy had a strong natural left-hand cast while Needle preferred to cast to her right. David worked on these weaknesses and before long he had both dogs casting equally well on either side.

The biggest problem affecting the performance of kelpies in trials was their tendency to 'come on' to their sheep too quickly. David put in a lot of time making sure that his dogs did not bustle sheep. He obtained permission to work them at the local showground and carted sheep in for the dogs to work. He was well aware that dogs usually worked better at home than away and that this had to be given consideration so that nerves did not affect performance.

David had been lucky to get two dogs with natures like their parents'. In David's view, Clancy and Needle had the right blend of temperament and working instinct. They were kept out of the yard and only worked on small, lively mobs in the hills. They were given plenty of casting practice along with mob work, and they were kept off three-sheep work until they were about eighteen months of age. Then David introduced them to obstacles.

When David could stop and sit Clancy and Needle a quarter-mile away and cast them right round the hill paddock above the house, he felt that he was more than three-quarters of the way along the track to Canberra. The rest of the training involved steadiness, positioning and off-balance work. Most good kelpies are born with instinctive balance. To get a dog to work off-balance is against a dog's natural inclination. At a sheepdog trial a handler is required to stand in a small circle at one side of each and every obstacle. To work sheep through these obstacles, a dog is actually working off-balance. A good obstacle dog must also be trained so that it can be moved freely from side to side. If a dog is too sticky in eye, or too hard in nature, it will not make a great obstacle dog because the sheep will nearly always beat it round the wings of the obstacle and cause a loss of points, and perhaps the loss of the trial.

There were a few freak dogs who were born obstacle dogs. The great black kelpie dog Wilga was one. David believed that to witness such a dog working three sheep at an obstacle was one of life's great experiences. He sensed that both Clancy and Needle possessed this wonderful old-time kelpie movement. It was not until he began working them on obstacles that he was absolutely sure of it. It was at this stage that he knew he had two young dogs he could take to Canberra. He did not even let on to his father what he really thought of Needle and Clancy.

All of this work was carried out over a period of a year or so. Training a sheepdog is not something you can do overnight. During this time David often worked his dogs either very early in the morning or very late at night, by moonlight. Only his immediate family knew how much time and effort he was devoting to his dogs, on top of his normal work on both properties.

Catriona began to take an interest in the training of Clancy and Needle, and sometimes accompanied David when he took the dogs off into the hills for steady work. She was still unsure about his feelings for her, although her own love for him was as strong as ever.

One day in late summer David came up for lunch to find his father waiting for him at the top of the steps. He could tell by the look on Andy's face that something was amiss.

'What is it, Dad?' he asked with some trepidation.

'It's real bad news, Davie. Tim Sparkes is dead.'

'Tim dead? Oh, no. Do you know any more than that? Did he die in hospital?'

'No. I'm afraid to say that he shot himself. Seems he left a note, saying that he wasn't going to live the rest of his life as a cripple. He asked for his papers, which he kept in a locked briefcase along with a pistol. That's how he did it.'

David sat down on the top step and tried to come to terms with what his father had just told him. It was almost impossible to believe that Tim was gone. He had always been so full of life. It was Tim who had taught him how to box, and Tim who had always come up with the right horse for him. It wasn't fair. Life just wasn't fair. Tim had so much to live for: a good life, a property and plenty of money. Tim had been a mate, the oldest mate he had, and now he was dead. David couldn't believe that he would never again read Tim's name in *Hoofs and Horns* magazine, unless it was his obituary.

'Hell, how could they have slipped up like that, letting Tim get hold of a pistol?' David said angrily.

'I reckon Tim knew what he was doing, Davie. He would have hated being totally dependent on other people.'

'But he's gone, Dad. Gone. We'll never see him again. Bloody hell. It sure makes you think about things.'

David got up and paced along the verandah. Andrew saw the tears in his eyes and had a good idea what he was feeling.

'Tim wouldn't want you to pull back on his account, Davie. No way. He would want you to go on.'

'What did Mum say?'

'She's having a good old cry. You know she had a soft spot for Tim. She had a bit of trouble getting used to him in the early days, like everyone did at first, but she soon woke up to the fact that he was a fair-dinkum bloke. A bit rough, but pure gold. It'll be a long time before we have a better friend than Tim. Wilf White's one. I reckon we have a lot to thank them for.'

'Aw, hell, I feel awful. We should have brought him down here where we could have seen him more often. Maybe he wouldn't have done it, then.'

'Don't crucify yourself, mate. It was Tim's decision. It's done, he's gone and that's that. Life has to go on. Make him proud of you, Davie. That's what he would have wanted.'

It was a long, tiring trip to Rockhampton, made all the more difficult because it was done in the knowledge that the larger-than-life Tim Sparkes would not be there to welcome them. The funeral was a big one, as Tim had been a very popular fellow on the rodeo circuit. There were many well-known roughriders and campdrafters in the church and at the graveside service. David and Andrew were depressed to know that they would never see Tim again. He had been such an individual character; a long streak of a man who had appeared to be indestructible. After the funeral they slipped away and, with David and Anne sharing the driving, they made a fairly quick return journey.

Life had to go on and the National was not all

that far away. This time they would be hiring two caravans, one for David and one for his parents. It would be the first time all three of them had had any kind of holiday together.

Following Tim's death, Andrew and Anne noted that David became very quiet. He would ride away into the hills with Clancy and Needle and they would not see him again for hours. When asked by his father how the dogs were performing he would fall back on his old response of, 'Well enough'. His work with the dogs did not abate, and if anything he seemed more fiercely determined than ever. Then, one evening, he walked into the house and without preamble addressed himself to his father.

'You feel like walking up to the top paddock, Dad?'

'Seeing you're inviting me, I reckon I do,' Andrew said. 'You got something special to show me?'

'Maybe,' David stalled.

Andrew was aware that David had built extra obstacles in his old casting paddock. These obstacles simulated the National Trial course exactly. He was also aware that David had been timing the dogs here. It was a tougher task to pen here than at Canberra because the sheep all wanted to bolt back to the top of the hill.

Andy sat himself down on the big log seat and waited for David to come up the hill with the two young dogs. He had been very keen to see these dogs in action, but David had put him off every time he had asked about them.

David tied Clancy up on the fence and sat Needle down behind him. He walked about twenty yards away and then cast her up the fence. She went out like an arrow and hugged the fence until she was perhaps thirty yards behind the sheep. From that point on the young bitch gave a flawless exhibition of control. When she had penned, Andrew clapped his hands and grinned.

'What do you reckon, Dad?' David asked as he walked back to Clancy.

'I reckon you've got yourself a real class bitch there.'

'You do, eh? Let's see what Clancy can do.'

After Clancy had completed his tasks, Andrew walked over to David and put his arm on his son's shoulder. He seemed so affected by what he had seen that words would not come.

'The best, the absolute best young dog I have ever seen, Davie. The bitch is good, but Clancy – well, he's very special,' he said at last.

'I'm pleased you like him, Dad. I reckon we can go to the National now.'

But two weeks later, tragedy struck. David was working Clancy on a hillside one morning and two wethers broke away. Clancy wheeled to block them and one big, rangy wether – which David thought was probably pea-struck – ran straight at the dog. It was travelling very fast, and it hit Clancy and threw him several feet to one side and hard up against a dead stump. David heard the dog's yelp and sent his horse plunging across the hill to where Clancy stood. Clearly, there was something badly wrong with one back leg.

David dismounted and knelt beside his dog. Clancy whined and licked David's hand. Part of Clancy's left back leg was swinging free. It had been fractured badly. There was no hope of taking Clancy to Canberra this year.

David lifted the dog in his arms and placed him across the saddle before mounting. 'I'm sorry if it hurts you, Clancy, but I have to get you to the vet.'

It was a very slow ride back to the homestead. David placed the dog on the front seat of the utility before going into the house to tell his parents what had happened.

'Clancy's got a broken leg,' he said as he walked into the kitchen. 'I'm taking him to the vet.'

'Is it bad?' Andrew asked.

'I reckon so. Looks as if it's broken right through.'

'Oh, David,' Anne exclaimed with real sorrow in her eyes. 'Does this mean you can't take him to Canberra?'

'Not this year,' he said, and without another word he walked out.

Anne's face fell. She knew how hard David had worked to get the two young dogs ready for the National and what it meant to him. And how would Catriona take another year's postponement?

Clancy returned home later that morning with a pin in his leg and the vet's assurance that his leg

444

would heal satisfactorily. David had stopped at the mailbox on the way in and he threw the pile of mail down on the table and slumped into a chair.

Anne put a cup of tea and some cake in front of him and glanced across at her husband. 'Why don't you go to Canberra with Belle and Needle, David?'

David looked at her and shook his head. He wasn't going to Canberra without Clancy. What even his father didn't know was that Clancy was a freak trial dog. Needle was very good and Belle was brilliant on certain sheep but Clancy was a freak. He reckoned he could get into the finals with both bitches, but he doubted if they would be able to win.

'No Clancy, no Canberra,' he said. 'He's the dog I need in that company. We'll simply have to wait another year.'

Anne picked up the mail and began leafing through it. 'There's a letter here for you, David,' she said, handing it over to him.

David didn't care about anything right now so he put the letter in his shirt pocket and went down to feed the dogs. When he had finished feeding them, he took the letter out of his pocket and sat down on Nap's log kennel while he read it. The letter was from a firm of solicitors in Rockhampton and its contents were startling.

It seemed that Tim Sparkes had left him his cattle property and all its livestock, not to mention a considerable sum of money. The news was so

445

breathtaking that he had trouble absorbing it. Surely Tim had close relatives he would have left the property to? David read the letter again. There was no mistake – he was the sole owner.

The ramifications of this news were staggering. Now, in terms of cattle and property, not even Angus Campbell would have more assets than the MacLeod family. They would actually own three or four times as many head of cattle than the Campbells. This wonderful gift meant that the MacLeods would be financially secure well into the future. They would now be real graziers, all because of good old Tim.

David went up to the shed where he had placed Clancy. The dog's leg had been put in plaster. David looked down at him and Clancy wagged his tail. 'We'll be there next year, mate. You get that leg healed up, and we'll be there.'

David made his way back to the house. He reckoned that when his parents saw the letter there wouldn't be much more work done for the rest of the day.

Anne's sharp eyes sensed immediately that David had received news of some kind.

'David, what's happened? More bad news?' she asked.

'Hardly,' he said, handing the letter across to his father. He reckoned he should read it since Tim had been his old mate. Anne leant over his shoulder as he read it through.

Dear David MacLeod,

In accordance with the Will drawn up by us
for our late valued client, Mr Timothy Gordon
Sparkes of 'Aberfeldy' Station, Broadsound,
Queensland, it is our pleasure to inform you
that you have been named as sole beneficiary
in the estate of the abovenamed Mr Sparkes.

The Estate comprises:

Firstly, the property 'Aberfeldy', west of
Broadsound and comprising 48 000 acres; and
all of the stock running on this property: 3500
head of cattle at last muster, and horses to the
number of about 100, mares, yearlings and
some older stock horses.

Secondly, a four-bedroom holiday home of about
forty-two squares on half an acre of land (two
blocks) at Yeppoon, which is in good condition
and was the retirement home of Mr Sparkes's
late uncle.

Thirdly, funds to the order of $223 000.

In his Will, our late client expressed the hope
that you would consider retaining the present
overseer, Donald Alan Morgan, as your overseer
or manager. Our client considered Mr Morgan
to be very competent and entirely trustworthy.

As you are now the beneficiary of the late Mr

Sparkes's estate, we would urge you to come and
see us at your earliest opportunity to complete
the necessary paperwork. In the meantime, a
phone call advising us of the receipt of this letter
would be appreciated.

We remain yours faithfully,

Tristram Jennings
Michael, Jennings & Duncan

David stood back and watched his parents' reactions.
His mother's eyes were glazed at first and then soon
filled with tears. His father had frozen, unable to lift
his eyes from the letter.

A hundred thoughts flashed through Anne's mind.
The uppermost was that this was a miracle. Now
David could marry Catriona! He was a wealthy man,
and – in terms of money at least – he could speak to
Angus as an equal.

Andrew reread the letter and let the facts sink into
his startled brain. He had worked hard all his life,
busted himself, so that they might have a measure of
prosperity in later life and so David would have a
future on the land. And now it seemed as if all their
financial worries were over. If anything happened to
him, Anne and David need never worry about money.
Tim's overwhelmingly generous gesture was just so
unexpected. Andrew didn't know what to say.

'I told you he thought a lot of you, Davie,' Andrew said at last.

'I would much prefer Tim to be alive and as we knew him,' David said in a broken voice.

'We all feel the same, David,' Anne said with tears running down her face. 'But it is wonderful that Tim thought so much of you he should give you all he had.'

'It was Dad who was Tim's old mate, and you always looked after him, Mum. He regarded us as family.'

'What a great help this would have been a few years ago,' Anne said. She was thinking of how Andy had not hesitated to return to shearing to help pay off Poitrel, and in so doing had brought on the stroke that had almost killed him.

'What's done is done,' Andrew said. 'No good talking of what might have been. Davie, you'll have to ring these solicitors first thing Monday morning. Now that you aren't going to Canberra we can shoot up there and see them before going out to the property. I think you should also advise them that Don Morgan is to be retained. That should put his mind at rest. Just as well we've got a new vehicle, as it looks as if we'll be making regular trips up north.'

'Not to mention that we now have another good reason to go – a holiday home,' Anne said.

'I think we should consider employing someone to help out here,' Andy continued. 'We can't keep relying on Kate. What we need is a reliable young person who can milk and do odd jobs as well as help out at shearing and crutching time. Davie, you can't do it all plus work your dogs and handle young horses. There's no sense in owning three properties and busting your gut forever.'

'I never thought I would hear you say that, Andy,' Anne said and winked at David.

'Just commonsense, Anne. I don't want to see David end up like me. Seriously, I think we ought to look at employing someone – but not just anyone: someone who is interested in stock horses and could learn to handle a few when things are slack. I would prefer to pay the right person a bit more money. What do you think, Anne?'

'I'm all for it. But we'll have to put it to Kate, since she is a director.'

'I think we ought to have Kate and Jean over for dinner tomorrow, to celebrate,' David suggested. 'Let's keep this news on ice until then. We can ask Kate about Dad's suggestion. She has to feel she's involved, too. Where would we have been without her?'

'The first thing Kate will ask is where an employee would live,' Anne said.

'Maybe we'd have to build a small cottage,' Andrew suggested.

'Well, Davie, I reckon this softens the blow about not going to Canberra,' Anne said.

'It does, but I'll still be going. Tim would have wanted me to go, and to do well.'

Chapter Twenty-four

The day after David received the letter from Tristram Jennings, there was a feeling of change in the air. David had ordered a new utility with the expectation that he would be working dogs at that year's National. He'd had a mesh crate made especially for it, modelled on what he could remember of Bruce McClymont's cage. The crate had a double roof to cut down heat, and four compartments. He brought the new crate back to High Peaks just before lunch. He was not back long when a thunderstorm passed over the property. There was a second one later in the afternoon, and between them the storms dumped over three inches of rain on the land. The hill country had been very dry and rain was just what was needed before the onset of cooler weather. But the storms did not clear the air. Sunday broke very humid and with the threat of more storms to come.

Catriona had asked if they could have a picnic in the hills. David had told her that he had discovered a very big cave on Wallaby Rocks and she was eager to see it. It was on the highest point of Poitrel and about the same height as the peak of Yellow Rock. David had breakfast and saddled his Sparkes-bred mare so that he would be ready to leave as soon as Catriona arrived. He tied a billy can onto a saddle and then buckled on a saddlebag.

'Catriona is just coming round the bend, David,' Anne called from the front verandah.

'Good. I hope she brought her rainskins.'

'Got matches?' Andrew asked.

David nodded. 'I think I'll leave the billy and some matches up at the cave I found. When things settle down a bit, we should all go up there for a picnic. I mean the lot of us: Kate and Jean, too.'

'That would be nice, dear,' Anne said. 'We haven't had a picnic for a while.'

David took the food he had prepared and hurried out to his horse where he waited for Catriona to arrive. She was driving a Ford utility and pulling a single-horse trailer. He could see that King was saddled with a stock saddle for the ride into the hills.

When Catriona pulled up she gave him her usual flashing smile and cheery greeting. 'Hi, David. We're sure to get another storm. Do you think we should be going so far?'

'I really want to go to Poitrel. I want to show you

452

that great cave I told you about. If we can get that far, the storm won't worry us.'

So they rode up through the foothills below Yellow Rock and then took a new track on the western side of the mountain. This slope offered far easier going than the dangerous eastern slope down which David had ridden Catriona's grey pony. The track led on to the boundary fence between High Peaks and Poitrel. They went through the mesh gate and then turned towards the east.

'We head up there,' David said. 'The highest point on Poitrel is almost as high as the peak of Yellow Rock but not as dangerous. Before we get to the top, we detour down the hill and along the face below the peak. That's where the cave is and that's where we'll have lunch.'

Catriona looked up at the rapidly darkening sky and thought that they would be very lucky to make the cave before the storm broke. There were ominous rumblings and the air was so heavy it seemed to be pressing them towards the ground. The clouds were purple-green and away to the east lightning ripped up and down in great jagged streaks.

'Not scared are you, Cat?' David asked.

'I'm glad I'm not doing this on my own,' she replied.

'To tell you the truth, I don't like storms either. Come on, it's getting close.'

The first big drops of rain started to fall as they rode off the slope and along the eastern face of

Wallaby Rocks. 'Head for that split tree,' David shouted above the noise of the thunder. He pointed to the remnants of a big dead box tree that had been shattered by lightning some time in the past. The tree was in amongst an area of massive rocks. Immediately below the tree, the track – which was really a sheep pad – dipped quite sharply, and off to her right Catriona finally spotted the opening of a big cave.

'Get off and follow me,' David said. He led his horse into the cave and Catriona followed closely behind. The area Catriona found herself in was only an entrance, a kind of anteroom, to a much bigger cave that was reached through an opening several feet across. 'Hang on to my bridle for a minute, Cat. I want to grab some wood before the rain soaks it.'

David dashed out of the cave and began picking up kindling and some bigger sticks. By the time he had gathered an armful, the rain had begun in earnest. Catriona watched him as he appeared through the curtain of water. He put the wood down and reached for the bridles. 'I'll tie the two neddies to that root,' he said, and pointed to where a thick tree root had thrust its way between two rocks. Then he unsaddled the horses and brought the saddles and rugs across to where he had dumped the pile of sticks. When he had spread the rugs on the ground near the back wall of the cave, he took from his saddlebag a motley collection of goods. There were two packets of food, a package wrapped in newspaper and two boxes of matches in clear plastic. The package in newspaper yielded a small amount of fine bark kindling, which he laid on the paper and lit. It flared up, and he fed the flame with small sticks from the pile beside him. When the fire was well under way, he took the billy and placed it on the ground at the cave's entrance. Water was pouring off the roof and the billy filled to overflowing in two or three minutes.

'We'll have a hot cuppa in no time,' he said.

Catriona stood and watched him as he worked. She always marvelled at the smooth way David did everything. 'Do you never forget anything, David?' she asked.

'Now and again, Cat. I had a first-rate teacher. Dad got me into the habit of making a mental check of everything I might need for a job. Too far to go back for something from here. I mean, where would we be if I had forgotten the matches? We'd be tea-less.'

'And I suppose you even remembered to bring the tea and sugar?'

'Sure did. They're in the saddlebag. Condensed milk, too. I never travel without those things. If the worst comes to the worst, you can always sit down and have a mug of tea.'

'Well, I brought fresh milk,' Catriona said. 'It's wrapped in crushed ice. It would go sour quickly in this weather.'

'Wow, what a team,' he said. He took off his hat and coat and lay down on his saddle blanket, his back propped against the cave's back wall. 'By the way, what do you think of my restaurant?'

Catriona gave what was the closest to a giggle he had ever heard from her. 'I guess we could be in worse places during a storm.'

David laughed outright. 'Safe as you could be here. Safer than at Inverlochy. Miles from anywhere and anyone. That's what you want, isn't it?'

Catriona paused in the middle of unpacking her saddlebags. Wild thoughts of desire flashed through her brain. Should she encourage him or remain detached? She knew she loved David, but they weren't married yet.

'What do you mean, David?' She saw that his eyes were fixed on her face and she forced herself to meet his steady gaze.

'You've fancied me for years. You've regarded me as your very own personal property,' he said.

'What if I did? Would you have any objection? I mean, have you got someone better in mind?'

'I once told you that there was nobody else.'

'David MacLeod, there is something odd about you today. I think I know you, and I say you are behaving very strangely. You have a different look on your face. If I didn't know you so well, I would say you are being smug.'

'Cat,' he roared. 'Me, smug? I hope I never am. Nothing of the kind.'

'You aren't a bundle of nerves because we're together in this cave?'

'I've always been very comfortable in your presence. Not like some of the young men who pant after you.'

'You mean you've always taken me for granted, just like one of your dogs?'

'Definitely not. Look, let's talk about this after lunch.'

Catriona handed him a plate of cold meat and salad which she had assembled from the contents of their saddlebags while he was building the fire. David took it and smiled across at her. Her heart began to beat faster and she turned away to hide her confusion. If only he knew how much she loved him. When he smiled at her like that she felt weak and strong at the same time.

'I'll make the tea,' he said, clearly wanting to change the topic.

They ate their lunch as they watched the rain pour off the lip of the cave and cascade down the mountain. In between watching the rain they covertly watched each other.

'What is it that you wanted to talk about, David?' Catriona asked at last as she sipped her tea. She couldn't contain herself any longer.

'I think I'll have another cuppa,' David said.

'You're enjoying this,' Catriona said.

'What?' he asked.

'Keeping me in suspense.'

'What do you want first? The good news or the bad?'

Catriona sighed. 'The bad.'

'I'm not going to Canberra this year. Clancy smashed his back leg. It's been pinned and he's now

457

in plaster. He'll be out of action for three months.'

'Oh, David, I'm so sorry. Poor Clancy. He looked so very good.'

'So my dream is on hold for another twelve months.'

'David, with all due respect, you may never win that blasted trial. There are too many good handlers with too many good border collies.'

'One man with a kelpie won the National five times,' David reminded her.

'Maybe he did, but there are so many more handlers now,' she said.

'Their dogs are no better,' David said.

'Well, David, how long do you expect me to wait for you? My parents are on at me all the time to marry someone else.'

'I know all that. Look, what would happen if you went home and told your parents that you were going to marry me? What would they do?'

'They couldn't *stop* me.'

'But they wouldn't like it.'

'We both know that already. But I've told you, I don't care.'

'Would having more money make a difference?' he asked.

'I suppose it might, but there are other things, too. Your father was a shearer.'

'Hell, Cat, there are millionaires who started off life a lot lower down the social scale than that.'

'You don't have to convince me.'

'Okay, so if I ask you to marry me, where do you stand? With your parents or with me?'

'I take it this is a hypothetical question.'

'You know I have to win that National. Not only for Dad but for Tim Sparkes.'

'David, that's ridiculous. Tim Sparkes is dead.'

'Tim believed in me and he has made it possible for me to marry you. Not that I wouldn't have asked you anyway.'

Catriona's eyes widened. 'David, what are you talking about?'

'I am the sole beneficiary of Tim's estate. He left me his cattle property with over three and a half thousand head of cattle, a house on the coast and a *lot* of money. He left it all to me.'

'Oh, David, this is wonderful news.'

'Wonderful isn't the word for it. Do you think it will alter your father's opinion about my suitability to be his son-in-law?'

'I should think it would be a huge help. David, does this mean you're asking me to marry you?'

David sighed. 'Cat, you have always known I would marry you. In your heart of hearts, you knew. I'm not a fancy fellow who knows fancy things to say. But I do know that if I can't have you, I don't want any other woman. I like having you close by me, and, Catriona, I do love you.'

Catriona felt her whole body melt with David's words.

'Are you going to kiss me?' she asked.

He took her in his arms and kissed her softly on the lips, hesitantly at first, then with all the passion in his heart.

Catriona felt his strength and closeness and sighed contentedly. 'I seem to have waited forever for this,' she said.

'I know you have, and I'm so lucky that you did.' They sat together with the fire's warmth soaking through them. Between kisses, Catriona asked, 'Where shall we live?'

'We can have a new home on High Peaks,' he said.

'Can you afford that?'

'I can afford a very nice new home wherever you want it.'

'What on earth will my parents say?'

'Cat, you're not to mention a word of this. Do not tell them we're engaged and do not tell them a thing about Tim's estate. Your father will take some handling, and I want to do it in my own way.'

Catriona sighed and leant back into David's arms. 'You know there has never been anyone else,' she said.

'I never doubted for a minute. Come on, let's have another cuppa and then we'll head for home.'

'Can't we stay a little longer? It's still raining, and I don't want to break the spell of this magic place.'

'The rain has almost stopped and we'll be late home as it is. Would you like to stay for dinner? Kate and Jean will be there, too. It's to celebrate our good fortune.'

'Now you tell me. How can I stay to dinner in these clothes? I smell all horsy.'

'I suppose you'll have time to go home and change,' he said.

'Come on then, quick. Let's pack up and go. I'll look after these things while you saddle the horses.'

The sun came out as they picked their way down the mountain. Grass, trees and rocks were transformed by the sun shining on the rain-soaked countryside. The air seemed fresh and brilliantly clean. Catriona thought it was a very good omen for their future.

Chapter Twenty-five

Sworn to secrecy about her engagement to David, and about his wonderful legacy from Tim Sparkes, Catriona went back to Inverlochy with her mind clear at last about the future direction of her life. If all went according to plan, she and David would be married the following year, after the National Trial, and they would live in a new house on High Peaks – after an unholy row with her family, of course.

Three days later David and Andrew left for Queensland. They were away about a week. Before leaving they had employed a young local man by the name of Greg Robertson as full-time station hand. He was a likeable fellow from a small farm close to town, and he considered himself very lucky to be working for the MacLeods. Greg was horse-mad, and he reckoned that David and Andrew would have to be as good a pair of horsemen as anyone in the country. Greg was put up in the house for the time being, and David and Andrew left High Peaks secure in the knowledge that their new employee could handle, under Anne's supervision, almost anything that came up.

After arriving in Rockhampton they made their way to the office of the solicitors who handled Tim's affairs. There, after half an hour's discussion, David was handed an envelope with his name scrawled across it. It was the last note Tim had written before taking his life. He had left instructions that it was to be given to David MacLeod when he presented himself at the solicitor's office. David put the note in his pocket and he and Andy walked out of the office into brilliant Queensland sunshine.

Later, on the road up to the cattle property that was now his, David stopped the utility and took out the envelope. It contained a single sheet of paper and the writing was very bad.

Dear David,

Your old mate is done for. I can't take any more of this lying in bed with nurses night and day. I reckon what I am going to do is the only sensible way to go.

I want you to know that I reckon you're a bonzer young bloke and one day you'll be a legend, like Lance Skuthorpe and Jackie Howe. I reckon the best way I can help you is to leave

you all I've got, which my old uncle left me.
There's enough income and money in the bank
to straighten up the old place in the way
I reckon you and Andy would want to.

Davie, your dad and mum are great people,
and so is Kate. I wish I had met a good woman
when I was younger. I would have liked a son
just like you. Maybe we'll meet again in the
next world, if there is such a place, but I'm
sure pleased I met you MacLeods in this one.

I know I am leaving everything I own in good
hands. I wish there could be another way out,
but there isn't, not for me. If I can't ride horses,
I don't want to live.

So long, Davie.

Your old mate,

Tim Sparkes

PS That Catriona was the prettiest girl I ever
saw. She must be really something by now.
Don't lose her, old mate.

David, who couldn't see clearly for the tears in his
eyes, handed the note across to his father. When
Andy passed the note back to him, David saw tears

where he had never seen them before. Tim sure had been one special bloke.

'I reckon that if a man meets one fella like Tim Sparkes in his lifetime, he's damned lucky,' Andrew said.

David nodded and wiped his eyes with his handkerchief. He folded the note and put it in his shirt pocket. 'Mum and Kate will want to read this,' he said. He sat and looked down the road for a few moments until he felt able to drive again.

'We'd better get on and see what needs doing at Aberfeldy,' he said.

As it happened, they found there was quite a lot that needed attention. Don Morgan took them on a tour of the property, and they considered everything from the perspective of ownership. Andrew was very critical of the Aberfeldy cattle, which he referred to as 'yaks'. They didn't appear to carry much meat on them, and he felt the whole herd required upgrading. David listened to Don's counterargument, which reflected his local experience and commonsense.

'I think there's good sense in what both of you say,' David said at last. 'The herd could stand a bit of improvement, but you can't ignore the fact that those "yaks" are hardier and handle these conditions better than a lot of the purebred cattle. But it's not much use running cattle just because they're hardy; we're trying to grow beef. Either that or we could look at selling live cattle overseas, in which case we should think about getting some good Brahmans and breeding our own bulls. Maybe we can do both. We should also consider upgrading the pastures. Let's see what we can do to keep the hardiness and at the same time put some more meat on them.'

There was also some fencing that needed attention, and the water reserves needed to be augmented. David had a horror of going into a drought with so many cattle and inadequate water. He didn't have any doubts, though, that Morgan was a competent man, so he decided to increase his salary to that of a manager's figure.

'Thanks very much, Mr MacLeod. I'm getting married later this year so the extra dough will be a big help.'

'That's great. Congratulations. Are you happy with the house? Does it need any work?'

'The house is all right for me, but a woman might not think so. There are a few things that could be improved.'

'Let's look at them while we're here,' David said.

Later that afternoon when they left Aberfeldy, David and Andrew were happy with what they had achieved. It was going to take time, but they would gradually get the property up to scratch.

'Don, if there's anything you're unsure about, you're to contact me. If I'm not there, talk it over with Dad. You manage the place and keep me informed.'

'Righto, Mr MacLeod,' Morgan said.

'And you can forget the "Mister" business in

future. My name is David and Dad's is Andrew. There's something else: I'd like to see you devote a bit more time to the horse side of things. Tim was a great man for his horses, and I'd like Aberfeldy to become even better known for its horses. I should think we'll need another good stallion here. I know you've got a good colt by the old horse, but we can't use him on his half-sisters. I'm not sure whether we should mix up the bloods or develop a stud of either quarter horses or Australian stock horses. If we did that, we could offer some at the stud sales. What do you think?'

'That sounds great. I'm pretty keen on horses myself. That's how I came to be here. I was working on a place running a lot of horses and Tim offered me more money to come here.'

'There's no need to give me an answer now. Have a think about where we should be going with the horses and let me know. Dad and I are hill-country men and used to a different type of horse to you fellows up here. You going anywhere particular for your honeymoon?'

'We haven't decided.'

'You can use the house on the coast if you like. Save you some money. Keep an eye on it and make sure it's kept in good order. Dad and I are going there now to have a look at it.'

'That's very decent of you, David.'

'Okay, you're the manager now, Don. Tim wanted you kept on, and if you do the right thing by us,

467

you've got a job here for a long time to come. Just keep me in touch. We must be going.'

As they drove away, David asked Andrew, 'You reckon Don will be okay?'

'I reckon so, Davie. He knows what needs to be done and he appreciates he's going to get some support. Tim and his uncle never worried too much about the place. Yeah, I reckon Don will be all right.'

They stayed the night at the Yeppoon house, which had a great view of the ocean. It was an off-ground weatherboard built for Queensland's humid coastal climate. You could stand up under the house and still have a foot of clearance over your head. The floor had been asphalted, and there was a long bench fitted with a vice and a grinder. Bits of leather hung from nails above the bench and there were still tools in racks. It was apparent that somebody – probably's Tim's late uncle – had been a leather worker.

Once upstairs – David lost count of the number of steps, and looked anxiously to see how his father was negotiating them – the view of the ocean was breathtaking. There was a long, narrow-roofed open verandah from which to view the coastline. By the look of the cane chairs and table, someone had liked this spot. The rooms were large but in need of paint, and they were all furnished. They also found that there was a new Kelvinator fridge and freezer, and an almost new ride-on mower. The whole under area of the house was latticed and could be locked by a large padlock. An open garage was attached to the house but that was empty.

'I reckon Mum would fancy a few weeks here,' Andy said when he'd had a good look through the house.

'It wants smartening up a bit, though,' David said. 'I'll arrange for Don to have some work done here. The bathroom and kitchen need modernising and the place needs a lock-up garage. Those improvements would make all the difference.'

All in all, Andrew and David were well satisfied with their trip north.

They returned to High Peaks and to the best winter for many years. The big wet was ushered in by the storms that fell the day David and Catriona had had lunch in the big cave. More heavy rain followed, as did unseasonably humid weather for autumn. There were floods on the coast, and old hands reckoned it was the best start to winter they could remember. The blowflies loved the sticky weather. All the sheep had to be mustered and jetted because a small army of stockmen would have been hard put to look after 6000 sheep in the paddock the way the flies were striking. Even though all the sheep had been crutched, it didn't prevent them being struck on the body. During this period David learned a lot about flystrike. Sheep that were yellow in the wool were the worst affected because their wool stayed wet longer and generated more odour, which attracted flies. The white-woolled sheep suffered least.

The indefatigable Kate loved mustering with David and his dogs. Her greatest pleasure was to work alongside David on weekends and on her days off. She especially enjoyed David's companionship when they boiled the billy for lunch somewhere up in the hills. David had once told his mother that Kate was as much a bushie as any of them, and Kate regarded this as a tremendous compliment. She rode a horse very well now, could handle a six-foot whip most adequately, and could do any job with sheep and cattle. She was also more than useful with young horses, which fitted in very well with David's plans for the future. Best of all, Kate was a tremendously cheery person who never allowed even the most adverse conditions to affect her.

Those days, David seldom had to tell his aunt anything at all because she could sense what he wanted before he even opened his mouth. When Kate had taken up residence at Poitrel, she had set out to make herself a top stockperson. She could even shoe a horse and make a good job of it, too. Andrew and David had started her off on quiet, well-schooled horses, and as her proficiency grew they put her on better and smarter horses. Kate had had several busters, but this had never affected her enthusiasm and she declared her readiness to take on campdrafting.

During this present period of fly trouble, David usually mustered the sheep and brought them down to either the Poitrel or High Peaks yard, where they treated the struck animals and jetted the mob. If Kate

470

was not working at the hospital, she mustered with David. He would gather up small mobs of sheep and take them to Kate, who would hold them together with one of the older dogs while David rode away again looking for more sheep. This procedure made hill-country mustering a lot quicker and helped them save some sheep.

There were now good sheep yards at Poitrel and these could be used for jetting, although all the shearing was done at High Peaks. On this particular Saturday morning Catriona was to have come up from Inverlochy to help with the mustering, but she had rung at the last moment to tell David the Campbells were expecting relatives from interstate and she would have to stay and help at home.

Kate was riding a new horse. It was a chestnut gelding that they had not long broken in, and Kate had fallen in love with him so much that she had offered to buy him. Kate had never asked for anything before so David had given her the horse, which she named Chief. David and Kate were mustering the last of the wethers in the highest paddock on Poitrel. It was murderously difficult country to muster, almost as bad as the worst of Yellow Rock, and sheep running in it became as agile and cunning as mountain goats. The country was dotted with dogwood scrub, manna gums and boulders of all shapes and sizes, with rocky gullies thrown in for good measure. It was also pitted with wombat holes, and wallabies loved it. The thick patches of scrub gave them protection in the open, and there were caves and ledges where they could shelter in bad weather.

David had gone round one side of a rocky ridge with Nap behind him and Kate had gone the other way. There were a few wethers on this last ridge and they were proving very difficult to extricate. Out of nowhere, a wallaby jumped from the rocks beside Kate, causing her new horse to shy.

When Kate did not rejoin him, David retraced his route and followed the track she had taken. What he saw sent shivers up his spine. Chief was standing with reins trailing and there was Kate lying prostrate on the ground. Her right leg was splayed across a rock and she did not seem able to move it.

David was off his horse in a flash and kneeling beside her. Kate gave him a sickly grin but her face was screwed up in pain.

'It's your leg, isn't it?' David asked, and through her agony Kate could not help noticing the tenderness in his voice.

'I can't move it, David. Ten to one it's broken. If you can sit me up, I'll be sure.'

David propped her up and held her while she gingerly felt her leg. She grimaced in pain as her fingers found the break she knew was there. When she nodded, David rocked back on his heels and considered the situation. If he put Kate up on the saddle with him, he risked damaging her leg even more, not to mention the pain she would have to go through. Should he try and splint the leg and take

Kate down off the mountain on his horse? It was a real dilemma.

'What are we going to do with you, Sister Gilmour?' He was trying to joke about the situation, but he knew there was nothing to be cheery about.

'My leg needs splinting and then we need a stretcher. And a couple of good men to carry it,' Kate said and grimaced again.

'I can probably find a splint or two, and I might, with time, even be able to manufacture a rough stretcher, but I can't produce another man or two.'

'I think you'll have to go for help, David,' Kate said at last.

'I don't like leaving you here on your own. I think I'll send Nap home.'

'Nap! Would he leave you?'

'I've sent him shorter distances when I was teaching him tricks. He's a very brainy dog. I can't be sure, though, whether Mum will see him. He wouldn't go to Poitrel: that isn't his home. He'd go through the High Peaks boundary and down the side of Yellow Rock. I think it's worth a try. If we don't turn up by nightfall, they'll come looking for us anyway.'

He sat down on a big boulder, took out his live-stock notebook and began to compose a note to his mother. He wrote down what had happened and then drew a rough map of where they could be found. He ripped the pages from the notebook and wrapped them in his handkerchief, which he then knotted and

473

tied to Nap's collar so that it hung down and could be seen easily.

'Home, Nap, home,' David ordered urgently and took a few steps in that direction. Nap looked at him rather queerly and then trotted off a few paces but stopped. He looked back at David with a quizzical expression on his face.

David repeated the command. 'Home, Nap, home, quickly.'

It took Nap a while to understand David was serious and not simply playing, but he eventually took off. David watched the dog until he was out of sight and then went back to Kate.

'I think he'll be right, Kate. Drink?' he asked and she nodded.

'First I'll fix up a spot of shade for you.' Kate watched him while he used his stock knife to sharpen some green staves which he drove into the ground with a lump of rock. Kate could not quite work out how he managed it, but within the space of a few minutes David had erected a canopy of green branches over her so that she was not lying exposed to the sun. He then walked up the hill and caught the chestnut gelding, which was nibbling grass among the logs and rocks. 'Steady, you billygoat.' Chief rubbed his head against David's shirt and seemed unaffected by whatever had happened.

'How did it happen, Kate?' David asked when he had tied both horses to saplings close by.

'A damn wallaby just came out of nowhere. It

must have been planted behind the rock and it just, well, took off. Chief put on a big shy, went half over and pitched me. One moment we were walking along nice and steady, and the next I was on the ground. It all happened so fast. My leg came down across that rock and I nearly passed out with the pain of it.'

'You never know what a young horse will do, and when you're breaking them in you can't duplicate every kind of experience you might strike. Now, I think a cup of tea is called for,' he said and grinned.

Kate's eyes widened. 'How on earth are you going to make tea?' she asked.

'Not far from here is that cave I mentioned. I left a billy there in case I ever needed it again. There's a spring right beside the cave and I have everything else we need in my saddlebag. I'll make a fire first.'

' 'Tis wonderful you are,' Kate said in the Irish brogue she used to embellish the many jokes she told. She watched David as he knelt and fed the fire with small sticks and then larger branches until he had it blazing well. Then he went to retrieve the billy, and when he returned he sat it between a couple of small rocks and switched his attention from the fire back to Kate.

'Should I try and splint that leg?' he asked.

Kate gritted her teeth, as her leg was hurting a lot, and she imagined it would be much worse when touched. But it needed to be made stationary. What she needed before anyone touched her was a pain-killer.

'It's going to hurt like hell but it should be splinted,' she said.

He nodded. 'I'll see what I can find after we've drunk this.'

He made the tea and propped Kate up while she sipped it from his pannikin. 'Oh, that's wonderful, David.' When Kate had finished, David made himself a cup, and while it was cooling he collected some more green branches and made a kind of cushion so Kate could sit up against a log.

'How long do you think it might be, David?' Kate asked.

David screwed up his eyes while he thought. An hour for Nap to get home and who knows how long before Anne noticed him and what was hanging from his collar. Nap would probably go to his kennel and stay there waiting for someone to tie him up. But once Anne did read the note she would get things rolling soon enough. That was the easy part. The big problem was actually getting people up there and then getting Kate down again. They really needed a helicopter, but the closest helicopter was probably in Tamworth. You couldn't get a vehicle within miles of where they were, which meant ambulance officers and police would have to ride on horseback up the mountain. And how would they get Kate down the mountain on a stretcher?

'I can't honestly say, Kate,' he said at last. 'If the police can get hold of a helicopter, which I've asked for, it might be only a couple of hours. A lot depends on how soon Mum sees that message.'

'And if there's no helicopter?' Kate asked anxiously.

'It could be quite a while. I'll need to collect more wood so I can keep the fire going to let people know where we are. I'll use green branches while the light holds. If Mum sees that message quickly, Catriona should be here before dark with blankets, food and some aspirin for you.'

'What an organiser you are, David. I'm glad you're here with me.'

Chapter Twenty-six

Anne was out in the vegetable garden watering her spinach when she heard the dogs barking. She had been working on their accounts and had slipped out for a few minutes to do the watering. It was unusual for the dogs to bark unless riders were returning or they heard a vehicle coming up the road. Occasionally a fox would come right up to the house looking for a meal, and the dogs would make a racket then. There were hens running loose with chicks and she didn't want to lose them, so she took down her gun from the rack, loaded it, and went outside to investigate the barking. The first thing she saw was Nap drinking from one of the horse troughs. His tongue was out and his sides were heaving. Her first thought was that David must have ridden across from Poitrel, but that did not make sense. David and Kate were mustering together on Poitrel, and Andy and Greg were jetting in the Poitrel yards.

Then she noticed the blue handkerchief – David's handkerchief – hanging from Nap's collar, and her heart missed a beat. Nap would never leave David unless there was trouble in the hills. Anne called Nap to his kennel and untied the knotted handkerchief. Two tiny sheets of notepaper floated down in front of her. She picked them up and read what David had written:

Mum,

Kate has broken a leg. I think bad. In pain. Call Dad, police, ambulance and Cat. Try REAL HARD to get police helicopter. Would be hell of a trip and take ages otherwise. Get Angus to drive Cat up with King. Give her blankets, food, small pillow and aspirins for Kate. Don't let her come if late, as she will get lost. I have fire going. We are on Wallaby Rocks (see map). Tell Cat it's near the big cave.

David

My God, Kate has broken her leg up on Wallaby Rocks! Anne's mind flashed back to the day they had ridden Poitrel before making the decision to buy the property. She recalled the roughness of the Poitrel top country and envisaged how difficult it would be to lift an injured person from that peak. Anne turned and looked down at the dog that had brought her this message. Nap was lying on his log kennel with his head pointed up towards the hills from where he had come.

'Oh, Nap, you wonderful dog,' she said and patted him on the head. 'I think I'd better tie you up so you don't decide to go back to David.'

Then she ran to the house. Please, God, let Jean be at Poitrel. She usually was when the men were working there. Anne fidgeted while waiting for her call to be answered. She breathed a sigh of relief when Jean's voice came over the line.

'Jean, is Andy down at the yards?' Anne asked.

'They've just gone back. Andy and Greg had lunch here.'

'Will you run down right now and tell Andy to come back to the phone? Tell him I said it is most urgent. Tell him to drop everything.'

Andy was doing the yard work and Greg Robert-son was doing the jetting. Andy still couldn't use his right arm very well, although there was more move-ment in it than there had been for quite some time. He could not do constant repetitive work, but he had learned to do most things with his left hand. He looked up in surprise when Jean began waving at him from outside the yards. Andy climbed over the fence and walked towards her.

'What's the matter?'

'Andy, Anne just rang. She said you're to come to the house and call her back, urgently.'

'Did she say what it was about?' he asked as they walked back to the house. Even with the limp in his right leg, Andy's long strides left her behind.

'No, but she did sound very worried.'

He reckoned that Anne must have been sitting right beside the phone because it had rung only twice when she answered. 'What's the problem, Anne?' he asked.

'Kate has broken her leg. She's up on Wallaby Rocks with David. Nap came home with the message. I've contacted the police, the ambulance and Angus while I was waiting for you. I'll read you David's note.' When she had finished she asked, 'Is there anything else I should do?'

'Hang on. I need a couple of minutes to think things out.' He saw Jean looking at him anxiously and tried to marshal his thoughts very quickly.

'David's right about the helicopter,' he said to Anne finally. 'It would be worth waiting until morning for it rather than try and carry Kate down the mountain. We couldn't make it there before dark anyway. Not by the time we get everyone here. If you can't get a helicopter, you'd better tell the police and ambulance driver to send people who can ride. You hold the fort there and Jean can stand by the phone here.'

'Poor Kate,' Jean said anxiously after Andrew had hung up the phone.

'She's in good hands. David knows what he's doing. That old dog should get a medal.'

'Andy, what can I do?'

'It would be great if you could make up several packs of sandwiches. I think we'll need them. You could also throw on a big pot of stew – something that can be heated quickly. Anne will ring back and let you know how many horses we'll need. Greg and I will see to that. If we can't get a helicopter this evening and have to head off with a party, we'll need to give them a feed before they leave. We'll take the sandwiches with us.'

'Andy, don't you overdo things,' Jean cautioned. 'Stress could bring on another stroke.'

'I'm as right as rain, Jean. It's just a matter of organisation.'

Anne had always had a quick brain, so when the local police rang back and told her they hadn't been able to locate a chopper, she rang the television station in Tamworth and gave them the whole story. The station put out a news flash that Kate was lying with a broken leg on one of the roughest parts of the Liverpool Range. The story was expanded for the evening news slot and beamed to the national services, heard up and down the east coast of Australia. Millions of people learned how a kelpie had been sent miles across rough country with a message for help for a woman who was still waiting to be rescued.

The police and ambulance teams arrived at Poitrel shortly before three-thirty p.m. At that stage of the rescue operation there was no suggestion that a helicopter would be available. There was a conference on the front verandah of the homestead while all parties considered the options.

'How do you see things, Andy?' Sergeant Hooper asked.

'It's a bad situation because Wallaby Rocks is about the most inaccessible spot you could find. We can't get a vehicle within miles, and if we go back through High Peaks we can only get a four-wheel drive to the foot of Yellow Rock. From there on, the trip would be worse than from here. How many of you can ride?'

The two police officers could handle horses well. Tom Chapman said he had ridden a little, years ago, while Eric Wood said he had never been on a horse before.

'This is the way I see it,' Andy began. 'If we go up on horses, we could make it before nightfall, but there's no way we could carry a stretcher back down in the dark. It would be bad enough in daylight but impossible at night.'

'What do you suggest?' Sergeant Hooper asked in his official manner.

'I think the first priority is to get these ambulance-men up. I wouldn't try and take a stretcher up on a horse because if we carry some rope and straps we can knock up a stretcher from saplings. Our best hope is that your man back at the station can locate a chopper, even if we can't get it here until morning. There has to be a chopper somewhere. The biggest problem is that Kate and David won't know what's going on down here.'

'Why don't we set a departure time?' Hooper said. 'If there's no chopper by nine a.m., we start back down the mountain with Sister Gilmour.'

'Good idea,' Andy said. 'Let's pack what we need and head off. One of you fellows had better stay and look out for things this end, to be here through the night and on deck first thing in the morning. I will leave Greg here in case he's needed. I'll guide you up. Sister Courteney has tucker ready and food to take with us. We'll need to pack some blankets as it's cold up there, even with a fire.'

It was nearly four-thirty before they got away. Sergeant Hooper was in the party and Constable Walker stayed behind at Poitrel. By that time Jean knew Catriona had left High Peaks for Wallaby Rocks. Angus had delivered Catriona and King to High Peaks within the hour. He had been keen to accompany Catriona, but was persuaded by Anne that this was not necessary. Together Anne and Angus rolled and tied the blankets and pillow that David had requested and then filled two saddlebags with food and other items. Angus threw in a bottle of scotch, which he said might come in handy.

'Are you sure you know where you're going, Catriona?' Anne asked.

'Quite sure. When you go through the boundary fence into Poitrel you follow the eastern side of the ridge and that takes you to Wallaby Rocks. David will have the fire going so I should see the smoke as soon as I get up on top.'

'Be careful, dear. Don't try and make too much pace. You will have to stay there the night. Do you think there will be anything else you'll need?'

'I don't think so. Bye, Daddy. Bye, Anne. See you tomorrow.'

Catriona trotted King past the dog yards and then down to the first gate. Angus watched her until she was out of sight.

'Anything else I can do, Anne?' Angus asked.

'I don't think so. We'll keep you posted.'

Angus shook his head. 'There must be a helicopter somewhere.'

'I rang the Tamworth television station and let them know about the situation. That might flush out a helicopter.'

'Terrific idea. Look, I think I'll take a run round to Poitrel and see what's happening there.'

Angus was always there when the whips were cracking. Anne had seen him tested several times and he had always come up trumps.

'I'd like to be there myself, Angus, but Andy told me to stay by the phone here, and I know I should.'

'Just imagine that old dog bringing David's message all that way!' Angus said before he left. 'No wonder David wanted him back.'

'Yes, it was a terrific effort. The TV people should like that for a story, especially if they could see the country he travelled through.'

Anne was right. The TV people did like it for a story. News teams were on their way within the hour.

Up on Wallaby Rocks, David had been busy collecting great heaps of firewood, fearing they would be on the mountain until morning and knowing it could get very chilly at that height. He kept their own fire going with a mixture of dead logs and green branches, and the beacon could be seen for miles.

Catriona saw it as soon as she came up onto the ridge from the High Peaks–Poitrel boundary fence. 'Good old David,' she breathed as she pointed King towards the smoke, chuffed that he had asked for her when he needed help. That was really something. And they would be together on the mountain all night.

David had bathed Kate's face and then scouted the ridge for saplings that could be used as splints. He came back to the fire carrying two branches, which he proceeded to shave smooth and flat on one side. When he had finished doing this, he produced a couple of pieces of redhide. She knew he always carried strips of redhide on his saddle or in his saddlebag as they often came in handy.

'Kate, it's crunch time. Do we do it over your jeans or cut the trouser leg off?'

'Well, David, I can't get up to take them off,' Kate said and forced a laugh. 'Cut the leg. I can always use them for shorts later.'

David used the portion of jeans he cut off to pad the two splints, and then with Kate holding the saplings in place he used the redhide strips to strap the makeshift splints in place. There was sweat on Kate's face when he finished and she looked a shade or two paler, but the splints cut down the pain a little.

In midafternoon he boiled the billy again and gave Kate another mug of tea. She was bearing up well, all things considered.

David didn't know what he would do without Kate. She was a cross between a second mother and an older sister to him. He sat with her and yarned awhile and tried to take her mind off her leg, which was difficult, as even the tiniest movement brought a grimace to her face.

The afternoon dragged on and when Kate looked at her watch she saw that it was just after five. She had come off Chief nearly six hours ago. It was clear to her that David was beginning to worry. It would be dark in under an hour. What if Anne hadn't found the message on Nap's collar?

'Kate, I'm going to climb up the ridge and have a look. I can see down into Poitrel from there and also along the ridge to where Cat would be coming from.'

After a few minutes Kate saw David wave from up on the ridge above her.

'She's on her way, and there are horses coming up the mountain from Poitrel,' he called.

She felt a huge wave of relief surge through her. David had done all that was humanly possible for her and now others could take over.

David noted the look of relief on his aunt's face as he came scrambling down from the ridge. 'Good old Nap. He did it. And good old Mum. I'll bet she had a fit when she read my message.'

'It's too late to go back down tonight, though, isn't it?' she asked.

'I reckon. But hopefully there'll be an ambulance-man or two in the party and you'll get a decent pain-killer. I must say I was starting to worry; Cat is cutting it fine for light. I'm not worried about the other lot because ten to one Dad will be guiding them. He could find his way here on the darkest night. I'll just walk up the track a little to meet Cat. I hope she's got some blankets. It's starting to get chilly.'

Catriona appeared on the high section of the ridge and saw the fire below the tall spire of dark smoke. And then she saw David walking towards her on a narrow sheep pad that led over the very top of Wallaby Rocks.

David's keen eyes picked out the bundle tied behind Catriona's saddle and he breathed a sigh of relief. At least they would have Kate warm when the other party arrived.

Catriona jumped out of the saddle in a rush, almost falling on David in the process. David took King's reins in one hand and one of Catriona's hands in the other as they walked down to the makeshift camp.

'How is she?' Catriona asked.

'Bearing up. You know what Kate's like. Her leg's in a mess and it must be hurting like blazes but she's very brave. Thank God Mum got my message. And thank God you were home. Well, King, you look more like a packhorse than a Champion Hack.'

Catriona knelt down beside Kate while David unstrapped the blankets and pillow. Catriona put the small pillow under the site of the break, as Kate instructed, and then covered her with a blanket. 'Better?' she asked.

'A lot, thank you. David, did you find the aspirin?'

'Coming.' David handed Kate two tablets and she washed them down with water.

'The other party is on its way, Cat,' he said. 'Now, I'll unsaddle King and put him near our horses. You can use his saddle for a pillow. I'm glad we've got these extra blankets – we're going to need them.' He threw the blankets over a rock and then laid out the packets of food Anne had packed.

'Feel like a sandwich, Kate?' he asked.

'I thought you'd never ask,' she said.

David and Catriona sat beside Kate and watched the sun go down behind the range. 'How's Mum?' he asked Catriona after he had finished his first sandwich.

'She's in control. She's even alerted the media.'

David smiled and looked up at the darkening sky. 'Just as well it's a fine night.'

'I must say it is very nice to have you here, Catriona,' Kate said with a wry smile.

'Any time,' Catriona flashed back. She had always admired Kate Gilmour. Even as a young girl she had been rather in awe of her. She had always seemed so

489

full of fun, and so wonderfully efficient. There were a lot worse role models a girl could have.

The sound of a stockwhip rent the quiet of the evening. David got up and went to where he had placed his saddle and whip. 'They can't see the smoke in this light. The whip will guide them here,' he said. He climbed back up on to the crest and let fly. Every few moments he swung the whip and listened for the answering crack. It was almost dark when the four riders came into view along the ridge.

Returning to the fire, he said, 'They're almost here, Kate. Four of them. I can pick Dad but not the others.'

He stood with Catriona and raised his hand in greeting as his father led the other three riders up to the fire. One man seemed to have difficulty staying in the saddle and David moved to help him off. The rider, who turned out to be Eric Wood, staggered and almost fell when his feet touched the ground.

'I'll never be the same again,' Harry said with a grin.

'Hi, Sergeant, Tom,' David said to the others. He was relieved to find two ambulance officers in the party.

There was a bustle of activity as gear was taken off the saddles and sorted into bundles. A light was set up beside Kate and, with Catriona in attendance, Eric and Tom took over. Kate was given an injection to dull the pain and David's rough splints were replaced.

'It's a pretty bad break by the look of things,' Eric

told the group. 'She has a bit of bruising as well.'

Andrew summarised the course of action they had decided on. 'We'll wait until nine in the morning and if there isn't a chopper here by then, we'll have to start back.'

'It'll be a hell of a trip, Dad,' David said.

'We realise that, but what else can we do? We can't stay up here indefinitely.'

David shook his head. 'Let me take Kate back on King. It wouldn't be any harder on her than getting thrown about on a stretcher.'

'Crikey, David, I don't know about that. You'd have to ask Eric and Tom what they think.'

'Either way it's a bad trip, but it would be a lot quicker if we did it my way. They could give her something more for the pain and I'd have her back in an hour and half. It would take three or four times that long carrying her on a stretcher.'

'I think we should delay making that kind of decision until we see what happens in the morning,' Sergeant Hooper said.

Andrew nodded. 'I sure hope Anne can get hold of a chopper.'

Catriona boiled the billy for everyone and they all sat in a rough circle drinking tea and eating sandwiches. The pain in Kate's leg had eased and she was warm under the blankets, feeling almost comfortable. She had the utmost confidence in the group gathered about her and knew that some way or other she would be in hospital the next day.

It grew steadily colder and David lit the other heaps of firewood so they could sit, and perhaps sleep, in a circle of warmth. There was plenty of dead wood, and some of the bigger logs would burn for a couple of hours. Catriona lay close to Kate, although her heart was with David. They all used their saddles for pillows and yarned on into the night by the glow of the campfire. Then Kate asked David to recite some bush poetry, which surprised Catriona. She had never heard him do this before. David recited several poems and his deep voice seemed perfectly in tune with their surroundings.

Eventually Catriona's eyes began to close.

'I reckon we should try and get some sleep,' Andrew said when the conversation began to wane. 'We'll need to be up and about fairly early.'

David replenished the fires and lay down a few feet from Catriona. He stretched out an arm and touched her reaching fingers. When he felt her hands relax he tucked her arm back under the warmth of her blanket. Kate's eyes were still open and David bent down and kissed her. 'Sleep well, Kate,' he said.

'God love you, David,' she replied softly.

Despite Kate's predicament and the rough nature of their camp, they had all experienced a magical night on Wallaby Rocks.

Soon the whole camp was asleep. The fires gradually burned down until David, waking at around four a.m., threw more logs on each heap. He went back to his blanket but did not sleep again and was up and about before daylight. He had the billy boiling when his father got up. It was very chilly and they stood and warmed their backsides until David said he would go and water the horses.

They took a couple of horses each and David led the way to the spring beside the cave. The water bubbled into a small trough of sand and rock.

'I didn't know about this,' Andrew said as he looked into the mouth of the big cave.

'Beauty, isn't it? Cat and I sheltered in there – and the horses, too – all through the storm.'

When the others got up they had to go and inspect the cave as well. 'It's almost worth the effort to get here just for the view and that cave,' Eric said. He was stiff in every joint and hoping like hell that he wouldn't have to ride again. With a bit of luck there would be a chopper and he could go back with Sister Gilmour.

Tom gave Kate another injection and while the horses were being saddled Catriona shared out the remaining food.

Shortly after, Andrew's keen ears picked up the characteristic beat of a helicopter's engine. 'Quick, throw some more green branches on the fire. I can hear the chopper,' he said urgently.

There was a furious burst of activity as his instructions were carried out. There was no wind at all and the smoke spiralled clear above the crest. The pilot couldn't miss it. The chopper was a mile or two south of them when it crossed the range and it soon veered around in a wide arc.

'Where will it be able to land?' Eric asked. 'Will we have to carry her a bit?'

'Over here,' David said, cantering off on his horse back along the ridge to the one spot that was clear of timber and rocks. The pilot knew where he had to land. David went back to the others, who were all standing with their faces upturned as they watched the chopper lose height right above them. It came down very slowly and seemed to almost kiss the ground it landed so gently.

The pilot was a lean, long-jawed young man wearing a red and yellow peaked cap, blue jeans and a cowboy shirt.

'Wes Moran,' he said, waving to the group. 'Sorry I couldn't be here last night.'

'G'day, Wes. I'm Sergeant Hooper from Merriwa. Where did you come from this morning?'

'Tamworth, Sarge. I didn't hear about this until after ten last night and it was too risky trying anything in the dark.'

'Would you like some tea, Wes?' Andrew asked.

'I'd love some. I had a dingo's breakfast this morning. But I'd better not, best press on. I reckon this lady here has been waiting long enough. You ready to go? I can take someone else along with us if you like.'

'Better take Eric,' Andrew suggested. 'He's sworn off horses for life.'

'Okay. If we put a blanket under the patient, we can carry her up to the chopper. Bring the pillow and some more blankets and we'll make her nice and snug. You want me to take her to Merriwa or Tamworth?' Moran asked.

'Merriwa,' Kate said sleepily. 'Merriwa, please.'

They placed the blanket under Kate and four men took a corner each, stretching it tight. Kate was carried up to the helicopter and positioned on the machine's floor. A pillow was put under her leg and a blanket was folded up under her head.

'Thanks for everything, David,' Kate whispered in his ear. 'Look after Chief, won't you?' were the last words David heard as the door of the chopper was slammed shut.

'I'll see that he never shies again,' he growled.

They watched as the chopper rose into the sky above them. It circled them once and then surged away towards Merriwa.

Chapter Twenty-seven

The party's descent to Poitrel was accomplished in little over an hour. When they rode into the house paddock they were surprised to see several four-wheel drive vehicles parked about the homestead. There were people everywhere: some in their vehicles and others with Jean on the verandah. There were cameras set up on tripods and they flashed wildly as the party neared the house.

'The newshounds are here,' Hooper growled.

Jean had heard the helicopter as it passed overhead towards Merriwa and she had a big breakfast waiting for the rescue party. There were sausages galore, eggs, tomatoes and plenty of tea and toast. They had never had a breakfast that tasted so good.

The reporters all wanted to see Nap and photograph him with his owner. They wanted to take David over to High Peaks for this purpose. He had been looking forward to a quiet ride home with

Catriona, but he knew they would find no peace until the reporters got what they wanted so he shrugged his shoulders and agreed.

Before heading off to High Peaks, Sergeant Hooper called David aside and said, 'Next time you're in town, come and see me.'

'I don't get to town often, Sergeant, but I reckon I'll be visiting Kate in the next couple of days.'

'Make sure you do, or I'll come back and see you. There's something you should know about. It would be a good excuse to have a look at that stallion of yours.'

David looked curiously at Sergeant Hooper, his eyes asking for more information.

'I don't want to say anything in front of Miss Campbell,' Hooper whispered.

'Okay. If I come in, I'll look you up. Thanks again for all your help.'

As soon as the procession of vehicles had left Poitrel, Jean rang Anne to advise her that Kate had been safely lifted off Wallaby Rocks and that the news crews were now headed for High Peaks.

Anne walked out on to the front verandah and soon enough a stream of cars came through their front entrance. She saw David get out of one vehicle and walk down to the dog yard. He was trailed by a score of men and women, half of whom were carrying cameras of some description.

Nap was found lying on his log kennel enjoying the morning sunshine. David had to demonstrate how he had attached the handkerchief to Nap's collar. Nap was photographed from every angle, with and without David, and then all attention was turned to Yellow Rock and the homestead. David had to retrieve the message he had written and this, too, was photographed. Anne was also photographed with David, and then at last the media representatives roared back to Poitrel, taking David with them at his request.

When he got back there David put Chief in his horse trailer and took Catriona and King back to Inverlochy. He didn't stay long, and drove straight on to High Peaks. He rightly judged that his mother would be anxious to leave for town to see Kate.

Anne had already rung the hospital and learned that Kate was in good shape.

'So that's that,' David said. 'It could have been a whole lot worse for Kate ... and getting her back. Kate was wonderful through it all.'

'Getting Nap to bring your message back was incredible.'

'I didn't fancy leaving Kate. Will you go in and visit her later?'

'I certainly will. If Andy's back in time, he might come with me. Though on second thoughts it might be too much for him. He's had a big couple of days. Would you like to ask Catriona up for dinner? There might be something about you on the telly.'

David spent the afternoon handling a horse and pressing a bale of crutchings. He then gave the dogs a run before feeding them. When he had finished he stood for a few minutes with Nap. 'You're a brainy fella, aren't you?'

Nap looked up at him and wagged his tail.

'I should never have let you leave here. Sorry about that, old dog, but we needed the money real bad at the time. I cheated on you and I still feel bad about it. Kate will probably spoil you rotten when she gets out of hospital. There'll be cooked lamb's fry and steak galore, if I know her. You did a great job, and tonight I reckon you're going to be famous.' He patted Nap on the head and went back inside.

That night he and Catriona saw themselves on television for the first time. Most of the footage centred around Nap and what he had done. They had expected to have a quiet night to themselves, but were quickly disillusioned because the news story generated one phone call after the other. The first caller was Bruce McClymont, who was overjoyed to see 'his' Nap in the news. Then came calls from David's grandparents in Sydney and Shaun Covers – and then there were the neighbours. After the fifth call David said he would take the phone off the hook.

'You can't do that,' Catriona protested. 'There might be an important call.'

'I'm sick of talking to people,' he growled. 'Why can't I just have a quiet night? I've been up since dawn.'

'Because you're in the news, darling. It will all be over tomorrow.'

Catriona was wrong. The next day there were more callers and special-feature writers wanting to do stories on the MacLeods and their dogs. The last call came from two representatives of a film company who wanted to sound David out about making a film. They were so serious about the idea that they even paid a visit to High Peaks a few days later, returning to Sydney with an enthusiastic recommendation. A research assistant and producer were then sent to make a more detailed assessment of the situation. The producer, like his earlier colleagues, became very excited once he had seen the spectacular scenery and the amazing feats of the dogs in action. The animals, especially the dogs, were simply magnificent.

But the producer, Laurence Singer, knew he needed more than just great dogs and horses to make a memorable film, so the research assistant, Helen Gray, set about digging out every bit of available information on the MacLeod family. She discovered how David had had to send Nap away for three years to help the family pay off its debt, and she even found out about his run-ins with Stanley Masters and the Missen brothers. The fact that David was a wizard with a stockwhip also added to his appeal.

A few weeks after their first visit, the film company began to make more ambitious plans. They formulated a rough script, which was posted up to David for approval. His initial reaction was not enthusiastic. He envisaged a lot of problems, mainly concerning how much time he and Catriona would be required

500

to devote to the project, him coaching the actors and Catriona doing some of the more high-risk horse work, like up Yellow Rock. There had been a television commercial for drenching filmed on Inverlochy and the cameramen had insisted on about twenty takes before they were satisfied. This might have made for good TV but it exhausted people and dogs. David was adamant that if he consented to do the film, he would not ask his dogs to repeat scenes. He doubted very much that he could spare the time to put into the film. He had three properties to oversee, plus dogs and young horses to handle. Moreover, his most important project was the next year's National Trial.

The producer said that the company would make the family's involvement well worth their while. He even increased his initial offer, which was a sum not to be sneezed at.

'I don't have time to stand on a hill and get a dog to do twenty casts,' David said. 'If I agree to do this film, I have to be given the right to tell you when I think a dog's work is satisfactory. I won't be dictated to by cameramen. These are my conditions.'

'You must understand that cameramen are very fussy people. They have to be – they're working with investors' money. Not only that but their work is looked at critically throughout the world. If we think a scene isn't good enough, it's done again until we're satisfied.'

'Mr Singer, I don't much care whether I do this

film or not. If I do it, you will get authentic work that meets *my* standards. If you aren't happy with that, you'll have to forget the whole thing.'

'You're a hard man, Mr MacLeod,' Singer said. 'A lot of people would jump at the chance we're giving you.'

'Then you should go and talk to them. Perhaps they're not as busy as I am. And another thing – I couldn't do much until well into next year, and I would want you to include in your script the build-up to the National Trial.'

'We'll have to think about it, Mr MacLeod. We'll get back to you.'

So that was that, and David went back to handling his dogs and young horses.

That afternoon he was in the horse yard when a police car pulled up beside him.

'Hello, Sergeant. Did you get tired of waiting for me?' he called as the big policeman climbed out of his Falcon. 'I'm sorry I haven't been to see you yet. I've only visited Kate at night,' he said by way of apology.

'I was out this way anyway so I thought it was a good chance to come and see you,' Hooper said.

'Got time for a drink?'

'I don't see why not. How's your dad?'

'Going well. He's over at Poitrel right now. We're upgrading the existing shed that Wilf let fall to pieces. Between you and me, Sergeant, we've also got our eyes on the place opposite. It's nearly all good breeding country and we could breed our replacement wethers there instead of buying them.'

Anne looked up in surprise when she heard voices on the verandah.

'Hey, Mum, we've got a visitor.'

'Well, bring him in, dear,' the imperturbable Anne said.

But Sergeant Hooper's entry to her lounge room did induce a feeling of alarm. The arrival of a police officer seemed to signify bad news. 'It's not Andy?' she asked in a strangled kind of voice.

'Nothing like that, Mrs MacLeod. Just some news I thought you people should know about.'

'Sit down, please,' Anne said. 'I'll just go and get some afternoon smoko.'

The big man sat down and looked about the room. It was the first time he had been inside the High Peaks homestead. There were photographs of dogs and horses on the walls, and the dresser was surmounted by large silver cups.

'I hear there's a film company chasing you to make a picture,' Hooper said, making conversation.

'How did you know?' David asked, knowing full well that you couldn't spit in town without someone knowing about it.

Anne came back into the room and placed a tray of tea and cake on the table.

'There was a young woman doing some research on you, David,' Hooper said with a big grin. 'She came to see me. Smart young woman. Really on the ball.'

'Oh, did she? What did you tell her?' David asked.

'Only the truth, David.'

David groaned. 'I wondered where they got their information.'

'Great cake, Mrs MacLeod,' Hooper said, taking a bite of Anne's lemon sponge. He hadn't tasted one like it for years.

'You said you had something to tell us,' David urged.

'Yes. We heard that Roy Missen had employed a top firm of Sydney solicitors to take up the matter of his boys getting early release from prison.' What the sergeant didn't say was that Roy Missen had mortgaged his property to find the money for the legal expenses.

There was silence in the room while David and his mother digested this information.

'Do you think it can be done, Sergeant?' Anne asked.

'I wouldn't have thought so. If a judge sets a non-parole term, then that is the minimum period an offender is required to serve in custody unless new evidence is brought forward. And a person is not necessarily released after the judge's stipulated period. Nothing may come of this, but there is mention of a QC being briefed so I expect that it will be taken to the highest level.'

'Are the Missens likely to be dangerous if they're released?' Anne asked.

'I can't answer that. But it pays to be prepared.'

'I'm not worried for my own sake, Sergeant,' David said, 'but Cat gets around a lot on her own, to town and to Tamworth – even to Sydney.'

'I don't want to cause alarm, but she might want to be careful.' Hooper got up and nodded to Anne. 'Thanks for the cuppa and the bonzer cake, Mrs MacLeod.'

'Thanks for calling, Sergeant. We appreciate it,' she replied.

'You reckon I could have a look at your stallion?' Hooper asked.

'You keen on horses?' David asked.

'Always have been. I was in the mounted police for a while. I've got a yen to buy a small place and breed a few thoroughbreds.'

'We aren't thoroughbred people. We took over some very good blood mares from Wilf White and we're using the best of them to breed stock horses. That black horse Catriona got Champion Hack with a year or so ago was bred from one of Wilf's old mares. Course, Cat did a great job with him. She's a good show rider – been winning awards in the show ring since she was a kid.'

'He's a bottler, old Wilf,' Hooper said. 'I saw him at the show. I used to go out and talk to him when I first came here. He had a terrific memory for pedigrees and race performances.'

'Wilf gave his mare Ajana to me as a present before we bought the place. I reckon this stallion mated with her should produce something. The stallion is just below the house. I'd be pleased to let you see him.'

They walked down the track towards the foal-rearing paddock and came to the big stallion yard they had built especially for Tim's stallion. It was more of a small paddock than a big yard because it was large enough for the horse to run around in and it included a stable and shade trees.

David climbed through the fence and walked up to the bay horse. 'He's as quiet as a kitten, Sergeant, but you never know with stallions and bulls. Wait there until I catch him.' He took a dog lead from his trouser pocket and clipped it to the stallion's halter. The horse rubbed its head against David's chest and David stroked its forehead in return.

'Now, that is a horse,' the sergeant said when David led him across to the fence.

'That he is,' David agreed. 'He was the top stock-horse sire in Queensland.'

'You taking mares to this fellow?' Hooper asked.

'No, not yet. Maybe never. We want a year or two of him for our own use. Greg is all for it, so we'll see how he shapes up before we decide. He isn't young, and we'd like to get as many foals by him as we can.'

'How are things going with Greg?'

'He's a top bloke and we think he'll make a good stockman. He's taken a big load off my shoulders. Not that Dad is useless, but we don't want him doing too much.'

'Damned shame.'

'Look, about your horse breeding. As I told you, we're negotiating to buy Glen Morrison, the place across the road from Poitrel. There's a piece of it that would be ideal for horses. It runs up into hills, which is what you need. The black country is too soft and heavy to produce good-footed horses. If we get that place I could cut you off that bit of ground.'

'But you don't owe me any favours. Why would you do that?' Hooper said.

'A lot of people have dreams they never realise. Maybe I can help you fulfill yours. I'd like to see you breed a few thoroughbreds. You might give Angus Campbell a bit of opposition. You should contact old Wilf and ask him for his ideas on making a start.'

'Is he still keeping well?'

'Seems to be. We exchange phone calls now and then. He still wants to know how his mares are doing. He even pays us a yearly visit; stays with Kate and Jean. Angus has been very keen for us to send Ajana to a blood horse, maybe on the shares. I might yet do it, mainly for Wilf's sake. I'd like to breed something from her that could win a race or two. It would give the old chap a big lift.

'How much land do you reckon there is in this section you refer to?' Hooper asked.

'Perhaps two hundred acres. There's a nice area on the road where you could build a house, put up sheds and grow some lucerne. There aren't many good little blocks available in this district.'

'You let me know if you buy that place, David. I'm interested.'

When Sergeant Hooper had left, David walked back into the house and sat down at the kitchen table. He was frowning, and Anne sensed that he was worried.

'You worried about Bill and Wade, David?'

'Sure I'm worried, Mum. They've got a mean streak in them a mile wide.'

But as the winter drew on there was no more word of the Missen boys' release. It now seemed that they would serve their full nonparole period, which would have them out in the next summer.

There were plenty of other things to occupy David's attention. He had agreed to do the film so long as he had technical control, and not until the following year. He compromised to the extent that he suggested some filming be done at shearing time and when they were bringing sheep down from the hills. This delay actually suited the film company because they had to engage child stars to play David and Catriona as children. These children had to be schooled in handling horses and dogs, and this would take time. In the meantime David had to try and win Catriona's parents over, and he knew this wouldn't be easy. Catriona was thrilled about the film, but he wasn't ready for it.

Shearing came and went and some filming was completed. This included routine sheepdog work around the yards and in the shed.

'I'd like to see some rain,' David said to his father one evening as they sat together on the verandah watching the last sunlight of the day slip away. They had experienced a wonderful autumn and had gone into winter with a big volume of feed, although the heavy frosts had dried and bleached the grass. There had been very little late-winter rain, and spring had been dry. Andrew said he had only seen seasons like that when he was a boy.

When September passed into October and there had been no worthwhile rain, David started putting out mineral blocks for the stock. Although there was plenty of dry feed, it had very little nutritional value, and sheep and cattle couldn't consume enough of it to convert into proper sustenance. The blocks contained urea, which broke down the cellulose in the dry feed and enabled animals to convert it more efficiently. But the cattle were not putting on much weight.

At the end of October, a dry westerly wind began to blow, and it blew for several days. It was at that time that the MacLeods received word that the Missen boys had been released. Stanley Masters, however, was kept inside after having been involved in a knifing incident.

Angus and David agreed that Catriona shouldn't be left on her own. Catriona complied very reluctantly as she felt that Bill and Wade would never be foolish enough to attack her again, especially without Masters. But the grudge Bill and Wade harboured was against David, not Catriona, and it had festered during their time in prison. Bill and Wade knew that if they stepped one inch out of line, David would come down on them like an avenging lion. But if they could get back at MacLeod without him knowing about it, that would be a different matter.

The dry spring and gusting westerlies provided the solution Bill and Wade had been looking for.

Kate was driving down the road from Poitrel on her way to surgery very early one morning when she saw a grey utility parked at the side of the road. Kate stopped her car and got out. There didn't seem to be anyone close by and her first thought was that someone might be trying to pot a rabbit or a wallaby. Shooters were rife in the area. She looked up the hill and saw two men trying to hide themselves behind trees. But that was not what sent her heart pounding. Just above where the men were skulking was a line of flames. And as she watched, the flames flared out across the paddock.

Kate took out her notebook and wrote down the number of the utility and then got back in her car, turned it around and headed straight for Poitrel. The first person she rang was David.

'There's a fire been started between here and your boundary. I think it might have been started by the Missen boys because I saw two men hiding in the trees, although they were a fair way away so it's difficult to say. There was a grey utility parked off the road as well – luckily I have its number. Please ring the police. I've got to get to the hospital. There's an emergency there. Ring Angus to get the fire engines going, and let the Hamiltons know the fire's near their boundary. Jean will stay here today and start the sprinklers, but the wind is taking the fire up the hill, not in our direction. I'll get her to bring the animals into the yards just to be on the safe side.'

'Good on you, Kate. And take your gun with you when you go to town. You never know what those mongrels might do.'

'I reckon they'll be long gone by the time I get there,' Kate said. 'But if I have to, I'll give the buggers a fright.'

Sergeant Hooper had to be woken but was all business when he heard David's news. 'Right, we'll spread the word and get a couple of cars out looking. What was the vehicle's number again?'

'Dad! Mum!' David roared as he put the phone down. His parents were still in bed and often got up a little later now they had Greg Robertson to help. Greg was living in a three-room cottage they'd had built for him during the winter.

'What is it?' they called.

'Kate's just rung. There's a fire in the front paddock at Poitrel. She thinks the Missens started it. They must have been out at dawn in the hope that they'd get well clear before anyone was about. The police are on the way. Mum, will you ring Angus and either Troy or Walter Hamilton? Angus can rouse out his fire team and the Hamiltons may want to shift stock. Hell, a fire with a westerly like yesterday and we'll be in real trouble. Dad, I'll get the horses. You and Greg better take some dogs and get up to Yellow Rock. We'll have to try and get what stock we can mustered and back here behind the creek. Maybe you could muster to the boundary and Greg could take them from you and push them back to the creek. Mum, can you look after the stock below us? Bring them all up and put them in the yards. It's the hill on Poitrel that's the big worry. If the wind gets up like it did yesterday, the fire will roar up that hill like a train.'

Fortunately it was dawn and the wind was little more than a breeze, giving the MacLeods and their neighbours time to get themselves organised. Later in the day, when the wind would be at its strongest, they would have little hope. And, luckily, most of the sheep had congregated around watering holes for their early drink and had not yet dispersed back into their daytime haunts. The bulk of the Poitrel wether flock was spread out across the hill country between the boundaries of High Peaks and Strath Fillan. These sheep had to be shifted first because they were in the most immediate danger.

By the time David, Andrew and Greg reached the High Peaks–Poitrel boundary fence, the fire had taken hold and was about a quarter of a mile further up the hill than Kate had reported. The smoke and flames had frightened the sheep up the hill so they were now in plain view of the riders. A fire travels very fast uphill, and with the westerly behind it all of the Poitrel high country could be devastated, or the slightest wind change could send it roaring off in a different direction. If the fire teams and their neighbours arrived in time, they might just be able to isolate the fire to Poitrel, but you couldn't get a fire vehicle very far up the hill. The pinching-off had to be done by men carrying backsprays and wet bags, which was dangerous business; the only refuges would be clumps of large rocks.

'We'll collect the sheep we can see in front of us and you take them down through Yellow Rock and over the creek. It doesn't matter if they get mixed up with the High Peaks sheep. You can take them all back. When you've got the first lot over, come back to Dad for the next lot. Push them, Greg. Time is everything,' David said urgently.

He left his father to gather in the nearest sheep and rode off across Poitrel to look for others. Andrew was using a black and tan bitch called Tess and he sent her out in a big sweeping cast that encompassed all the sheep they could see directly in front of them. These sheep were uneasy in the smoke-laden air. David left that lot to his father and rode on. The mobs were smaller now and in rougher places. He put two small mobs together and pushed them hard with Nap and Clancy, who was back in action again at last. Greg had not returned by the time David pushed his mob through the gate into High Peaks. He saw his father coming from the direction of Strath

Fillan with another mob of perhaps 300 sheep. The fire was now about halfway up the hill and the wind was definitely picking up. He splashed some water from his water bottle into his hat and gave Nap and Clancy a drink. Although still early morning, it was oppressively hot and the dogs were tonguing. They had had a fast run from the house through to Yellow Rock to begin with.

David paused before riding back into Poitrel. As he looked down the boundary fence, he saw a line of men climbing the hill. Crikey, the firefighters have moved, he thought. They would never stop the fire front-on with the wind blowing it in their faces. So much depended on the wind. Right now the westerly was driving the fire uphill towards Wallaby Rocks. If it reached there – and David knew there was nothing to stop it – the fire could go down the other side and perhaps burn for days in the rough country on the eastern side of the range. Out of the corner of his eye he saw a familiar horse come into view from the direction of High Peaks – it was King with Catriona riding him hard.

'I left Stuart with Anne,' she said. 'They're bringing the cattle and ewes up to the house. And you won't want to know this, but three of the film people are on their way here.'

David slapped his hand against his thigh. 'Hell. I forgot they were due here today. But at this hour?'

'They stayed in town last night and heard from someone at the hotel that there was a fire here and they apparently shot off as fast as they could. They arrived at High Peaks about half an hour ago and got Anne to saddle them three quiet horses. They've followed me down to the creek.'

'Then they'll lose themselves on Yellow Rock,' David said.

'No. They've teamed up with Greg.'

'Can they ride?' David asked.

'Not very well, and one is carrying a big camera.'

'The mad buggers will kill themselves on the mountain. Crikey, Cat, I don't have time for this!'

'They said they wouldn't get in the way; they just want to be here.'

'Jesus. Cat, keep your eye on them, will you?'

'Okay. Is there anything else I can do?' she asked.

'Make sure the fire doesn't come in behind you and those blokes and cut you off. You can take that mob Dad is bringing now down to Greg. That will save some time.'

'I haven't got a dog, David.'

'I know that. Take Nap. He'll work for you. I'll use Clancy.'

When Catriona arrived back from driving the first lot of sheep down to Greg, she found Andrew holding a small mob of about a hundred sheep. Andrew was looking into the pall of smoke that now covered the upper hill country. Not far from him the three men from the film company had set up their camera and were filming the activity around them.

Just at that moment David appeared from out of

515

the smoke with another fifty or so sheep. 'They're getting harder to locate,' he said. 'I saw another lot near Wallaby Rocks.'

'David, let them go,' Andrew cautioned.

'I've still got time. I can't let them burn to death,' he said.

'Better the sheep than you,' Andrew said grimly.

And then David was gone and, as a gust of wind momentarily cleared the smoke, they saw him heading along the side of the ridge for Wallaby Rocks. At that moment the fire roared up over the ridge and they knew that unless David saw it and galloped back, he would be cut off. The film-makers captured him turning in the saddle and looking behind at the fire, but he had sent Clancy after some sheep and he would never leave his dog.

'David,' Catriona called out desperately, but he wouldn't listen. Even above the roar of the flames they could hear David's voice calling, 'Clancy, get up. Get up, boy.' Clancy pulled himself up over one big boulder after another until he was sitting right on top of a mammoth bare rock half the size of a house. And then the fire roared across the ridge and down the other side. Finally they could see David no longer. He was lost in a sea of smoke.

Chapter Twenty-eight

Catriona was screaming and crying alongside Andrew as he looked grimly into the fire-ravaged scene of desolation. Two of the film-makers were gazing with open-mouthed horror at what they had just seen, but this didn't stop the third man filming. Catriona made an attempt to ride closer, but Andrew caught King's bridle and brought her back. She was still screaming hysterically, and finally Andrew threw a pannikin of water in her face. That stopped the screaming but great sobs still racked her body.

There was absolutely nothing anyone could do until the fire burnt itself out on the ridge and the main fire front passed down the eastern slope.

It took more than half an hour to burn up the scrub and dead timber on the ridge and then the fire surged on down the slope, more slowly now that the wind was not behind it.

'Where's David?' Greg asked, appearing from behind.

'In there,' Andrew said, pointing into the thick, choking smoke on the ridge. 'Tie the dogs up so they can't follow me. They'll burn their feet if they do. I'm going over there to find him, one way or another.'

'I'm going with you,' Catriona said through her sobs.

'It would be better if you didn't,' Andrew said gently.

'No, it wouldn't. King will take me anywhere.'

'All right,' Andrew said with resignation. 'Pick your way. There's a lot of logs still burning, and trees. Keep clear of them. If your horse collects a hot cinder, you'll have a job getting him any further. Greg, you hold this mob here until we get back.'

'Where's Nap?' Catriona asked.

'I thought he was with you,' Andrew said.

'He was and then he wasn't,' Catriona said.

Andrew shook his head in despair at the devastating situation. 'Those Missen boys have got a lot to answer for.'

They picked their way across the blackened, smoking ridge and bypassed burning stumps and logs. Their horses, well-schooled though they were, were nervous of the flames and smoke. They reached the monstrous boulders up which Clancy had climbed, but there was no sign of the dog. They continued riding right around the rocks. No dog, dead or alive, greeted their anxious eyes.

'Look, there's a burnt sheep,' Catriona said. 'And there's another.'

Andrew's concern increased. If these sheep were in the mob David had tried to rescue, the fire must have overwhelmed them. But why only two? They did not find any more burnt sheep or see any sign of Nap or Clancy. As they dipped down off the ridge towards Wallaby Rocks, the smoke and flames were thicker; there were more logs and they were still burning.

'Catriona, there's just a chance ...' Andrew said hesitantly. 'That big cave. David would have had that in his mind all the time, to fall back on.'

'Do you think he could have made it in time?' Catriona asked.

'If I know David, I reckon that's where he would have made for.'

Together they rode along a sheep pad in an eerie world of smoke and burning bushland. A tree crashed down on the ridge above them and caused their horses to prance nervously. It was getting difficult to see much for the smoke, and Andrew handed Catriona his big handkerchief. 'Tie it over your nose and mouth.'

'Please, God, let David be there,' Catriona said.

'Better get off,' Andrew said.

He waited until Catriona had dismounted and then they picked their way across the still-smoking ground towards the front of the cave. Catriona dropped King's reins and ran ahead. Andrew picked up the reins and followed more cautiously.

Catriona stopped at the cave's entrance and peered inside. The scene that met her eyes was one she would never forget. The first thing she saw was a red and tan dog, which she knew was Nap by the grey on his muzzle. He stood sentinel at the mouth of the cave with his head pointed towards a small mob of sheep. And then, as Catriona's eyes became more accustomed to the gloom and smoke inside the cave, she saw David, his horse and another red and tan dog. David was dripping water from his water bottle onto Clancy's feet and the dog was making little whimpering noises.

'David,' Catriona screamed as she ran towards him. Crying, she fell to her knees beside him.

David put his arms around her and waited patiently for her sobs to subside. And then he looked beyond her and saw his father standing at the mouth of the cave with the horses.

'I reckoned you'd find your way here,' Andrew said grimly. He looked at his son, who was covered in black soot, and a great wave of relief passed over him.

'You crazy, crazy man,' Catriona said. 'You should have left those damned sheep. And how did Nap get here? He was with me. What's wrong with Clancy?'

'He's burned his feet quite badly, I think. He must have waited on the rock until the fire passed by and then come looking for me. I think he saw or smelt Nap go by like the wind. Nap picked up this mob and we got them in here. After a while Clancy found us but he couldn't stand up any longer. Don't know how he got this far with those feet. Dad, how are you? How's the fire?'

'I think we've saved most of the Poitrel sheep. There's a couple of dead ones up top and there's probably more elsewhere, but some of those we missed could have got in among the rocks. We'll have to winkle them out or they'll starve. What's our next move?'

'Dad, we either get the hell out of here or else we can all sit down and have a drink of tea.'

Andrew and Catriona stared at him in amazement. And then Andrew laughed so uncharacteristically that Catriona wondered if he, too, had become a little crazy.

'If it comes to that, I reckon we've earned a drink of tea,' Andrew said. 'Especially as we went without breakfast. But what about Greg and those film blokes? God knows what they're thinking.'

'Catriona knows where the billy is and I have tea things in my saddlebag. We'll have no trouble finding some burning wood! When you get the billy going, you might care to ride up to the top of the ridge and wave to Greg. And then we'll have to see what's happening elsewhere and get those film blokes home. And someone is going to have to take Clancy to the vet. He's in a lot of pain.'

'Poor Clancy,' Catriona said as she patted the dog's head.

'I want you to get him in to the vet's as fast as

you can,' David said. 'I reckon he'll be lucky to work again. Greg can go with you. He can keep his eyes open for the Missens. Oh, and I'd call in at the house before you leave. Your face is very sooty.'

Catriona put a hand to her face and grimaced when it came away black.

'I must look a sight,' she said.

'Not to me you don't,' David said. 'You looked like an angel when I saw you standing there.'

Later, when Andrew had returned from the ridge and they had all drunk their tea, David got to his feet. 'I suppose we'd better make tracks.'

'What about Clancy?' Andrew said.

'Heave him up to me when I get on.'

Clancy whined softly when Andrew lifted him on to the saddle in front of David. 'You'll be right, old mate. The vet will give you something for your pain.'

They rode back through the devastation with Nap shepherding the sheep behind them. Only a dog with superlative holding ability could have held sheep together under the conditions that prevailed on the ridge, and David had never been prouder of a dog than he was of Nap that day.

Greg rode across the ridge towards them, pointing back behind him. The film men were still shooting as they approached. The western sky was full of dark clouds and away in the distance they could hear the low rumble of thunder.

'We're going to get a storm,' Andrew said to David

and Catriona. 'There was a storm came up after the fire that went through Inverlochy. It came after a westerly like this one. Rained a dollop. Let it be quick.'

But the film-makers were not concerned with the likelihood of a storm. They were beside themselves with joy because they had just shot one of the best and most authentic pieces of film they could have hoped for. And as they had filmed the sooty trio emerging from the smoke, with David holding Clancy across the pommel of his saddle, the figures had been obscured enough for them to pass for their leading actors. Even Clancy's burnt feet were real, and though not in the script, they would have no trouble working it in.

David hardly acknowleged the film crew. His immediate concern was to get Clancy to the vet.

'Greg, I want you to take Clancy and go with Catriona back to the house and then on to the vet. You can take the ute. There's a shotgun under the seat.'

'Cat, tell the vet that no matter what it costs he's to try and get Clancy right. If he doesn't know much about burns, have him call in a specialist. Be very firm about it, okay?'

'I understand. I'll have to leave him there, won't I?'

'No doubt. Tell the vet I'll ring him later on tonight.' He handed Clancy across to Greg and waved them away. Just before they left, he leant over and kissed Catriona on the cheek.

'See you later, Cat. Go for your life. I'll get King back to you after this is all over.'

David wheeled his horse and walked it across to where the three men from the film company were talking together. 'You fellows should follow Cat and Greg, but you'll need to hurry or you'll lose them. Dad and I won't have time to look out for you. There's a storm on the way and your gear will get soaked.'

The three men got on their horses and set off after Catriona and Greg.

'Thank God they're out of our hair,' David said as he and Andrew trotted their horses down the hill towards the men working along the flanks of the fire. It had burned into High Peaks but had been stopped by the firefighters on a ridge below Yellow Rock. It was now burning itself out among the jumbled rocks and stony gullies. But there was a lot of smoke coming from the far boundary of Poitrel, and David wondered whether the fire had burned into Strath Fillan. The problem was that they couldn't be in two places at once. Their main worry was the fire that had gone down past Wallaby Rocks. If the wind changed, it could spread into Jimmy's Mountain and come back over the hill behind the homestead.

'It should be raining within two hours, if we're lucky,' David said.

As they continued on down the hill towards the Poitrel–Inverlochy road, they saw a rider approaching. It was Angus Campbell on a Poitrel horse. He lifted his hand in greeting as he came up to them.

'You fellows look a bit worse for wear,' he said in his usual deadpan way.

'We had a brush with the fire. Cat will tell you about it later on,' David said.

'Where *is* Catriona?' Angus barked.

'She and Greg have taken Clancy to the vet. His feet were burned in the fire. Where is it now?'

'I think this side of the fire is under control,' Angus said. 'Thank God for the rocks. You can get in and do something when there's rocks to break it up. There's a team over on the Hamiltons' and they're having a hard time of it. I've just sent another ten men over there, but getting water up for the backpacks is the killer. It's a hell of a caper in this hill country.'

'We know,' David said. He looked up at the sky, which had darkened considerably, and the thunder was much louder now, too. 'Looks as if we might get some help.'

'I sure hope so. I suppose the head of the fire is still heading east?' Angus said.

'It is at the moment. It would take an army of men to stop it in that country. Of course, it could turn and come down on us from behind Jimmy's Mountain.'

'Hopefully we won't have to worry about that. You might remember, Andy, that our fire was stopped by a storm that came up just like this one,' Angus said.

'Yes. Well, things could be a lot worse. If Kate hadn't spotted it early, or if it had started yesterday, we might have lost the lot,' Andrew said.

'Did you lose any sheep?' Angus asked.

'We did see a few dead ones and don't know how many more there could be. And we'll have a bit of fencing to do,' David said.

'There's no doubt that those Missen boys are pure poison,' Angus said.

'If it was them – and Kate was certain it was – I feel really sorry for Roy and Bessie. This will kill them. They borrowed a lot of money to get the stupid buggers out and they're not out five minutes and they're in trouble again. Have you heard anything on the radio?' David asked.

'Too damned busy,' Angus said.

Two hours later David and Andrew rode home in pouring rain. They were thoroughly soaked, as were their dogs beside them. They rode into their horse yard with an anxious Anne waiting for them on the front verandah. After they had had hot baths and a good feed and changed into some clean clothes, Catriona and Greg came racing up the front steps to the verandah.

'You'll never believe what's happened!' Catriona said. 'Bill and Wade have been killed. There was a car chase on the Bunnan Road. Their car skidded, ran off the road and smashed into a tree. They were going so fast their ute was literally wrapped around it. They were both dead when the police arrived.'

'Oh, dear,' Anne said. 'Who could have imagined those two boys would end up like that? Poor Roy and Bessie.'

There was silence on the verandah as the rain continued to pour down. Nobody knew what to say.

'What's the news on Clancy?' David asked at last.

'The vet said he thought that in time the pads would grow a kind of lining, but his feet would never stand much work. You could use him for a stud dog or perhaps put boots on him so you could show off with him, but that's about all. The vet wants you to go and see him.'

'I don't know what you put that poor dog through up there. You're a crazy young man, David,' Anne said. 'Catriona, why you would ever want to be involved with a man of this family is beyond me. Why don't you consider a doctor for a husband? Or a vet?'

'I've waited a long time for this man,' Catriona said, smiling across at David.

'Just as well, I suppose. I am getting old and one mad MacLeod male is enough for me to handle.'

'Nonsense, Mum,' David said. 'You're far from being old. And Nap was trying to save *our* sheep. I cheated on him once when I sent him away for three years, and I wasn't going to let him down again. I knew I could make that cave if the worst came to the worst. The only tragedy is Clancy's feet. Will they recover enough for me to work him at Canberra? I'll work him in boots if I have to.'

'There's a hoodoo on Clancy,' Andrew said. 'The

dog is a genius, the like of which a man gets only once in a lifetime, and yet you can't take advantage of what he has to offer.'

'I'll get him there this time,' David said grimly. 'I don't care what it costs me.'

The story of Nap's feat spread like wildfire and he made the national news for the second time. The story 'Kelpie saves sheep in bushfire' was seen by millions of viewers in eastern Australia. Bruce McClymont saw it and was beside himself with joy because his Nap dogs were the boom kelpies of Australia. Two animal welfare organisations initiated moves to honour Nap's courage in first helping Kate Gilmour and then sheep threatened with death by fire. These awards would take about a year to be formalised.

Later that afternoon, with the rain still coming down in torrents, the MacLeods sat and discussed what needed to be done in the wake of the fire.

'Fencing first,' Andrew said.

'You'll not touch one piece of fence, Andy,' Anne said. 'You're to take a couple of days off after today. Just sit down and read the papers.'

'Mum's right, Dad. Forget the fencing. I'll get a contractor onto it. We've got the money now. More important than anything right now is Clancy. First thing in the morning I'm going in to see what the vet has to say about him.'

Clancy's feet were encased in bandages but his tail wagged furiously when he heard David's voice in the surgery the next day.

'G'day, David. They tell me you had a close shave up there yesterday,' Eric Chalmers said.

'It was close enough,' David replied.

'That old Nap must be a marvel. He thinks like a human being.'

'He keeps on surprising me, that's for sure, and I thought I knew him backwards,' David said.

'Those kelpies of yours must be about the best dogs in the whole damn country.'

'I don't know how we'd get on without them. Now what's the news on Clancy?' David asked with a frown.

'It could be worse, but then again it could be a lot better,' Chalmers said with a grin. 'I've consulted with the Vet School in Sydney and also with a human doctor who's a burns specialist. They agreed with my own treatment and prognosis, although there are a couple of new options available for humans so I'll try one of those medications. Clancy's pads have been cooked and most of the skin has either sloughed off already or will do soon. We believe he will grow new skin but it will be thinner. It won't have the toughness of his old pads, but we can look at perhaps toughening it artificially. There are a couple of things we can try. You would probably be aware that some of the old hands used a wattle-bark solution. I can talk to you about that later. I should warn you, David, as I told Catriona yesterday, that it is very unlikely Clancy will be any good for hard work,' Chalmers said.

'Okay, so he won't be able to do hard work, but could he still run a trial?'

Chalmers looked David up and down. He had more time for this young man than almost anyone else he knew. 'How good is Clancy, David?' he asked without answering David's question.

'Only Dad and I know about it, so let's keep it between us. Clancy is the best trial dog in Australia. He's a freak. Nap is perhaps a better sheepdog, but Clancy would wipe the floor with him on three sheep. If I can get Clancy to Canberra, I think I can win the National with him, even as a Maiden dog. That's how good he is.'

'And Andy agrees?'

'Dad hasn't worked him before but he says he's never seen a better dog,' David said.

'If we have to, we can put boots on him. If Clancy is that good, he's worth putting a lot of effort into to try and get him right. We don't have a lot of time in terms of healing, so the sooner we can get the new skin to grow the sooner we can start toughening up his new pads. You won't be able to work him until the last month, and I'd work him in boots right up to the last. You should get him well used to working in boots in case you have to use them at the trial. How many runs would he have to do?'

'Depends on how he scores. Top Maiden dogs go into the Open. If he gets into the Open and then into the Open final, he would have three runs.'

'Gee, that's forty-five minutes of running. It's not much for a seasoned dog but a lot for a dog with wonky feet.'

'I have to give Clancy the chance. I may not make it to Canberra again. That's why this next National is so important to me.'

'You'd better leave Clancy here for a few more days. I'll watch him closely, and when I'm satisfied that his pads are healing, you can take him back and continue with the treatment.'

'That's fine by me,' David said. 'The money doesn't matter. It's getting Clancy better that matters. His smashed leg put him out last time, and now this. You get a dog like this once in a lifetime, if you're lucky, and these things happen.'

'That's life, David. You go and get your fencing up and leave me to worry about Clancy.'

So David left the vet's surgery with mixed feelings. Well, he thought, if Clancy did have to wear boots at the National, it would be a talking point in the caravans all over Canberra Showground.

David was fortunate to be able to get hold of a fencing contractor almost immediately. It was important to get the fencing done as quickly as possible because High Peaks was now running nearly double its usual sheep flock. Feed had come away well after the big storm and this helped with the heavy stocking on High Peaks. David took the opportunity while the wethers were all together to drench them, and then the Poitrel sheep were drafted off by earmark and taken back to their old paddocks. Here the feed had come away wonderfully well since the fire and all the burnt ground was covered in sweet new grass. The wethers trotted away and in the space of only a few minutes were spread out across the hills.

'They know where they are, Dad,' David said to his father as he watched the sheep move quickly across the paddocks to old haunts.

'They sure do. Well, they've got some fresh new grass now and they'll do real well on it. The fire would have killed all the worm eggs, too. Things could have been worse. Looks like we lost about fifty sheep in all.'

'And Clancy's feet,' David added sombrely.

They rode back through the green paddocks with a sense of relief that conditions were back to normal: the Poitrel sheep were back in their old paddocks and High Peaks had reverted to its usual stocking rate. They were within a squeak of purchasing Glen Morrison, the property opposite Poitrel. It ran back in the general direction of the Cassilis Road and, except for a section of hilly country, it was first-class grazing land very similar to Inverlochy country. It was probably too rich for merino sheep, though the famous Collaroy strain of merinos had been grazed there way back in the early days of settlement. It was also very good cattle-fattening country, and this fitted in with David's idea of taking some of his Aberfeldy cattle there.

David reckoned he had enough on his plate for

two men to handle, but he loved his work. He just hoped he would have the time to put in with Clancy before Canberra – and he hoped the wattle-bark solutions would shape up to be as good as the old hands reckoned.

Chapter Twenty-nine

Now that the fencing had been completed and Glen Morrison was as good as theirs, David turned his attention to the next major consideration – his marriage to Catriona. So far their engagement had been kept secret, although Anne had had her suspicions. Angus had not yet got wind of David's Queensland inheritance, which was a minor miracle in Merriwa. It was only the fact that it was a legacy from interstate that kept the news from spreading. But when Angus learned that the MacLeods had bought Glen Morrison, he was likely to be just as upset as he had been when Wilfred White offered them Poitrel. Jack Carruthers, who owned Glen Morrison, had a lot of time for the MacLeods and was pleased to be selling to them. He was also happy about not paying an agent's commission, which amounted to a good few thousand dollars.

Meanwhile, David had Catriona to consider. He

knew that he could not put off talking to Angus any longer. Catriona was adamant that they be married after the National, with or without her parents' approval. She was even prepared to get married in a registry office, although that was a last resort. David knew that deep down Cat did want a grander wedding with all her friends around her, and if she was prepared to fly in the face of her parents' wishes, it was up to him to front up to Angus and lay their situation on the line.

A few days earlier, Catriona had ridden up to see David and they had boiled the billy down by the creek.

'Darling, it's no good going on like this,' Catriona said. 'Mum and Dad are at me all the time about this or that fellow. I can't keep stalling them forever. I've waited all this time for you. I want you and I know you want me. If we're to have a future together, you'll have to tackle Daddy one day. Let's do it and get it over with.'

'What if Angus digs his toes in?' David asked.

'I think we can expect that,' Catriona said. 'You'll have to tell him we are getting married with or without his approval. Tell him we'll get married in a registry office if we have to. That should rock the boat a bit.'

'You don't want to do that, do you, Cat?'

'Of course not. Ideally, I'd like to be married in Sydney and in a ceremony I'll always remember.'

David walked up and down beside the creek. He

had always known that it would come to this. It was not that he was afraid to face Angus – what concerned him were the consequences of such a confrontation. The atmosphere could get nasty. Catriona could be cut off from her family, and would be extremely upset; it wouldn't be the ideal start to a successful marriage. But things couldn't drag on. Catriona was being pushed to marry someone else, and David wouldn't abide that.

'Come here, Cat,' he said. He put his arms around her and kissed her gently. It was a very long kiss, and by the end of it Catriona was close to tears.

'You're going to tell me something, aren't you?' she asked.

He nodded. 'I'm going to see Angus. I can't have you hassled to marry someone else. One way or another, we'll be married after the National.'

'Oh, David, you darling,' Catriona cried. 'I'm sorry you have to front Daddy, but I can't bear the suspense any longer.'

They sat with their arms around each other's waists, Catriona's head on David's shoulder, each knowing that the die was cast and, come what may, they would be married.

So several days later, on his way back from town where he had been finalising details for their purchase of Glen Morrison, David stopped off at Inverlochy. Angus was attending to his mail and invited David into his office.

'Got Poitrel all fenced again?' he asked.

'All fenced, and the Poitrel sheep back in their old paddocks.'

'I hear that you and Andy have been up north,' Angus said as David seated himself in one of the big leather chairs. 'Looking at horses or cattle?'

'Both, actually,' David said noncommittally.

'Wouldn't think you'd need to bring cattle from up there. Your herd has improved out of sight. You'd not be buying a bull up there, would you?'

'No, we weren't thinking of doing that. Listen, Mr Campbell, I have come here to talk to you about something more important than cattle.'

To Angus Campbell there weren't many things more important than cattle, and suddenly David had his full attention.

'Is that a fact?'

'I want to talk about Catriona. We want to get married after Canberra next year, and I am here to ask you for her hand.'

Angus shook his head. 'You're a nice fellow, David, and you've achieved a lot in your young life. I like you as a man and as a neighbour, but I can't give you my permission to marry Catriona.'

'That's a pity,' David said. 'Would you mind telling me why?'

'I don't have to give my reasons,' Angus replied.

'Is it because you think Catriona could marry someone wealthier?' he persisted.

'That's one reason,' Angus agreed.

'And is it because I didn't go to a private school?'

'That has to be taken into consideration also.'

'And is it because a son-in-law with a father who's a shearer is not acceptable in your circle?'

'There's no need to be offensive, David.'

'You should know that Catriona and I will be married whether you give your approval or not. Naturally, she would prefer your consent. Catriona is prepared to be married in a registry office, but it needn't come to that. We'd both prefer a proper wedding.'

'No doubt. But the fact remains that I won't give you my permission. I have to think about my grandchildren, too. I would want Catriona's children to be properly educated, as Catriona has been. My daughter could marry anyone she likes. She's had a string of proposals – young men from the most prominent families in the country.'

'But Catriona loves me, Mr Campbell.'

'What is love, David, if you don't have security and prestige?'

'You are a damned snob, Mr Campbell, and a patronising one at that,' David said vehemently.

'You can't talk to me like that,' Angus said with his face growing even ruddier.

'I can and I will. Catriona and I will be married whether you like it or not. If you really want to know the truth, we have been engaged for months. In fact, there's a lot you don't know, Angus Campbell. You mentioned Dad and me having been up north. You want to know why? Tim Sparkes left me everything. Everything, you hear. You know what it amounted to? A cattle property running over three and a half thousand head, plus over a hundred good horses and a holiday house at Yeppoon, not to mention two hundred and twenty-three thousand dollars in the bank. So I own a damn sight more cattle than you do. What do you think of that?'

'Well, er, I had no –'

David didn't wait for him to finish. 'I have just come from town where I signed a contract to buy Glen Morrison. As of today, the MacLeod family now owns four properties. Not bad for a shearer and his son. We own more land, more cattle, more horses and as many sheep as you do, Angus. I didn't want any of this information to influence your decision about Catriona and me. As far as I'm concerned, you can go to the devil. We will go ahead and make all the necessary wedding arrangements, and pay for them, too. It's up to you whether you come or not. Now, good day, Angus,' David said and walked out of the office and down the steps to his vehicle.

He was still fuming when he arrived home at High Peaks. His father and mother were outside drinking tea on the front verandah. Anne could see that David was agitated as he threw himself down on a chair beside them.

'Is something wrong? Did the sale fall through?' she asked.

'No. Glen Morrison is ours, but I just had it out with Angus. I asked for his permission to marry Catriona and he refused.'

'Oh, David. You didn't tell us you were engaged! And Angus has refused? What will you do now?'

'Get married anyway. I told him we would pay for everything. Catriona is coming over here tonight. We can discuss all the arrangements with her then.'

'Did Angus tell you why he wouldn't give you his blessing?' Anne asked.

'Only after I pushed him. You should have seen his face when he heard what I had to say to him.'

Anne looked at Andy, who was grinning broadly. 'You approve of all this, do you?' she asked sternly.

'Damned right I do,' Andy said. 'One hundred per cent.'

'I don't suppose either of you have considered what sort of position this puts Catriona in. The poor girl will feel terrible. Her people have given her everything her whole life and now she has to turn her back on them.'

'We always knew it would come to this,' David said grimly. 'Cat told me she would marry me with or without their permission. And she wants to get married as soon as possible after I get back from Canberra – if I get to Canberra. It's her parents' fault. They're just damned snobs.'

'That they are, but they're trying to do the best by Catriona and her children,' Anne said. 'You can't blame them for that.'

'Any children we might have won't want for anything,' David said. 'It's what Cat wants that matters. Anyway, they can't stop her. Imagine how it would look if we had the wedding without them. They would never live it down. Any tea left?'

'I'll make some more,' Anne said.

'About time someone tore a few strips off Angus,' Andy said when Anne had left the room. 'He'll either hate you forever or respect you for this, David.'

'I've got more to think about than him. I wanted to talk to you and Mum about putting up a house for Cat and me,' he said.

'What's all this?' Anne asked as she came back into the room carrying a full teapot.

'I'll need to build a house for Cat and me, Mum.'

'Of course you will. Where?'

'Well, we could live at Glen Morrison, but I don't really want to leave High Peaks. This is my home and this is where I want to live. I thought I might build close to Creek Paddock.'

'You should know you can build anywhere you like, David,' Anne said.

'That's good, because I had a yarn to a builder this morning. He could make a start about the time we're due to go to Canberra.'

'If we go to Canberra,' Anne pointed out. 'How is Clancy coming along?'

'Very steadily. We started him on a drug called formalin and now I've got him onto a wattle-bark mixture. Mr Chalmers has had a couple of pairs of soft boots made up. I'll pick them up in a few days' time. They'll be better than the bandages. It's going to be touch and go, but I'm working on Needle in the meantime. As for Belle, she's a pro – doesn't need any extra tuition at her stage in life. The main thing is to keep her in good working condition. Everything depends on Clancy. If we can't get him fit, we won't be going to Canberra. It's as simple as that.'

'Where does that leave you and Catriona?' Anne asked. 'You used to say you wouldn't get married until after you'd worked at Canberra.'

'Canberra or no Canberra, we'll be married. A fellow can't keep a girl like Cat waiting forever.'

Anne clapped her hands. 'The Lord be praised! You have at last come to your senses. I must say it's about time. How wonderful, David. Congratulations. Oh, I can't believe it. I can't wait to tell Kate and Jean. A wedding at long last.'

Angus Campbell went storming out of his office in search of his wife.

'Jane,' he roared. 'Jane, where the blazes are you?'

'In here, dear,' she called.

'Are you aware that Catriona and David MacLeod are unofficially engaged?' he asked.

'No,' Jane said. 'Are they?'

'David has just asked for my permission to marry Catriona and then had a go at me when I refused. Told me some story about having been left Tim Sparkes's property in Queensland with thousands of cattle thrown in plus a holiday home on the coast. And the MacLeods have just bought Glen Morrison.'

542

'Fancy that. They have come up in the world.'

'Come up in the world? They own more than we do. That's if what David tells me is true. I don't think he'd lie. What do you think about your daughter marrying David?'

'Well, it's not what we had in mind, Angus. I know Catriona always liked David a lot but I did think she would get over it. Apparently she hasn't, and won't.'

'So what do we do now?' Angus asked.

'Catriona doesn't need your permission to marry now that she is of age,' Jane reminded him. 'You can try and dissuade her but I think you'll be wasting your time.'

'Does that mean we have to accept this . . . this . . . situation?'

'I don't see what else we can do, Angus, without making Catriona very unhappy. Do you want that?'

'Damn it, Jane, I don't want any of this! And I can't believe that Catriona made this arrangement behind our backs. Damn David MacLeod. He made me look small when he gave Catriona her black horse and now he's done it again. He didn't tell me about the other properties before asking me about Catriona. He sure let me have it with both barrels.'

'Catriona could do worse, you know,' Jane said.

'I must say you are taking this more calmly than I expected,' Angus replied.

'The fact is we've lost, Angus. David will be our son-in-law and that's that.'

'Bloody hell,' he roared and stormed away again.

He was still breathing fire when Catriona drove in that afternoon. She had no sooner walked onto the front verandah than he confronted her. 'In here, Catriona,' he said, pointing towards his office.

'What is it?' she asked.

'Your mother and I are very disappointed in you,' he said. 'How could you not see fit to tell us, your parents, about your engagement to David MacLeod?'

'Because I knew you wouldn't approve of David. You never have,' Catriona said calmly.

'Well, the boy has no breeding, even if he does own four properties.'

'I am going to marry him and that's all there is to say. It's my life. I love him.'

'Don't be so ungrateful. We only want the best for you and our grandchildren.'

'They will have the best,' Catriona said firmly. 'And they will be brought up in a home full of love.'

Angus did not know what else to say.

Right up to the last week David was unsure if he would get Clancy to Canberra. The formalin and wattle-bark treatments had done the trick in toughening up his pads, which meant he could now run for short periods without boots, but he was hesitant in his moves. For the first few runs he was very diffident about stretching out, and he gingerly picked his way over ground that was at all rough. David tried him with the boots and saw the dog move with far

544

greater freedom. From then on Clancy did not hesitate to run. The problem was that the rough ground played havoc with the specially treated basil and David urgently sent away for half a dozen more pairs of boots. He didn't fancy going to Canberra short of the precious boots. Of Clancy's ability David had absolutely no doubt. The dog was a freak. It would not be lack of ability that hindered him if he got to Canberra – it would be his feet.

When David finally announced that the trip to Canberra was a certainty, a mood of relief swept over High Peaks and Poitrel, for they all knew that the wedding was sure to follow.

Catriona was relieved, too, because there was a very strained atmosphere at Inverlochy. Her father hardly spoke to her and her mother seemed not to know how to handle the situation. Catriona could hardly wait to leave for Canberra.

She was to drive down with David – their first trip away together – and she would stay at a nearby motel. David had presented his mother with a new air-conditioned Ford Fairmont, which she would be driving with Andy to Canberra. They had booked a caravan right next to David's.

Anne sensed that Andy was excited about the trip, which made a nice change for him as he never got excited about anything. Following his stroke, Andy had been living from day to day, and he very much wanted to get to Canberra. For all his years with kelpies, he had never been to a trial the scale of the

National. He had read of the great dogs and handlers who had won there, and he knew that some of them would be working against his son. He also knew exactly what the National meant to David. The one thing David could give his father, something that no money could buy, was the National Championship. That would put the seal on a lifetime of achievement in perpetuating the MacLeod kelpies.

Everyone associated with the MacLeods seemed to be excited about Canberra, too. Everyone but David, that is. He was concerned that virtually everything depended on the thin layer of skin tissue that covered Clancy's pads. The dog had a great heart and would give it everything he could, but his pads might just let him down. David thought about taking the safer option by working Clancy in boots, but that would slow him down, and nobody could predict how much of a handicap that might be. Otherwise he would just have to take the risk and work him without boots in the hope that his pads would hold up.

And so they went to Canberra. The showground was actually in the suburb of Hall, but the great event was always referred to simply as 'Canberra'. Kate had been invited, too, but she had elected to stay and oversee things at home.

The dogs were housed in separate, straw-filled pens in the handsome crate on the back of David's utility which was parked between his caravan and the one his parents were staying in. Each morning, following an early cup of tea, David and Andrew drove out to a nearby property to give the dogs a run. The property owner was a kelpie crank who the previous year had invited David to visit. 'You want to give your dogs a gallop, or work 'em on a few sheep, you come on out,' Ed Somerville had told him.

David wasn't interested in working his dogs on sheep. He said that if his dogs couldn't handle the sheep by now, they shouldn't be in Canberra. He was more interested in trying out Clancy's special basil boots and giving his dogs a decent run in safe surroundings. Keeping bush dogs tied up for a week without exercise wasn't ideal for good trialling.

Anne would have breakfast ready for them when they returned, and a bloke or two would be waiting to talk sheepdogs. Bruce McClymont would drop in to the van for a cuppa and a yarn, mostly about the formidable task facing David's two novice dogs. Unlike their mother, Belle, who had won trials in the past – therefore automatically qualifying for the National Open trial – neither Clancy nor Needle had ever worked in a trial, let alone won one. They would have to work in the Maiden trial, and only a handful of top-scoring dogs from this were admitted into the Open. A dog had to be in the top half-dozen or so to make it. It was a tall order to expect that young, relatively inexperienced dogs could make the final of the Maiden, much less do well in the Open.

But David felt that the months of his preparation with his young dogs couldn't have been better. The first opportunity to test them came just after lunch on the second day of the trials when Needle was listed to work. After giving the young blue and tan bitch a walk around the ground, David headed confidently to the peg. The strange conditions did not seem to be affecting Needle. As soon as she heard her handler's warning hiss, she was all business. Her keen eyes picked up the three sheep as soon as they were let out into the arena.

After one quick look at the jumbucks, Needle switched her attention to the hands of her owner. His hands were important to her. As soon as the starting bell rang, David cast Needle to her right, which was her best side, and she surged away and ran three or four yards out from the arena fence. Her cast was almost perfect, although some extra-tough judges might have docked her a point for finishing a shade short. Her stop, lift and draw down the ground could not have been faulted, and she did not strike any real trouble until she had the sheep placed at the first obstacle. A staggy wether took her on, and despite Needle trying to hold him tightly in front of the obstacle, the wether broke away down one side before she could get him back. A couple of points lost there. The same wether challenged Needle again, this time on the bridge. He went outside the wings just once before she managed to block him in. She might have lost another point for the sheep being very slightly off course between the bridge and the pen, but she penned with three minutes to spare. David felt it was a fairly good round considering Needle had a bugger of a sheep to deal with. He was happy with her score of 92 points. This was the second-top round up to that point of the trial, and the top score by a kelpie.

Bruce McClymont had a grin a mile wide as David and Needle came off the ground. 'Just like her mother, David. Chip off the old block.'

'Not a bad run for a first time on a trial ground, Bruce,' David said.

'Bloody terrific. You opened a few eyes, let me tell you. If you hadn't had that staggy wether to deal with, Needle might have scored anything.'

'That's trialling, Bruce.'

That night David sat with his parents and Catriona and discussed the importance of tomorrow's outcome. They had eaten dinner in the caravan, and David and Catriona had held hands under the table.

Anne sensed the tension in her two men. She knew them both so well. Andy, usually taciturn and un-demonstrative, was strung up beneath the surface, and she didn't like that one bit. David, although apparently nerveless, had so much riding on the events of the following day. Catriona also realised, even more than the others, how much this trial meant to David and his father.

Anne tried to prepare David for the worst. 'David, you know this is a chancy business. Clancy might not have a good run. Don't get your hopes up too high. Andy, you know. Tell David.'

'I already have, and David knows that. I'm not going to roast him if the dog does no good. He's done all anyone could do to get the dog right. Nobody could have done a thing more.'

'Clancy won't let us down,' David said grimly. 'The dog's too good for that. It's his feet that worry me. If they hold up he'll do the job and he'll do it so well people will remember him for years.'

Later, as he drove Catriona to her motel, David sought to reassure her that, win or lose, they would be married within three months.

'No matter what happens tomorrow, or for the rest of the trial, we'll be married, Cat. Nothing will stop us being together now. Go and have a good night's sleep and I'll see you in the morning.'

They kissed briefly before David drove back to the showground, thinking that none of them really knew how much he wanted to win this trial for his father. Andy might not be around in a year's time if David needed a second chance to win. It was now or never.

As for himself, the thought of having Catriona as his wife was so wonderful he could not put it into words. They would begin a life together, and he would have to put her needs and wishes above his preoccupation with dogs. But for now, tomorrow was perhaps the most critical day of his life. He had to put up a good score with Clancy to get him into the Open. If he couldn't do that, he wouldn't have a chance of winning or even being placed in the final.

Clancy was due to work midway through the morning and, despite David's doubts about the dog's feet, he appreciated that Clancy was his main hope. The crowd had built up from the previous day and there were several interstate kelpie enthusiasts in attendance. Bruce McClymont was sitting with Andrew, Anne and Catriona as David walked onto the ground.

David sat the big red and tan dog well behind him and waited for the bell. When it rang, Clancy followed the direction of David's hand and cast out to the right as his sister had done. He was not a foot out from the fence as he made his out-run, and this time no judge could have faulted his cast. He was dead in line with David when he stopped. The three wethers took one look at him and came down the ground at a run. In so doing they veered slightly to one side, and Clancy had to work wider to steer them back on course. He would have lost something there, but at the race he was perfect and his work at the bridge was quite wonderful. The wethers would not face Clancy like their mates had faced his sister. When they looked into his eyes, they seemed to simply move away without any resistance. He would have lost a point at the pen when something outside the fence startled one sheep, but when the gate was closed David was happy with the round.

It had been a fairly fast round so Clancy hadn't had to run much, for which David – and Clancy's feet – were thankful. It was a two or three point better run than Needle's effort the previous day, and it was good enough. The 94 Clancy scored made him equal top dog, and he held that position almost to the conclusion of the Maiden trial. Only then did a very experienced border collie from Victoria take the lead with a score of 95. When the Maiden trial concluded, Clancy had been placed second and Needle fourth. The important consideration was that both dogs were now through to the Open, and despite a border collie being top scorer, it was the efforts of David's two kelpies – neither of which had previously worked in a trial – that had attracted the attention of almost everyone on the ground.

Up in the grandstand was a very old man whose name had become a legend in sheepdog circles. Wrapped in a thick overcoat and tartan scarf, there was a gleam in his knowing eyes when the Maiden trial concluded. He had been a border collie man all his life, although his dogs had had a splash of kelpie in them to sharpen them up; but he was not biased towards one breed. Back in the 1930s, when he had begun his long career with sheepdogs, he had worked against three wonderful kelpies that had wiped the floor at every trial. He had seen two of these score the possible 100 points, and the youngest dog of the trio had once or twice beaten those 100-point dogs. One of the three dogs had such power over sheep that they just walked away from him once eye contact had been made. The dog could put the sheep wherever he liked. Over the years, this old man had seen quite a few good kelpies, including the legendary

Johnny, but he had never seen one that could hold a candle to these three. He had seen Johnny win every one of his five National Trials and he attributed these successes more to the late Athol Butler's mastery of the handling art than to Johnny's innate ability. No, he had seen nothing to compare with those three great kelpies – until today. He had liked the work of the young blue and tan bitch, Needle, but she could not be compared with the red and tan dog called MacLeod's Clancy. Here, at long last, he seemed to have found a real kelpie, but he knew better than to praise the dog too highly after just one run. So he kept his counsel. Yet for all that, the old man was very excited. He was not concerned that Clancy had been beaten into second place by a very experienced dog. In terms of natural ability, the kelpie was streets ahead of the border collie. He could not wait to see Clancy work again.

The following day the Open trial began, and it was Belle's turn to show what she could do. The brilliant bitch did not let her owners down. Andrew and David had always claimed that she was a real natural who required very little training; more than that, she was the modern embodiment of the great kelpies of the past. David was determined to illustrate this claim. To Belle, three-sheep trials on a perfectly flat arena were simply a game after mustering wethers on rocks and in dogwood scrub on Yellow Rock. That was real work, compared with which trial work was child's play.

As with all the MacLeod dogs, Belle's cast was near perfect and her field work was outstanding. Head bowed into her sheep, she floated across the ground in her unique, effortless way, always seeming to know what the sheep would do. Her anticipation was so acute that she had sheep stopped before they had even begun to move.

When they arrived at the pen, David put his hands in his pockets and left the penning to Belle. There were no strident commands because Belle did not need them. Her holding ability was breathtaking and she was extremely fast. One sheep broke quickly but Belle skidded to stop him within seconds, although at the bridge she was not quite as strong as most of her kennel mates. Her gifts were holding sheep in the open and her wonderful cast. It was a top round which scored her 94 points. Bruce McClymont was ecstatic.

David had to wait another day before it was Needle's turn to run in the Open. She struck trouble on the lift when one sheep bolted back to the fence, and she had to do some great work to hold the three sheep together. Her score of 89 was very good in the circumstances, but would not be high enough to get her into the final.

The following day it was Clancy's turn again and, despite Belle's good score, David felt that if he were to win the National, it would depend on the way Clancy handled his sheep that day. David was very nervous before the trial, but as soon as the bell was rung his nerves left him, as he concentrated on what he had to do. It also seemed to him, knowing the dog so well, that Clancy was different this time around. He had gained in confidence and was really on the job.

But it was not all plain sailing for Clancy. When they reached the pen, one sheep broke out to the side, just as had happened in Belle's round. Hating sheep to beat him, Clancy skidded to block it, and prevented losing any points. It was a brilliant piece of work, but as David closed the gate of the pen, his heart missed a beat. Clancy was holding up his left front leg. Even before he let the sheep out of the pen, David raced over to Clancy and inspected his foot. His worst fears were confirmed – half of the pad had sloughed off. The enormous friction generated by Clancy's skid across the grass had been too much for him. Even so, the dog put his foot down and shepherded the three wethers off the ground. David hardly heard the score of 96 as it was announced over the loudspeaker.

Bruce McClymont was beside himself. He had dogs at home by the sire of Clancy and he had a good Belle bitch as well. The value of these dogs had increased considerably because of what the MacLeod dogs had already achieved in this tournament. It was a dream come true for Bruce, even if the dogs went no further.

The old man who had picked Clancy as a freak after seeing his first run turned to his old cobber and said, 'That red and tan dog is a genius, and so is the fellow who's working him.'

Harry Marchant, who was sitting nearby, nodded his head in agreement. 'You're right there. That fellow won his first trial at ten years of age and I was there when he did it.'

But the High Peaks contingent was grim-faced when David walked the limping Clancy back to his caravan. Andrew nodded his acknowledgement of the round, and that was sufficient reward for David. Like his son, he knew that a lot of dogs would keep working on ruined pads, and leave blood on the ground while they did it, but they could not move as quickly as sound-footed dogs. In a trial of this stature, you could not afford to begin with a handicap – that could be enough to lose you the trial.

'Half his pad has gone. It was that last block at the pen that caused it.'

Andrew nodded. 'What do you reckon about it, Davie?'

'I'll bandage it and try him with one boot and see how he runs. If it throws him off balance, I'll put boots on both front feet. I reckon we'll have to find a vet and get him to give Clancy a pain-killer before he works again.'

Next morning, when they took the dogs out to Ed Somerville's property for their run, David experimented with the boots. To his relief, the single boot did not seem to inconvenience Clancy at all. He and Anne had put cotton wool on the pad and then bandaged it very slowly and carefully. Then finally the boot was pulled over the top of that. David did not risk running him without a pain-killer, which the vet administered by injection.

Back at Inverlochy, Angus was having a battle with his conscience, and his pride, and Jane was behaving very strangely. She had always made much of the fact that their daughter should marry well. Now she was worried that she risked permanent estrangement from Catriona if they did not give their blessing to her marrying David.

'Damn it all, Jane. You had more to do with Catriona than anyone else. You told her that she should marry well.'

'And you agreed, Angus. But we're going to lose our daughter if we don't give in, and I don't want to lose her.'

Angus didn't want to lose Catriona either. He was also disturbed about his standing in David's eyes. Clearly, David had a low opinion of him as a man. He had never concerned himself with what other people thought of him before. As chairman of every board and committee he sat on, he knew he had the respect of his peers. But David's opinion had come to matter, now that he was a person of real substance. The MacLeod family had done more and accumulated more property than anyone else he knew. Catriona would not be marrying a nobody. And now David was down in Canberra with his dogs – and Catriona was with him – and Angus had a sudden urge to know what was going on.

'Ring the motel and leave a message for Catriona to contact us,' Angus said to Jane. 'I want to know how David is doing.'

When Catriona rang back with the news that David had two dogs in the Open final, Angus made a quick decision.

'Throw some clothes together, Jane. We're going to Canberra. Damned if I'm going to miss all the excitement. I reckon I'm big enough to wish my future son-in-law well before the final,' he said.

To which Jane replied with a simple, heartfelt, 'Thank you.'

Chapter Thirty

When the last of the Open dogs had worked, David had both Belle and Clancy in the eight-dog final. Belle had received the second-lowest score of the qualifiers and Clancy the second highest. It was the best result for kelpies in the past twenty-five years. The other finalists were all top border collies from three states, and the men who owned and handled them were real professionals. One mistake against such competition could put David right out of the running – and didn't he know it. He had waited years to win this trial for his father, and he had a wonderful young woman standing by while he acted out his dream.

'So this is it, Davie,' Andrew said as they ate lunch in the caravan on that last day. The finals were due to begin in a little over an hour.

'This is it, Dad,' he agreed.

'Well, you've got two dogs in the final, and that

is really something in this company. Don't be disappointed if you don't win it. I want you to know that I couldn't have done one bit better, if as good, as you've done. I couldn't be prouder of you than I am right now. And anything could happen. The breeze is getting up and I know that these sheep can be hard to handle here when there's a wind.'

Andrew's prediction about the wind turned out to be prophetic. The first finalist was crossed by the sheep and disqualified immediately. The second dog, a vastly experienced border collie from Victoria, handled the sheep well but lost several points trying to hold them on course. He finished up with a total of 92.

The next dog to work was Belle. Unfortunately the sheep quickly beat her to the left side of the ground as they ran into the wind. She pulled them across to her handler but was down a few points from the outset. She was used to lively sheep, though, and was very quick in her movements. The sheep were nowhere near as difficult as the rogue wethers on Yellow Rock and Jimmy's Mountain, where she had worked all her life. She penned for 92, which gave her a combined total of 186.

Because David had two dogs in the final, Clancy would be the last to work, making David the final competitor in that year's National. When David walked back to the caravan after Belle's run, he had a quick word with his father. They were both concerned that the sheep would be running into the wind. As soon as the wethers were released and smelled the wind blowing in from the mountains, they immediately moved off into it. This meant that there was no big cast on the left side of the ground for fear of a dog crossing, and a dog cast to the right could not get around to head the sheep before they were off course. Every dog had lost points for being off course when it picked up its sheep.

'Davie, the very instant the bell goes, don't wait to see where the sheep end up. Cast Clancy to the left and send him fast. That's the best chance you've got not to lose points for being off course.'

'Okay,' David said. He looked as grim as his father had ever seen him; grim and determined.

David knew that what it came down to was having confidence in his dog. He would have to rely on Clancy not crossing if he cast him to the left, but would get to the head and hold the sheep in the middle of the ground. That done, he could bring them straight down the ground to the handler's peg. Easy in theory, but could it be done?

David walked to the gate of the arena and looked back at the people in the stand. He noted his father and mother and Catriona – and, sitting beside her, Angus and Jane Campbell. From the smiles on their faces, David reckoned things were going to be okay at Inverlochy. Andy had his notebook and pencil on his knee so he could do his own judging.

Away to the right David quickly noted Laurence Singer standing beside his film crew. They had filmed his earlier rounds and were now in position to record this, the last and most important round of the National Trials.

David took a deep breath and stepped out onto the ground. When he walked out to the peg there was absolute silence around the ground. The crowd had increased significantly and there were even many dignitaries in attendance. David knew he had to score another 96 to win. If the sheep ran well off course, that could lose him enough points to beat him in the opening moments of his round. Belle was in third place and would be fourth if Clancy scored above her. Even so, third place in the National would be a very satisfactory result. But it was Clancy he now had all his faith in; he was the blend of two of the greatest kelpies, Nap and Belle. Combining Nap's brains and Belle's moves, Clancy had it over the pair of them. What really made the difference, what really set Clancy apart, was his extremely rare hypnotic power over sheep. This gift had been the hallmark of legendary kelpies like Coil, Biddy Blue and Boy Blue. After sheep looked into the eyes of these dogs, they seemed to come under some spell and moved under their direction. This was something entirely different to a dog's power to frighten sheep.

David's father had told him about this rare trait when he was a small boy. It was found in certain strains of pure-blood kelpies that had not been contaminated by other bloodlines, and traced back to the old Quinn and King and McLeod strains. Andrew

MacLeod's dogs had these strains. But a dog needed more than this to be a good sheepdog. Clancy had it all. The first time David had worked him on sheep, he noticed that they neither fought nor ran from him but simply moved away quietly. That was when he first suspected he had a dog to be reckoned with on the trial ground. He would have to make the three sheep look at Clancy long enough to be drawn in by his hypnotic power.

Only one other person on the ground outside David and Andrew recognised what made Clancy so different from any other dog competing at that year's National Trial, and that was the legendary old sheep-dog man swathed in a heavy overcoat and scarf who was sitting up in the stand near David's family and friends.

David tried to put all his fears about Clancy's dicey feet into the back of his mind and concentrate on the dog's great gift as he made his way out to the centre of the ground. As soon as the first clang of the starter's bell rang out, David signalled Clancy to cast left. He used a very different-sounding whistle than normal, the whistle he used when he required his dogs to run at top speed to collect rogue wethers bolting for rough places. Normally David liked his dogs to run their casts at a steady pace so they could concentrate on what they were doing, but right then the priority was to get Clancy out and around the sheep before they ran into the wind and veered off the tight course.

Clancy understood what the piercing whistle

meant and he shot away like an arrow discharged from a powerful bow. He was a very fast dog, and despite the boot on his front paw, there was no exception to his speed today. It looked as if the pain-killer in Clancy's foot was doing its job.

The sheep had hardly smelled the wind before Clancy was behind them. There David held him, and held him even longer, while the sheep looked deep into his big eyes.

'What's he doing?' someone in the stand asked the legendary old man.

'What is he doing, you ask. By crikey, this dog is going to mesmerise his sheep. When they turn away, they'll do just what that dog asks of them.'

'Why is he wearing a boot?' a lady near them asked.

'I heard he was burnt in a bushfire,' her husband replied.

'Oh, the poor little dog. I hope he wins,' she said.

The crowd looked on in amazement as Clancy cast his mesmerising spell over the sheep. Soon enough, as if in a slow-motion movie, the three wethers turned away and walked very slowly down the ground towards the handler's starting peg. Clancy steered them around the peg in a very tight semicircle so that they were not even a fraction off course, and then pointed them in the direction of the first obstacle. The sheep moved in a dream-like manner, almost as if they had been drugged, and passed through the race only seconds after David arrived at the handler's circle. He moved off towards the bridge and was there to check the sheep on the near side as Clancy covered them on the right. The sheep turned and looked at Clancy again and David let them soak up the dog's unique power. Then they turned away and walked sedately up the ramp of the bridge onto the bridge itself. There they stopped momentarily and David brought Clancy up the ramp and onto the bridge. The sheep jumped off and walked a few steps before stopping and looking back. To the spellbound watchers, it almost seemed as if they were waiting for the dog to dictate their course.

David walked to the handler's ring at the pen and let Clancy bring the sheep to him. This was a tricky part of the course. If the sheep left the pen before he had closed the gate, he would get no score at all for this component of the trial.

Clancy circled to the right to drive the wethers back against the gate, and then blocked them when they moved an inch towards David. One sheep looked back at Clancy and then trotted into the pen. The other two followed suit. David sat Clancy down, left his circle and shut the gate. He touched Clancy briefly on the top of his head before opening the pen to take the wethers off the ground. And then there was an enormous roar and a spontaneous burst of clapping from right around the ground.

'What did I tell you?' the old legend said to nobody in particular. 'You can take it from me, you may never see the likes of that dog or his handler again, if you live to be a hundred.'

'What did you score him?' Harry Marchant asked, turning to the old man.

'In my book, you couldn't get him for a point. It was just as perfect as Johnny's run in 1952.'

Anne clutched Andrew's arm in excitement. 'What did you score him, Andy?' she asked, knowing full well how hard a judge her husband was of sheepdogs.

Andrew showed her his notebook.

'Oh, my God,' she exclaimed, and whispered something in Catriona's ear, which she in turn passed on to her father. Angus had sat spellbound as he watched David in action. It had been a class act. The fact that this young man was going to be his son-in-law was something to think about.

David took the three wethers to the collecting pen with the noise of the crowd drumming in his ears and his heart pounding wildly in his chest. His eyes scanned the ground for his family and Catriona, but in all the commotion he couldn't make them out. He knew that Clancy had just worked the best round he had ever seen. He had thought Belle's 99 at their local trial was just about perfect, but Clancy's round was the ultimate. But would the judge think so?

And then the noise of the crowd died away and there was a hush right around the arena as the judge walked over to the officials behind the starting peg. A man approached the microphone to announce the score. David heard, as if in a dream, the words 'one hundred points' come over the loudspeaker. Clancy – a Maiden dog – had scored the possible 100 points, equalling the performance of the legendary Johnny. Clancy, the novice, had won the National Trial.

Now the sound was almost deafening as David walked back across the ground, soaking in the atmosphere of this incredible occasion. He had wanted this win, here, for his father, more than anything. Now all Australia would know about the MacLeod kelpie dogs.

As he walked the last steps to the gate through which he had entered the arena, his eyes at last found the faces of the people who meant so much to him. There was his mother, her face covered in tears as she looked on at David, who, in turn, desperately sought his father. Anne's face was beaming as she watched Andrew. She thought she even saw tears on the old fellow's face.

Anne was so enormously proud of both men she could hardly speak. Words seemed to choke in her throat. Her son had done what he had set out to do, what he had said he wanted to do ever since he was a boy. He had given his father the greatest prize a sheepdog breeder could aspire to. Twice Clancy's progress towards this great prize had been threatened by injuries, but today his great class had finally prevailed. It was almost too much to bear. And for as long as Andy lived, whether it was for a week or a month or for years, he would have this day, and Clancy's great effort, to remember.

David approached his father, the iron-hard bushman whose skill he had inherited, his father who

567

had almost killed himself to give his family financial security. How much more could Andy have done with dogs if only he had not chosen to work so hard?

Andrew could hardly believe what he had just witnessed. Clancy had worked the greatest round of three-sheep work he had ever seen. Like Anne, he was so proud of his son that words failed him. His dogs had been virtually unbeatable at local trials, but it was the National that separated great dogs from the rest. Clancy had now joined the band of legendary dogs that had won the National, and the MacLeod name would be enshrined in sheepdog history. Andy thought of all these things as he reached out to clasp his son's hand. What a man David was! He had given Andy's life new meaning.

Now David was being thumped on the back by Bruce McClymont, who had just seen something he never expected to see. Everything else paled into insignificance when compared with what David and Clancy had just done. As David's eyes continued to search the enthusiastic crowd of well-wishers, he saw Laurence Singer and the film crew bustling their way through the crowd, and then Angus and Jane Campbell and, behind them, with her gorgeous hair blowing across her face in the chilly wind and her brown eyes shining with love, Catriona. Catriona, who had loved him and waited for him all these years, and who had defied her parents for him. And then she was clinging to him, her arms around his neck and her lips pressed against his cold cheek. Oblivious to the people crowded about them, David and Catriona were, momentarily, lost in a world of their own. When they reluctantly drew part so David could acknowledge the congratulations of fellow handlers and others, their eyes were still locked on each other.

People were all around him. They were shaking his hand and patting his dog. Clancy stood quietly with his intense hypnotic eyes staring up at David.

'Jump, Clancy,' David commanded, and Clancy leapt up into David's arms, causing another outbreak of cheers and applause to erupt. David rubbed the dog's head and ears and then put him down beside him. Clancy soon seemed bored with proceedings now that his job was done.

The presentation was made with David still in a daze. A big old man, stooped by the years, came up and shook his hand. David learned later that he had shaken hands with the greatest handler of border collies Victoria had ever seen. 'Young man, if I die tomorrow, I will be happy for having seen you and your dog work today. I once saw one dog like your fellow and that was a long time ago. Don't let that strain die out.'

The old man's words, like the words of so many others that magical afternoon, were whirling around in David's head as he stood with his prizes and talked to the media.

And then Bruce made his play. He had reaped a profit of over $45 000 from his kelpies the previous year, and he reckoned that if he owned Clancy he could up that figure significantly. But even more than the prospect of the profit was McClymont's vision of becoming part of the legend that would surround this day.

'David, would you take twenty thousand dollars for Clancy?' he asked in a voice that could be heard above the noise of the crowd.

David looked across at McClymont and shook his head. 'I wouldn't sell Clancy for twice that figure, Bruce. This dog is not for sale. I don't need the money, and that's not why we keep the dogs. You can have first crack at a good dog by Clancy, Bruce, but I wouldn't part with him for anything in the world.'

When everyone had had their say and all the photographs had been taken, the afternoon was almost done and it was becoming quite cold.

'I think this calls for a drink,' Andrew said. 'In fact, it's too damned cold not to have a drink. What do you say, Davie?'

'I reckon you're right there, Dad,' David replied.

So they went back to the caravan and cracked open a bottle of whisky, which Anne had packed in anticipation (she knew Andy wouldn't drink champagne). Catriona had refrained from joining them just yet; she knew this was an emotional time for the family and, much as she felt close to the MacLeods, she wanted to give them some space. David reached for the beautiful sash that had been presented to him as winner of the National Trial.

'This is for you, Dad,' he said.

'Get out of it! It's yours, Davie,' Andrew said.

David shook his head. 'They're your dogs, Dad. All I did was work them. This is for all the years you couldn't take your dogs to trials because you were too busy paying off the place. I want you to have it.'

'Nobody else could have done it but you, mate,' Andrew said. 'I doubt that I could have. Nothing I can say would be enough to tell you how proud and how thankful I am of you and what you've done.'

'That's reward enough for me, Dad.'

A tap on the van's door interrupted their quiet celebration. It was Bruce McClymont and, behind him, the three Campbells. They were invited in and Andrew dispensed more whisky.

David and Catriona made their way into a quiet corner, desperate for a few minutes alone. They sat on a bed and looked into each other's eyes, while around them a friendly argument raged – both Bruce and Angus wanted to take the MacLeods to dinner. Anne solved the dispute in her usual practical fashion by suggesting that if they absolutely had to shout dinner, they should share the expense. With this suggestion, the glasses were filled and clinked again.

The conversation hardly registered with David and Catriona. They had eyes and ears only for each other.

'So you did it,' Catriona said. 'I can hardly believe it. You seem to have been telling me about this trial for as long as I've known you.'

'Crikey, surely not that long?'

Catriona nodded. 'Those dogs were always the most important things in your life. I was just a distraction and a pest,' she said, laughing.

'Aw, Cat, a bloke has to put on a front. I didn't want people thinking I was soft.'

'Well, now it's just you and me, David. I can't believe we're almost there. And, David, I can't tell you how pleased I am that Daddy has come to his senses.'

'Your father is a realist, Cat. He's also a bigger man than I gave him credit for. Anyway, I'm as pleased as you are – now you and your mother can plan the wedding to your hearts' content.'

On the way to dinner, Anne stopped to ring Kate and give her the great news. Kate was beside herself with joy. She'd always had faith that David would do great things. Now he had proved it.

At the restaurant, David held Catriona's hand tightly under the dinner table. He felt her leg against his calf, and he smiled with sheer delight. Now that he had done what he had set out to do, he felt more relaxed and somehow quite different. Now what mattered most was the girl sitting beside him. Catriona had never doubted that David was the right man for her. She had never really complained about being made to wait for him, and she had never even been tempted by the dozens of young men who had doted on her. David couldn't believe that before too long he would finally marry this girl in a million and live with her on High Peaks.

Presently Angus got to his feet and, with the waiter pouring champagne, had his say. He spoke of the years he had known the MacLeod family and of how they had worked to own two properties, and now owned four. He also spoke of Andrew's great ability with dogs and horses and of how he had passed on that same great talent to David.

'I would like to make a toast,' he said, 'to the best trial dog I have ever seen, to the two best dog handlers I have ever seen, and to the very best neighbours and family-in-law a man could ask for.'

'Hear, hear,' Bruce roared. He was feeling wonderful and wanted the night to last forever. He felt he had played his own small role in today's miracle by honouring the agreement he had made with David to return Clancy's sire, Nap. After Angus had had his say, it was Bruce's turn to get to his feet.

'My co-host has very eloquently given you a toast which echoes my own thoughts. Unlike Angus here, I haven't had the privilege of being a neighbour of the MacLeod family, and, unlike Angus, I never saw Andrew work a dog, but I want to say that it has been a privilege to know and do business with the MacLeods. This has been one of the greatest days of my life. Now I know why the kelpie made such an impact on Australia all those years ago.

'David, you and Clancy will leave Canberra tomorrow, but what you did today will never be forgotten by the sheepdog fraternity. Your feat will pass into legend. If you never break in another kelpie,

573

your name and Clancy's name will be enshrined in sheepdog lore. To you, David and Catriona, and to Andrew and Anne, my thanks and very best wishes for the future.'

When Bruce sat down, Anne leant over and kissed him. 'Thank you, Bruce,' she said.

'Do you realise you're a living legend?' Catriona whispered in David's ear.

'That may be the case, but I know what I would rather be right now,' he whispered back.

'You'll just have to wait for that,' she said with a glint in her eye.

Eventually the night had to end, so the MacLeods and Bruce McClymont returned reluctantly to their caravans and the Campbells to their motel.

The next morning, as they were packing to go home, some of the handlers who had stayed the night came across to say goodbye. There were enquiries about pups and whether David would bring his dogs to their trials. David's replies were noncommittal. He told them it would be some time before he could trial again.

With the dogs safely installed in the back of David's ute they were almost ready to leave, but just then Bruce emerged from his van.

David and the kelpie breeder walked across to the now deserted arena. 'Will you come back here next year?' McClymont asked.

David shook his head. 'I doubt it, Bruce. We've got four places to look after now. We bought this last one so we could breed our own replacement merino ewes and perhaps use some of it to top off our Queensland steers. I want to see how that works out. It may be that we try and get hold of some more country just to fatten steers. There's a lot of work in running four places. No, Bruce, I don't think I will ever come back here. And, anyway, there's no need. I've done what I wanted to do. I could never top Clancy's effort. Besides, I shall soon be married, and when a bloke is lucky enough to have a girl like Catriona, he can't neglect her. Look, if you ever feel like coming up for a visit some day, do spend a few days with us.'

'That would be terrific, thank you, David. You don't imagine I'm going to forget you. I'm going to want more dogs in future.'

'Okay, I'll see what we can do. Now, we'd better hit the track if we want to be home tonight. Thanks for the great evening last night, and don't forget to come and see us. Bring Mona next time.'

They made their way back to the vans and Bruce said goodbye to Andrew and Anne. Yet still he lingered and seemed reluctant to leave.

'Goodbye, David,' he said at last, and with that he drove away.

David turned and walked back to the picket fence that surrounded the arena. His eyes took in the scene so that it would live in his mind forever. He had once thought that dogs and horses were all that mattered in life. But now he had priorities and responsibilities

575

that counted for more than anything. He was well on the way to becoming a very wealthy man, and it had all been because of his father's industriousness and unselfishness, Wilf White's benevolence and Tim Sparkes's wonderful generosity. And he could not forget his Aunt Kate, who had given them all the financial support she could afford when they needed it most, and who had helped them in so many other ways. It would be irresponsible for him to go on trialling dogs and drafting horses, as enjoyable as those pastimes were, after what these people had done for him. And of course there was Catriona. Before long, he hoped they would have children, and David's role in life now was to secure their future as his own father had done for him. No, he would never come back to Canberra. There were other dreams on the horizon.

When he turned away from the ground, he found his father standing behind him.

'I want you to know, mate, that I doubt very much if I could have done what you did, even in my best days. I didn't know Clancy was that good. I know you did all this for me. Davie, if I drop dead tonight, I want you to know that I never dreamed I would have a son like you. Don't know what I did to deserve it. Thank you.'

'Come on, Dad. We've got a lot on our plate, and I've got a girl to marry.'

Kate and Jean were waiting for them at the gate into the High Peaks house yard. Over the gate they

had made up a sign which read 'Congra
David and Clancy'.

David picked up each woman in turn and
her.

'I'll put the kettle on,' Kate said.

'And I'll see to the dogs,' David replied. 'Th
be pleased to be back home after being cooped up i
a fair bit this last week.'

Kate watched David's tall figure stride down the
track. She loved him dearly and had missed him.

'Well, I must say I'm pleased to be home,' Anne
said. 'Canberra was nice for a break, but there's no
place like home.'

'Especially when there's a wedding just round the
corner,' Kate reminded her.

'We'll get no sense out of you three until that's
out of the way,' Andrew said.

'Andrew MacLeod, I'm sure I don't know how *you*
ever got married. You've no romance in you at all,'
Kate flashed.

'I had enough to get me the best woman in these
parts, so stick that in your pipe and smoke it,' he shot
back at his sister-in-law.

'Hey, you two, no shadow-sparring,' Anne protested. 'First few minutes home and you're already at it.'

'Ah, it's just a bit of good-natured arguing. We do
agree on most things, you know,' Kate said.

'Agree on what, Kate?' David asked as he came
into the kitchen.

'That you should go out and bring in some wood or the stove,' she replied.

'Nothing like a few chores to bring a man back to earth,' David said. 'Yesterday a legend and today a wood carter.' But he was smiling broadly as he spoke.

Chapter Thirty-one

A couple of days before the wedding, David decided to take a day off and have a ride into the hills. He packed some lunch, added tea, sugar and condensed milk, and rode off on his favourite mare – the one he and Andy had brought back from Aberfeldy. She was a dream to ride and draft on, although he didn't ride her often, but she made him think of the lanky Queenslander who had had so much faith in him. He reckoned that if Tim had been looking down on the National, he would have been mighty pleased with the result.

Nap, as usual, was running behind him. Clancy whined to be let off, but David knew that his pads would never again stand up to a day in the hills.

He rode first to Yellow Rock, and let his mare pick her way up the narrow track that led to its peak. He dismounted and rested for several minutes at the spot where Catriona and her grey pony had gone over the ledge. He tried to remember how Cat had looked that day. She had been crying a lot and the tears had made little channels down her dust-streaked face. He had been very frightened about jumping her pony off the rubble heap, but if he had shown any hesitation at all, his father would not have allowed him to make the attempt. Yet the idea of Cat crying her heart out at the thought of losing her pony had been too much for him to bear. He supposed he had felt something for Cat even then.

At the top of Yellow Rock he looked out across the range and breathed in the sharp, clean air. He remembered the time in his life when he first realised that he loved this country, and knew he would never live anywhere else. Some part of him would wither if he did.

He climbed back up on his horse and headed for their boundary gate into Poitrel, making his way along the ridge to Wallaby Rocks. Except for the standing burnt trees, there was little to show that a fire had passed over this country. The big storm and further falls of rain had brought life back to the grass and scrub in no time. The new fences were up, and life was proceeding more or less as it always had.

On Wallaby Rocks he noted where Kate had broken her leg and the rock over which he had sheltered her. Now the shelter was gone, destroyed by the fire. And the Missen boys were gone, too. Here Kate's rescue party had camped for the night and he first experienced the joy of having Catriona so close by, yet agonisingly not close enough.

He dismounted, hitched his mare to a tree and walked the last few yards to the mouth of the big cave. There was a wallaby sitting on a rock just outside the entrance, and on sighting him it vanished in three or four swift bounds.

It did not take long to start a fire and boil the billy, and he sat down, with Nap beside him, to eat his lunch. Nap lay with his eyes on David's face, waiting patiently for the pieces of meat sandwich he knew would be forthcoming.

'I don't know what I did to be lucky enough to own a dog like you, Nap,' he said aloud. Nap's agate-coloured eyes gleamed with a flash of light, just as they usually did when he was being spoken to. 'I'd give anything to know what you were thinking when I sent you away with Bruce. Did you think I was the biggest mongrel in the country? I'll never do it again, I promise. I know you know where home is. You really are a clever dog, old mate. Now, I have to go away for a bit, but I'll be back before too long. Mum will look after you, and Dad, too. And when I get back, Cat will probably spoil you rotten. She's going to learn how to work one of your pups.'

David knew that if anyone heard him talking to his dog they would reckon the hills had finally got to him, but if a man couldn't talk to his dog, especially a dog who could understand everything as Nap did, it was a poor show.

David looked around the cave and thought of the day he had brought Cat here. It was the first time he had experienced intense longing for her, and she had known it. He had seen the response in her eyes.

He lost track of time as he sat in the cave with his dog and thought about the past, and it was late afternoon when he finally rode down the mountain and came in sight of his new house. He had erected an old-fashioned hitching rail under a kurrajong tree at the back of the house, and he tied his mare to it before going up the path to the new building. It wasn't locked. Country people rarely locked their houses. He walked from room to room sniffing the smell of fresh paint and marvelling at the newness of the interior. The carpets and curtains were in place and there was new furniture in most rooms. He sat down on the edge of the big double bed and tried to imagine what it would be like living there with Cat. It was almost too much to imagine that she would be with him for the rest of their lives.

Nap was lying beside the mare when he came out of the house. 'Time to feed you fellows,' he said, and with Nap at his heels he walked up to the dog yards, grinning from ear to ear. It had been the kind of day he wanted – needed – before going away to be married.

The wedding turned out to be everything Catriona had dreamed of. It was held in late June, and, true to her Scottish lineage and Presbyterian background, Catriona chose St James's in Sydney as the venue. She was piped out of the church by a piper wearing the tartan of Clan Campbell.

When David had turned to watch Catriona come down the aisle on her father's arm, he saw tears on his mother's face, and then he saw Catriona and his heart began to pound. She looked breathtakingly beautiful. Her gown was made of brocaded satin encrusted with the palest opalescent design. It was made in a traditional style – tight at the waist, with a full, voluminous skirt, long pointed sleeves and a long train. She carried a bouquet of lily-of-the-valley and wore her mother's milk opal brooch. Her head-piece was made of the same brocaded satin as her dress and featured a fingertip veil. Her four brides-maids wore gowns of pale-aqua brocaded satin cut in much the same style as Catriona's Deb gown, and they carried bouquets of baby pink roses.

All the words of the service prior to David's 'I do' passed in a blur. He just could not concentrate while watching Catriona. He had liked, then loved her for years, but he had never imagined it would come to this. They had overcome so many obstacles, but it seemed that fate had been on their side. Now he knew that he really loved her, nothing would stand in their way.

Catriona gave a little sigh as she spoke the words 'I do'. For her, the long wait was over. She had always wanted David MacLeod. Always. Her mind flashed back to the day he had saved both her and her pony, and damaged his shoulder in the process. She remem-bered with fearful clarity how he had belted that awful Masters boy, and later, years later, had rescued her the night of her debut. Thinking back, she realised David had never looked at another girl, and she was sure he never would. He was hers now and they would be together as long as they lived.

When it was time for David and Catriona to leave there were still tears in Anne's eyes, and although Kate was trying to be brave, eventually she cried, too.

David threw up his hands in despair and then wrapped them both in bear hugs.

'I promise to look after him,' Catriona whispered in Anne's ear as the gathering farewelled them.

'I know you will, Catriona, and I couldn't be happier,' Anne said.

'Thank you. You have always been my ally and confidante,' Catriona said, kissing her fondly.

Catriona was radiant as she and David left the reception. She settled in her seat and then turned and looked behind her.

'What are you doing?' David asked.

'I'm just checking to make sure you haven't sneaked Nap or Clancy into the back.'

'I can assure you that I haven't given my dogs a thought all day, nor will I for the next three weeks. There are other things in the world, you know.'

Catriona felt her heart race. These were going to be the best three weeks of her life.

It turned out to be an idyllic honeymoon, and even several inches of rain did not dampen their spirits and happiness. It was the first real holiday that David had ever had, and Catriona was determined that he would enjoy it. They stayed for two weeks at the Yeppoon house, eating enormous candlelit dinners and sleeping in much later than they had ever done. From Yeppoon they drove up to Aberfeldy for a few days, where they spent most of their time riding over the property. As wonderful as it all was, Catriona sensed that three weeks away was long enough for David. He felt the pull of the hills and wanted to go home.

When they returned, Anne could tell by the stars in Catriona's eyes that they were extremely happy and that the honeymoon had been everything they had hoped for, and more.

Anne watched them as they walked hand in hand from the car to embrace her, and the pain in her heart was unbearable. How could she spoil their happiness? But David had to know. The news could not be delayed.

David sensed immediately that his mother was holding something back.

'What is it, Mum? Is something wrong?'

'It's Andy, dear,' she said. 'He's gone.'

'Gone? What do you mean "gone"?' he asked urgently.

'Andy died last night, David. He just said he was tired and wanted to go to bed early. He died peacefully in his sleep.'

'Oh, Lord,' he cried in a stricken voice. 'Mum,' he sobbed and fell on her.

All the joy of the past few weeks and his home-coming dissolved in an instant. High Peaks could never be the same without his father.

'Shhh, David. He didn't have any pain and he was so very happy for you and Catriona,' Anne said. She had dreaded this moment because she knew how much her son loved and respected his father. They had been almost inseparable from the moment David could crawl.

'I wasn't here, Mum. I should have been with him. Should have been with you.'

'Don't be silly, darling. You couldn't be in two places at once. Try not to take it so hard. We need to find strength in each other right now. Andy was so very proud of you. We talked about you all the while you were away. He said that the day you won the National was the proudest day of his life. It was the fulfilment of everything he could have hoped for with his dogs. To have a son cast virtually in his own image and to do what you did made his life perfect.'

'And having a loving wife as wonderful as you.'

'It's all up to us now, though it has been for some time, hasn't it?'

'Dad should have lived years longer. He wasn't old, Mum. Just fifty-six,' David said.

'I know, but he almost died when he had that first stroke.'

Anne's eyes met Catriona's and she found sympathy there. But what could she or anyone else say that would soften this blow to their lives? Andy had been such an inspiration for his son.

'Where's Kate?' David asked.

'She's making the necessary arrangements. I wanted to be here when you arrived.'

He nodded and then sat down on the top step with his head in his hands.

'He's being buried on the hill, isn't he?' David asked at last.

'Yes, of course. That is what he asked for, to be buried where we both shall be.'

'Then he will never really die. Not while we have this place and his dogs, and by God I shall have both while there is breath in my body.'

'That's what he wanted, David,' Anne said.

'And what do you want, Mum?' he asked.

'To see my days out on this place that holds the happiest memories of my life. To see my grandchildren grow up here.'

'At least we've got each other,' David replied, and then asked, 'When is it?'

Anne knew just what he was referring to. 'The day after tomorrow,' she said.

'There are people who need to be told,' David said. 'Bruce McClymont and Wilf White, to name just a few. And unless you have other ideas, I'd like to give the eulogy at the church.'

'Whatever you want, David,' Anne said.

Later, much later, David realised how selfish he had been in not recognising his mother's suffering.

She had done her crying and then marshalled all her remarkable strength and spirit in readiness for his return. Having to give him the news of his father's passing must have been about the toughest task Anne had ever had to do. He had thought only of his sadness at losing his father, without really comprehending that his mother had lost her companion of half a lifetime.

Two days later David stood up before the congregation to deliver the following words:

'Those of you who are here today and who knew my father would remember him as a gun shearer, horsebreaker and campdrafter, sheepdog breeder and triallist, and a successful grazier. My father was all of those things and much more. Some people have said that Dad was a hard man, but he was also the fairest man I have ever known. If he thought you were worth helping, he would do whatever he possibly could. When he took over the management of High Peaks it was heavily in debt. Dad cleared this debt by sheer hard work, and then some.

'My father was a gifted man in many ways. He was a wonderful whipmaker and could craft anything in leather. But what made Dad really stand out was his natural ability in handling dogs and horses. In the hundred or so years since the kelpie came into being, we have had a handful of people with the ability to both breed and handle the working kelpie. These men really understood what the breed was all about. My father belonged to this small group. His knowledge of sheepdogs and his ability to handle them transcended ordinary standards.

'I could not have done what I did on my own. It was my father who taught me everything I know. Everything I am, so far as sheepdogs are concerned, I owe to him. History and legend may largely remember me and my dog Clancy, but I know better.

'But what was especially great about my father was that he was my best mate. He was my mate from the first day I could follow him, and from the first time I could sit on a pony that he led. Dad was there the day I won at Canberra, and his final piece of advice probably made the difference between me winning and losing that great trial.

'In a little while my father will be buried alongside his parents on the hill above our home, so for me his spirit will never die. I speak now for both my mother and myself. My father was fortunate to have a wife like my mother who was there for him every day of her life. Life for her will never be the same without her Andy, but I don't doubt that her incredible strength and wonderful spirit will carry her through. If Dad were here, he would want me to say that for him there was only ever one woman in his life, and that was my mother. I had the two best parents a boy could wish for. For Mum and me, Dad will never be far away. We will carry our love for him in our hearts forever. Every time I drink tea with my mother I shall see my father sitting in his chair, and every time I work a dog or ride a horse I shall remember Dad's words of advice.'

Here David put his hand in the pocket of his coat and brought out a sash of rolled silk.

'This is the sash that I won with Clancy at the National. It is the most precious award in our possession. For me, because I wanted so very much to win it for Dad. I wanted him to have this sash but he wouldn't accept it. But, Dad, if you can hear me now, I want you to know how much I appreciate what you meant to me and what you did for me. This is my final thank you.'

David moved across to where the coffin lay and spread the silk sash across it. He looked into his mother's tear-streaked face and nodded. Catriona, Kate and Jean were crying, and Bruce McClymont, who had dropped everything to come to the funeral, was crying, too. Even Angus Campbell was close to tears. Sitting behind Angus and his family were Wilf White and his sister, Gertie. Kate had rung Gertie with the tragic news and said that they would understand if Wilf couldn't make the funeral at his age. Gertie had said Wilf would attend if it killed him. Wilf, David could see, was very upset.

Finally David took his place between his mother and his wife and felt the pressure of their hands on his arms. 'Thank you, David. That was lovely,' Anne whispered.

So Andrew MacLeod was taken to the grave that had been prepared on the hill above High Peaks. It was a clear, sunny winter's day and a gentle breeze was faintly stirring the leaves of the big kurrajong and box trees above the gathering by the graveside. All that remained of Andrew was lowered into the ground. Anne's roses from the garden close by and David's sash crowned the coffin. All other flowers were placed on an adjacent mound of earth. Andrew MacLeod was at rest.

By midafternoon everyone but Bruce had left. He and David walked down to the dog kennels and sat on the big hollow log kennels. 'I'll be heading off now,' Bruce said.

'You sure? You'd be most welcome to stay the night,' David said.

'I know that. I think it should be just family tonight,' Bruce said.

'Well, thank you for coming. It's a long trip and we appreciate it.'

'I'm just sorry it had to be for a funeral. You will miss him.'

'More than anyone will ever know.'

'You've won yourself a pretty decent mate in Catriona.'

'Yes, I've been lucky in many ways. I am doing what I most want to do, surrounded by land and people I love. I couldn't imagine being anywhere else.'

'You will keep the dogs going, won't you?'

'Of course I will. I may not trial again, except locally, because I have a big job in front of me. Nothing will change with the dogs. I'll keep them going in the hope that there will be another Andrew

MacLeod who has the gift of working sheepdogs.'

'That's good news. Not that I really thought you would let them go. I'd better push off now. I can get a fair way down the track tonight. I'll be back when you have those dogs ready for me.'

David stood with his wife and mother and watched McClymont's vehicle disappear around the bend of the road.

'Well, that's that,' Anne said at last. 'I must say it's been quite a day. Well, life must go on. There are chooks to feed and eggs to collect, and –'

'The cow to get in for Greg and dogs to feed,' David said.

'And Tess's pups due next week,' Catriona added.

'Go and feed your dogs, David,' Anne said. Her eyes were clear now and he knew his mother would be all right.

So he went down to the dog yard and peered inside. There was Nap, who, as usual, looked him straight in the eye and seemed to anticipate what he was thinking; and there was Clancy with his injured front foot still booted; and there was Clancy's mother, the brilliant Belle; and Belle's old mother, now the matriarch of the stud; and Tess, with her distended belly full of pups for which there had been enquiries from all over the country; and King II, named after the dog who had been his father's last top male dog after Ben; and the other bitches of the strain his father had maintained and made famous.

David cast his eye over the lot of them. In his view

there were no dogs better than these and none would ever take their place. 'Come on, you lot. Let's see you run off some steam down the paddock.'

Anne and Catriona watched his tall figure walk down the track towards the creek. The dogs streamed past him in their enthusiasm to run, all save Clancy and Belle's old mother, who followed sedately at David's heels.

'Thank God for that son of yours,' Catriona said.

'Thank you for waiting for him. I hope you have another little Andrew MacLeod before too long,' Anne said.

'There will only ever be one Andrew MacLeod,' Catriona said. 'And only one David MacLeod.'

The Potato Factory
Bryce Courtenay

Always leave a little salt on the bread . . .

Ikey Solomon's favourite saying is also his way of
doing business. And in the business of thieving
in thriving nineteenth-century London, he's very
successful indeed. Ikey's partner in crime is his
mistress, the forthright Mary Abacus, until misfortune
befalls them. They are parted and each must make
the harsh journey separately to the convict settlement
in Van Diemen's Land.

In the backstreets and dives of Hobart Town,
Mary learns the art of brewing and builds The Potato
Factory, where she plans a new future. But her
ambitions are threatened by Ikey's wife, Hannah, her
old enemy. The two women raise their separate
families, one legitimate and the other bastard. As each
woman sets out to destroy the other, the families are
brought to the brink of disaster.

A thrilling tale of Australia's beginnings

Tommo & Hawk
Bryce Courtenay

Brutally kidnapped and separated in childhood, Tommo and Hawk are reunited at the age of fifteen in Hobart Town. Together they escape their troubled pasts and set off on a journey into manhood. From whale hunting in the Pacific to the Maori wars of New Zealand, from the Rocks in Sydney to the miners' riots at the goldfields, Tommo and Hawk must learn each other's strengths and weaknesses in order to survive.

Along the way, Hawk meets the outrageous Maggie Pye, who brings love and laughter into his life. But the demons of Tommo's past return to haunt the brothers. With Tommo at his side, Hawk takes on a fight against all odds to save what they cherish most. In the final confrontation between good and evil, three magpie feathers become the symbol of Tommo and Hawk's rites of passage.

An epic tale of adventure and romance